# QUEEN
## OF
# FATE

FAE OF WOODLANDS & WILD

BOOK 3

## KRISTA STREET

BOOKS BY KRISTA STREET

SUPERNATURAL WORLD NOVELS

## Fae of Legends & Lore

*Stone of Legends*

*Bindings of Lore*

*Keeper of Stars*

## Fae of Woodlands & Wild

*Kingdom of Faewood*

*Veil of Shadows*

*Queen of Fate*

## Fae of Snow & Ice

*Court of Winter*

*Thorns of Frost*

*Wings of Snow*

*Crowns of Ice*

## Supernatural Curse

*Wolf of Fire*

*Bound of Blood*

*Cursed of Moon*

*Forged of Bone*

## Supernatural Institute

*Fated by Starlight*

*Born by Moonlight*

*Hunted by Firelight*

*Kissed by Shadowlight*

## Supernatural Community

*Magic in Light*

*Power in Darkness*

*Dragons in Fire*

*Angel in Embers*

## Supernatural Standalones

*Beast of Shadows*

Links to all of Krista's books may be found on her website.

**www.kristastreet.com**

Cover art created by Maria Spada.
Map illustration created by Chaim's Cartography.

# WELCOME TO THE FAE LANDS

*Queen of Fate* is the final book in the *Fae of Woodlands & Wild* trilogy, which is a slow-burn, fae fantasy romance.

*Fae of Woodlands & Wild* is the fifth series that Krista Street wrote in her *Supernatural World*, but while all of Krista's fantasy and paranormal romance books take place in the same setting and have similar world-building references, each series is entirely separate so may be read in any order.

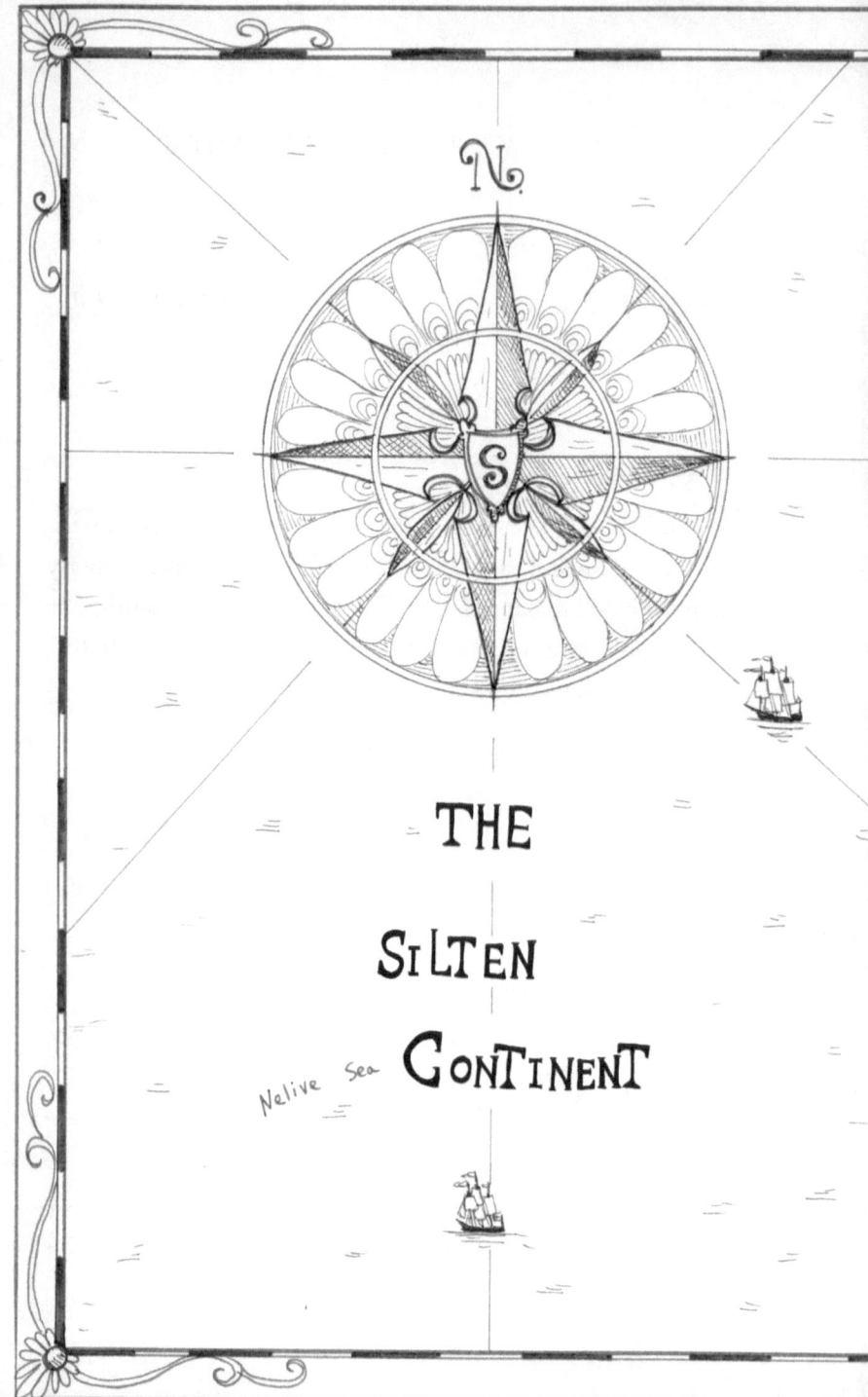

# THE

# SILTEN

Nelive sea **CONTINENT**

# GLOSSARY

## **Kingdoms of the Silten Continent**

*Faewood* – southeast kingdom, colors are turquoise, white, and dark brown. Elowen's kingdom. Magic is elemental.

*Ironcrest* – southwest kingdom, colors are silver, magenta, and dark orange. Magic is sensory.

*Mistvale* – northwest kingdom, colors are bright yellow, dark purple, and deep red. Magic is mental.

*Stonewild* – northeast kingdom, colors are forest green, gold, and sapphire blue. Jax's kingdom. Magic is shifting.

## **Seas of the fae lands**

*Adriastic Sea* – the ocean to the west of the Nolus continent and to the east of the Silten continent.

*Brashier Sea* – the most northern ocean in the fae lands, large icebergs often present.

*Nelive Sea* – the ocean to the west of the Silten continent.

*Tala Sea* – the ocean to the south of the Solis continent.

## **Fae races**

*Silten fae* – the Silten fae reside on a continent surrounded by ocean. Silten fae have numerous subspecies. The Silten species that is considered most powerful are the *siltenites.* Siltenites have bodies like humans, pointed ears, and varying skin and hair shades. The other Silten species are called *wildlings.* Wildlings have primitive Old Wood magic, which connects them to aspects in nature. Wildlings typically have animalistic features: horns, scales, hooves, and tails, yet are often as intelligent as siltenites. Wildlings that don't reside in cities, usually live in underground dens, hollow logs, or wooded forests. Their ages vary based upon their subspecies, but siltenites live thousands of years.

*Solis fae* – the Solis fae reside on the icy, most northern continent of the fae lands planet. Solis fae have silvery white hair, crystalline blue eyes, and wings. They typically live for thousands of years.

*Nolus fae* – the Nolus fae reside on the central continent. They often have various shades of colorful hair, pointy teeth, glowing skin, and otherworldly strength. They typically live two to three hundred years, but royal Nolus fae live for thousands of years.

*Lochen fae* – the Lochen fae reside on a southern continent, islands, and in the seas throughout the fae lands. They can morph into fish-like creatures, similar to mermaids, but they can also walk on two legs and live on land. There are subspecies of Lochen fae who live in freshwater rivers, lakes, and ponds. The Lochen fae typically have green eyes and varying skin shades and hair colors.

## Silten Fae Species

*Cerlikan* – a small wildling fae with large eyes and a furry body. Highly intelligent and capable of language. They live in dens in the Wood and have an intricate community in which their chatter often fills the Wood with sound.

*Fusterill* – a huge monstrous wildling fae, with the strength of a giant.

*Half-breed* – half-breeds are Silten fae of siltenite and wildling descent. They are able to procreate at a faster rate than siltenites, and some half-breeds are magically powerful. Because of this, procreating among siltenites and wildlings is against the law. Half-breeds that do come into existence are shunned in the Silten culture.

*Siltenite* – Elowen's species, considered the superior species among the Silten fae due to their appearance being most similar to the Nolus, Solis, and Lochen fae, and their ability to harbor and wield powerful magic. The siltenites have human-like bodies and a varied range of hair, eye, and skin color. They usually live thousands of years.

*Wildling fae* – fae of the Silten continent who aren't siltenites. Each wildling species has some animalistic trait or feature. Intelligence along with language abilities vary among the wildlings.

### **Fae Terms**

*Calling* – the term used when Elowen travels to the Veiled Between to interact with the semelees on another's behalf.

*Full season* – equivalent of one year.

*House* – each kingdom has ten noble Houses that oversee land, businesses, and fae within their kingdom. House nobles are very wealthy and hold a considerable amount of power.

*Kingsfae* – the law of the land in the four kingdoms, similar to police, and commanded by the kings.

*Lady* – a noble title for a female fairy.

*Lorafin* – a female siltenite who possesses rare magic. Lorafins can venture to the Veiled Between. This is where the semelees reside.

*Lordling* – a noble title for a male fairy.

*Rhifilyte Gem* – a magical gem formed in Harrivee's floating meadows.

*Salopas* – a fairy version of a bar with no serving staff. There is a bartender and magically enchanted trays that serve patrons.

*Semelees* – all-knowing shadow creatures that live in the Veiled Between. They are neither dead nor alive, yet they are able to be commanded by lorafins.

*Veiled Between* – a plane of space between universes that is neither a realm of the living or the dead but rather an alternate reality in between.

## Fae plants and food

*Cottonum* – a plant similar to cotton.

*Leminai* – a bright-green alcoholic drink common throughout the fae lands.

*Saggerwire* – a common shrub in the Stonewild desert. The center of its leaves holds water.

*Wintercrisp fern* – a plant on Stonewild's royal crest and a leaf that symbolizes trust and strength.

## <u>Fae animals</u>

*Brommel stag* – a stag or deer-like creature that can run so swiftly hardly any fae can hunt them.

*Colantha* – a large cat that resides in jungles.

*Dillemsill* – a messenger bird whose magic allows it to travel instantaneously throughout the realm.

*Ligersail* – a winged creature that lives on the Solis continent and is used in their mines.

# PRONUNCIATION GUIDE

## Names

*Elowen* – Ell-oh-when

*Jax* – Jacks

*Alleron* – Al-err-on

*Lillivel* – Lill-ih-vell

*King Paevin* – Pay-vin

*Mushil* – Moo-sheel

*Esopeel* – S-oh-peel

*Phillen* – Fill-enn

*Trivan* – Triv-en

*Lars* - Larz

*Bowan* – Boe-en

*Lander* – Land-err

*Saramel* – Sarr-uh-mell

*Archon Severell* – Sev-err-ill

*Penneveer* – Pen-uh-veer

*Saroly* – Sare-oh-lee

*Master Fistideeous* – Fiss-stid-ee-us

*Lorasbelle* – lor-ass-bell

*Miramim* – mere-uh-mim

*Isobel* – iss-oh-bell

## **Fae Races**

*Lochen* – Lock-uhn

*Nolus* – Naw-luss

*Silten* – Sill-tun

*Solis* – Saw-liss

# QUEEN
## OF
# FATE

# CHAPTER 1

The crown prince's half-breed brother sat on a chair, entirely catatonic, as we all stood in a circle around him. The hustle of Leafton's nightlife hummed through the windows of Jax's private suite at The Silver Hand. Life carried on outside these walls. Yet we'd come to a standstill.

Large permanent antlers rose from Bastian's temples, and he still wore the same dirty, homespun trousers and top that he'd been wearing in the Wood's underground caverns. But despite being among his friends and family again since we'd rescued him, Bastian had done nothing but sit on the chair we'd placed him on.

Glazed eyes stared at nothing in particular, even when we waved a hand in front of his face, and he had absolutely no emotional response. He breathed, but that was his only sign of life.

"How are we going to get Bastian to the Solis continent like this?" Lander gestured to Jax's despondent brother, his voice its usual monotone.

Frowning, I wondered the same thing because according to the semelees, traveling to the Solis continent and finding the creator of Bastian's anklet was the only way to have it removed. And it was imperative that we got that jewelry off him because the semelees had also confirmed that the gem within his anklet was how someone was controlling Bastian's mind.

I momentarily ran a finger along my collar, hoping against hope that whoever had created Bastian's anklet had also forged the irremovable jewelry that controlled my magic. I knew it was unlikely, as I'd been told my collar could never come off, but now . . .

I quickly shoved that envious thought away. Right now, our focus was Bastian. Not me.

Everyone glanced at one another, and Lander's question still hung heavily in the air.

Jax's brow furrowed, his midnight eyebrows drawing together until a sharp groove appeared between them. "I suppose we'll have to carry him."

Trivan scoffed, and the lean blond placed a hand on his hip. "Carry him *everywhere* on the Solis continent? Won't that look rather odd?"

"I don't think we have a choice," I chimed in. "The semelees said Bastian needs to be present to have his anklet removed by the Solis female who forged it, and if the only way we can move him is by carrying him, then we'll have to."

"What about an enchanted carpet?" Lars asked. The quiet redhead had hardly said a word since we'd retrieved Bastian over an hour ago. Phillen, Jax's other private guard, stood beside him. "Maybe we could place him on one?"

Alec nodded, and the light caught on the dark-brown hair of the Graniteer House noble. "A carpet would certainly be the easiest way to move him, especially if we're going to Harrivee's floating meadows. An enchanted carpet could also help us travel while we're there."

Jax placed his hands on his hips, his fingers tapping rhythmically. "That would work, and like you suggested, Alec, a carpet would also help us traverse the Solis landscape. Good idea, Lars."

The redhead dipped his chin.

I cocked my head. "Will it be easy to find an enchanted carpet?" Dealers of the magical forms of transportation could be hard to come by. Usually, they were sold out.

Jax drifted closer to me, his pine and spice clouding around me. "I know someone in the capital who can get us one."

I smirked and said teasingly, "Of course, you do."

His lips curved, and he set his hand on my lower back. Our mate bond hummed inside me with contentment at that simple gesture.

I still couldn't believe that Jax and I were actually mated now and that I was mated to a *crown prince*. Our bond was still so newly formed that we hadn't had a chance to even enjoy it yet.

As though recognizing where my thoughts had turned, his eyes heated, and he leaned down and kissed me on the neck.

An array of shivers blasted down my spine.

Trivan coughed, but it did little to hide his snicker in our direction.

"What about Quinn?" Lander arched an eyebrow. "We'll need to let him know that we've left Leafton and are going to Harrivee's floating meadows."

His practical reminder pulled me back to the conversation, and I reluctantly stepped away from Jax.

Jax sighed. "I'll send a dillemsill."

Phillen, the brawniest of the bunch, crossed his arms, then scratched his cheek through his heavy beard. "I'll fetch one in the morning."

I scrunched my nose up. "Can dillemsills even find a crowfy shifter who's currently in shadow form?"

Bowan shrugged, and his earring flashed in the fairy lights with the movement. "Some can. It depends how much magic the bird possesses. They're all slightly different in strength."

Jax nodded. "In fact, Phillen, make that two dillemsills. Royal protocol also requires me to send word to the Solis royals that we're planning to visit their continent, so I'll need to send a message to Norivun too. And as for Quinn, take more rulibs and pay the higher fee for their most magical bird."

"Any news from Quinn?" Lars asked Jax.

Jax shook his head. "No, but I'm not surprised we haven't heard from him. Trying to find out how the kingsfae knew about our raid in Possyrose Forest is probably going to take a bit of time."

"Or rather, how the *king* knew," I corrected. After all, it was King Paevin who directed the kingsfae to seize Jax and his raider band that night. I'd found out what the kingsfae were planning and had managed to reach Jax in time, but we all narrowly missed that arrest.

But as for how the king had been aware that Jax and his band of raider friends would be there . . .

None of us could answer that. But hopefully Quinn discovered something soon.

Phillen ran a hand through his auburn hair, making his biceps bulge. "Will do, my prince. I'll get two dillemsills first thing in the morning when the shops open."

"I'll go too and get that carpet," Bowan offered.

Jax nodded curtly. "It's settled then."

Lander nodded toward the clock. "'Tis near midnight. We should all rest. It's been a long day."

"Agreed." Jax crouched by his brother's side again. "Bastian, we'll move you to a bedroom chambers to sleep for the night." He waited as though hoping against hope that his brother would suddenly respond, but of course, he didn't.

Bastian continued sitting unmoving, staring docilely. It was such a strange position for a male who appeared so large and powerful.

Like Jax, Bastian was tall with broad shoulders and had a lean yet muscular build. He had fae-tipped ears and siltenite features, along with high fae limbs, feet, and hands. All of him appeared as any other siltenite would, except for the antlers. Unlike Jax, who could magically manifest his stag antlers at will and then make them disappear, Bastian's antlers were permanent since he was a half-breed.

But their facial features were similar. Like Jax, Bastian's eyes were a beautiful shade of blue, and his bone structure was rugged, his chest defined, his thighs muscled. His skin was a shade darker than his brother's tanned complexion, yet Bastian's hair was lighter than his brother's. Whereas Jax had black hair, Bastian's was dark blond.

Still, it was so obvious they were brothers. All one had to do was look at them, and the resemblance was apparent. I couldn't believe I hadn't recognized it initially when Jax had asked me to locate his brother in the Veiled Between all those weeks ago, but I'd never suspected such a thing was possible because, until Jax, I'd never heard of any royal siltenite in any kingdom having an illegal half-breed brother. *No wonder the king of Stonewild Kingdom banished Bastian.* If anyone saw him, they would likely question his lineage.

Pain puffed in my mate's aura as Bastian continued to sit unmoving. I kneeled at my mate's side, placing a hand on his waist. "We'll save him, Jax. He'll come back to you."

Jax's jaw ground together, and he nodded stiffly, but the movement looked forced. "I hope so. It's hard to see him like this."

My heart squeezed. "It is." Even though I never met Bastian prior to our rescue tonight, the unwavering way Jax loved him and strove to protect him spoke volumes for the kind of male Bastian was.

Saramel, Phillen's wife, had once told me that Jax and Bastian were incredibly close, that they spoke every day, and that they were fiercely loyal to each other. I couldn't imagine having such an unbreakable bond with a sibling, especially since I had no brothers or sisters, not that I knew of at least, but the love Jax felt for Bastian was evident. It was why he'd abducted me from my guardian after all. Sheer desperation to find Bastian had made Jax seek out the only lorafin living on the Silten continent, someone who could travel to the Veiled Between and get him answers, someone who would surprisingly end up being his mate.

How much had changed since Jax and I had met.

I squeezed Jax's hand again. "Come. It's getting late. We should all get some sleep."

EVERYONE FINALLY STOOD and retreated to their individual bed chambers for the night. Once Phillen and Lars had carried Bastian to an empty room, Jax used his magic to clean his brother's soiled skin and change him into clean clothes. The fact that Bastian was streaked in grime and dust and didn't even react when Jax bathed him or dressed him broke my heart all over again.

Jax's pain drifted toward me along the mate bond as he cared for his brother, and I wished I could fix all of this for him, but it was as though Bastian was no longer there, that his large body was merely a puppet for whatever puppet master was controlling him.

Nerves coiled my stomach, and my gaze shifted to the anklet that Bastian wore. Similar to my collar, a purple stone was secured at its center.

We still didn't have full answers from the semelees. All we knew was that someone was controlling Bastian with that gem, but we had no idea who, and it was possible we would never know.

But getting that anklet off Bastian was imperative. Nothing good came from jewels that had been placed upon fae to control them. The Goddess knew I'd learned that lesson over and over.

I ran my hand along the smooth metal at my throat. At my collar's center, the purple stone barely throbbed. At least now it was mostly dormant, since my guardian had used his adaptor to release me from its suffocating hold. But it still suppressed my magic to some extent, and it would never allow me to become a queen of the semelees. With it in place, I would always be a lorafin princess only.

"Elowen?" Jax's quiet question had my hand dropping. The room was dark, moonlight only penetrating the windows. Jax pulled the covers over his brother, who was lying motionless and supine. Bastian remained staring straight ahead, so Jax ran a hand over his face, closing his eyelids. Pain again reverberated from Jax into me along our bond.

Heart breaking, I questioned if Bastian had even blinked since we'd saved him. I reached for Jax, and when I spoke, my voice was slightly hoarse. "Come, my love. It's late."

Jax clasped my hand, his palm warm and smooth. A shiver raced up my arm, and my magic naturally billowed toward his. A low hum sounded in his chest as he led me from the room.

I still couldn't believe that just last night, Jax had laid claim to me, bonding me as his mate, and this morning I'd done the same to him.

We were still so newly mated that I couldn't believe that it had happened. Everything with Bastian had taken centerstage since our bond had formed, yet Jax—Prince Adarian, the crown prince of Stonewild Kingdom—was my mate. The gods and goddesses had chosen him for me and me for him.

At the threshold to Bastian's chambers, Jax gave his brother one last look, then extinguished the fairy lights, and closed the door. For a moment, he stayed there, eyeing the lock while standing in the hallway.

He took a deep breath, then muttered a spell, and a coating of magic sealed the lock and frame. Pain again engulfed Jax's aura and billowed toward me on our bond.

"I'd like to think that my brother would never hurt me, or you, or any of us, but"—his throat rolled in a swallow—"the male in there looks like my brother, but it's not him. I don't know where my brother has gone, but that's not him."

I laid a hand on his cheek, my heart clenching at the sheer agony strumming from him. "I know, Jax, but tomorrow we'll venture to the Solis continent, and then we'll find that female. We'll find a way to remove that anklet and truly save your brother once and for all. We won't stop until we do."

# CHAPTER 2

Bells tolling in Leafton's square roused me from sleep. I stretched, and heat from Jax's side warmed my skin. Turning, I wrapped my arm around his waist, and his stomach tightened, a low groan rumbling in his chest. Outside, the sun kissed the horizon, and a pulse of magic bathed the realm. A sleepy smile lifted my lips. I loved sunrises. I loved everything about this time of day when magic from the universe called to my own.

"Good morning," I whispered. I kissed the back of Jax's neck and ran my hand up his middle, my fingers dancing across his skin.

His aura began to pulse. "Good morning, mate," he replied in a husky growl.

He abruptly spun and pinned me beneath him, getting a giggle out of me. "It's about time we had a moment to ourselves. Yesterday's wakeup didn't exactly go as planned."

His eyes blazed like liquid cerulean. Dark hair draped across his forehead, and the muscles clearly defined in his shoulders bulged against his skin, begging me to touch them.

I arched into him, a low throb beginning in my lower stomach. Jax dipped his head, kissing along my neck, and then trailed soft kisses across my collarbone.

Power thrummed in his aura, calling to my magic. The mating mark on the back of my neck tingled, and the need to be with this male, to claim him, to own him . . . it filled me up as though a force greater than myself demanded that I be with him.

"I love you," I whispered, and an answering pulse of love strummed along his bond.

He cupped my cheek, his eyes heated with want. "Love doesn't accurately describe what I feel for you, Elowen. You are my realm, my stars, my moon, my life. You are everything to me. *Everything*."

I pulled him in, our mouths clashing together. A low growl rumbled in his chest, and his fingers grazed against the side of my breast in a soft caress.

"Has it only been a day since I felt you inside me?" I rasped when his mouth finally left mine. "It feels like I haven't felt you in weeks."

A discontented sound came from him. "I shall indeed fix that."

I closed my eyes, relishing the power that radiated from him. His head dipped again, and my fingers tangled in his hair. He moved lower, deliberately, and I knew immediately where he was headed.

I parted my thighs, my need making me quiver like a trembling leaf.

He inhaled, and a sharp spike entered his aura. "I could smell your arousal all day, and it wouldn't be long enough." Humming in satisfaction, he settled himself between my legs, and his tongue flicked out.

I bowed off the bed, a cry parting my lips.

Another groan came from him, and he began to lick me in earnest, but then a shout came from down the hall.

Jax's head lifted just as a crash against a wall reverberated through the suite.

Another garbled yell that sounded more animal than fae pierced my ears.

"What in the realm is that?" I muttered.

Both of us bolted upright, and I pulled the covers up and around me just as Phillen burst through our bed chambers' door.

Ragged breaths lifted the guard's chest. "Jax! Bastian broke out of his room. He charged right through the wall. It's not good."

The crown prince of Stonewild shot out of bed as though he'd channeled God Zorifel's power. Naked, he flew across the room, only snagging a pair of pants on his way out.

A crash came from somewhere else in the suite, then grunts and banging.

*Stars Above.* I rushed out of bed too and dressed hastily, then ran out of the room after them.

Hurrying, I was still trying to get my hair tied up and out of my face when Lars flew through a door into the hallway right in front of me. I skidded to a stop.

The redhead's body slammed into the wall and fell to the floor. Dust wafted up in the air around him.

Gaping, I stepped toward him, but before I could ask the groaning guard if he was okay, Bastian was standing in the hall, having charged through the broken door after Lars. He was only three paces in front of me.

Warily, I met his gaze.

Standing tall, he was as imposing as Jax. I took a step back, then another, and Bastian's head swayed. His antler rack brushed the ceiling. Dead-looking eyes regarded me, as if he didn't really see me.

"Bastian?" I said tentatively.

He abruptly moved, bending low as if about to charge. His gaze locked onto mine, but it was as though he looked right through me.

"Bastian?" I stumbled back more, but he positioned his antlers to strike.

"He's in the hall!" someone yelled from elsewhere in the suite.

Bastian charged.

I leaped back as he barreled toward me.

Jax, Phillen, and Bowan flew into the hall from a hole in the plaster in another room.

There was a hole.

In the wall.

That was big enough for fae to fit through.

"Elowen, get back!"

It was the only warning I got before a rush of fire erupted from Bastian's hands. The fireling half-breed's flame shot toward me at an impossibly fast rate while his antlers were only inches away from penetrating my stomach.

A wave of Jax's magic exploded out of him, but before Jax's power could reach his brother, my own magic reacted.

Potent lorafin energy rushed up from my internal well and engulfed me in cold shadows.

Bastian's fire hit my magic in an explosive array of flames just as his antlers tried to pierce me. Fire licked against my magical barrier, and the scraping of his antlers shoved and searched for a way in, but even though I could sense his fire and bone-like antlers, I didn't feel them.

Coldness seeped from my pores, dousing Bastian's

magic and strength. In a blink, my magic overpowered his, tempering his flames and halting his efforts to impale me.

It was enough time for Jax to throw himself on top of his brother. Phillen and Bowan quickly followed, piling on top of the half-breed. All three of them had cuts and bruises on their faces and bodies that were quickly healing, and a look of anguish twisted Jax's expression as he attacked his brother.

Panting, I calmed my magic, and my shadow magic disappeared.

But even though three fae held him down, Bastian began to rise, his face entirely impassive, his eyes glazed.

It was as though a puppeteer was commanding a puppet, and Bastian wasn't even aware of what his body was doing.

"Hold him!" Jax yelled through gritted teeth.

"I . . . can't." Bowan's jaw ground together. "Dammit, when did he get so strong?"

Phillen grunted.

Farther down the hall, Lander stumbled into the hallway, holding his head. Blood seeped through his fingers. Groaning, Lars pushed to a stand from where he'd fallen. The redhead cradled his head as well, just as the sound of the front door opening and closing came.

Alec came into view, sauntering toward the kitchen. He carried a tray of steaming mugs of coffee. "Who's ready for some fresh—" Alec's jaw dropped. He lunged toward the counter, trying to set the tray down, but his movements were too hurried.

The coffee fell to the floor in a tumbling array of tipped beverages. Hot coffee spilled everywhere, and all of the mugs shattered into a hundred pieces. But Alec didn't even pause. He leaped toward the others.

Every single one of them descended upon Bastian, Lander and Lars joining too. It was a mess of flailing limbs and grunts.

Yet Bastian kept rising.

"How is that possible?" I whispered.

Grunting, Jax and his friends grappled for Bastian, groaning and heaving.

I plastered myself to the wall to stay out of their way as the strong scent of coffee permeated the air.

"You're going to have to knock him out," Lander panted. He sat on Bastian's leg, but impossibly, Bastian began to push him off.

"He's right. It's for his own good." Phillen's biceps strained when Bastian tried to wrench out of his grip. "It's the only way we're going to stop him. Nothing else has worked."

Jax's brow furrowed, his expression crestfallen, but then in his commanding Mistvale voice, he said, *"Bastian, go to sleep. Now."*

Powerful Mistvale magic spiraled toward Jax's brother, engulfing Bastian in a sweep of energy.

I waited for him to pass out. Waited for his eyes to close. Waited for this craziness to end.

But it didn't.

Bastian kept moving, still rising inch by inch. It was as though Jax hadn't even spoken.

My eyes flashed wide. "That anklet's control of him is repelling your magic, Jax."

Wildness filled Jax's eyes, and I couldn't help but wonder if it was the first time anyone had ever resisted his Mistvale command.

"Shite!" Bowan flew back when Bastian swung his head and nearly impaled Bowan with his antlers. He grabbed Bastian's left antler at the last moment, dodging the blow. "What are we going to do?"

"We can't take him to Harrivee like this." Phillen grunted again, then ducked when Bastian swung a huge fist for his head.

"*Bastian. Stop!*" Jax tried again in his commanding voice.

But Bastian kept fighting.

Looks of terror descended upon all of their faces, and my mind raced.

With my eyes flashing wide, a thought struck me. I would have to call on the semelees. I hadn't done such a thing since I was a child, and I didn't know if I safely could now, but we were out of options.

Breathing heavily, I closed my eyes and dove my

concentration inward, down to my bottomless well of power.

My soul instantly detached and hurtled through the galaxy, and not even a second later, I punched through the Veiled Between's mist as though it were tissue paper.

*Come to me. Now! I need you in the fae lands,* I commanded the nearest semelee.

It swirled forward, eager to do my bidding, its demeanor curious, its fangs dripping with venom.

Fear cascaded through me. I needed to maintain control of the shadow creature. They were pure power, complete might. One wrong command on my end and—

I faltered. Images of what had happened when I was five assaulted my mind, but I shoved those thoughts away.

*Hurry. I need you in the fae lands.*

The semelee paused. *You wish to twist fate? But you're not—*

*No, I don't want to twist fate. I just need more power. Yours. Join me, for just a moment.*

*Yes, my princess.*

My soul slammed back into my body, and somebody gasped.

I opened my eyes to see the semelee's inky shadow body coiling around me, lifting my hair and igniting my skin with its power. Its huge serpentine form swirled in the hallway, staying close to my side. Its head's width was easily the length of my arm, and its long body would have stretched all the way to the kitchen if it lay flat.

"What in the realm . . ." Lars's eyes grew wide.

The others inched back, only Jax staying put.

"*Subdue the half-breed male,*" I commanded the semelee. "*Make him sleep.*"

The shadow creature swirled forward, like inky mist in the fae lands—both see-through yet whole. Its serpentine body glided through the air, defying gravity, and the outline of its silver eyes and razor-sharp fangs were apparent in the morning light.

"Dear Gods," Phillen muttered and surged back even more.

Jax leaped out of the way just as the shadow creature reached his brother. Bastian pushed to a stand, his dead eyes still staring at nothing. He swung toward the door and took a step toward it, but the semelee swirled around him, encompassing Bastian with its godlike power.

All it took was one squeeze from the ever-powerful semelee.

Bastian slumped to the floor, his eyes closed, his body asleep.

The semelee hissed, its body still wrapped around Jax's brother.

"*Release him. Come to me.*" Magic bled out of me, and pants lifted my chest. It'd been so long since I'd commanded a semelee like this.

A slight sting came from my collar, and I staggered. The semelee swirled around Bastian again, then glanced toward Jax and his friends. Venom dripped from one of its fangs, and its mouth opened.

"*No. Come to me!*" I said in a more forceful tone.

Slowly, as though reluctantly, the semelee released Bastian once more, then drifted to my side.

It wrapped around me, its power humming with mine. I had just enough stamina left to tether it to my soul before I shot us through the galaxy.

The Veiled Between's mist parted slowly, and it took every drop of my concentration to return the semelee to the plane between planes.

With every second that passed, I grew more fatigued and sluggish, but I had enough power left to release the shadow creature before I shot back to the fae lands.

My breath sucked in when I returned to my body, and when I opened my eyes again, it was to see Bastian unconscious on the floor and Jax and all of his friends staring at me with slackened jaws.

Relief hit me momentarily.

I'd done it, and I was still standing, still alive. And I hadn't killed anybody this time.

But then my vision tunneled. Darkness pressed in. The realm spun, and I crashed to the floor.

I AWOKE to the feel of someone draping a cool cloth over my forehead.

Twitching, I moved my head from side to side.

The cool cloth lifted. "Elowen?" Jax said.

I opened my eyes to bright sunlight streaming into our bed chambers. My mate sat beside me, and a heavy dose of worry pulsed in his aura.

"Hi."

"You're okay?" He ran a hand over my forehead, feeling my temperature.

"I don't have a fever." I smiled despite the fatigue rolling through me. "I'm not sick."

He glowered. "You passed out."

"Yes, but that was from being tired. My collar still suppresses me too much despite its loosened state."

A frown marred his features, and his sapphire eyes swirled in a myriad of blue colors. "You commanded a semelee in the fae lands."

"I know. I haven't done that since—" My throat rolled in a dry swallow, and I hastily looked around for a glass of water. One sat near the bed, on a table. I pushed up more and reached for it.

Jax instantly placed it in my hand, and I greedily consumed most of it.

Once my mouth no longer felt dry, I set it down, but I refused to meet Jax's probing gaze. A second ticked by, only the sounds of the city on the streets below filling the quiet.

He cocked his head, and his voice turned soft. "Does your hesitation right now have anything to do with what happened when you were young?"

My attention shot to him.

An understanding look spread across his face. He settled onto the bed more, his aura billowing around him. "Have you ever spoken of it?"

For a moment, I couldn't respond. Of course, Jax knew immediately where my thoughts had turned. He always had an uncanny knack for reading me, and since we were bonded, he could probably feel my wariness too.

Squeezing my eyes shut, I tried to forget what happened all of those summers ago, but the screams had stayed with me. I could still hear them.

Finally, I shook my head. "No, I've never spoken of it."

"Do you think it would help if you did?"

Tears moistened my eyes, but I blinked them away. Drawing my knees up, I wrapped my arms around my legs. "I can still hear them, Jax. Their screams when they died still haunt me."

His throat bobbed, and a groove appeared between his brows. "You were a child, Elowen. You didn't do anything on purpose."

"But I *killed them*. Twenty-one fae died at my hands that day."

"How old were you?"

"Five."

His breath sucked in, and he inched up the bed until he sat closer, then slipped an arm around my waist so he could lean into me. "And where was your guardian when it occurred?"

My chest tightened, but I forced myself to calm and inhale deeply. "He was beside me."

A muscle began to tick in Jax's jaw. "And who was the one that pushed you to venture to the Veiled Between when you were only five summers old and probably had no idea what you were doing?"

I swallowed, my throat again feeling dry. "Him."

"And when you called the semelees back to the fae lands with you, did you do it on purpose?"

"No!" The shout left my lips before I could stop it, and I drew my legs up even tighter. "I didn't even realize I'd done so, not until I saw them swirling at my side. Truth be told, I'm not even sure how I returned them to the Veiled Between after they—" With a shaky hand, I grabbed the water again and took another hasty drink. The cup trembled in my grip.

Once finished, Jax took the glass from me and set it back down. He tucked a strand of hair behind my ear, his eyes softening. "Yet you did return them, with nobody helping you learn how to do that. At five summers old, you stopped them from killing more fae."

I dropped my attention to my hands and began to play

with my fingers. "But *I'm* the reason twenty-one fae were killed that day. I still destroyed twenty-one families."

He cupped my jaw, forcing my chin up so I had to face him.

Hardness coated his expression, and a muscle ticked even more in his jaw. "*No*, Elowen, you didn't. Your guardian is to blame for that. No adult should be demanding that a child risk her life and other lives by forcing her to learn her magic too quickly when she's not mature enough to understand it herself. You are *not* to blame for what happened that day. *He* is."

A tear rolled onto my cheek. Voice catching, I replied, "But he said it was my failure that caused their deaths. He always said I was to blame. He used that event to convince the courts that I should be enslaved. It was after that day that he put his collar on me."

A spike in Jax's aura flooded the room, and his chest rose quickly. Malevolent energy suddenly swirled around him. "Do you think your guardian asked you to call the semelees that day in hopes it would result in deaths? Because if it did, he'd then have a reason to enslave you to him."

My lips parted. "You think he wanted fae to die?"

"You and I both know he has no bounds to his treachery. That event may have been planned by your guardian all along." Jax took several deep breaths, but his aura still swelled in steady, thickening waves. "You've seen more of his true character in the past few weeks than you've probably seen in your entire life. Do you still think he's innocent of any wrongdoing that day?"

My forehead furrowed, and all of the memories flooded back of what my guardian had revealed in the Ustilly Mountains and the days since then. The lies. The betrayals. The murder he committed against my own mother.

Slowly, my heartbeat began to calm, and my chest didn't feel quite so tight. "No, he's not innocent. He's far from innocent."

"And do you feel that you genuinely warrant all of the self-loathing you've inflicted on yourself since that horrible event?"

I nibbled on my lip, my brow furrowing more. I'd been five summers old. *Five.*

I shook my head. "No, I never would have tried to venture to the Veiled Between that day if he hadn't insisted on it. I only did so because he promised me chocolate syrup on my ice cream that night if I tried."

Jax's lips curved up in a sad smile, and he cupped my jaw again, caressing my face. "Do you see it now for what it truly was?"

A tear hit my cheek, but instead of guilt causing it, a bolt of relief did. "He took advantage of me again that day, and like you said, maybe it was all planned from the beginning."

"Exactly. Yet he convinced you that it was your mistake, and I have no doubt he twisted the truth when he went to the courts. And since the fae near you that day all perished, my guess is the courts issued that decree out of an abundance of caution, especially when your guardian put that collar on you that guaranteed it would never happen again."

A rushed breath escaped me, and for the first time since that horrible day, my chest didn't feel so crushed. So constricted. "I never would have killed those fae that day if my guardian hadn't been involved."

A genuine smile lifted his lips. "No, you wouldn't have."

I sat there for another moment, processing all of what we just discussed, and for the first time in my entire life, an emotion entered me that I'd never felt before when I thought of that day . . . forgiveness. Forgiveness to myself and the child who had been abused.

Remorse still filled me and likely always would. But for the very first time, the self-loathing eased, and a ray of hope entered my soul that I wasn't entirely at fault for what had transpired that awful day.

Once again, it was becoming apparent that, like so many other events in my life leading up to this moment, I had been a victim too. A child caught up in a treacherous adult's plan.

And I wasn't to blame for that.

# CHAPTER 3

Since I assured Jax I was fine, he left to check on his brother.

I got up and stretched. The sleep had helped the fatigue I'd felt from commanding the semelee. Not to mention, the revelation I'd had while speaking with Jax had lightened my soul in a way I'd never felt before. Once again, he was right. My guardian was more to blame for what I'd done when I was five summers old than I ever should be.

But one thing still faded my spirit. The collar was slowly restricting my magic again. Twice now it had activated. The first being when I ventured to the Veiled Between right before we found Bastian, causing the semelees to pull back and put a restriction on the number of questions I could ask. And then this morning when I tried to command the semelee back to my side while it'd been wrapped around Bastian. It'd tried to resist and had almost turned its attention on Jax and his friends versus listening to me.

No matter all that I'd done, I was still *caged.*

I balled my hands into fists and padded across the room.

After changing into clean clothes, I slipped through the door into the bathing chamber. My reflection greeted me in the mirror. Tangled hair fell around my shoulders, and dark smudges lined the skin beneath my eyes.

In the ignited fairy lights, the gold collar on my throat gleamed like a blade.

*If only I could rip it off.*

I grabbed a brush and vigorously began working it through my hair.

The purple gem at my collar's center flashed in the light with every swipe of the bristles against my scalp. That magical gem was behind my imprisonment. Each time the gem's magic had surged slightly, it'd alerted the semelees to my magic's full potential still being doused, and they'd paused. The collar's suppressing effects had been minimal, but its controlling pulses had been just enough to jar my magic and cause me to lose my grip on the semelees while tiring me in the process.

Sighing, I finished brushing and pushed the hair from my face. The semelee's response was a grim reminder that soon, even if it took months to fully activate again, eventually the collar would contain me completely.

I nibbled on my lip and plated my hair into three strands, then began braiding it. In the bathroom mirror, I studied the slight smudges under my eyes again, the only remaining evidence of my venture to the Veiled Between this morning. But my green irises were bright and alert, and my chestnut hair now looked shiny and clean. The cozy emerald sweater Jax had gotten me weeks ago in Fosterton adorned my top, and simple black breeches covered my legs. For the most part, I felt good and strong. It was nothing like I used to feel when I ventured to the Veiled Between with a fully active collar, so I tried to take some comfort in that.

Behind me, Jax's reflection suddenly appeared in the mirror. I started at his silent approach, which got a roguish grin from him.

"Scared you?" He raised his eyebrows.

"You wish."

His lips stayed lifted in a crooked smile, and he leaned against the door frame. Casually, he crossed his arms and watched me.

The movement made his chest muscles press against his shirt. Strong biceps were visible when his elbows bent. Dark midnight hair swept across his forehead, and eyes so blazing that they always reminded me of sparkling sapphires regarded me.

My breath caught, and I quickly finished with my hair. Jax's beauty and powerful physique still totally and completely took my breath away.

Clearing my throat, I tied a ribbon around the end of my braid. "How's Bastian?"

Jax frowned. "Still sleeping."

"What about food and drink? Were you able to get him to eat?" I'd been wondering since we took him if he'd consumed anything recently. Bastian certainly couldn't feed himself in the state he was in.

"Phillen managed to get a cup of water down his throat. It took a while, but at least we know he's had that."

"What about food?"

His lips pressed into a line, the fleeting lightness on his face vanishing. "No, nothing yet. We can't get him to swallow bites, so I'm not sure how we'll get him to eat."

I nodded and faced him, then placed my hands against the cool stone counter behind me. "He doesn't look too thin, so he must have been eating at times."

"You're right. Maybe whoever's controlling him"—a muscle bulged in his jaw when he clenched his teeth— "commands him to stay nourished." Oscillating expressions of remorse and anger crested over Jax's features, and I crossed the distance between us.

His arms were around me before I could finish enclosing him in my embrace. "He's survived this long, Jax, and we have him now. He's with us, and we'll find a way to get that anklet off him. We *will*."

"Do you have any idea how long that semelee's magic on him will last? If he becomes agitated again like he did this morning . . ." He released a frustrated sigh and rested his chin on the top of my head. "I don't think any of us are strong enough to keep him held down. That anklet's magic seems to give him superior strength."

My brow furrowed. I eased back enough to see him better, then trailed a finger across his forehead, gently pushing a strand of hair away from his eye. "I don't know how long he'll stay asleep, but I imagine it will be for a while. At least through the day, maybe even a few days. Or perhaps longer." I shrugged. "Honestly, I'm unsure how much magic the semelee used on him. I'm not in-tune enough with them to sense that." I brushed a finger along my collar. The gold choker-style necklace hummed slightly, and its gem released a tingle of energy.

"Has your collar been bothering you more?" His gaze settled on my throat.

"Only slightly. My magic is still mostly free."

"We'll have to work fast because I don't want you risking yourself in the Veiled Between again if Bastian becomes animated once more."

"Do you think whoever's controlling him tried to get him to return to those caverns in the Wood? And that's why he suddenly became so active this morning?"

He nodded. "That's what we're all guessing too."

"Then you're right. We don't have any time to waste. His controller obviously knows Bastian's escaped."

Jax's nostrils flared. "And he wants him back."

IN THE LIVING AREA, everyone was dressed and ready to go. Quinn still hadn't returned, and none of us knew when he would, but the dillemsill had found him and reported our plans to the crowfy shifter. So at least Quinn knew we were venturing to the Solis continent.

"Have the Solis royals been notified of our arrival?" Lander asked, his eyes narrowing shrewdly.

Jax nodded curtly. "The dillemsill I sent returned while Elowen was sleeping. Nori knows our plans and approved them. He said he'll try to meet with us, but he has a few council meetings he has to attend first. If he's unable to join us, he said he'll send his brother instead."

Trivan chuckled. "Ah, Nuwin. I remember him. Cheeky bastard, that one."

Already wearing a cloak and dressed warmly for the Solis continent, Phillen lumbered to the couch in the living area where Bastian slept. Jax's brother lay lifeless again, his eyes closed, his chest rising in small, evenly spaced breaths.

With a groan, the burly guard hefted Bastian off the

sofa, then strode back to us, carrying the large half-breed dangling over one shoulder.

"I bet you're glad we found an enchanted carpet this morning so you won't have to carry him the entire way." Trivan snickered quietly.

"Oh, I don't know," Phillen replied easily. "It's been a while since my muscles have had a proper workout. Sparring with you lot certainly isn't taxing enough."

Bowan laughed, and with widening eyes, I realized how busy all of them had been while I'd been unconscious. A large enchanted carpet was rolled at our feet, and Jax held several long cloaks. Everyone was dressed warmly, wearing heavy pants and thick long-sleeved tops. Sturdy boots covered all of our feet. No one had been sitting idly.

"Does everyone have a portal key on them?" Jax asked as he handed out the warm garments to everyone, each long cloak brushing the floor. They were all navy with gold trim. The one he handed me was even lined with fur. "I want everyone to have a way to return should something happen and we become split up."

Each of his friends slipped on their cloak, then patted their pockets, indicating they'd all stored their keys safely away.

Jax handed a key to me too, and I tucked it into an inner pouch within my cloak.

I'd only recently become aware of the tiny traveling keys. Quinn had procured a jar of them from Drachu, the Lochen king. I'd been told the tiny magical keys had been crafted in the *other* realm, but even that didn't bother me since the keys allowed one to travel instantaneously from one location to another. They were incredibly useful, and we were lucky that Quinn had obtained so many.

Jax swung his cloak around his back, and the long piece of clothing settled around his broad shoulders. "Ready?" he asked.

We all nodded, and a moment of excitement filled me.

I'd never been to the Solis continent, but Jax had warned me that the entire northern land mass was perpetually covered in snow and ice and was freezing season-round.

Once his cloak was secured, Jax held his hands out. "Let's go."

THE REALM SPUN AROUND US, twisting and jarring me as I gripped Jax's and Phillen's hands. In a rush, my booted feet hit powdery snow, and I swayed momentarily until I got my bearings.

I opened my eyes to a sea of white. Harsh, cold wind bit into my skin, and fierce gales blew the cloak around my legs.

The portal key that Jax had been holding fizzled out of

existence as I took in the frozen, icy terrain that we transported to.

Everywhere I looked, snow and ice greeted me. Rolling hills graced the horizon, all covered in sparkling white blankets of winter frost, yet the harshness of this land didn't captivate my attention long. Instead, it was the floating meadows above us.

Gasping, I tilted my head back.

Soaring hundreds of feet, and some even miles above us, hovered Harrivee's floating meadows. They hung suspended in the sky. Dozens and dozens of huge pieces of land dotted the atmosphere. They all shifted and swayed as though controlled by a phantom breeze. Some were so large they blocked out the sun entirely. Others were smaller and looked barely big enough to hold more than fifty fae on their surface, but it was the sheer magnitude of how many there were that took my breath away.

"What is this place?" I asked, awestruck.

Jax placed his hands on his hips. "Harrivee Territory's floating meadows. The larger meadows contain mines deep within them, and I've been told the power of these hovering islands infuses the gems and stones with potent magic."

"And you learned this how?" I arched a quizzical eyebrow at him. In all of my studies, I'd never heard of this place.

"Norivun told me about it once when I had a visit in

Solisarium. Most fae in our realm don't know about these floating islands. The gems and precious stones harvested in these meadows are revered by the Solis. They don't sell them, and they don't allow them to be traded on the open markets. They keep the meadows' contents a closely guarded secret." His gaze shifted to the sky. "But until this day, I've never seen them."

"None of us have," Alec commented.

Like us, the House Graniteer noble's attention was fixated on the sky.

"Right then, should we go?" Trivan unfurled the large enchanted carpet in the snow.

Lars nodded. "No time to waste."

Carefully, Phillen lowered Bastian to the carpet's center, and the sleeping half-breed fell limply onto it.

Jax issued a command, and a whisper of magic puffed around the carpet. It levitated until it hung suspended a hand's width off the ground.

One by one, we all stepped aboard.

"Where do we go from here?" I asked Jax.

"Norivun said to go to the central floating meadow, the largest one. He said we can't miss it." Jax issued another command, and the carpet began to rise, lifting into the sky but staying horizontal. We went up and up and up, like a floating platform that levitated effortlessly.

My vision swayed when the ground disappeared beneath us, and the floating meadows grew closer.

Cold atmospheric wind blew around us. We rose higher and higher, and the floating meadows grew more apparent. The one nearest us came into focus, and I was able to make out its pointy underside better. The meadow was constructed of solid rock. Harsh angles of its stony exterior looked like an upside-down cone, yet at the very top, the meadow's surface appeared flat and had bits of grass dangling from the edge.

"How peculiar," Lars whispered.

Out of nowhere, a Solis fairy dipped around one of the floating meadows above us, his huge leathery black wings flapping. He held a weapon in his hands, and a uniform covered his frame. My breath sucked in when another Solis fairy careened around the meadow behind him, dressed exactly the same.

Another appeared, darting between two smaller meadows that were suspended in the air only a few paces apart from one another.

And then more fae flew toward us, their numbers growing with each breath I took.

All of them had flapping wings, holding them aloft as their weapons trained on us. And a quick look at all of their identical clothing told me who they were. Guards.

"Do you think they're here to greet us?" Bowan muttered sardonically.

Jax sighed. "I was worried this would happen. Norivun said he would send word of our arrival, but he wasn't sure if his message would get here in time. He warned me that Solis guards patrolled the floating meadows."

"Which means . . . what?" Phillen shifted on the carpet, his hand going to his sword.

Jax scowled. "Which means, we may have some explaining to do."

"Is that before or after they try to kill us?" Lander's eyes narrowed when one of the Solis fae, who was rapidly approaching us, aimed his weapon.

"You're trespassing on sacred Solis land!" the guard yelled, and his finger tightened on his crossbow. "That's against Solis law and punishable by death!"

A swell of magic emitted from Jax. "Apparently after."

# CHAPTER 4

The Solis fae guards flew toward us, weapons aimed to shoot. A huge rush of magic shot from Jax, exploding into the air around us.

Jax's magic hit the Solis fairy closest to us first. He shrieked, his movements suddenly turning erratic and uncoordinated.

"I'm blind!" the male yelled.

Jax's magic continued its outward ascent, and each Solis fairy stopped their forward momentum. Their wings held them aloft, but their limbs began to thrash, and more than one scrubbed at their eyes.

"They've blinded all of us!" a female shouted. "Call for reinforcements!"

Jax cursed beneath his breath, then issued a command to the carpet that had us flying upward at an accelerated rate.

Cold wind rushed over my cheeks, and Phillen and Lars both crouched and placed their hands on Bastian to keep him from rolling to the side.

When the carpet was close enough for the Solis fae to hear us more clearly, Jax shouted, "My name is Prince Adarian Willip Jackson Stagthorn, crown prince of Stonewild Kingdom and heir to one of the mighty four thrones on the Silten continent. I gained permission from the Solis royal family to venture here today with my friends. Your royal family, specifically Norivun Deema Melustral Achul, has sent a message to your commander that grants us permission to visit here today."

A few of the fae nearest us swung their heads from side to side, as though trying to see. Snow began to fly in the air, swirling around everyone, making it even harder to read facial expressions.

Heart beating erratically, I stood stiffly, but one fleeting thought registered. Jax's full name was Adarian Willip *Jackson* Stagthorn. I was guessing Jax's nickname had come from his second middle name, but as soon as that epiphany struck me, I returned my attention to our surroundings.

The first fairy who had flown at us, likely the leader of their group, huffed. "We'll have to verify that information before you can proceed farther." His nostrils flared. "Is it you who's blinded us?"

"Yes, it was me, and I apologize, but I couldn't have you

harming us." Jax sighed heavily, his hands fisting. "I will return your eyesight to you, but if you threaten me, my mate, or my friends again, I will take it again just as fast."

The Solis male seethed but dipped his head. "Understood. If you're indeed who you say you are, I apologize for our aggression today. Had we known a foreign royal was visiting with permission from the Solis royal family, this wouldn't have occurred."

"Thank you." Jax dipped his head even though none of them could see it. "I shall return your sight now, and we'll wait here until you grant us permission to go farther."

In a blink, Jax's suffocating Ironcrest magic disappeared, and the dozen fae who hovered near us released collective sighs of relief. All of them stayed put, their wings continuing to flap and hold them aloft, but the first swirled around and raced back to where he'd come from. The rest stayed, circling us, weapons still in hand.

Lander growled low in his throat, probably because one of the weapons was trained right at him, but there was less fury in the Solis guards' auras. It was as if they kept their weapons up out of the training instilled in them versus wanting to actually use them.

Their close proximity, however, did give me a moment to study them, and everything I'd ever heard about the Solis fae proved to be true. All of them had silvery or white hair, and each had blue eyes. Their uniform tops were a light yellow, and black breeches covered their legs. If I remembered right, the territory color of Harrivee was yellow, so that wasn't surprising.

In addition to the uniform tops, all of them wore gloves, and thick scarves encircled their necks. It was obvious they were equipped to fly in freezing temperatures, yet I couldn't help but wonder if their clothes were enchanted to keep them warm or if their bodies had simply adapted to the cold, and they didn't feel it like I did.

Shivers continually wracked my frame, the cold atmospheric wind not helping, and I had to keep my jaw locked so as not to tremble with cold.

Thankfully, we didn't have to hover in the freezing temperature for long. A shout came from above, and the initial fairy who had confronted us zoomed back our way, dipping and weaving around the smaller floating meadows.

He stopped a short distance away and made a gesture with his hands. All of the fae surrounding us lowered their weapons.

"Prince Adarian is right. This foreign royal and his friends have been granted permission to visit the meadows. We're to take them to Hartivul Mine." The guard inclined his head. "Apologies, my prince. Follow me."

Jax commanded the carpet to keep pace with our fae escort. We glided in the center, the guards surrounding us, and everyone dipped and wove up and around the floating meadows.

We flew higher, the solid land below now distant. Cities on the ground's surface became visible too, but they were just specks, too far away to clearly see.

My eyes widened more as the meadows grew closer. Impossibly, on the tops of most of them were plants and grasses, growing and blooming on the flat surfaces. Some even had flowers. Yet, it was still *freezing*. Snow dotted all of the meadows, but the vegetation didn't seem to mind. Miraculously, the plants grew through it.

"How is that possible?" I gaped when we sped by an entire field of budding roses emerging from crisp white snow.

"Magic," Jax replied. "This land is blessed with immense magic that allows plants to grow in their frozen climate. They call it *orem*."

"Look at that." Phillen nodded toward a cascading waterfall on one of the floating meadows. Ice coated the waterfall's sides, but the pond it fell into was mostly open water. From there, the pool wove into a small river that snaked along the meadow's surface. The river swept all the way to the edge of the meadow, where it dripped off, falling in a perpetual waterfall to the ground. It was one of the largest meadows that we'd passed. Rolling hills and a small mountain on its surface graced its landscape.

"This is so beautiful," I whispered.

Jax inched closer to my side, his pine and spicy scent filling the breeze. "We're very lucky to witness this today. Most fae in our realm are never granted this privilege."

"Are you friends with the royal family here? Is that why they were so welcoming?"

Jax shrugged. "Norivun and I are of similar age. I grew up seeing him at sporadic royal events held among the four continents. I suppose you could say we're friends, although we don't frequently see each other, and we don't talk often, but we've always gotten along."

"Our destination is straight ahead," the fairy guard leading the way called over his shoulder, his flapping wings obstructing my view of his face.

Jax's and my conversation halted, and my jaw dropped when I beheld the *huge* floating meadow we glided toward. It was the largest one I'd seen so far. The depth of the floating meadow had to plunge at least a thousand feet below its surface, and the width of it stretched several miles.

Despite its massive weight and the rocky sides that tapered into a cone shape beneath it, the enormous meadow hung suspended in the air as though it was as light as a feather.

Fae working on the meadow's surface could be seen as we drifted closer to the center. All of them had silver hair and black wings. Some stayed put, calling out orders to those around them. Others emerged from what looked like the entrance to a cave, which I guessed was the mine, as they walked to a large winged creature that lay docilely on the meadow's surface.

The creature was an animal I wasn't familiar with, but it appeared to be asleep since its eyes were closed and its scaled head rested on the snowy ground. Its body was covered in furry white feathers, and I couldn't tell if it was a bird or reptile, but it had wings folded at its side, and strapped to the animal's large frame was a harness with several large buckets attached to it.

The fae who approached the sleeping animal did so readily, as though not scared of it. When they reached it, they placed whatever they were carrying into the large containers harnessed to the animal and then secured the bucket's top flap.

"What is that flying behemoth?" Trivan called to the Solis around us, pointing to the animal.

"A *ligersail*," one answered. "We use them to bring the mine's harvest back to the ground. It's easier than the mineworkers carrying heavy sacks. More secure too. Ligersails can be trained to detect deceit. If anyone working in the mines attempts to steal the harvested stones, the ligersail makes its displeasure known."

Bowan laughed. "I bet that makes catching criminals easier."

The guard grinned slyly. "Indeed."

We flew closer to the cave, and the fairy guard pointed to a flat area near the mine's entrance. "Land there."

Jax followed his command and settled the carpet on the meadow's snowy surface. Back on solid ground, my body still swayed. The floating meadow dipped and moved beneath us. It was an entirely disorienting feeling.

"Wait here." The fairy guard folded his black wings behind his back, lifting them so they didn't drag on the ground, then strode toward the mine's entrance.

A fairy who was standing resolutely by the mine and issuing orders inclined his head to the fairy guard when he reached him. Behind them, banging and groaning sounds came from deep within the mine shaft, and I couldn't be certain, but I could've sworn that small puffs of magic emitted from the entrance as well.

The two males spoke to one another quietly, and I couldn't hear what they said, but they both glanced our way a few times.

The fairy at the mine's entrance, who I could only assume was the male in charge, lifted his hand and beckoned us closer.

Trivan huffed and grumbled under his breath. "Is that any way to treat a crown prince?"

But Jax just shrugged. "We'll do as they request. Come."

All of us stepped off the carpet, save Bastian. Jax's brother was none the wiser that we were currently standing miles above the realm's surface on a gigantic floating meadow.

As a group, we ambled toward the male in charge, and when we reached him, Lars and Phillen moved to guard Jax's flank, their attention continually swiveling around.

The fairy guard bowed. "Prince Adarian, may I present the Hartivul Mine's lead archon, Khristian Severell. He may assist you further."

The rest of the Solis guards who'd accompanied us all took flight, leaving us alone in the archon's company.

The archon drew himself up taller, and the tips of his black wings shone like obsidian in the sun. He glanced behind us, his gaze alighting on Bastian's still form. Eyes narrowing, he shifted his attention back to the prince.

"Prince Adarian." The archon bowed. "I've received word that you're to be allowed information regarding our mines."

"Thank you." Jax inclined his head. "We're here today because we have reason to believe at least one stone, and possibly many more, were taken from these mines either illegally or were sold legitimately to someone on the Silten continent—"

"The Silten continent?" Khristian's chest puffed up indignantly. "We don't sell our gems to Silten fae."

Jax paused. "In that case, we'll assume they were taken illegally. Whatever the case, the gems that we believe came from here were crafted into jewelry that have been used for nefarious purposes and are currently being worn by Silten fae. We believe the gems are controlling their minds, and we would appreciate any help you can give us in locating the fairy who forged the jewelry."

Khristian's forehead furrowed over his snowy eyebrows. "Gems from our mines? Forged for *Silten* fae? Truly?"

"That is what the prince said," Bowan all but growled.

The archon huffed. "But we don't allow gems from our floating meadows to leave the continent."

Annoyance flared in Jax's aura. "Nevertheless, we believe that's what's occurred, so I would appreciate your help in locating the forger." Jax glanced back at his brother. "One gem is on the male there. We believe many more are on other fae on our continent, and there's also a possibility that one's on my mate, and in a device that we own." Jax turned toward me, his eyes softening. "Elowen? If you would please show him."

I stepped forward and angled my head. "The purple stone at my throat is magical."

The second the archon caught sight of my collar, his eyes widened. He stepped forward, his movement swift until he stood right in front of me. He lifted a finger to touch my collar.

Jax growled and shifted closer to my side. "No touching." A flash of light appeared in Jax's eyes, the same territorial gleam that he'd portrayed in the Wood, the morning we'd been searching for Bastian and Alec had held my hand.

Khristian's wings ruffled, and he dropped his curious fingers, but his gaze sharpened. "Where did she get that stone?"

I bristled. "*She* didn't get it anywhere. This was placed on me."

Khristian's gaze swept across all of us, and his wings rippled again. He jerked his chin toward Bastian's sleeping form. "Is the same stone on that male?"

"We believe so. Both jewels look similar, but of course, we have no way to confirm that." Jax waved toward the floating carpet. "And his was forged into an anklet, not a collar."

The archon's nostrils flared. "And you say there are *more stones* like this on the Silten continent and in a device?" His voice was so sharp that it cracked like a whip.

"Yes, we believe there are many more," Jax replied evenly.

Huffing, Khristian strode to the carpet, his strides fast and agitated. He stopped when he reached the carpet's edge and planted his hands on his hips as he assessed Bastian.

We followed him, and Jax crouched and lifted the hem of Bastian's pants, revealing the anklet secured above his brother's foot. The metal flashed in the sunlight, the jewel at its center gleaming.

Khristian's breath sucked in. "*Where* did you get that stone? I must insist that you tell me."

Jax took a deep breath. "We don't know. That's why we're here. We need to find who forged them so they can hopefully be removed."

Khristian's fingers, still wrapped around his hips, began tapping against his waistband in quick succession. "Upon looking at them, it does, in fact, appear that they came from our mines, but I will need to test them to affirm that." He glanced toward the mine's entrance and beckoned someone with two fingers. "Penneveer, bring the wand."

My spine snapped upright. *Wand?* My guardian's adaptor was also like a wand.

A female wearing a uniform similar to Khristian disappeared into the mine shaft. She emerged a minute later. In her hand, a slim wand flashed in the sunlight.

My heartbeat increased erratically. Another wand. Another device. I could only pray to the gods that their wand couldn't control me.

Jax stepped in front of me and growled low in his throat. "What is that device?"

"It's used to test the potency and identity of the stones that are harvested from our mines." Khristian glanced at Jax, as if only registering the energy that soared around him. His tone turned haughtier. "It won't hurt anyone. It's merely a testing device."

I stepped from around Jax and suppressed my irritation. I couldn't help but think that this archon was used to issuing orders versus having to answer questions. Whatever the case, the archon's arrogance was starting to get on my nerves. Shoulders tensing, I waited for whatever was to come.

Penneveer neared, and despite her thin form, the female carried herself as confidently as the archon. "Archon Severell, as you instructed." She held out the wand to him.

He snatched it from her and faced me. "I'm going to set this against the gem at your throat. It will confirm whether that stone came from our mine. Hold still."

Jax seethed and stepped closer to the archon. "Remember, that's my mate you're speaking to." A puff of anger filled his aura, and his magic wafted closer to the archon.

The second Jax's power hit him, the archon gasped. "I meant no disrespect, my prince." He bowed, the movement awkward, as though—like having to answer questions—he was out of practice in bowing too.

I took a deep breath. Sweat lined my palms, the moisture cooling my hands in the icy breeze. But even though my entire body wanted to retreat, I held still as the wand loomed.

With slower, less rapid movements, the archon placed the wand at my neck. A tingle of magic puffed against my skin when it touched the stone. My collar heated and warmed, and the wand began to glow until several colors emitted from its base in a series of undefinable order.

The archon's eyes widened, and he pulled the wand away. He turned stunned eyes on Penneveer.

"Impossible," she breathed.

The archon swung back to Jax and me. "It *is* a gem from our mine." He focused on me. "Who placed this on you?"

My heart began to pound with hope. My collar's gem *was* from here. But I focused on his question. "My former guardian put this on me, but I have no idea who he purchased it from. This was locked upon me when I was a child. At the moment, it's irremovable."

"Does it suppress your magic?" the archon asked.

My heart jolted. "Yes."

He inclined his head. "I'm not surprised. This stone is a *rhifilyte* gem. It's a rare jewel that our mines only produce on rare occasion, but the potency of its magic is known for its ability to cage and control any type of magic. For many winters, we haven't seen any of these gems produced until a few months ago, when we had a rather prolific production from one of our shafts. Over two buckets were crafted by this meadow in two days, but that explosive production was short-lived."

"A few months ago, did you say?" Alec asked, coming up behind us. The wind ruffled his mahogany hair.

"That's what I said," the archon replied.

All of us gave one another a side-eye, because a few months ago was when Bastian was taken.

The archon glanced down at Bastian. "Is he unwell?" He arched an eyebrow.

I nodded. "He is. That's also why we're here. We believe that his current state of mind and lack of awareness are due to that anklet."

The archon frowned heavily, his expression turning grave. "That could very well be true." He crouched and placed the wand against Bastian's anklet. Sure enough, the same heating and glowing appeared at the wand's end, and the colors it emitted matched the colors it had shone when it'd been against my throat.

The archon seethed quietly. "This one is also from our mines."

"What about this?" Jax withdrew Guardian Alleron's adaptor from his pocket. The slim piece of metal also held a small rhifilyte gemstone.

Khristian quickly tested the adaptor's stone too, and when his wand confirmed that *three* rhifilyte jewels were in his midst, he drew himself up, his nostrils flaring as indignation rose in his aura. "But this truly makes no sense. The mine hasn't produced any more rhifilyte gems since that rare explosion a few months ago. And rhifilyte gems are considered dangerous by many. Nobody would ever sell them, especially not to your fae, so this couldn't have come from us."

"Can these gems be created anywhere else in the realm?" Lander asked, crossing his arms. His brown skin shone in the sunlight, his complexion looking even richer against the snowy backdrop.

"Well . . . not that I'm aware of," the archon replied.

"Then isn't it fair to say both of these gems *did* come from this mine?" Lander pushed. "Even if you can't explain how?"

Before the archon could respond, I said, "Can I ask something? You mentioned that a few months ago, two buckets of this jewel were created here. How many pieces of jewelry could be forged from that amount of this gem?"

Still appearing flustered by Lander's comments, Archon Severell raised his chin. "I daresay thousands, perhaps ten thousand? But like I said, we carefully stowed that production away. None of those stones have been crafted into jewelry or have left our storage facility."

"Are you sure?" Jax asked. "When was the last time anyone officially confirmed they were still under lock and key?"

The archon's chest puffed up again. "What are you implying?"

"We're not implying anything." I dropped my tone into a less challenging one. "We're truly just trying to figure out how these gems came to be on our continent and who forged them. All we know for certain is that the forger is a Solis female."

Khristian's eyes narrowed. "How do you know that?"

"The semelees told me."

"Semelees? Who are they?"

"They're all-knowing creatures that reside in the Veiled Between. I'm a lorafin. I'm able to communicate with them."

The archon looked my frame up and down, and another low growl came from Jax. Drawing himself up once more, the archon stated, "Well, I know nothing about semelees, but never mind all that. Whatever the case, I can assure you all rhifilyte gems mined from here are indeed locked away. We've had no thefts."

"That you know of . . ." Trivan muttered under his breath.

The archon's nostrils flared. "But seeing as how two of these gems are currently placed on the both of you, and one being in that device, I will have to begin an inquiry as to how they've come to reside on your continent."

Trivan snickered. "Please do. That would save all of us a lot of trouble."

Jax gave Trivan a side-eye and addressed the archon again. "Is there anybody you know who's capable of acquiring these gems and turning them into jewelry?"

The archon's wings ruffled anew. "Of course, Hartivul Mine has many employees on staff who do just that. Our forgers are paid to craft our gems into jewelry, among other things, and they are the only ones on the continent with the specific training required to do so, but none of our employees would do *this*."

Jax inhaled, and his annoyance strummed to me along our bond. I stepped closer to him and wrapped my hand through his.

"Would you be so kind as to give us a list of the fae employed by your mine who are capable of creating jewelry such as what me and this male are wearing?" I asked the archon.

Khristian gazed down his nose at me. "That is confidential information."

"Even if that request comes from *me*?" The mask of the crown prince descended over Jax's face.

Khristian sputtered. "This is highly irregular. We normally do not share any information like that, even with outside royals."

But Jax's lips only thinned more. "I believe the Solis royal family will be quite displeased to hear that you've defied my wishes."

For the second time since meeting him, the archon's haughty expression faltered, but just as fast, he squared his shoulders. "Even so, it is quite unusual to reveal such privileged information."

Jax stepped closer to him, and my mate's blazing blue eyes turned into chips of ice. "And it is also quite *unusual* for fae I care for to have been subjected to the potent power of the gems locked around their limbs. I'm sure you can appreciate our need for such information. The sooner these devices are removed, the better, and according to the semelees, the only one who can remove that male's anklet is the forger." Jax pointed at Bastian.

The archon scowled. "But—"

"I'm also more than happy to return these gems to your mine as soon as we accomplish that task," Jax added. "We would like to be rid of them as assuredly as you would like to reclaim them."

The second Jax revealed that he would surrender the gems to the Solis continent, the archon's face brightened, and a small smile played upon his lips. "Ah, in that case, of course, my prince. I'm very pleased to hear that you endeavor to do the right thing and return these gems to their rightful owners."

Behind me, Trivan muttered something under his breath, and even Lars snorted a sound of disbelief.

I stepped closer to the Solis archon. "How many fae are employed in your mines who can forge jewelry with these stones?"

Khristian canted his head. "Our metalwork affinity fae would be the ones to do so, and at last tally, I believe there were thirty-four of them on staff."

My eyebrows shot up. "Thirty-four? In that case, will you please provide us a list of all of the females that have such an affinity?"

"Only the females?" the archon asked, his voice rising

in surprise. "You're truly certain it was a female who crafted these?"

"Yes, females only." But while I was certain it was a female who crafted Bastian's anklet, we didn't know for certain that the same fairy had crafted my collar. Yet right now, we needed to get the anklet off Bastian. The way his mind was being controlled was entirely dangerous. His needs took precedence.

"What about your collar?" Jax asked me, his brow furrowing.

I lifted my shoulders, and even though I wanted desperately to get my collar off me, I also knew that right now it wasn't our top priority. "We can always come back here if we reach a dead-end with my collar. Just knowing that the gem is indeed from here is a start to figuring out if its forger is able to remove it from me or not."

He frowned, and I could tell he wanted my collar off as much as he wanted Bastian's anklet removed, but this trip wasn't about me. It was about Bastian.

"You heard my lady," Phillen said gruffly to the archon. "Please fetch us that list, and do make haste."

All of us glanced at Bastian. The half-breed still slept, his breaths deep and even.

But we had no idea how long his slumber would last.

# CHAPTER 5

The list that Khristian provided us contained the names of each female fairy employed by the mines who had a metal-work affinity. In total, there were twenty, and it was very possible one of them had crafted Bastian's anklet.

The parchment fluttered in my hands as we studied the names. We were still on the huge floating meadow, yet Khristian had retreated momentarily to the mine's entrance, leaving the eight of us alone.

The archon was currently sending word to the Solis royal family that he'd done as asked and supplied Jax with the information requested. But since we were now demanding admittance to the location where the fae with metalwork affinities labored so that we could question them, he needed to have that request cleared.

According to Khristian, the fae employed by the mines all lived in the surrounding cities and all worked at a nearby secured facility, which was where they also stored the gems brought down by the ligersails.

Supposedly, according to Archon Severell, the gems never left that facility unless they'd been approved for sale, in which case, they were carefully transported to fine jewelry or weapon markets throughout the continent. Yet each purchase was still tracked. Every single Solis fairy who owned a gem harvested in this mine had their name, address, and other identifying documentation recorded.

One thing was for certain—the Solis fae didn't allow folly with the unique magical stones created by the floating meadows, so for so many to have appeared on the Silten continent, unbeknownst to them, was entirely concerning.

"If Bastian's anklet, and even my collar, were both crafted here, then someone snuck them out of that facility and effectively stole them." I mulled that over, nibbling on my lower lip. "It's the only way to explain it. There's no way the Solis fae would have legally relinquished these gems to our land."

Jax nodded. "I agree."

"As do I." Alec also dipped his head. The others quickly did the same.

"It would appear they have a traitor in their midst whether that archon wants to believe it or not." Trivan sneered. "Sounds like someone needs a visit from a certain *someone* from our land."

He kept his words vague on the off chance anyone

could overhear us, but we all knew who Trivan referred to. Whoever had crafted my choker and the anklets being used to control the half-breeds did indeed deserve a visit from the Dark Raider. Because our jewelry had only been created with malicious intent and malicious intent only.

"Do you suppose that every single anklet that is being worn by a half-breed on our continent came from that facility?" Lander scratched his chin, his expression thoughtful, yet his voice was its usual monotone. "Or do you think it's possible someone stole the jewels directly from the mineshaft shortly after this floating meadow produced them? Perhaps before any of the Solis fae were even aware of their creation? Maybe it produced more than two buckets, and that archon doesn't realize it."

"What about the ligersails?" I asked. "The guards said they also help detect theft. Wouldn't that animal have noticed if someone left the shaft with gems stuffed in their pockets?"

Lander nodded. "Good point."

Trivan shrugged. "Maybe that flying behemoth missed it."

"You all raise good questions," Jax said, his brow furrowing. "We'll have to ask Khristian more about the mine's security."

My frown deepened as I thought more too. "But even if someone stole them directly from the mineshaft without Khristian's awareness, someone with a metalwork affinity still crafted them into jewelry. Who else on this continent would know how to do that apart from the fae who work for these mines?"

Phillen scratched his chin. "Another fairy with a metal-work affinity who isn't employed by the mines?"

"I suppose that's possible," I replied, "but Archon Severell said it takes specific training to learn how to create the magical jewelry." I ran my finger along my collar, and a slight tingle of magic pulsed against my skin. "In all likelihood, one of their employees forged these, or someone who used to work for them did. And even if they stole the gems directly from the mine shaft, logic deems that they were indeed crafted here and then transported to our land. A Silten fairy would have no idea how to forge this kind of jewelry. And remember what Guardian Alleron admitted in the Ustilly Mountains? He hired a forger to create my collar in a land far away. He didn't even know where it'd been crafted exactly, but I would bet rulibs it was somewhere near here."

Bowan clapped me on the back, a jovial laugh erupting from him. "Look at you, Elowen. You've turned into quite the investigator."

I rolled my eyes but couldn't help my smile.

Lars cleared his throat. "I agree with Elowen. It seems most likely it was a Solis fairy who's either still employed by these mines, or used to be, who's behind it all."

Pride shone from Jax's expression, and he shifted

closer to me and slipped an arm around my waist. He pressed a kiss to my neck and whispered, "Beautiful and intelligent . . . how did I get so lucky?"

The bond hummed inside me. I turned my head, and his lips found mine. His kiss was searing, possessive, and my body instantly responded.

Breathless, I finally pulled away from Jax, only to find everyone looking respectfully away. Cheeks heating, I sagged into my mate's side, embarrassed at how easily he elicited reactions in me.

His only response was to nip my neck again before saying to his friends, "I'll still inquire about security in the mineshaft, just to be sure it's not possible more gems were created unbeknownst to the archon, but I think you're right. We should focus our efforts on the Hartivul staff who could have created Bastian's anklet, and possibly Elowen's collar, which means we have many fae to question."

"What's the plan now?" Alec pulled his cloak tighter around him. A fierce wind had picked up, bringing with it blowing snow that hit one's skin like icy needles. He leaned down and straightened Bastian's clothing as well, covering the half-breed's exposed hands.

"Now, we wait for admittance to that facility," I replied, relieved that my voice sounded even, following Jax's kiss. "Then we have our crown prince begin questioning the fae with metalwork affinities. If he uses his

Mistvale commanding voice, they'll be forced to reveal the truth of what they know. Because even if none of them match the description the semelees showed me, it's still possible one of them will know something about the anklets, or if a past employee created the anklets, they may be able to direct us on where to find them."

Phillen's eyebrows shot up. "Did you really just speak that casually about Jax using his Mistvale magic?"

Bowan laughed. "Oh, Elowen, I really am growing to enjoy you. You didn't even blink when you suggested that."

A blush warmed my cheeks, and Jax chuckled and nuzzled my neck. "For you, my love, I'll command *anyone.*"

WE WAITED for Archon Severell to return with word from the Solis royals on whether we could visit their facility.

Wintry weather continued to blow around us, and I cupped my hands, breathing into them, but despite trying to warm myself, my fingertips grew numb, and I could no longer feel my toes.

Jax stepped closer to me, his booted feet crunching quietly in the snow, and he pulled me into his embrace.

Warmth from his chest penetrated my cloak, and his arms felt like hot steel bands around me. He ran his hands up and down my back, then dipped his mouth to my ear. "Are you cold, my love?"

My only response was a shiver and chattering of teeth.

A low, discontented growl came from his throat, and a puff of magic emitted from him. The air around us abruptly warmed. Heat enveloped my frozen limbs, and it felt as though a warm ray of sunshine burned down upon us.

I sighed in bliss. "Have I ever told you that I'll never get sick of how many elements you control?"

He chuckled. "I'm glad my abilities please you. And have I ever told you that every time my magic aids you, I get a strange jolt of pleasure?"

I murmured something halfway intelligible. I was too distracted to do more as I soaked up his heat, but when my mind actually processed his words, my lips curved into a smile. "Is that our mating bond talking?"

"It is." He wrapped me tighter in his embrace, then rested his chin on the top of my head. I nearly moaned in pleasure since he kicked his heat up another notch. "Every time I meet your needs, I feel wildly satisfied."

Sighing, I managed to reply, "Well, in that case, don't let me stop you. I would hate to interfere with that *wildly satisfying* feeling of yours."

Another laugh rumbled in his chest, and he pressed his lips to my ear. His voice dipped to a husky whisper. "Do you know what else I find *wildly satisfying?* Those little sounds you make when I—"

But before he could finish his sultry remark, a flash of magic billowed in the air around us.

I squeaked.

A *huge* Solis male stood before us, having appeared as though from thin air. And considering he wasn't holding a portal key that fizzled out of existence, I knew that he'd mistphased.

The new male was as tall as Jax and just as broad. Tangled silvery hair flew around his head, and eyes as crashing as the Adriastic Sea regarded us. Large black leathery wings—taller wings than I'd ever seen on another fairy and tipped with talons—folded together at his back.

I felt the urge to step away. Whoever this male was, he was powerful, given the energy in his aura, and wealthy too. Finely woven clothing, which reeked of hundreds of rulibs, adorned his frame. The woolen material was mostly black but also had silver and blue embellishments.

Somehow, I managed to hold my ground, but it was hard. The only other male I'd ever felt that kind of strength from was my mate.

But as soon as I finished taking in his appearance, another flash of magic zinged through the air, and four more Solis males appeared right behind the first one.

I started from their abrupt arrival.

All of them had two swords in a crisscross pattern peeking out from beneath their wings, and my brow furrowed as I took in their clothing. They wore what guards did.

One of them had hair shorn close to his head, was tall and lean, and had a grumpy expression on his face. Another had a thick white beard, a strong stance, and large hands. The third had round cheeks and smiled readily, and the last had a long braid down his back that settled between his shoulder blades. And all of them had large leathery black wings folded at their backs.

Despite five huge new males appearing from thin air, Jax just laughed.

"Norivun." My mate grinned and stepped toward the first male, bringing his fist to his chest and bowing.

*Ah, so this is Norivun.*

"Adarian, nice to see you again." Norivun returned the traditional greeting, then inclined his head to the four males behind him. "My guards decided to join me. You remember Nish, Sandus, Haxil, and Ryder?"

"How could I forget?" Jax nodded behind him. "And you remember my friends and guards?"

All of the males brought fists to their chests simultaneously and bowed.

Norivun's guard with the braid cocked his head. "Where's Quinn?"

"Who knows." Trivan shrugged, and a lock of blond hair fell across his forehead as he straightened.

With our pleasantries finished, I realized all of them knew each other.

"And who's this?" Norivun asked, turning his attention on me.

"My mate, Elowen." A smile filled Jax's words.

I brought my fist to my chest and bowed. "It's an honor to meet you."

"Likewise," Norivun replied. His icy blue eyes assessed me, and his face reminded me of chiseled stone.

My mate slipped his arm around my waist and pulled me closer to his side. "I'm glad you could join us, Nori. I hope we didn't interfere with the meetings you had to attend this morning?"

A small smile curved Norivun's lips, cutting through some of the harsh planes and angles of his face. "Trust me, I welcomed the excuse to leave."

Alec laughed, and the pattering in my heart slowed, yet my lorafin magic wanted to rattle inside me. It seemed my magic also recognized the lethal power in this male despite his non-threatening demeanor.

"I do apologize, however, for not getting here sooner." A strand of Norivun's silvery hair, which sat around shoulder length, caught on the wind and brushed against his chin. He pushed it back with a thick finger and curled it behind his tipped ear. Crystalline blue eyes that were nearly as bright as my mate's regarded Jax. "How has Archon Severell been treating you?"

Trivan scoffed. "Well, in my opinion, he's a real—"

"He's been fine," Jax interrupted. "Archon Severell is prideful, as Trivan was about to hint at, but he answered our questions. In fact, we're waiting for him right now. He was trying to contact your family to see if we could venture to the facility where the staff work and the mine's stones are stored."

Norivun nodded. "I know. That's why I'm here. I thought I could kill two birds with one stone—come and see you while also letting him know that I approve your admittance."

As soon as the fae working at Hartivul Mine realized their sovereign was in their midst, they became a flurry of bows and slackened jaws. More than one fairy kept their distance, their expression telling me they both feared and revered this royal male, while others rushed forward to get a look at him and his guards.

I didn't know how to interpret that since I didn't know much about this continent's royal family. But since Jax didn't seem concerned about Norivun and instead acted genuinely happy to see him, I decided that I didn't need to share their fear.

Archon Severell's haughty arrogance also vanished entirely. He became a tongue-tied mess around Norivun, only managing to bow profusely after every sentence he stuttered.

It was both painful and amusing to watch.

Yet Norivun took it all in stride, and I couldn't help but wonder if he was used to this kind of reaction from his fellow fae.

"I'll accompany you to the facility." Norivun glanced down at Bastian's sleeping form, his brow furrowing. "Why does this male appear unconscious?"

"Because he is." I glanced at Jax, wondering how much we should reveal about his brother.

Jax seemed to understand my questioning stare because he added, "We had to use my mate's magic to subdue him. What's locked around his ankle is nefarious. We can't remove it, but it's allowing another to control him."

Norivun's head cocked. "Control him how?"

Jax quickly summed up Bastian's puppet-like behavior this morning and the destruction that had occurred at his residence. "Not even my Mistvale magic could stop him."

Norivun arched an eyebrow. "Yet your mate's magic could?" He turned his attention to me. "And may I ask what your magic is?"

"I'm a lorafin."

His eyebrows shot up, and all of his guards' mouths dropped.

Haxil, the jovial one, grinned. "I've read about your kind in the history books, but I've never met a lorafin before."

I shrugged. "Now you can say that you've met one in the actual flesh."

Haxil's grin stretched, and Norivun chuckled. Even the grumpy-looking guard standing at Norivun's back—I thought his name was Nish—cracked a smile.

But my mate's expression quickly sobered. "I can't guarantee how long Bastian will remain asleep." Jax inclined his head toward his brother again. "If he awakens, it won't be good for anybody. Whoever's controlling him demands obedience. It's like his body can't deny them. We need to get that anklet off of him and the choker off my mate too, if we're able. She's worn hers for far too long."

Norivun's gaze flashed to my throat and to the collar locked upon it. "Is anyone controlling you?" His expression turned grave.

"In a way, yes, but my collar is only used to suppress my magic. Thankfully, my mind remains clear."

Norivun cocked his head. "Why would anyone suppress your magic?"

I raised my shoulders sadly. "Apparently, they fear it."

The royal's eyes narrowed. "There's nothing I hate more than suppressing a female simply because she's powerful . . ." His jaw locked, and a pulse of magic, like blackness and death, wafted in his aura. It felt as though Lucifer had come from the underworld to claim my soul. His magic felt so strong, and the sheer *power* of this male made me once again realize he was just as strong as my mate.

Sucking his power back inside him, Norivun straightened. "It seems swift answers are in order. Follow me."

# CHAPTER 6

Norivun and his friends circled our carpet while the eight of us stepped onto the enchanted material. Bastian stayed sleeping in the center, and luckily, he remained quiet and unresponsive. Everyone crowded around him, Lars and Phillen holding him securely again. Bowan, Lander, Trivan, and Alec flanked his sides, and Jax and I stood at his front.

Even though it was crowded, we had room for more fae, but instead of joining us on our magical form of transportation, Norivun and his guards spread their massive wings.

Norivun pointed south. "It's a short flight to get to the facility. All you need to do is follow me. My guards will keep pace behind your carpet, and I'll keep us on an easy path so your carpet won't have any problems keeping up."

Jax inclined his head. "We'll stay close."

Norivun gave a mighty push from his legs, and he shot into the sky, his black wings flapping violently in the strong winds. His guards took off just as fast.

Jax quickly commanded the enchanted carpet to rise. Soon, we were soaring through the cold atmosphere once more. The huge floating meadow containing Hartivul Mine fell behind us. Other floating meadows filled the sky, making us dip and weave to avoid colliding with them.

Some of the fae guards who we'd seen earlier flapped in the skies near us, patrolling the floating meadows. All of them nodded respectfully to Norivun and his guards, each of them pausing their flight to hover in midair as we passed.

Thankfully, Norivun flew on a glided path downward, not too steep, which made it easy for Jax to command the carpet to follow him. The royal brought us closer to the realm's surface, his guards flapping on the wind behind us. And while it certainly wasn't warm even as we drifted downward, being nearer to the ground helped keep the fierce atmospheric wind at bay.

Despite that, Jax still enacted his air element. We'd been in the cold for hours now, and even though their shifter blood kept the stags from freezing, I wasn't so lucky.

Of course, my mate seemed to sense that because he erected a solid shield of air around us, stopping the wind and warming the bubble of air that cocooned us. It made traveling over the ground pleasantly comfortable.

Our carpet stayed a few stories above the ground as we followed Norivun over hills, icy streams, and snowy valleys. Above us, the floating meadows continued to shift and sway in the sky, and I wondered how much distance they covered. The meadows seemed to go on forever.

But on the ground, everywhere I looked was crystalline snow and ice. Forests were visible, too, in the distance, and a few crops appeared as well. The entire Solis continent was a wintery wonderland, yet amazingly, life still grew here.

It didn't take long to reach the facility that held the gemstones. The building kissed the edge of the nearest town, and the city appeared to be rather small, maybe several thousand fae in residence. Farther into the city, shops and homes were visible. Smoke curled from chimneys. Flying fae dotted the skies. And the sound of the town's hustle whistled to us on the breeze.

The facility we traveled to wasn't overly large either. It stood about a story tall, but it spread out over two blocks.

Norivun landed lightly at the main doors, and Jax glided our carpet to land on the snow at his side. His four guards touched down just behind us.

"Ock, weather's brisk today," the grumpy one—Nish—commented.

Haxil clapped him on the back, his round cheeks bright with cold. "'Tis a lovely northern day, Nishy. The

Mother has blessed us. Don't you all agree?" he asked me and Jax's friends and guards.

I offered a polite smile while Jax's guards all commented on the weather, chests puffing up since, as I was guessing, none of them wanted to admit they felt the cold.

As the male boasting continued, I turned my attention to the facility. My heart began to strum once more. Inside this building, answers might be waiting to questions I'd been asking my entire life.

Constructed mostly of metal, the facility blended into the landscape. It had no windows, only the entrance doors, and a sign hung over them reading *Hartivul Mine Processing Facility.*

I couldn't help but wonder if the vague name was to deter any would-be thefts. While I was certain it was common knowledge to the residents in this city what occurred behind these walls, I had a feeling most fae on the Solis continent were ignorant of the precious gems locked within it.

Jax drifted closer to my side, his brow furrowing. Inhaling my scent, he dipped his head. "We'll not stop until we find that female who forged the anklets and, hopefully, your collar too."

I took a deep breath and nodded.

As the other males and guards turned their attention to the facility, Norivun strode toward the double doors, and when he reached them, he knocked on one sharply. Both doors were frosted, impossible to see through, but a shimmer appeared around the middle of one, and then a male's face appeared from inside.

I jumped, the door's magic and security guard taking me by surprise, but Norivun calmly stated, "Good afternoon, my guests and I would like admittance, and I'll also need to speak with the archon in charge here."

The guard's eyes widened when he beheld Norivun's imposing figure. Through the door, he uttered, "Of . . . of course." He bowed quickly, and then another shimmer appeared around the door's handle.

The lock holding it in place disengaged, and all of us strode inside, save Bastian, who Phillen had to carry.

We entered a simple reception area. Several metal chairs, and a small fire burning in a hearth waited before us. In addition to the woodsmoke, metallic scents permeated the air. Phillen shuffled to the nearest chair and set Bastian down. The half-breed slumped to the side, barely maintaining a sitting position.

The security guard twisted his hands and bowed at Norivun. At his back, his wings stayed closely locked together. "I'll, um, still need you to pass clearance. I do apologize for the formality." He waved toward a crystal ball at the metallic reception desk.

Behind the desk, another wide-eyed male was watching all of us with a slackened jaw. Like all Solis fae, both the receptionist and security guard had white hair, blue eyes, and black wings.

"No need for apologies. I would expect nothing less," Norivun replied as he strode to the crystal ball. "Appearances can be deceiving, especially if one has an illusion affinity or is skilled at glamours."

"Yes, precisely." The guard bowed again. "If you would." He waved toward the crystal ball. "Your guards and guests will need to do so as well."

One by one, we all placed a hand on the crystal ball while the receptionist watched on.

With each new palm that was placed on the sphere, the ball warmed, then our names and addresses were scrawled across the reception ledger. The only fairy who wasn't scanned was Bastian. Both the guard and receptionist eyed Jax's brother curiously as the ball's magic accurately identified each of us, cataloging our identities and residences.

"As you can see, I'm who I appear to be." Norivun smirked slightly.

"Indeed. It's truly an honor." The receptionist brought a fist to his chest and bowed, then glanced at the security guard. "Those that have been cleared may go back. I can take them to Archon Oniville."

The security guard grunted and nodded toward Bastian. "This one will have to stay here since he hasn't been identified."

"Bowan and Lars, would you stay with Bastian?" Jax asked them.

"My guards can stay with him too," Norivun added. "For extra security."

Bowan, Lars, Nish, Sandus, Haxil, and Ryder all moved to stand around the sleeping half-breed, effectively caging him in. Bastian, unbeknownst to the fact that he was surrounded by six large males, still slumped unconscious on the chair.

The facility's security guard frowned, and I could only imagine what he was thinking. I would have bet rulibs that the last thing he expected on his shift today was for a group of foreigners, multiple guards, and two royals to show up with an enchanted carpet and an unconscious half-breed stag.

The receptionist cleared his throat. "The rest of you may come with me."

We followed the receptionist through the back door into a hallway. Gray shiny flooring spread out before us, along with cream metallic walls. The sharp scent of metal grew the farther we wove into the facility.

At the end of another long hall, the receptionist rapped sharply on a closed door, and a shimmer of magic appeared around it. Similar to the front door, another face appeared through a circular hole in the frosted pane, and given the male's uniform, I figured it was another security guard.

The receptionist drew himself up taller. "Our

sovereign and his guests would like to speak with Archon Oniville."

The guard's eyes widened when he saw all of us hovering behind the receptionist, and he quickly disappeared from view. Only a few seconds passed before the door opened, and a female fairy emerged.

She had pure silver hair and blazing blue eyes. Small wings graced her back, and she brought a fist to her chest and bowed deeply at Norivun. "It's an honor, truly." She slowly straightened. "I had no idea you planned to visit us today, but I'm at your service for whatever you may need."

I studied the archon's silvery hair pulled back in a severe bun. Her astute blue eyes traveled over the rest of us before returning to her royal.

Norivun waved toward Jax. "My friend, the crown prince of Stonewild Kingdom on the Silten continent, is in need of our help. Prince Adarian's mate and another male —still in the front reception area—are both wearing jewelry that we believe may have been crafted in this facility. Rhifilyte gems, mined from Hartivul Mine, are encased in both."

The archon's eyes widened, and a surprised huff escaped her. "*Our* jewelry with gems from *our* mine are on Silten fae?" Her wings ruffled behind her, and she cast her narrowed eyes my way.

"Indeed," Norivun continued. "Archon Severell's wand has confirmed it."

"Is that so?" Archon Oniville stepped in front of me, and her gaze focused on my collar. "May I?" she asked, lifting her fingers.

"You may." Appreciating the fact that she asked for consent first, I inclined my head, and she ran her fingers along my collar. Puffs of magic emitted from her fingertips, magic that I hadn't felt the likes of before. With each magical emittance from her, my collar vibrated and tingled.

Eyes widening, she finally dropped her probing hands. "Unbelievable. My magic recognizes the pattern used to construct such a piece. This is indeed a collar from our facility, but how could such a thing have happened?"

My heart leaped at hearing her confirm that my collar had originated here. Voice straining with hope, I managed to get out, "This was constructed sometime in the previous twenty-three to twenty-eight summers. It was placed on me when I was five summers old."

Her eyes widened even more. "You've been wearing such a device nearly your entire life?" She recoiled and brought her hand to her chest. "But that collar is brimming with suppression magic. Why, it must have felt like you were trapped underwater for all these seasons."

My throat rolled in a swallow. "It has."

"Can you remove it?" Norivun asked. "To cage a female like this"—his jaw pumped—"is not something I condone, and it certainly isn't something I would like the Solis fae known for."

"No, certainly not. I completely agree." The archon took a step back, her lips thinning. "But from what I just felt, strong magic was used to forge that collar. Only one of our strongest fae would have been able to create that. Not very many would be capable, and I'm afraid I cannot take it off, but perhaps its wielder could."

"Do you know who created it?" Somehow, I resisted the urge to wring my hands.

"No, but there aren't many who could have. Maybe five of my employees over the seasons would have been capable of producing what I just felt in your necklace."

*Five? Only five?* Hope pounded through me.

"Are they"—my throat suddenly felt dry—"here?"

"Three are here today." Her wings tightened more behind her. "But two have since retired and moved away."

"How many of those five are females?" Jax crossed his arms, his black hair flashing ebony in the lights.

"Two." She cocked her head. "Why do you ask?"

"Because we know for certain that a female forged the anklet our friend is wearing. He's still in the reception area," Jax replied.

Her eyes narrowed. "How do you know that a female did such a thing?"

"The semelees told me," I explained. "I'm able to walk the Veiled Between."

When her brow only furrowed further, Norivun said, "Elowen's a lorafin, a rare type of Silten fae. Her particular breed of magic isn't common, so don't be alarmed if you've never heard of the Veiled Between or the magic she harbors. But I can tell you that if a semelee told her a female forged the anklet they speak of, then it was certainly a female."

"What about your necklace?" Her gaze pierced the collar encircling my throat. "Did a male or female forge yours?"

"I'm afraid I don't know. The semelees didn't reveal that."

"I see." The archon stood straighter. "Well, regarding your friend, that will help narrow it down if you're certain it's a female."

"We also have this." I thrust the piece of parchment toward her that contained the list of names Khristian had supplied to us. "Although, if you already think you know who it may be, perhaps you don't need it."

She took the parchment and perused the names. "I see that someone's done their homework."

Jax and I shared a side-eye, while the rest of our friends shuffled their feet behind us. Anxious energy puffed in all of their auras.

My mate leveled the archon with a penetrating stare. "Of these two females you spoke of, are either here today?"

The archon nodded. "Indeed, Angim Holz and Saroly Yimmperfae are both working today."

An explosive array of hope burst in my chest, and a

cataclysmic response, just as strong as mine, came from Jax along our bond. Archon Oniville had just narrowed down our list from twenty fae to *two*.

Jax slipped his hand through mine. I squeezed him tightly, and my heart threatened to beat out of my chest.

A sting came from my collar, just the barest brush of magic cascading through me, but it triggered enough to whip Archon Oniville's attention back to me. "Your necklace just *activated*."

I gave her a weak smile. "It's common for it to do that. Emotions bring it out."

Norivun's eyes narrowed and grew glacially cold when he said, "And where might Angim Holz and Saroly Yimmperfae be at the moment?"

"Why, they're both working at their stations." Archon Oniville waved to the room she'd emerged from.

Norivun inclined his head. "Excellent. In that case, please take us to a private chamber and then bring each of them to us alone. Prince Adarian has some questions he would like to ask them."

The archon bowed. "As you wish."

# CHAPTER 7

It felt as though I was going to jump out of my skin as we waited for the first fairy to arrive. Archon Oniville had taken us to a room just off the facility's main floor that I guessed was normally used as a meeting area.

A fire crackled in the chamber's small hearth, and a large metallic table sat at its center. Around the table were chairs also constructed of pure metal. Everything in this facility was made of similar material, which I supposed wasn't surprising since some fae who worked here had a metalwork affinity and had probably crafted everything we touched.

Norivun sat at the table, drumming his fingers against the cool surface. His wings draped behind him, relaxed and loose in the chair's divots.

Everyone else had taken a seat with the Solis royal, including Jax, but I couldn't. I paced back and forth, nearly twisting my fingers off as I wrung my hands over and over. Alec, Trivan, Phillen, and Lander all watched me with worried expressions while Jax wore a perpetual scowl.

"My love," my mate said for the third time. "Please, come sit with me."

From the edge in Jax's voice, I knew his mating instincts were not pleased with how I was feeling, but I shook my head. "I can't. I need to keep moving." I paced again when I reached the far wall.

"Has that collar truly suppressed you since you were five?" Norivun asked quietly when I swung back around to stride the other way. "You said it commonly activates."

All I could manage was a nod as a low growl rumbled in Jax's chest. "She's been abused mercilessly with that collar."

Norivun's jaw locked just as the door opened, and Archon Oniville appeared with a female in tow.

"I do apologize for the wait, but may I present Angim Holz." The archon waved toward the newcomer.

I spun toward her, hope bursting through me, but the second I saw her face, my shoulders fell.

She wasn't who the semelees had shown me. She didn't match the image at all with her long silvery hair, stooped shoulders, and wide eyes. She was *very* old, much older than the fairy I was shown.

Jax cast me a look. "She may still know something," he

said quietly. "If not about Bastian's anklet, then perhaps about your collar."

I nodded swiftly. He was right.

"Will you please check your storage vaults now to ensure all rhifilyte gems are accounted for?" Norivun asked Archon Oniville.

She bobbed her head. "Of course, I'll report straight away with the amount we have stored after we've done a thorough accounting."

The archon bustled from the room, leaving Angim Holz with us.

Frowning, the old fairy assessed us warily. Watery blue eyes regarded us, and despite having long hair that one commonly saw in youth, deep wrinkles grooved the skin alongside Angim's eyes. She pushed her glasses up her nose, and when her attention fell upon Norivun, she brought a fist to her chest and bowed. "It's an honor, truly."

Norivun inclined his head and waved Angim to the chair across from him. "Please, have a seat."

Angim's wings hitched up when she sat, her wings also fitting into the divots on the chair's back.

Norivun drummed his fingers on the table again. "My friends have a few questions for you."

Angim swallowed audibly and tugged at her shirt. "Oh? May I ask what about?"

Jax leaned forward, his dark hair shining as black as ink in the fairy lights. "It's in regard to my mate, Elowen, and a friend of mine named Bastian." Jax's attention slid to me. "Elowen? Would you please show Angim your collar?"

Stomach tumbling, I pulled out the chair beside the female and lowered myself down, then faced the old fairy. Angim's gaze immediately fixated on my collar. Eyes widening behind her spectacles, she assessed my chestnut hair, green eyes, and wingless back.

"But you're not a Solis fairy. Where did you get a collar infused with a rhifilyte gem?" Genuine confusion filled her expression.

"We're hoping you can answer that," Norivun replied, his tone as cold as the frosty landscape outside. "There's also an anklet on a male in the reception area, the one named Bastian, who also wears a gem harvested from our mines. That's two pieces of jewelry we need to account for, and apparently, there are many more anklets on other fae on the Silten continent as well. *And* there's a device with the gem too that's been used to control this female."

Angim straightened, her wings flexing slightly behind her. "But how is that possible? We don't sell our gems to them."

"Exactly," Norivun growled.

"But I've never seen this female before." A blast of indignation shot into Angim's tone. "And I know nothing about any anklets."

"*Have you ever seen that collar before?*" Jax asked, his words laced with a Mistvale command.

Magic flowed in the air at my side, and Jax's magic hit Angim square in the chest. Words tumbled out of Angim before she could stop herself. "No, never."

"*What about an anklet with a rhifilyte gem? Have you ever seen one?*"

"No."

"*Did you craft Elowen's collar?*" Jax persisted.

Angim's eyes widened anew. "No."

"*Have you ever forged an anklet?*"

"Once, many full seasons ago, but not with a rhifilyte gem but rather a *sarupeem* stone. Anklets aren't commonly requested by our jewelry stores."

Despite her innocent answers, Jax continued. "*Do you know who crafted Elowen's collar?*"

The old fairy's throat rolled in a swallow. "No, but only a few fae would be strong enough to do so."

Jax and I shared a look. Her answer aligned with what Archon Oniville had told us.

"*Do you know how to take Elowen's collar off?*"

"I'm . . . I'm unsure." As if of their own accord, Angim's hands rose to my neck. Her fingers danced over the cool metal, and a hum of her potent magic encircled my throat.

Forehead furrowing, she took her time, her magic assessing and probing.

Finally, she dropped her hands and shook her head. "No, I cannot take it off. It has a locking mechanism at its back that's magically hidden, but my affinity can't undo it. Only its creator can. This collar will never come off unless the creator wills it."

*Unless the creator wills it.* My heart soared. That meant it could be removed if only we found the creator. It was the same as Bastian's anklet. Only his could be removed from who forged it.

Jax leaned forward in his seat. "*Have you ever heard of anyone illegally creating any jewelry of any kind with rhifi-lyte gems?*"

"No."

"*Do you know anything about anybody stealing gems from this facility?*"

"No." Sweat appeared atop Angim's brow, and a moment of sympathy filled me.

With each answer she'd given so far, it was obvious she knew absolutely nothing about my collar or Bastian's anklet. Yet Jax's questions continued. Similar to how he'd questioned Guardian Alleron in the Ustilly Mountains, he looked for any loophole that would allow Angim to withhold information.

By the time he finished, Angim looked positively nauseous, and it was apparent that she truly didn't know anything about my collar or Bastian's anklet.

Everyone frowned, and Norivun began to drum his fingers on the table again.

I sighed, trying to hide my disappointment that Angim had been a dead end.

Finally, Jax inclined his head. "Thank you for your honest answers."

Angim looked between him and Norivun, fear bleeding into her expression. "May I go now?"

"Yes, you may leave." Norivun leaned back in his seat. "Please tell Saroly Yimmperfae she's required next."

Angim's chair scraped sharply against the floor in her haste to exit the room.

Anxiety pulsed around me, and I again twisted my hands.

"We still have another fairy to question, Elowen," Alec said from down the table.

Lander nodded, and even Trivan offered me an encouraging smile.

"We're not out of options yet," Phillen added. He then looked to Jax, but try as he might to hide his concern, I could feel Jax's emotions along our bond. He felt as anxious as me.

I forced myself to sit still, even though my knee wanted to bounce, but I kept thinking of what would come if the next fairy also wasn't the anklet's creator.

Jax's stare barreled into me, and when I glanced at him, a glow flared in his eyes. Protective and possessive energy surged from him, wrapping around me in a warm cloud. I took some comfort in the feel of his and the group's unwavering support, but before I could voice any gratitude, the door reopened, and a new female appeared who I could only assume was Saroly Yimmperfae.

My jaw dropped.

Saroly's eyes widened when she beheld the table full of Silten males and her sovereign.

Phillen closed the door behind her, then gestured to the empty chair. "Sit," he said sharply.

On bated breath, I waited for her to sit beside me.

# CHAPTER 8

Saroly's throat bobbed, and her gaze darted to me, widening slightly when she saw my collar, and I was just as speechless.

Because it was *her*.

The female who matched the image the semelees had shown me stood right before me. The forger of Bastian's anklet had been found.

With wild eyes, I glanced at Jax and nodded, then mouthed, *She's the one.*

Darkness gathered in Norivun's aura, the royal's gaze cutting to the female while a vicious smile curved my mate's lips.

Saroly glanced at the door again, but before she could bolt, Jax's command cut like a whip. "*Sit.*"

Potent magic speared the Solis fairy, and on stiff limbs, she moved to the chair beside me and sat.

Up close, I was better able to see her. She appeared middle-aged, not as advanced in seasons as Angim, and fear wafted from her. Pure, genuine fear.

My heart began to race.

"We have a few questions for you." Norivun leaned back and folded his arms over his chest. "We have reason to believe that someone in this facility has been stealing gems from Hartivul Mine and selling them to fae on the Silten continent who are using them for nefarious purposes." He nodded to me. "This female has also suffered her entire life because of that collar upon her neck, and there's a male in the entryway whose mind is currently being controlled by another due to a piece of jewelry around his ankle."

Saroly's nostrils flared, and since I was sitting so close to her, I was able to see her chest rise in short, shallow breaths. "I assure you," she said quickly. "I know nothing about this."

Norivun arched an eyebrow, then glanced at Jax. "Prince Adarian, question her at will."

An angry clash of energy rose in Jax's aura, and I couldn't help but wonder if he'd also reached the same conclusion that I had, that Saroly's fear and rapidly rising chest when she saw my collar meant it was possible she was not only the anklet's creator but my collar's as well.

"*Have you ever seen her collar before?*" Jax pointed at me, his potent Mistvale magic lacing his question.

Saroly's jaw worked, her teeth clenching together, but one word hissed through her lips. "Yes."

It felt as though my heart stopped.

I fell back in my seat, my mouth going slack. She'd said yes. *Yes!*

Jax's jaw muscle pumped, and his eyes blazed. *"Are you that collar's creator?"*

Saroly's nostrils flared sharply, and her thigh muscles clenched as though she was trying to rise so she could run from her chair, but Jax's earlier command to *sit* held firm. "Yes," she replied, her answer no more than a whisper.

The entire room fell silent.

Hope surged in me, so strongly that I had to squeeze my hands into fists, using my sharp nails digging into my skin to keep myself grounded. I wanted to rise and shout in elation, then dance around the room. *We found her.* After so many seasons of torture and abuse because of my collar, its creator sat before me, and she might have the power to remove it.

*"And what about anklets that are currently being used on the Silten continent to control fae? Did you create those too?"* Jax's expression turned lethal.

Saroly hissed, her lip curling, but Jax's magic forced her response. "Possibly."

*"Explain."*

Fury flooded Saroly's expression, and her jaw worked, but Jax's command held firm. "I recently created many anklets with rhifilyte gems, but I don't know who they were put on."

The air around Norivun dropped to freezing temperatures, and frost licked the table in front of him. "You *stole* gems from our floating meadows and sold them to other continents? Even crafting rhifilyte gems into jewelry knowing how dangerous that is?"

Saroly flashed him a look of contempt.

"*Answer his questions,*" Jax commanded in a deadly low voice. Malicious energy rose in his aura, clouding around him until it filled the room.

"I did exactly that." Saroly lifted her chin.

Norivun's breath sucked in, and his aura rose even higher, pounding through the room until the magic from the two royal males was so strong that my head began to spin.

Sharp zings of magic abruptly emitted from my collar. Gasping, I reached over and grabbed Saroly's hand. "Take this off me. Now."

Saroly whipped her hand out from under mine, her gaze darting around the room. Heightened energy strummed from her sovereign, Jax, and all of his friends. But at the moment, I didn't feel rage toward this female. I only felt a desperate need to have her undo all of the hurt that her magic had caused me.

Jax rose from his chair, his tall and imposing form filling the room. A wave of potent magic radiated from him, directed entirely at Saroly. *"Can you remove her collar?"*

Saroly bared her teeth but hissed, "Yes."

My breaths turned so rapid that I grew lightheaded, yet I didn't want to hope too desperately that my collar could be removed. If something went wrong, and Saroly couldn't . . .

It would destroy me.

Jax's attention cut to me, and the ruthlessness of the Dark Raider shone upon his face, but it fractured for a split second when he saw me, and his features softened.

*"Do what she said. Remove that collar from her immediately, and ensure she is not hurt in the process."*

Daggers shot from Saroly's eyes, but she turned in her chair, and even though I'd done nothing to this female and in no way deserved her wrath, she looked ready to spit in my face.

But Jax's magic had also commanded her not to hurt me, so even if she did want to rake her nails down my cheeks, she couldn't. Just like she couldn't resist his command to remove my collar.

My heart pounded painfully.

Lifting her hands, Saroly settled cupped palms around my throat. Her magic heated my skin so much that it felt as though I should be burning, but no pain came, only potent magic that had its own feel and fragrance. Sharp scents of gold wafted up to greet me, then magical tangs of silver and iron followed. Saroly closed her eyes, her jaw muscles pumping in rage while her body begrudgingly followed Jax's command.

Not even a second later, a click came from the back of my neck.

A new texture on my collar rubbed against my skin, right by my mating mark. My fingers flew toward it of their own accord. A locking mechanism, which had magically appeared under its maker's instruction, brushed against my fingertips.

Still scowling, Saroly swatted my fingers away and pinched the mechanism. A click followed, and my collar sprang open.

Just like that . . . *it opened.*

Eyes wide with shock, I watched as Saroly pulled back, bringing my unlocked collar with her.

Cool air rushed around my throat. Air that I couldn't remember ever having felt upon my skin bathed me in freshness. I ran my fingers over my neck, around my throat, and against my mating mark just beneath my hairline. Naked skin greeted me. *Naked skin.* My collar was gone.

As soon as that realization hit me, a rush of cold energy blazed from the depths of my stomach, soaring upward through my frame as all of my lorafin magic coasted free. Shadows unfurled within me. My magic sang. My power surged. The sense that I'd had previously, that there was a missing piece to the puzzle of my magic, disappeared. The last final essence of my power clicked into place, and the second it did, for the first time in my life, I felt *whole*.

Magnificent, heady power barreled through me. I jumped up and shouted, glee filling me so completely that I raised my arms and began to twirl in place.

Magic cascaded through me, around me, in me. So much magic. So much power. And I had access to all of it now, because I was *free*.

Finally, blessedly *free*.

Shadows blazed around me as tears filled my eyes, streaming down my cheeks. Thickness coated my throat. I cried in relief and joy, so overcome that I couldn't see through the pool of moisture flooding my eyes.

But then the hazy image of Jax was there, standing before me. He wrapped me in his embrace. Strong arms held me, crushing me to his chest, and I hugged him back just as fiercely.

"My love." His voice was husky and thick with emotion.

I held him just as fast. "I'm free." My words came out choked as disbelief still filled me. I'd wanted this for so long. Full seasons of hope had been leading to this single moment, and at last, it was here. Finally, the suffocating magic that had caged me my entire life was gone. Blessedly and completely *gone*.

Tears of amazement continued to pour from me. I couldn't hold them back. Couldn't stop my reaction to the reality that had just occurred. For so many summers, I'd dreamed of this. But it'd always seemed to be just that—a dream. My entire life I'd hoped that one day, what had just happened, would finally be true. And now it was.

Sobbing, I clung to my mate.

Jax gripped me hard, his face buried in my neck as I cried and cried in happiness. Finally, *finally* I was allowed to say goodbye to the slave life that I'd always known. I was a caged lorafin no more.

My potent magic continued to cascade through me as Jax held me, but I didn't explode. I didn't grow out of control. I had mastered my magic long ago, and I *knew* I was no longer a threat to others.

Another sob shook my chest, and Jax pulled back, just enough to cup my cheeks and kiss me.

I kissed him back just as hard, a laugh bubbling out of me. He joined in, his deep laugh joining my own. I suddenly became aware that his friends around the room were cheering and thumping the table in their excitement.

And when I finally wiped my eyes enough to clearly regard everything that was happening, it was to a sea of smiling faces.

Only Saroly wasn't rejoicing, but for the life of me, I couldn't find the will to care.

THE GOLD COLLAR, the choker that had been placed upon me, literally choking the magic out of me my entire life, sat on the table in front of us. Sitting there, it looked innocent. Harmless. Yet I knew if I slipped it around my neck and allowed that deadly lock to engage once more, its magic could affect me all over again.

Jax seemed to realize the same thing. Because after our celebrations finally calmed and reality set in for what Saroly had done, he commanded her to destroy the magic she'd infused into it.

Removing its potent magic wasn't as easy as it'd been for her to unlock it. Sweat soon lined her forehead, and magic rolled from her in continued waves. Her cupped hands remained around the collar for much longer than they'd been around my neck.

But eventually, a clash of magic shook the walls around us, and the collar evaporated. It happened in a clang of power, as though a bolt of lightning shot from the skies, and in one blinding moment, its magic was destroyed, and the collar was obliterated.

When the energy calmed, only the gemstone remained, the purple jewel bouncing along the table until the energy diffused completely. But it remained a loose rock, looking entirely harmless, even though it was one of the deadliest jewels created in our lands.

But the amount of energy it took Saroly to fulfill such a task made the magnitude of the collar's might hit me anew.

And to think I'd been wearing that thing for twenty-three summers.

Before anyone could say anything further, the door banged open, and Archon Oniville appeared. Face pale, her gaze sought Norivun's.

She bowed quickly. "I've just come from our vault, and I . . . I . . ."

"Spit it out," Trivan growled.

She bowed again. "I'm so sorry, but you were right. All of the rhifilyte gemstones in our vault that were harvested several months ago and over the seasons . . ." She gulped. "They're all gone. Someone had cast a glamour over their container to make it look as though they were all present, so when routine accounting was done, it didn't appear that anything was amiss, and"—her face paled even more—"I'm so sorry. As the archon here, I'm entirely responsible for—"

"Are the other gems in the vaults accounted for?" Norivun cut her off. "Have more been stolen?"

The archon bowed. "We're doing a thorough inventory right now, and I've called a spellcaster to come in to ensure no glamours or illusions remain. I'll return when I know more." She quickly fled the room.

Norivun growled low in his throat, and his cool gaze met Saroly's.

But the fairy only faced him straight-on. The fear she first exuded when she entered this room was now entirely absent.

"We'll get to the other missing gems in a minute," Norivun finally said. "Adarian? Would you like to continue?"

Seething, Jax shoved a hand into his pocket. He pulled out my guardian's adaptor. "*Destroy this too.*"

Spiteful eyes met Jax's when he tossed the adaptor her way. But Jax's face was carved stone. Unyielding rock. There was no mercy in his expression as he gazed down at Saroly.

Hissing, Saroly grabbed the adaptor.

It took her just as long, but the same clash of magic eventually shook the room, booming like thunder. Finally, the adaptor was destroyed too, leaving only the small rhifilyte gem it'd held bouncing along the table.

Two loose gemstones now sat before us, but nobody dared touch them.

"And now Bastian," Jax said in a cold, hard voice.

"I give my permission to have him brought back here, even though his identity hasn't been verified." Norivun's wings tightened. "If the receptionist gives you any trouble, notify me."

Jax signaled Phillen, and the guard left the room. Only minutes later, he returned with the half-breed dangled over his shoulder and Bowan, Lars, and Norivun's four guards in tow.

I still didn't know if Norivun knew that Bastian was Jax's brother, and considering the bargain I made with

Phillen's wife, Saramel, I couldn't ask him outright. I made a mental note to ask Jax to relieve me of that bargain once we were home, since he was the only one who could do so given the bargain's conditions. We'd been so busy recently that the thought hadn't even occurred to me.

"Where do you want him?" Phillen lumbered into the room.

Jax pointed to the table. "Lay him down here."

Saroly's lips thinned when she caught sight of the anklet around the half-breed's ankle.

Phillen carefully lowered Bastian, and Lars and Bowan jumped in to help straighten his limbs and support his antler rack. Despite that, Bastian's large antlers knocked against the table's surface, creating a tinny sound that rang through the room.

Once Jax's brother was supine and appeared relatively comfortable, Jax returned his attention to the metalwork fairy.

*"Did you create his anklet?"*

I could have sworn Jax held his breath after weaving his Mistvale magic around her.

Saroly's nostrils flared. "Yes."

A collective sigh of relief flowed from all of our lips.

*"Did you create all of the anklets with rhifilyte gems that were sent to the Silten continent within the last few months?"*

Her lip curled. "Yes."

Jax closed his eyes, as though needing a minute to collect himself. When he opened them, he leveled her with an unforgiving stare, but he spoke in a normal voice when he said, "You're going to remove this male's anklet, and then every fairy your creations have been placed upon will be found, and you'll be required to undo all of them."

"And when you finish that, you'll answer to me." Norivun's eyes were as cold as the Cliffs of Sarum when he stared at the female. A puff of his mighty affinity curled around her, and for the first time, true fear shown on Saroly's face as the Solis continent's Death Master's might filled the room.

Jax crossed his arms, and powerful magic once again filled his tone. *"Remove his anklet and ensure he's not hurt in the process."*

Saroly's hands shot out, cupping Bastian's anklet as she fell victim to Jax's Mistvale magic once more.

Like it'd been with me, it didn't take more than a minute before a click sounded from the anklet, and then it was falling away, clanging softly onto the metallic table.

*"Destroy that anklet now,"* Jax commanded.

Still seething, Saroly cupped the jewelry while the rest of us surged forward, eagerly peering down at Bastian. Breaths held, we waited for him to awaken.

Minutes later, a final clash of magic abruptly shook the walls, and Saroly sagged back in her chair. Like my collar, the anklet had been destroyed, its gem now loose, but in that time, Bastian hadn't roused.

"Do you suppose his mind is injured?" I placed a hand on Jax's forearm.

His brow furrowed, worry lining his expression. "I don't know."

"I can seek a healer if needed." Norivun's comment was calm, yet he wore a look of concern.

I began to worry that Bastian would never wake because the semelee had used too much of its power on him to make him sleep. I surmised that I might have to return to the Veiled Between to find a semelee to undo what the first had done, but just as that thought struck me, the barest moan came from Bastian's mouth.

The half-breed's breathing increased, his chest puffing more with each breath. And with a loud groan, he brought a hand to his head, right below one of his antlers.

Hope soared across Jax's face. "Bastian? Can you hear me?"

Eyes cracking open, Bastian lifted his head, his antlers swaying across the table's surface as he looked left, then right. Eyes widening more, he sat up. "Stars, my head is *pounding.*"

Jax's smile turned into a grin, and he launched himself across the table, enclosing his younger brother in an embrace so fierce that Bastian fell back.

"Whoa, calm down, bro," Bastian said, laughing softly. "I seriously have the most massive headache."

Trivan, Lars, Phillen, Bowan, Lander, Alec, and I began to whoop in joy, everyone clapping and hugging while Bastian embraced his brother back, confusion still evident in his expression.

Bastian's forehead furrowed even more when he assessed his surroundings. "Um . . . where am I?"

Jax's laugh turned into a sob. Tears streamed down my mate's face. I climbed onto the table beside him and wrapped him in a hug.

Bastian's look of shock when Jax kissed me fiercely only made me grin more. Joy radiated through my mate and along our bond, and when we pulled apart, Bastian looked between the two of us, his confusion giving way to a small smile.

"Is someone going to fill me in on what's going on?" The look on Bastian's face grew entirely playful. "Why do I feel like I missed something?"

## CHAPTER 9

Archon Oniville returned and reported to Norivun that more jewels had indeed been stolen—it wasn't just rhiflyte gems. And if Saroly had been working alone, then the traitorous female had indeed been busy. She'd stolen *thousands* of precious stones.

Fury strummed from the archon's aura, but she called for a hydration tea, then made sure Bastian was comfortably seated and warm by the fire. She apologized to us, explaining she would have ordered Bastian food too, but their facility didn't allow food on the premises in order to keep their work areas decontaminated.

"There's a salopas down the lane." Norivun's guard with the long braid nodded toward the exit. Ryder, I thought was his name. "They serve excellent food. I'm sure they would be happy to serve you if you would like a meal."

Sandus, the guard with a beard, nodded in agreement. "It's where we usually go when we travel here."

Archon Oniville also inclined her head. "Our staff usually ventures there during their breaks. I also recommend it."

"Bastian? Can you hold off on eating for a while?" Jax asked his brother.

Bastian lifted his mug toward the archon, his playful and affectionate aura filling the room. "As long as you keep this tea coming, I'll be just fine."

I leaned against the wall, closer to Jax, and watched it all. Even though I didn't know Jax's brother at all, I was beginning to understand why Jax was so protective of Bastian and felt so deeply about his brother.

A natural charm, a truly charismatic aura, surrounded the half-breed. There was something about Bastian that made one want to smile and laugh. A feeling, or perhaps his energy, called to those around him, putting them at ease and making them want to play. The true Bastian was nothing like the catatonic male we rescued from the cavern. And I just thanked the stars and galaxy that we'd gotten him back.

As though reading my mind, Jax's attention slid my way. Utter relief and pure joy still filled his expression. But as Jax's brother leaned back in his chair, sipping his hot beverage, the crown prince of Stonewild returned his attention to the metalwork fairy across from us.

We still hadn't finished what he started.

Archon Oniville bowed at Norivun. "I would like to stay here while the rest of our inventory is accounted for." Her expression hardened. "I need to learn more about what Saroly has done."

Norivun inclined his head. "Of course." The royal regarded Saroly coolly, his aura swirling around him in barely controlled pulses.

And once again, Jax's expression turned glacial. "I have some more questions for you."

Archon Oniville pulled out the chair beside Jax. "We both do."

Saroly sagged in her seat, and even though insolence still radiated from her, she seemed resigned to the fact that she'd been caught.

Jax crossed his arms. *"How many anklets total did you create for someone on the Silten continent?"*

Saroly shrugged. "I don't know the exact number, but it was close to ten thousand."

My breath sucked in, and Alec and I shared a shocked look. Someone had wanted to enslave ten thousand half-breeds. *But why?*

*"Who were you working for?"* Jax's Mistvale command again coated his words.

She shrugged once more. "I have no idea. Our communication was all done via dillemsills, and payments were delivered to me anonymously by someone working for whoever commissioned the anklets."

All of us shared a frustrated look. If Saroly had no idea who she was working for, whoever it was had kept their tracks covered well.

Jax continued his questioning, not letting up, while Norivun's guard, Haxil, took careful notes of everything that Saroly revealed. It soon became apparent Saroly had crafted *all* of the anklets that the half-breeds at the Centennial Matches had been wearing.

But her acts of treason didn't stop there. She'd also stolen other gems and made other illegal jewelry over the seasons—my collar being only one of those creations. The only blessing was that she'd been working alone, and there wasn't a large criminal network that the Solis authorities would need to track down.

We spent hours in the room, learning just how far Saroly's treachery went. It turned out that she had been swindling gems, of various varieties, from the Hartivul Mine for hundreds of full seasons. Her treachery hadn't started with the half-breeds' anklets. It hadn't even started with my collar. She'd been doing it for *centuries* . . . long before I'd ever been born.

Initially, her thefts had been small, only a gem or two once a winter, and she'd initially sold the gems loose, not constructing them into jewelry or weapons. When asked how she'd done so, she explained that she devised a way to break into the facility's vaults, wield a powerful glamour, and steal what she wanted, effectively covering up her tracks as she went. And since the vault's gems were never all utilized at once for legitimate projects, and stock was continually replenished by the mines, her ploy had worked. The female was a genius really, not only blessed with an incredibly strong affinity but a cunning mind as well.

It was just unfortunate that she'd chosen to use her skills for selfish gain versus the good of others, because over the seasons, her thefts had grown, and her creations had advanced. She often constructed her nefarious pieces of jewelry at home, working on them when she wasn't crafting metallic items in the facility. Which was how she'd gotten away with it for so long, since nobody knew what she was doing.

Jax's questions continued as Jax helped Norivun and Archon Oniville uncover everything that Saroly had done.

When he finally finished every line of questioning they could think of, I was horrified to learn that Saroly's metallic jewelry had likely affected more than five thousand fae in the centuries she'd been stealing, and that didn't include all the anklets she furiously crafted in the previous months. Apparently, since all of the anklets were the same, and she'd grown so practiced in her magic, she was easily able to duplicate them, making a huge amount of the jewelry all at once.

The female was truly powerful, and I prayed to all the gods and goddesses that most of the ten thousand anklets she created hadn't been put on any half-breeds yet, but in reality, we didn't know. After all, we had no count of how many half-breeds were still in the Wood's underground caverns.

Of the other five thousand individuals that she'd affected over the seasons, most of the fae were scattered throughout the realm, not only residing on my continent and the Solis continent but also on the Nolus continent and Lochen islands as well. Saroly had even gone so far as to sell the stolen gems to creatures in the *other* realm, something that had nearly made steam rise from her archon's ears.

And when Saroly finally revealed why she'd done such crimes, I was sickened to hear that the reasoning was as unforgiveable as they got. A noble reason might have made my heart soften slightly, but Saroly had done it all for rulibs. She proudly admitted that she was wealthier than any fairy in Harrivee Territory, unbeknownst to anyone around her.

Hearing that made her archon scowl. "And over the seasons, when you've disappeared on your trips and have taken your extensive time away, were you using your rulibs to fund those ventures?"

Saroly sneered. "Of course. I've been living like a queen for hundreds of winters. I have many properties scattered throughout the realm and dozens of servants at my beck and call." She laughed lightly, and for the first time seemed to enjoy the line of questioning. "None of you ever even knew. That was the best part of it all. You all thought I was just another fairy toiling away in this despicable facility when in reality, I was outsmarting you all."

My hands balled into fists when her purely selfish motives came to light. While Saroly was living like a noble from a House, thousands of fae had been suffering because of her choices.

Trivan was right. She did deserve a visit from the Dark Raider.

Norivun's aura surged as he stood and began reviewing the notes Haxil had taken. It would likely take many, *many* summers to track down all of the fae who had been affected by Saroly's treacherous deeds and to recover all of the stones that had been stolen. And given Norivun's barely controlled rage, I knew that ultimately, that task could very well fall on his shoulders.

A twinge of pity rose in me for the gigantic headache that had just been thrust upon the Solis royal.

Finally, when Norivun and Archon Oniville confirmed that they had all of the information they needed, Jax looked toward his brother. "Are you doing okay?"

"Fine, I'm just fine." Bastian cocked his head, making his antlers sway. He'd probably downed a dozen cups of hydration tea since the questioning had started. "On second thought"—he patted his stomach—"I'm seriously starving, bro. Can we at last get something to eat?"

Jax laughed, and the rest of us stood up to join him as Nish and Sandus clamped Saroly's arms behind her back, then told Archon Oniville to call for the Fae Guard. The corrupt metalwork affinity fairy wouldn't be enjoying her freedom again anytime soon. And her days of living like a queen had finally come to an end.

JAX, his friends, Bastian, and I sat around a table in the local salopas that'd been recommended down the road. Norivun and his guards had stayed back at the facility to issue orders to the mine archons and other authorities in the area as they began the needed process of cleaning up Saroly's mess. Even though Saroly had been working alone, there were many wrongs that had to be made right, the security of the mines and the vault's storage being paramount. Because if she'd been able to break into them, others might be able to devise a way to as well.

"It was very kind of Norivun to assist us as he did," I murmured to Jax. Music filled the salopas from a band playing on stage while locals drank and ate, more than a few giving us curious looks. I had a feeling a group of Silten fae hanging out in their local eating establishment wasn't the norm around here.

Jax inclined his head and took another drink of ale. "I owe him a debt."

Bastian looked up from the bowl of stew he'd just finished. He raised a hand to the barkeep, signaling that he wanted another. He'd already eaten an entire hen, two salads, and a bowl of rice, but he didn't appear to be slowing down anytime soon.

"Have you at least had enough now to answer some questions?" Jax asked his brother, his tone amused.

Bastian took a huge gulp of his ale, then set his drink down and wiped his mouth. "Okay, now I'm ready, but I'm still hungry."

An enchanted tray floated toward us and deposited another bowl of stew in front of Bastian. He picked up his spoon, but instead of taking a bite, he eyed his brother. "So, what the guys were telling me"—he nodded toward Bowan and Lars—"while you were questioning that fairy, is actually true? For the past three months I've been under the control of someone because of that anklet I was wearing?"

Jax nodded, his mouth a firm line.

"You really don't remember anything about that time?" Bowan cocked his head, and his earring caught the light. "Not even this morning when you attacked us?"

Bastian's eyebrows, similar in shape to Jax's, shot straight up. "I *attacked* you?"

Alec nodded. "I spilled several mugs of coffee in the

process. You owe me the cleaning bill on my pants. Those were my favorite ones, and I had to change."

Bastian snickered, and his antler rack swayed slightly. "I wish I could have seen that. I love when your pretty clothes get messed up."

Alec slugged Bastian in the shoulder, but a smile spread across his lips.

"You truly did attack us," Lars said quietly. "You threw me through a door."

Some of the amusement slid from Bastian's face. "I did? Stars, I'm sorry. I didn't mean to. I never would have done that if I'd been in control of myself. Well, unless we were wrestling. I do love beating you lot when we spar."

Trivan clapped him on the back. "It's good to have you back, Bas, even if you are a poor sparring companion."

Bastian laughed and flicked Trivan's hand with an antler. "Care to take those words outside?"

Trivan grinned. "Any day, stag."

The laughing and joking continued, and Jax grinned. I leaned into him, soaking up the newly elated emotion puffing along my mate's bond. In all the time I'd known him, I'd never felt such intense relief from him. His brother truly did mean everything to him.

When the teasing finally slowed enough for him to ask a question, Jax said, "What do you remember, Bas? Do you recall anything about the summer or the past three months?"

Bastian took another bite of his stew, his jaw working slowly as he chewed the meat and vegetables. "The last memory I have is walking to work at the end of spring. It was dark. My shift started early at the shipyard that day. I wasn't really paying attention to my surroundings, just ambling along, and then . . ." A heavy frown descended over his features. "Nothing. I don't recall anything past that."

I cocked my head. "Do you remember hearing anything unusual that day? Before your memories disappeared?"

Bastian shook his head. "No."

"Do you think he was attacked from behind?" A heavy groove appeared between Lander's eyes when he swung his attention to the group.

"I'm assuming so." Jax scratched his chin, then took another drink from his tall mug. "Do you recall sensing someone else's presence? Even if you didn't hear anything?"

Bastian shook his head again. "I don't. I don't remember anything other than thinking of Anna while walking. She and I were planning to share a meal that night. I was supposed to cook it, and I was trying to figure out what to make that would impress her." He grimaced. "Oh, shite. *Anna!* I just realized I haven't seen her in months, even though that morning feels like yesterday to me. Do you know how she is? Has she been asking about me?"

"She has." Jax explained what he knew, sharing that she was one of the first fae he had his staff contact after realizing his brother was gone. "I couldn't contact her directly, obviously, since she doesn't know we're brothers, but one of my staff did. Anna's been searching for you too, asking questions all over town since the day you disappeared. She's been very anxious to find you, and like me, she hasn't given up."

"Really?" A hopeful expression grew on Bastian's face. "Does that mean she didn't find anybody else in the past few months?"

Jax shook his head. "She hasn't, not last I heard. She's still loyal to you. About as worried sick as I've been if my staff are to be believed."

Bastian perked up and quickly ate the rest of his stew, then slugged the remainder of his drink. "I need to get home. I have to explain to her that I never would have left her on purpose."

But when he tried to rise, Jax clamped a hand on his shoulder. "You will, and soon, but not until we figure out who took you."

Bastian slumped back in his seat.

"Your brother's right," I chimed in, my voice gentle. "Until we know who's behind this, there's no telling if they'll simply abduct you again, and according to Saroly, the fae who commissioned those anklets bought *thousands* of them. Who's to say they won't simply put a new one on you?"

Bastian glowered and scrubbed his cheeks. "Stars and galaxy. I hadn't thought of that."

"So now what?" Phillen asked. The burly guard sat at the end of the table, looking as tense as a board. "I wouldn't mind getting back to our continent too. All this makes me nervous, and I'd like to check in with Saramel and ensure she and Cassim are okay."

I nodded sympathetically. If I had a three-summer-old child, I would want to ensure his safety as well.

Jax made a move to stand. "We can portal key back to Leafton now if everyone's ready. We'll need to make a few more appearances as we allow word to spread that we're done at the Matches."

"Then let's get out of here." Bowan elbowed Trivan, who sat at his side, and everyone began to slide out of the booth.

The local Solis fae cast us more curious stares, but we all moved to the door and out into the snowy night before anyone could approach us.

The night sky loomed above, even more colorful and dazzling this far north. Freezing wind blew through the streets, and I pulled my cloak tighter to my chest.

Jax fished a portal key from his pocket, and everyone moved into a circle, while Phillen explained to Bastian that Quinn had amassed a jar of portal keys, which made traveling extremely easy.

"How peculiar." Bastian scratched his head when Jax showed him the key.

I clasped my mate's hand and gave him a heavy look. "You do know what this means, don't you? Since Bastian can't remember anything, and he doesn't know who's behind his abduction, and Saroly didn't either, I'll have to venture to the Veiled Between again to get answers. It's the only way."

Jax's nostrils flared as my comment sank in. Because even though all communication between Saroly and whoever had hired her had been done via dillemsill— which indicated that it might be a Silten fairy behind it since dillemsills were native to our continent—that didn't necessarily mean it was. It could be anybody. Perhaps a Lochen, Nolus, or another Solis fairy was to blame. We had no idea since Saroly hadn't bothered pursuing more information. All she'd cared about was amassing rulibs. She was so much like my former guardian it was sickening.

Jax finally inclined his head. "I know."

But even though his answer was accepting, his concern for me still strummed along our bond. The effects his calling had on me seemed to be long-lasting, but I'd proven the last time I've ventured to the Veiled Between that I was stronger now, that using my magic didn't hurt me anymore like it once had, and with my collar now completely removed, I was likely even better off.

I squeezed his hand. "Trust me. I'll be fine. I'm no longer restricted by my collar. My magic is fully untethered. The semelees should now see me as their queen, which means they'll bow to me completely."

Alec rocked back on his heels. "She's right, Jax. She survived her last trip to the Veiled Between just fine, and if she goes again, everything could be answered."

The crown prince of Stonewild Kingdom nodded. "You're right. My mate is now likely a queen of the semelees. I daresay she's probably the most powerful female fairy on the Silten continent."

A feeling of pride swept through me, and a tingle of excitement followed. "It's about time I embraced my birthright. I *will* find us answers."

A heated glow filled Jax's eyes. "My mate, the lorafin queen. Who would have thought I'd end up so lucky?"

Intense joy abruptly flooded me, and I could only hope that, eventually, his parents would feel the same. The king and queen of Stonewild Kingdom still had no idea that their son had mated himself to a non-royal commoner.

But since we were going back to Stonewild soon, I knew it was only a matter of time before they found that out too.

But all in good time. First, we had to discover who created Bastian's collar and put a stop to them.

We used a portal key to travel back to Leafton, knowing our presence would inevitably be missed if we didn't stick to our original schedule of enjoying the Match Finals.

Bastian's eyes grew wide when he beheld the destruction of the Stonewild royal suite at The Silver Hand.

"I did this? *Seriously?*" He swung his head back and forth, surveying the damage. Then he laughed. "I have to say, it's actually quite impressive." He flexed an arm.

Phillen snorted, and Bowan laughed.

But Trivan rolled his eyes. "Rubbish, this was all from that strength the anklet gave you. I can still beat you sparring. Fairly easily, I'd like to remind you."

Bastian dropped low, knees bent. "Oh, is that right? I see your ego hasn't changed in the slightest while I was comatose. Maybe it's time I remind you how easily I can best you?"

Trivan grinned, and the two of them tackled one another, getting a chuckling laugh from Jax even though more furniture began to fly.

I couldn't help but laugh too when another chair crashed into the wall, even though it added to the damage that would need to be addressed.

Alec shook his head. "Children, I swear. We can't take them anywhere."

While Trivan and Bastian's boastings and wrestling continued in the living area, the others set about cleaning up the mess from earlier this morning. Unlike the spilled coffee, which a cleaning charm had easily taken care of, the broken walls and exploded plaster would take longer to reconstruct and would require purchasing advanced construction charms. Lars and Phillen volunteered to venture into the city to buy what was needed for the task.

I tugged on Jax's sleeve as the others got to work. "I'm going to our chambers. I need to venture to the Veiled Between while the rest of you clean up so we can finally have full answers. We can't delay this anymore. We need to know who's behind it all."

My mate's midnight brows slanted together. "I'll stay with you, just in case you need my help to return."

I slid my hand through his, knowing that I very well could need help, because while my magic was now entirely free, I was still new to navigating the Veiled Between without my collar. I'd had to use the pull of Jax's magic once before to find my way back when I inadvertently traveled there during a dream. There was nothing to say I wouldn't need his help again until I learned to command my magic fully, even if I now was a lorafin queen.

We entered our chambers, and I shut the door behind us.

"You'll stay at my side?" I asked quietly, then lay on the bed.

Jax kneeled beside the mattress and took my hand. A fierceness entered his expression that took my breath away. "I'll never leave it."

# CHAPTER 10

I took a deep breath and closed my eyes. Magic cascaded through me, as though eager to be released and used. I felt different but in a good way. Whereas I'd always felt the collar's restricting hold previously to some extent, even after Guardian Alleron had loosened it, now, I was *entirely* uncaged.

I called upon my lorafin powers and asked them to take me away. It was so simple. So easy. Without my collar in place, my magic surged forward. The warning vibrations from my collar were gone. The pain that would follow for using my magic unchecked had been obliterated. Pure *power* throbbed around me.

My soul shot through the universe instantaneously, and the Veil's mist appeared at my fingertips. I parted it, cutting through the Veil so swiftly that all it took was a whisper of magic, and I was inside.

The second my soul crossed into the Veiled Between, a pulse of my newly released powers vibrated out of me, as though a rock had been dropped into a pool, and a swell of ripples shot through the water around me, alerting every semelee within the Veiled Between that I'd arrived.

That'd never happened before.

*She's come,* a semelee whispered, eagerly surging forward.

*And she has so much power. Do you feel it?* another replied.

Before I could so much as utter why I was there, semelees were swirling around me, twisting through my limbs, caressing my soul, sliding across my back. It was as though they wanted to touch me. Needed to.

*Stop,* I said, my voice deeper and more commanding than it had ever been before. Magic barreled through me. So much power. So much *might* lay at my fingertips. The heady feeling coursed through me once more, but I tempered my wonder.

Every single semelee halted their movements the second I requested it until not even a flap of time stirred around me, not even a whisper of the cosmos. It was as if the entire Veil had stilled.

*I need answers, and I have many questions.*

*Yes, my queen. What do you seek?* the nearest one asked.

For a moment, I hovered in their midst, entirely

speechless. *My queen.* How long I'd waited to hear those words. And that statement meant it was true. I'd fulfilled my birthright. I was finally, fully in control of them.

Another heady sense of power filled me. I could twist fate now if I wanted to. Such an act was illegal, and I would never do such a thing, but as their queen, that was my ability.

For a moment, I allowed myself to revel in pure wonderment. I had the power to alter the fabric of time, to change the very course of our universe as though I was Goddess Verasellee, the Goddess of Time, in the flesh.

But to do so was not to be taken lightly. I didn't know much about past lorafins who had twisted fate, but the practice had been made illegal for a reason.

Returning my attention to the semelees, I said, *I need to know who's responsible for the half-breeds being locked in those caverns in the Wood outside of the Centennial Matches.*

A large semelee shot forward, almost as though it wanted to prove itself and show its loyalty to me. *It's King Paevin.*

If my soul could have stumbled, it would have. *King . . . Paevin?* I somehow managed to get out.

*Yes,* another replied. *He commissioned that Solis fairy to create the anklets that are controlling the half-breeds. It is the Faewood king who's behind it all.*

I let that bit of information digest, and only one reaction billowed through me—shock. When I finally felt I had my wits about me again, I asked, *And what about Bastian? How was he captured?*

Another replied, *A fairy the king commissioned found Bastian and determined he was a powerful half-breed. That fairy captured Bastian and placed the anklet around him before taking him back to the king.*

I frowned. *So earlier, when you told me Bastian was being controlled by another, that fairy was King Paevin?*

*Yes,* a dozen semelees hissed at once.

*But why? Why is the king doing this?*

The semelees began to circle me, growing more vibrant and bolder with every swirl.

*The king is harnessing the half-breeds' ability to procreate at a faster rate than siltenites,* one responded. *Half-breeds have much higher rates of fertility than siltenites, and some of them are very magical, meaning their offspring can be quite powerful. The king would like to have those children under his control. And since they have few rights in your society, nobody cares when half-breeds go missing. It's allowed the king to capture many of them and use them for his gain.*

Another moment of speechlessness hit me, and I recalled something I'd heard in the tunnels the night we rescued Bastian. One of the guards had spoken of breeding. A sick feeling coasted through me. Stars Above.

I snapped my attention back to the semelees. *But how is King Paevin breeding them? Half-breeds are given a potion at birth to stifle their ability to reproduce. And more importantly, why is he wanting to breed and control them?*

A third semelee drifted forward, one who hadn't spoken yet. *The king has given them a counter-potion that he's spent full seasons having his spellcasters develop. This potion has returned their fertility. And the king has done this so he may raise an army of magical half-breeds to do as he commands.*

*An army?* My stomach bottomed out.

*Yes*, they all hissed in unison.

*Do the king's plans have anything to do with why there are so many half-breeds at the Centennial Matches right now?*

The semelee nearest me, a large one with ribbed scales, nodded emphatically. *Yes, my queen. Initially, when King Paevin devised the plan to develop a secret army, he sent spies throughout the kingdoms to search for powerful half-breeds to capture. This was many full seasons ago, and he's slowly been capturing them. But that method was proving to be too time-consuming. Over the seasons, because half-breeds are so reclusive and often hide their abilities, the king feared he wasn't finding the most powerful, so when his kingdom was invited to host the Centennial Matches, he opened up the Matches to half-breeds. That is why so many are there and why they're being allowed to compete. He wants them to come to him, so that during the Match Finals, he's able to determine who the most powerful half-breeds are. He's captured those who are magically superior, and he's enslaved them using the anklets. He's keeping them hidden in those caverns beneath the Wood, and he plans to breed them to build his army.*

Another wave of sickness filled me, and my soul swayed. I couldn't believe what they were telling me. It was beyond disgusting.

But I recalled a half-breed I'd seen in the arena at the Match Finals, the one who'd resisted a poisoned dart and who'd been able to weave illusion magic. That half-breed had been immensely strong, and now, according to the semelees, since he revealed how magical he was, he was likely already wearing an anklet and enslaved beneath the Wood. That half-breed had thought he would be competing in the Centennial Matches, but in reality, he'd offered himself to the king like a prized treasure.

*Gods and Goddesses,* I whispered more to myself than to the semelees. *How do we stop King Paevin?*

The largest semelee near me curled around me until its cool skin met my fingertips. *You could twist fate, lorafin. You are a queen now.*

I jolted away from it. *No, I will not disrupt the fabric of time. Such an act is illegal. Tell me how to stop King Paevin in the fae lands. A just way. A fair way that will stop any forward progression of his plan and will free the half-breeds he's captured.*

Another semelee slid along my side. *If you refuse to twist fate, it will not be easy. You will need to enact the help of the other kingdoms. The kingsfae in Faewood are under King Paevin's command. They will only listen to him. You will have to bring all of the kingdoms' Houses into your confidence and share what you've discovered. It will result in much bickering and numerous squabbles. Many won't believe you. Some will. It is those who have an open mind that you must convince. Only the three other thrones, and the four kingdoms' Houses, working together against King Paevin will stop him. He's already grown too powerful. The king sees and knows too much.*

Hearing that reminded me of something that had happened with the Faewood kingsfae earlier. The night that I overheard them at the Venapearl Fountains, speaking of how the king had issued an order to arrest the Dark Raider in Possyrose Forest. King Paevin had known Jax would be there . . . and we'd never figured out *how* he'd known.

I swirled among the semelees once more. *How did King Paevin know the Dark Raider would be in Possyrose Forest the other week? How did the kingsfae know to be there looking for Jax?*

The semelee at my left made a sound, as if wanting my attention. *The king used one of his newly born half-breed children to find the Dark Raider's whereabouts. That half-breed child has only recently come into her power. She's still very young, but she's incredibly strong and wields Mistvale psychic magic. Her magic is more powerful than the most talented siltenite psychics. That child was able to see where the next raid would be. That was how the king knew where your mate would be in the forest that night.*

It felt as though my heart stopped. A child. The king was using a half-breed *child* who he'd bred in captivity to learn things that no other fairy could know. King Paevin was just as horrid as my guardian and Saroly, if not worse.

And equally troubling, if the king's enslaved child psychic could do that once, he could force the child to find Jax again, which meant that Jax would never be safe as long as King Paevin ruled Faewood Kingdom with no consequences.

*How long has the king been breeding half-breeds? How long has he been doing this unchecked? And how old is that child?*

*The king started his plan seven summers ago. Initially, he only captured a few half-breeds since he was finding it hard to locate powerful ones. That child is one of the first enslaved children to be born under his plan. She's only six summers old right now, but her magic grows stronger with every day that passes.*

My soul whirled as worry and revulsion pummeled through me. That half-breed child was only six. I hadn't been much different in age when my guardian had also manipulated me to use my magic for his bidding.

I called to the semelees again, *How many half-breed children are currently enslaved to the king and have been born in such a way?*

The semelee nearest me curled around my ankles. *Only that child and twelve others, all born to the same couple. Seven summers ago, he wasn't able to acquire enough anklets to have more than one breeding couple as he kept the remaining anklets he'd purchased to use on the children they planned to have. It wasn't until the Hartivul Mine had an explosive production of rhifilyte gemstones a few months ago that his plan really catapulted. Originally, King Paevin thought it would take over a hundred full seasons to create his army. But with the mine producing so many of the gems that he needed at once, he took advantage of that. He commissioned Saroly Yimmperfae to create as many anklets as the mine's production allowed, and he took it as a sign from the stars and galaxy that the gods wanted him to continue his plan since the mine had produced so much.*

If I could have vomited, I would have. No wonder the king had been so insistent that Jax sell me to him when I arrived at his side. King Paevin wanted to acquire me too. He probably would have put an anklet on me in addition to my collar, all so he could own and control a lorafin. Perhaps he even would have bred me.

Stomach tumbling, I forced my questions to continue. *Where is he keeping the child that located Jax?*

*She's living in the caverns with the others. Since the king's acquirements of half-breeds have grown, all of his captives have been moved there. Previously, he kept his breeding couple locked in his palace, hidden away from prying eyes in a secret chamber, but now that he's enslaved so many half-breeds, he's had to find larger accommodations.*

I nodded. That also aligned with the timeline Esopeel had told me of when strange occurrences had begun in the Wood. And to think, it was the Hartivul Mine's creations of so many rhifilyte gems at once that had been the catalyst for all of this. If so many gemstones hadn't been created and harvested, the king wouldn't have been able to enslave so many half-breeds. He needed that gem's potent power to control their minds.

I turned to another semelee, one that hadn't answered me yet. *How many adult half-breeds does the king currently have in his caverns?*

The semelee immediately bowed submissively. *Sixty-two.*

*And you said he currently has thirteen offspring from his breeding couple, but there are no other children currently born?*

*Correct.*

*And how many spare anklets does he still have?* I asked another.

*Nine thousand, eight hundred and fifty-seven. He keeps his collection of anklets in a locked chest in the caverns, and he seeks to acquire many more half-breeds. Each child born is to wear an anklet as soon as their magical abilities begin to manifest. The anklets he's purchased will remain stored in the chest until needed.*

I blanched. The king could potentially have an army of close to ten thousand, just as Saroly had reported, and given the strength of the child who foresaw Jax's raid in Possyrose Forest, and the strength of that single half-breed I'd seen in the Match Finals, the semelees were right. The other kingdoms didn't stand a chance against an army with that kind of power. The child psychic alone could tell the king exactly how to win each battle.

Rage seared through me, and my power crackled. *Well, none of that is going to happen if I have any say in it.* I seethed inwardly. The king was still on the hunt for more half-breeds to create his offspring, but we now knew the majority of his anklets were reserved for the children to come.

And to think, just one of the children he had enslaved had nearly brought down the Dark Raider. It would be unfathomable what thousands of children with that kind of power could accomplish . . . or destroy.

And the king's plan was moving rapidly forward. His one breeding couple had already produced thirteen children in only a few summers. And given how powerful the psychic child was that he already had at his disposal, I cringed to think of what the other children were capable of.

Stomach turning, I began to back up. *Thank you, but I must go. I have much to do.*

The semelees followed me to the Veil, and since I hadn't drifted far into the Veiled Between, I didn't need Jax's magic to assist me back. And I wasn't sure I would have needed it. Without my collar, a tingle of magic pulsed through me, sharpening my focus and intrinsically directing me toward the Veil. That had also never happened before.

The second I was free of the Veil's embrace, magic swelled inside me and catapulted me back through the galaxy to the fae lands.

I came to, on the bed, sucking in a huge rush of air. Eyes flying open, I was greeted with tousled black hair right in my line of sight.

Jax, who'd been kneeling at my bedside, shot to standing.

"You're back." His gaze swept over me, his irises like burning sapphires.

In the hall, banging and sweeping sounds could be heard as the others cleaned up the mess from this morning, and given the heady scent of magic permeating the air, I had a feeling Phillen and Lars had returned with the construction charms.

"Yes, I'm back. Oh, Jax." I sat upright and slipped my legs over the bed. Movements swift, I got to my feet, then grabbed his hands, holding onto him tightly. It only struck me as I stood tall that I wasn't tired. For the first time ever, I wasn't fatigued after a calling. "You're not going to believe this. King Paevin is behind everything. The king is doing horrible, *horrible* things and has been for many summers."

"What?" Broad shoulders tensed under Jax's woven shirt, and his hands pumped around mine, warming me in the process. "How? Tell me what the semelees told you."

I explained everything in rapid-fire. When I finished, Jax's mouth dropped open.

He let me go and began to pace, then raked his hands through his hair, and his lip curled. "King Paevin took my brother from me."

"He couldn't have known Bastian's your brother. Nobody could have known that. They took him because Bastian has strong fireling magic, and they somehow learned that about him."

Jax swung toward me. "But if the king has an enslaved child psychic and that child was able to know my whereabouts in the Possyrose Forest, then it's possible that child could be forced to find Bastian. The king could already know he's here."

I placed a hand on his arm, stopping his frantic steps. "That's unlikely. If the king already knew where Bastian was, he wouldn't have tried to call Bastian back to him by using the anklet this morning. And remember, it's the Match Finals right now. Thousands of fae from the other kingdoms have flocked here to watch it, and if the king is hand-picking the half-breeds from the arena who he wants to be enslaved to him, well . . ." I shrugged. "King Paevin likely has many things he's focused on right now. With any luck, he won't force that child to track down Bastian anytime soon."

"But for how long will he be distracted? If the king tried to bring Bastian back to heel this morning, he'll try again. And even though we left no survivors in the caverns, it's possible the king thinks Bastian was rescued versus broke out. He could be looking for us too."

My brow furrowed. He was right. "The only real way to prevent all of that is to stop King Paevin."

Jax nodded curtly. "We'll return to Stonewild. I'll alert my father and mother. I'll force them to understand how serious this is so they'll act immediately. And then we'll tell the other thrones and all of the Houses. We'll expose what King Paevin is doing."

"Do you think they'll believe us? The semelees said the hardest part would be convincing them of what we know. They'll only believe it if they don't think I'm lying. After all, I'm just a lorafin. We're asking them to believe me simply because of what I am."

His eyes hooded, and he stepped closer to me. Pine and spice wafted around me, and my galloping heart slowed when I inhaled his inherent scent. "We're not asking them to believe you just because you're a lorafin, Elowen. We're also asking them to believe me, their crown prince, and you, their future queen."

# CHAPTER 11

I knew Jax thought presenting me to his parents as a supremely magical lorafin would sway them to our side and would convince them to believe me about King Paevin. He also thought they would accept me as his future bride, given what I was and that we were mated. But the reality of my lineage couldn't be forgotten. I was a commoner. I might have godlike power, and they might relish having a lorafin in their court, but it was entirely different to welcome one into their family, as the future Stonewild queen nonetheless.

But Jax held my hands in our bedroom chambers as a dillemsill swirled in a tornado of magic at our feet. Jax had just finished telling it his message, and the dillemsill was on its way to Stonewild's palace to deliver it to his parents.

"We're really going to tell them about King Paevin's

plan *and* that we're mated?" The urge to wring my hands grew even stronger.

"It'll be all right, my love." Jax squeezed me again. "The dillemsill will tell my parents that I need to meet with them privately, that it's urgent, and that I want to introduce them to someone before we share some disturbing news. Have faith in me, my love. I'll make them come to accept you. You'll see."

I took a deep breath and nodded. Elsewhere in the suite, now that the damage from Bastian's attack this morning had been entirely fixed, everyone was packing in a hurry, readying for our departure from Leafton. Considering what kind of despicable fairy King Paevin truly was, none of us felt obligated to carry on with our ruse of enjoying the Match Finals. In the coming days, word would eventually reach the king of what we were accusing him of, and all of us were fine with drawing that line in the sand between us now.

But despite everyone's eagerness to leave, I couldn't stop knotting my fingers together and picking at my fingernails. I was going to meet Jax's parents tonight. As his mate.

I joined Bastian in the living area as Jax went off to see if everyone else was ready to go.

Bastian was sitting on one of the chairs. Several bags lay packed at his feet, and his antler rack appeared a dark beige in the low light.

He hunched forward, elbows on his knees, and a troubled look was upon his features. "It was truly the Faewood king who ordered my abduction and enslavement?"

I dipped my head and paced to the other side of the room. "Yes. King Paevin is an absolutely wretched fairy."

Bastian's lips thinned into a tight line, and his furious expression reminded me so much of his brother that I was astounded nobody had realized the likeness between the two. But on the other hand, I wasn't that surprised. Nobody had reason to suspect the Stonewild king of infidelity or that he had banished a secret half-breed child.

Bastian huffed. "Jax will find a way to stop him. Just wait, Elowen. You'll see. My brother's unstoppable when something's driving him."

I stopped my frantic movements and forced myself to sit beside him. Sounds of the others carried from down the hall, and I knew they were almost ready to go. "You're right. I should stop worrying and have faith that not only will your parents accept me, but we'll stop King Paevin too. After all, your brother's desire to find you is how he and I met and got us to where we are now."

Some of the ire on Bastian's face lifted. "Is that right? So, really, you should be thanking King Paevin for taking me. If he hadn't, you may have never met your fated mate."

His teasing tone had my wringing hands loosening. "Or perhaps I should thank *you* for enduring what you did for the past several months, all so I could meet your brother."

The lightness in his face lessened. "Do you think they forced me to . . . breed . . . while I was down there?"

My breath caught. "I don't know, but I can ask the semelees next time I'm in the Veiled Between. Would you like that?"

"Yes, I need to know." An air of heaviness settled around Bastian, like a cloak of despair. "Please understand, Elowen, I would never have knowingly or willingly been unfaithful to Anna. Even if she and I can never have children."

I scooted closer to him. "I can see that. You seem very committed to her."

"I am committed. I plan to wed her, which I know some think is crazy since we've not known each other long, but she's the one for me." He clasped his hands together, and his head dipped. "But if I've bred a child with another half-breed, I've not only broken the law and can be executed for it, but I've also betrayed Anna."

My heart broke when his face entirely crumpled, and I placed my hand over his. "No, you *didn't* betray Anna or do anything illegal. King Paevin is the one who should be held accountable for all of these crimes and for everything else that's happening in the Wood. Not even the supernatural courts could hold you responsible if an illegal half-breed child has been born. If you had knowingly bred such a child, they may hold you responsible, but you never consented to it. Both you and that child would be victims in all of this."

His shining blue eyes lifted to mine, but despite trying to reassure him, they didn't lighten. "I hope you're right, Elowen, because by the stars, if you're not . . ." He hung his head again. "I really hope you're right."

WE ARRIVED BACK in Jax's private tower in the Stonewild palace by mid-evening, the portal key depositing us down the hall from the enchanted chambers Jax had initially held me in. It'd already been such a long day, but I straightened my spine, knowing the hardest part was yet to come.

Outside the palace, the bustle of the city was going strong. On the horizon, the sun was setting, casting the city in an ethereal glow. Through the windows, everything looked so beautiful and alive, but all I could think about was that every single citizen in this city had no idea of the atrocities currently being committed just south of their kingdom's border.

In the hall, it was quiet, yet Bastian glanced around warily even though no servants were in sight. He scanned everything—the tall walls, the hanging tapestries, the rich carpet with its thick, woven fibers—he took it all in as though he'd never seen it before, and I couldn't help but wonder if he'd ever been in the palace.

"Do you think *he* has any idea I'm here?" Bastian asked Jax. All emotion had wiped clean from Bastian's face, yet his eyes gleamed with something dark and unforgiving.

Jax's mouth tightened. "No, our father is none the wiser as to what occurs within my tower. My wards see to that. He can't hurt you here."

Lander glanced around as the others did the same, but we were truly alone. In his usual monotone voice, Lander said to Jax, "So the plan is to meet in the main hall at nine for the supper meal, after you've had a chance to speak privately with your parents and introduce them to Elowen, correct?"

Jax's princely expression fell into place. "Correct. I've asked my parents to be there at eight so Elowen and I can speak with them before the rest of the court arrives for the evening meal. I have no idea how that discussion will go. Be ready to defend Elowen and me if needed."

Lander, Trivan, Alec, and Bowan all nodded and then headed out together. I could only imagine they were returning to their Houses to bathe and dress for the evening meal before returning to the palace once more.

Lars and Phillen still stood at our sides, but Phillen kept glancing at the stairwell.

Jax followed his line of sight. "You're both dismissed.

Feel free to check on Saramel and Cassim, Nellip. Just be in the hall by nine. We'll see you both then."

The guards bowed to their prince, and Lars added, "After I bathe and dress, I'll check on her guardian before supper, to replenish his stores if needed."

Jax inclined his head, and my lips parted. A jolt of shock shook my system. Guardian Alleron. I'd nearly forgotten about him.

My former guardian was still confined within one of Jax's chambers and had been so since we'd left for Leafton. He'd been alone for days, with food and water left behind to nourish him, but I doubted Jax had given him back his voice. His isolation was likely driving him mad. But for the life of me, I couldn't find an ounce of will to care.

Both guards hurried off, leaving Jax and I alone with his brother.

Jax cleared his throat. "I'll show you where you can stay, Bas, while we sort things out. You'll be safe here."

Jax clasped my hand, and that simple gesture soothed my bond.

I followed the brothers down the hall, and my thoughts whirled with what was to come. Before leaving Leafton, Jax had prepared me, telling me that supper was served precisely at nine each night, often with nobles of the ten Houses in attendance, so it would be the perfect opportunity to tell the other lordlings and ladies of what King Paevin had done.

And hopefully, our private discussion with his parents beforehand would go smoothly. With any luck, they wouldn't hate me, and they would accept our newly formed mate bond.

My stomach was a mess of twisting and turning knots as I followed Jax and Bastian to the end of the hall, and I was in such a worried state that it took me a moment to realize that Jax had led us to the same enchanted chambers where he'd once kept me.

I paused at the door. "You want Bastian to stay here?"

Jax gave me a sly smile as he laid his hand against the door's lock. A shimmer of magic clouded around his palm, a click sounded, and then the door opened. "You asked me once why I'd created this chamber with its strong enchantments and fogged windows to hide any prying eyes from seeing in, and it was for one reason." He opened the door more, and the familiar furnishings inside greeted us as we stepped over the threshold.

Jax closed the door behind us, and Bastian turned in a slow circle, whistling low beneath his breath. It was obvious from his wide-eyed surprise that he was as taken by the chamber's elegance and large size as I'd initially been.

A pulse of Jax's magic emitted over the lock again, freezing it, then he faced us. "The reason I created this chambers was in case I ever needed to hide my brother." He gave Bastian a sad smile. "It's warded. Seers can't penetrate its protective magic, and I'm hoping the king's child psychic can't see into it either." He slid his hands into his pockets and eyed Bastian. "What do you think? Do you like it?" The prince's expression was guarded, but I still caught the undercurrent of hope in his aura.

"This is where you want me to stay?" Bastian put his hands on his hips and surveyed the suite.

Jax raked a hand through his midnight hair. "Only for the time being. I know you want to get back to Anna, and I promise to get word to her that we've found you and you're safe, but I don't think it's a good idea for you to return home yet. As Elowen's pointed out, there's nothing to stop King Paevin from capturing you again."

Bastian's brows folded together, and he nodded. "As long as you tell Anna so she knows that I'll be back at her side as soon as I'm able to, it's fine if I need to stay here for a while." His eyebrows shot up. "Or . . . do you think I could have a looking glass and contact her myself? At least then, she and I could talk. I won't tell her anything about where I am or who you are, obviously."

Jax laughed softly. "Yes, if you'd rather tell her yourself, I can get you a looking glass."

Bastian grinned. "Perfect. Our plan's settled. I'll hang out here, talk to Anna every day, and enjoy a life of leisure while you go save the kingdoms." I burst out laughing, and Bastian winked at me. "Just let me know when it's safe to head back to Anna. But in the meantime, if I can talk to her, you don't need to worry about me. Being able to speak with her will tide me over. Not to mention, it'd be nice to spend my mornings sleeping in. The shipyard's schedule can be brutal."

Jax released a breath, and his face lightened. "Oh, brother, how I've missed you." He laid a hand on Bastian's shoulder, but before Jax could pull back, Bastian seized him and yanked him into a hug.

"I never thanked you properly for what you've done for me, J." Bastian's words turned gruff, his joking nature calming. "You risked your life, your friends' lives, your *mate's* life . . . all to save me."

Jax's throat worked in a swallow as the brothers held each other, and a sharp ache formed in my gut. Relief filled me that he finally had Bastian back at his side, but I would have been lying to myself if I didn't also feel a twinge of envy. I was so thrilled the brothers were back together, but a part of me wished for that too . . . to have a sibling so I could experience what they had.

Jax squeezed Bastian tighter. "You know I would do anything for you. You're my brother."

I could have sworn a coating of moisture filled Bastian's eyes. "And you're mine, but it's more than saving me from the Faewood king that I'm thankful for. You've never seen me as a half-breed either. Never, in all the seasons since you found out I was your brother, have you ever treated me any differently. I don't know if I've ever properly thanked you for that."

Jax pulled back, his gaze sharpening. "That's not something you ever need to thank me for, and you shouldn't. Everyone should treat you with kindness and respect regardless of who your father and mother are. It's despicable that our culture allows half-breeds to be treated as they are, as *you've* been treated your whole life."

A burst of pride and love bloomed through me as the fierceness of Jax's words penetrated my soul. He believed that, truly believed that, and not for the first time I saw the courage and perseverance that made my mate who he was.

It was Jax's unwavering belief that *all* Silten fae—both siltenite, half-breed, and wildling—deserved equal treatment and fair laws. Those beliefs and seeing the injustices in our land had forged his path to becoming the Dark Raider. And I had a feeling that if the day ever came where Jax was the king of Stonewild, it wouldn't be just his raider acts that strove to perform justice. It would be his ruling hand as well. Real change would come under Jax's leadership. I was certain of that.

"Elowen," Bastian said, grinning over his brother's shoulder, and I realized he'd been staring at me as I remained wrapped up in my love for my mate. "Come here and join us." He opened his arms to me, Jax doing the same, and before I knew it, the two brothers had me crushed against them as the three of us embraced.

I laughed, and Jax did too.

"My brother's a lover and a jokester," Jax said in a chuckling tone. "I did warn you of that, didn't I? Expect to get hugs regularly from him."

I laughed more. "I can get used to that." I'd received such little affection in my life, and I was coming to learn I quite enjoyed it.

Hugging them one last time, I finally pulled free of the two large males. Standing apart again, Bastian surveyed the chambers. "So now what?"

Some of the lightness in Jax's expression vanished, and he placed his hands on his hips. "I'll get you a looking glass so you can talk to Anna whenever you want while the others and I work to stop what King Paevin's doing. Once I'm certain it's safe to return you home, we'll get you back to Anna."

Bastian nodded, and then, in a sudden burst, he jumped backward and landed on the bed with his arms spread out. His leap was so big some of the pillows bounced off the mattress, and one flipped upward and wedged right between his antlers. He freed the pillow and flung it to the side. "I suppose I can get used to this in the meantime. I've never lived in luxury before."

Laughing again, I nodded toward the walls. "And when you're hungry, all you have to do is ask the enchantment for whatever it is you want. It'll deliver any kind of food you're craving." I eyed Jax teasingly. "Someone forgot to mention that tidbit when I was caged here. I thought servants were sneaking in when I wasn't looking to deliver food. It nearly made my heart stop in fright."

"Wait, my brother held you captive *here*?" Bastian's eyes grew entirely round.

Jax scrubbed his cheeks. "It's not one of my proudest moments."

"Don't worry, Bastian," I added. "I've forgiven him, even though he nearly starved me."

Jax hissed, looking sheepish. "Damn. I'm a horrible captor, aren't I?"

I grinned and pinched him teasingly. "Good thing you eventually made up for it."

A sly smile lifted his lips, and he drifted closer to me, putting his hands on my hips and then drawing me against his chest. "Perhaps you could join me in my private chambers now, mate? Considering I don't intend to let you sleep in any other chambers ever again?"

I arched an eyebrow. "Keeping me captive again?"

"Definitely, but your new captivity comes with *lots* of fucking. An added perk. It'll be better than the first go-around. I promise."

Bastian covered his ears. "That's your cue to leave, you two. I'm glad you've found your mate, J, but I don't need to hear the details."

A flush of embarrassment rushed up my neck, but so did a bolt of *want*. It hummed through me, and Jax's burst of hunger—that had nothing to do with food—shot toward me on our bond.

I draped my arms around his neck. "Well, with a promise like that, how could a female refuse?"

# CHAPTER 12

Since I'd enjoyed an extensive tour of the palace with Alec right before we'd left for Leafton on the royal ship, I was vaguely familiar with the royal residence's layout.

"I'll make sure you're properly oriented to the entire palace in the coming weeks," Jax said to me as he led me through his wing.

This area was entirely quiet and completely new to me. I followed him closely, soaking up the feel of our bond humming pleasantly from him into me.

The palace was so huge that I knew it would likely take me months to fully learn each turn. And since all of the rooms, corridors, and passageways that Alec had shown me were in common areas, I hadn't seen many places of the palace.

Of course, at that time, the purpose of Alec's tour had been to reveal my face, which was why we'd only visited places that House nobles and a multitude of servants frequented. All of that was to ensure I was recognizable, so it wouldn't be a shock if I began turning up at court events with the Dark Raider and his band since I was to be his indefinite captive. However, things had now changed. I was no longer Jax's captive. I was his mate, and someday he wanted me to be Stonewild's queen.

As my feet swished through the carpet, I said, "Before I forget, will you remove the bargain Saramel and I agreed to about Bastian?"

He arched an eyebrow. "I suppose I could. You do seem fairly trustworthy," he added teasingly.

I pinched him playfully, and we stopped in the silent hall. Jax took my hands and ran a thumb over my inner wrist, a common area the gods used to seal their bargain marks.

"Elowen Emerson, lorafin of Faewood Kingdom, and mate of my heart, as by my right according to the terms you agreed to in the bargain created with Saramel Highcrest, siltenite of Stonewild Kingdom, I—Prince Adarian Willip Jackson Stagthorn, crown prince of Stonewild Kingdom, and heir to one of the mighty four thrones on the Silten continent—hereby abolish the bargain you both agreed to, rendering you both free of its consequences."

A clash of magic clapped the hall, gone as swiftly as a distant boom of thunder. A searing flash lit up my wrist, and the wintercrisp fern that the gods had branded me with fizzled out of existence.

I ran a hand over my skin, smooth once more, and felt a moment of relief I was no longer tied to the gods in a bargain.

Jax chuckled. "I bet that took Saramel by surprise."

I made a face. "Hopefully, it didn't scare Cassim when her bargain mark flared."

"I'm sure he'll be fine. And now that that's done . . ." Jax entwined his fingers through mine and led me down the hall, moving even farther away from Bastian's chambers. We passed several closed doors, and Jax nodded at one. "That's where your guardian's being kept."

I listened intently but didn't hear a thing. "Are his senses still gone?"

"Only his voice, and we forced a potion in him to cage his fire element, but he can still see, hear, taste, touch, and smell."

No movement came from behind my guardian's closed door, and I wondered if he was sleeping.

My brow furrowed, and I tallied how many days my guardian had been caged within that chambers. But given all that he'd done to me, I once again found that I didn't care and stopped trying to add it up.

Jax kept walking and led me to the very end of the wing. We went past the staircase that I'd used in my initial escape. And when we reached the hall's end, Jax stopped in front of a wall in which a long banner hung. "You enter my upper tower this way."

I frowned. There were no doors anywhere, but with a sly smile, Jax swept the banner to the side.

I gasped when an arched entryway to another stairwell appeared. The banner hid it completely, and I would have never known it was there if Jax hadn't shown me.

"So clandestine," I commented in amusement.

He smirked. "I like my privacy, and in this palace, I'm awarded very little of that."

I stepped into the circular stone staircase, and a wash of powerful magic prickled my skin. "Is this stairwell warded too?"

"Indeed. Wards encircle my entire tower in various places, which keeps certain fae out of areas I don't want them in. Only a few of my most trusted staff have access to the upper floors."

"Do all of the palace's servants have access to this floor and the lower ones?" I distinctly remembered the feel of his wards when he'd initially brought me into the palace, when I'd still been blinded, and the feel of another ward when I'd done my mad dash down the stairs in my attempts to escape.

Jax shook his head. "No, very few servants are able to cross my wards at all. Even fewer can access this stairwell."

I began following him up the steps. "Where exactly are we?"

"Still in the west tower. This entire area is mine."

My breaths turned to pants as we climbed up. And up. And up. Windows dotted the stairwell, allowing natural light in while also revealing sweeping views of Jaggedston.

Fairy lights hung intermittently as well, and they shone off Jax's dark locks. "The enchanted chambers I created for Bastian are on the third floor of my tower, but my private suite is at the very top."

We climbed an additional five flights of stairs to get there, and the size and monstrosity of the Stonewild palace once again took my breath away.

"Is it normal for a crown prince to have this much space to himself?" I asked when we finally reached the top floor. I was panting heavily, not having the endurance of shifters despite my potent lorafin magic.

Jax shrugged, not even winded. "As their only official child, I will admit that my parents have indulged me." His voice turned sharper. "Perhaps if I'd had a legitimate sibling, that wouldn't have been the case, but as it is, all of this is mine, even though half of it should be Bastian's."

I followed him down another hall, which was wide enough to park two carriages side by side. Windows lined one of the walls, and imposing portraits of males and females looked down on us from the other. Each portrait held a name plaque beneath it. They were all Stagthorn family members.

The setting sun set everything aglow, but twilight had

begun to set in, and one of the moons had risen. Outside in our night sky, the colors of our galaxy were coming alive.

"Did you do the decorating?" I asked when a particularly sinister-looking male gazed down his nose at me from a large portrait. Shivering, I wanted to hurry past it but found myself stopping to stare at it.

Jax halted at my side, looking up at the male. "No, I can thank my mother for that. She won't admit it, but I have a feeling the reason she insisted on placing family portraits here is to remind me of who I am every night when I go to bed. Having my ancestors stare at me each day is supposed to instill in me a sense of duty and purpose. I dare say my mother has sensed some of my discontent with our family's line."

I cocked my head at him. "And has it? Instilled a sense of duty and purpose, I mean?"

"It has, although not in the way my mother intended." He nodded up at the dark-haired male staring at us. "That's my grandfather."

My eyebrows shot up, and I studied the severe-looking fairy again. Like Jax, he had midnight black hair, chilling blue eyes, and strong features. I couldn't recall seeing a picture of Jax's father, but if my mate resembled his grandfather this closely, I imagined it was the same with his da. "When did he pass?"

"Eighty full seasons ago, when I was twenty summers old. He lived to two thousand, one hundred, and eighty-seven summers and ruled this kingdom for over fifteen hundred of them. He abdicated the throne to my father around four hundred summers ago, as is common in our kingdom when a royal is nearing the end of his life."

"And his name?"

"King Jackson Persevious Adar Stagthorn, ruler and creator of Stonewild Kingdom, king of the stags, and commander of the north." A throb of Jax's aura puffed out of him, enveloping me in his scent. A trace of bitterness coated the pine and spice, and I glanced at my mate to find a contemptuous look on his face. "My grandfather claimed the Stonewild throne after the elvish wars ended, and he managed to hold on to it despite all of the strife and polit- ical maneuvering during that tumultuous time." His eyes narrowed, and he scratched his chin. "But whenever I see his picture, I don't see a male blessed with a cunning mind and courage to declare an entire kingdom his."

He paused, his brow furrowing. "No, instead I see a male who began the ostracization of our culture. It was my grandfather who declared that wildlings should be in serving positions only. He felt their inferior magic deemed them lesser." His jaw locked, and he began to stride away, as though looking at his grandfather for any length of time infuriated him. "I have no doubt if my grandfather were alive today, he would have agreed with my father on the treatment of Bastian."

I hurried after him, taking one last glance over my

shoulder at his imposing grandfather. The artist who'd painted him had also drawn antlers along the bottom of the portrait, and I couldn't help but notice their size and shape were similar to the antlers Bastian had permanently and the ones Jax could call forth with his magic.

"His name was Jackson, and one of your middle names is Jackson," I commented.

Jax glanced over his shoulder at me, and a sly smile lifted his lips. "It was, and it is."

I offered a teasing smile in return. "I suppose I won't need to ask Saramel, after all, where your nickname comes from."

He chuckled softly and stopped when he reached a set of large double doors in the middle of the hall. "I suppose you won't."

I cocked my head. "What about everybody else's true names? Come to think of it, I'm only certain of Nellip and Alec's birthnames. Alec told me everyone's nicknames were roughly their true names spelled backward, but he never actually told me what they were."

He made a low sound in his throat. "How remiss of me. You're correct that Phillen's true name is Nellip. Lars was born with the name Sarl. Bowan is Nathob. Trivan is Navani. Lander is actually Edwin. Like me, Lander chose a middle name for his nickname. And Alec . . . is Alec. We call him Cal on our raids."

"And Quinn?"

Jax shrugged. "He's just Quinn. We never gave him a nickname since he's usually in shadows and has such few interactions with actual fae."

I contemplated all of their true names. Nellip, Sarl, Nathob, Navani, Edwin, Alec, and Quinn. I made a face. "I have to say, I quite enjoy their nicknames more."

He smirked. "That makes two of us, or rather seven of us. All of us prefer our nicknames, and as you may have noticed with Bastian, it's also what my brother prefers calling me." He grasped one of the door handles of the double doors we'd stopped at, and a shimmer of his magic disengaged the lock.

But before he could open it, I thought back to the picture of his grandfather and asked, "Brommel stag shifter blood must run strongly in your family, and the land's magic here must want your line to continue having that shifter ability."

He faced me more, and his azure eyes looked stormy in the dying sunlight. "It does run in our family, and you're right. My line keeps producing brommel stags. My great-grandfather was also a stag shifter, as was my grandfather, father, and now me."

Unconsciously, I put a hand to my stomach. If Jax and I ever conceived a child, I had no doubt if I birthed him or her here, he or she would also be a stag. Or perhaps it wouldn't matter which kingdom I was in at the time. It certainly hadn't with Jax. He possessed magic from all *four* kingdoms—a true anomaly.

Jax's attention dipped to where my hand was, and another low sound came from his throat, part content rumble and part possessive purr.

Stepping closer, he slid an arm around my waist and pressed his lips to my ear. "Soon, mate, I shall place a child in your belly and watch it grow. Nothing would give me greater pleasure than to see you with my seed swelling you round the middle."

A throb of lust shivered through my insides. "Perhaps we could enjoy a few summers first with just the two of us? If the stars and galaxy eventually decide to bless us with a child, that is."

Nostrils flaring, Jax drank in my scent, then opened the door to what I assumed was his private suite. A sultry smile curved his lips. "I could be persuaded to wait. But I shall insist we practice conceiving a child many, *many* times in the interim. Now, come, my love, this chambers is now just as much yours as it is mine."

I stepped over the threshold, Jax still in front of me, and a strong wash of magic prickled my skin. I arched an eyebrow. "Another ward?"

He turned, his large frame blocking the view of his residence. "Of course. This is my private suite. I don't allow anyone in here, not even the servants. Only you have access now, in addition to me."

"Truly? You do the cleaning yourself?"

"It's nothing a few charms can't take care of."

"And you've never allowed anyone in here? Ever? Not even your friends? Or your parents?"

"No, not even them. Much of my life"—his brow furrowed—"hasn't been mine. It's owned by others, but here, within these walls, it's truly a haven for me. Nobody disturbs me when my doors are shut, not even the king and queen."

My breath caught. "Are you seriously telling me I'm the only one to have ever stepped over that threshold?"

He nodded. "Since I moved up here eighty summers ago? Yes. Only you."

"And you're truly telling me you've never had another female up here? Not even for a night?" It was a ridiculous question. If he had, I didn't want to know, but in response, he only stepped closer to me.

"No, Elowen. You are the only female ever to pass through my ward. Nobody has been in here since I claimed this as my private residence. Only you, my love."

Warmth bloomed through me, and he finally moved so I could see the chambers that he'd now opened up to me.

I gasped, my gaze alighting on the circular stone walls holding dozens of tall windows. A thick, plush carpet graced the room's center, and a large canopied bed sat by the far wall. The bed was large enough to easily hold three, even four, fae and was perfectly made without a wrinkle or crease in sight.

The bed's large coverlet was a deep navy with stone-gray sheets peeking out beneath it. Matching dark-wood tables graced the bed's sides, and across the chamber directly facing the bed waited a huge fireplace.

Surrounding the fire were two chairs and a sofa. I couldn't help but imagine us one day curling up on that couch, letting the fire warm us on a cold winter night, as the sounds of Jaggedston drifted to us faintly from the city streets below.

On the far wall of the chamber sat a huge bookshelf filled with hundreds of books. Next to that was a writing desk covered with a stack of parchments and quills. And beside that was a wall of swords, crossbows, and bows and arrows.

I smiled playfully. "Do you do a bit of training up here as well?"

He chuckled. "I like having my weapons close." Jax waited patiently, a content smile on his face as I explored his private suite. "I'll make room for whatever you would like added to our chambers as well. There's plenty of space."

I couldn't help but grin as I continued my wander. In the chambers' corner, a door waited. The door led to a large bathing room, putting the one attached to the suite Bastian had to shame. Unlike that suite, the windows in this one were crystal clear and awarded one a breathtaking view of the Adriastic Sea glimmering along the coast.

I eyed the monstrous tub and fluffy towels beside it. Jax and I could both easily fit in that tub, and the thought of doing so sent a shiver through me.

"Do you like it?" he asked quietly from the doorway.

I swirled toward him. "I love it."

"Come. I have something to show you." He beckoned me, then wrapped his hand around mine.

I followed him out of the bathroom to another door that I hadn't spotted since it lay close to the chambers' entryway and was easy to miss behind the double doors.

Jax stepped through it, and I followed, only to stop dead in my tracks.

A *huge* wardrobe stretched out in front of us, but instead of only holding clothes for the crown prince, half of it held female garments.

My heart began to pound when I eyed rack upon rack of beautiful sweaters, cozy tops, breeches in every color imaginable, billowy cottonum pants, simple dresses, and shelf after shelf of underthings in every shade of color. And at the far end of the wardrobe in a very small space, was a rack of opulent gowns.

Slowly, I made my way down the ginormous closet, feeling the clothes along the way. I stopped at the end, near the gowns, and my fingers trailed along their material. Every single gown was made of comfortably silky cloth.

None of them had restricting corsets or endless tulle or plunging necklines meant to titillate.

Tears formed in my eyes when I swung back to face Jax. "Is all of this . . . for me?"

He stood just behind me, having followed me silently, an unsure look on his face. "It is."

"When? And how?" I somehow managed in a choked whisper.

"I hired a dozen seamstresses the day that you broke out of your chambers. I knew that I couldn't let you leave, and I wanted to take care of you. It made my instincts absurdly happy to provide this for you, even if you didn't know about it and I was keeping you captive."

Another burst of warmth coasted through me. "So, it wasn't just the green gown you had crafted for me that I wore to meet King Paevin, or that chest of clothes you brought along to Leafton?"

His throat bobbed. "No."

"You had all of this made just for me?"

"I did. I made it very clear to the seamstresses what your tastes were. I hope I got it right." He raked a hand through his hair, suddenly looking unsure. "If I didn't, I'll—"

I wrenched him to me before he could utter another sound and kissed him.

His lips crashed into mine, his hands automatically going to my waist to pull me closer. Our mouths moved as one, and his taste flooded my senses. He tasted of wind and pine, hope and love. He tasted of home.

When I finally pulled back, I was breathless.

A smoldering look filled his gaze. "I take it that I got it right?" He smiled cheekily.

"You did." I ran a hand over one of the sweaters near me, still panting and breathless from our kiss.

My fingers encountered thick and soft material. I held the sweater up. It hung to mid-thigh and would be warm and comfortable when strolling through the chilly halls at night. "But this isn't the regal sort of attire a queen wears."

Jax cocked his head. "Perhaps not usually, but who's to say that can't change? Why should a queen be required to wear restrictive, uncomfortable gowns from dusk until dawn while the king wears comfortable pants and woolen tops or tunics and breeches?"

The tears in my eyes grew so thick that I could barely see. Blinking, I glanced at the gowns at the very end again. "And those are for when duty requires me to wear such finery?"

I surveyed the collection. There were around four dozen gowns, each of a different color with unique embellishments.

"Traditionally, we dress formally each night for the evening meal." Jax came up behind me and encircled my waist. "But if you don't like them, we'll get rid of all of them."

I laughed, the sound between that of joy and disbelief. I ran my fingers along the dresses. They were just as soft as the sweaters. "They're beautiful, Jax. No, not just beautiful. They're perfect. And I'm not entirely averse to wearing gowns, you know. It's simply that in my life with my guardian, I never had a choice, and he always chose ones of styles that I didn't favor. But these . . ." I pulled out one.

The dark navy dress had a fitted top encrusted with thousands of shimmering dark sapphires. From the waist down, the skirt was layer upon layer of fine, sheer-like material. It flowed like water to rest in a pool around my feet. And attached to the shoulder area of the gown's top was a cape made of the same sheer material, but at only one layer thick, the cape was slightly see-through. More glittering sapphires adorned the cape's clasp and seams.

The gown was breathtaking. Bold. Utterly beautiful. Yet I could tell from the cut and feel that it would be comfortable to wear for an entire day.

"I love this one."

His lips curved in a satisfied smile. "Try it on for me. You can wear it tonight to meet my parents if you like."

My cheeks warmed under his husky declaration and the arousal coasting from him into me along our bond. I swirled my fingers to indicate that he should turn around, then I quickly undressed and slipped into the gown.

It easily slid up my body, and the clasps in the back

were something I could even clip together myself, nothing like the stays and hundreds of buttons that commonly befitted the gowns my guardian had insisted on. I didn't even need a lady's attendant to wear this dress.

Once done, I smoothed the navy material over me, marveling at how perfectly it fit, then I clasped the sheer cape around my shoulders, hooking it to the dress in clasps just above my breasts.

Jax's large frame blocked the mirror at the wardrobe's entrance, but looking down, I was able to see that while the gown showed off my figure, it wasn't revealing, and the sheer layers of the skirt were lightweight and airy but not see-through. This gown would be easy to move in and wouldn't make me feel exposed. Yet it was beautiful enough that I felt regal.

"Well?" Jax asked, still turned away. "The suspense is killing me."

I laughed lightly. "You can turn around."

He spun slowly, and the second his gaze alighted on me, a predatory look stole over his face. He looked me up and down, his expression turning *hungry*. It reminded me of all the times I'd seen that look on his face previously, before I'd known that he was my mate.

He stepped closer, his intent clear. Liquid heat rushed between my thighs, and I instinctually backed up.

He *tsked*, yet a wild glow lit his eyes. "No running, mate. I fear I'd give chase."

I was already breathless by the time he pinned his hands to the wall behind me on each side of my head, caging me in. Leaning down, he ran his nose up my exposed throat, drinking in my fragrance.

"Is that arousal wafting up from you that I scent?" He pressed a kiss to my neck. "Why, I think it is. Is there something you're wanting, my love?"

I rubbed my thighs together, the friction delicious against my aching core. He nipped my neck, and I moaned.

"I believe I asked you a question." He trailed a finger up my thigh, dragging the gown with him until his hand slipped beneath it.

His fingers grazed over my leg, moving up, up . . . *up*.

Teasing, he traced his fingers along my hip, moving toward my center, right to where I was already throbbing for him.

When he reached my core, he tapped the bundle of nerves, and I cried out. "An answer, my love. *Now*. I believe I asked what you wanted?"

His dominant tone sent a spark of need spiraling through me. "I want you," I somehow managed through breathy pants. "I want you inside me."

A possessive rumble shook his chest, and he hoisted me up, parting the dress completely. He backed me into the wall until my spine was flush against it, and my legs hooked around his waist.

My hands went to his waistband as he hiked the dress

up entirely. The slippery, sheer material easily draped over my thighs to spill behind me, and I let out a loud moan when his cock sprang free.

He rubbed himself against my entrance and groaned. "So wet."

He lined himself up and slowly pushed into me. His large girth filled me with every inch he won, and my core clamped around him, holding him tightly. Gasping, I clung to his shoulders, already drunk with lust.

A harsh breath escaped him, and in a shimmer of magic, his antlers appeared. A wild glow filled his eyes, and he growled, "*Mine.*"

He plunged himself entirely inside me, and I cried out when he filled me so deliciously. Hands running up his chest, I tangled my fingers in his hair and then encircled his antlers with my palms.

A grunt came from deep within his throat, and his look turned feral. He began to pound into me, his cock thick, and my body hummed with need. The bond inside me burned, tying me tightly to my mate, and every time I grasped his antlers harder or caressed their rough length, his hips bucked, and his thrusts increased.

He rutted with me against the wall, slamming into me over and over. It'd felt like so long since we'd last done this, and I wondered how in the realm we'd managed to go as long as we had without touching.

"You're mine, Elowen. *Mine*," he rasped. "My mate. My queen. You're fucking *mine*."

I was a mindless mess by the time he slammed into me the final time. We both came together, our screams trapped in each other's mouths when we kissed fiercely. Wave after wave of pleasure spiraled through me, and he swallowed each of my sounds as he emptied himself inside me.

Many breaths later, he finally dipped his head, and his antlers winked out of existence.

Panting, I cradled him to me since my legs were still locked around his waist, and he was still buried deep within me. "Do your antlers always come out when you're . . ." I let my words hang, not entirely sure if it was simply sex that elicited them or something else.

He shook his head. "No. Only with you. Only you have the ability to bring out that side of me. Every time I'm with you, my mating instincts take a hold of me."

A thrum of satisfaction coursed through me that no other female had ever seen him that way. I ran a hand along the back of my neck, on the mating mark he seared into my skin back in Leafton. Then I ran my finger along his mark, the eye of a semelee, on his inner wrist. He shuddered.

"Good," I said simply and then draped my arms around him and kissed him languidly.

He kissed me soundly in return, his tongue dancing

with mine. *Gods and Goddesses*, but this male had the power to consume me.

A faint bell began to ring in the distance, and when it reached seven tolls, I realized what time it was. We were expected in the dining hall at eight, and with how monstrous this castle was, it would likely take a while to reach it.

Regretfully, I tore my mouth from his. "We should probably start getting ready to go. We don't want to be late to meet your parents."

He kissed me again, but instead of releasing me, he began to harden inside me. "We still have an hour. One more time . . . or two, or three . . . are in order. I haven't had nearly enough time to properly fuck you, my love."

My hair spilled back when he began to move, his thick length rubbing deep inside me and demanding that I respond. Our mating bond burned brightly, and his growing arousal coasted into me.

Moaning, I dragged him back to my mouth, kissing him thoroughly as he began to thrust into me again and again and again.

WE MADE love two more times. The second time we joined was again in the wardrobe, and the last was on the couch near the fireplace. It was well and truly close to eight by the time we'd both fully dressed again. But in a way, I was glad Jax had insisted on making love again. It'd certainly been a heady distraction. I hadn't thought even once of his parents or what was to come tonight.

In a rush of Jax's magic, he cleaned his seed away that had begun to slide down my thighs, and then, in another whisper of his magic, cleansed my folds too.

I gasped when his magic touched me *there*.

He smirked and kissed me softly before whispering in my ear, "Get used to it, my love. I plan to touch you in *every* way possible for many summers to come with my hands *and* with my magic." A caress of his air element danced down my spine, and damn him, but another stirring of longing began to pulse inside me.

Chuckling, he ran his hands over my gown, straightening it until it fell in a beautiful pool around my legs. Nobody would have known what we'd just been doing in his private chambers for the past hour.

Jax had changed into a pair of navy trousers and a crisp white buttoned-up shirt, covered with a navy jacket. He looked elegant and commanding, exactly as a prince should.

At the end of the wardrobe, near the door, a mirror waited.

I gazed at our matching attire, and for a moment, my breath was taken away. I knew most of my beauty came from my lorafin magic, but even I had to admit that we made a striking pair.

A smile tugged at his lips. "You're gorgeous, Elowen, absolutely *gorgeous*."

Warmth rushed through me, yet as we walked out of his suite, the doors locking automatically behind us, it truly hit me what we were about to do.

I was going to meet the king and queen of Stonewild Kingdom while their son declared me his mate, and then we were going to drop the news on them of what King Paevin had done.

This night had the possibility to end in triumph . . . or complete disaster.

# CHAPTER 13

"Come. I'll show you a faster way to exit my tower." Jax tugged me down the hall, going the opposite way of where we'd arrived. Behind us, the circular stone stairwell that we'd climbed to reach his suite grew farther away.

Near the hall's other end, he stopped at a large painting. The artwork was of the countryside, a beautiful rendition of the Wood full of vibrant color. Jax hooked his finger behind the frame on the top right. A click came, then the painting swung open. It moved on hinges as though it were an actual door.

"What in the realm?" I whispered.

A floating platform, encased within the stone wall, waited behind the painting.

Jax grinned. "It's a lift. If you're ever too tired to climb the stairs, you can simply take this."

I snorted. "Now you tell me."

He laughed and clasped my hand. We stepped over the tall stone lip to stand on the platform, and a fairy light instantly ignited, brightening the space around us. Stone walls encased the lift, no more than an arm's length away on all sides.

Jax swung the painting shut, and a moment of fear hit me that we were locked inside, but he quickly showed me the latch that would open the painting again. "Just press here."

He touched a small pad on the side, and the portrait immediately swung open. He even waited for me to try it too, seeming to sense that I was afraid of becoming trapped in this stone cylinder.

Once my fear abated, he grinned. "Ready?" As soon as I nodded, he stated, "Lift, take us to the first floor."

The platform instantly began to lower, and the stone walls rushed past us. But it didn't move so quickly that my stomach dipped, and it was definitely faster than taking the stairs. Similar to most lifts that inns and businesses used, we quickly passed multiple floors.

Laughing, I said, "I'm assuming this lift is enchanted, like Bastian's suite, if all you had to do was call out your wish?"

"It is. Just tell it what floor you want, and it'll take you to the correct painting to exit."

We passed floor after floor of paintings on our way

down. Their frames and the backs of each piece of art were visible as we glided past them.

When we descended seven floors, the lift stopped, and a pulse of green light emitted from the frame's release pad.

I cocked my head. "What does that green light mean?"

"It indicates that there are no servants or fae in the corridor. Nobody will see us if we exit now."

I gaped. "Does anybody know about this lift?"

He shook his head. "No, only me, and of course, now you."

I warmed internally again. Like his private chambers, I was once again being welcomed into his secret space, and that invitation was for me and me alone. "Does that light emit another color if someone's about?"

He nodded. "If you get a pink light, you need to wait until it turns green."

I cocked my head. "So if nobody but you and me know about this lift, who created it?"

"Me. I installed it when I created Bastian's suite."

My eyes bulged. "You? Truly?"

He laughed. "Don't look so shocked. I've been told I'm quite skilled when it comes to inventing magical creations."

I laughed with him, and his look turned entirely devious. "And as I told you, the west tower is my private residence. I've created many things within these walls that neither the servants nor my parents know about."

I laughed anew, his sly demeanor making me giggle. "But how did you construct it?"

"A lot of magic. A lot of cursing. And a lot of trial and error. The first lift was a disaster. I was locked in it for six hours until I could undo the magic I'd created to seal it."

My heart pattered faster just imagining that.

He drew me close and kissed my temple. "Don't fear, my love. It's fully functioning now."

"But if only you know about it, are you sure it'll work for me?"

"Of course, it will. I changed all of my wards and spells the day after I brought you to the palace. Well, all except for the door to Bastian's suite. I kept that one locked."

"The day after . . ." My jaw dropped. That'd been when I'd still been locked in Bastian's chambers, when I'd been convinced Jax and I would never see each other again after I did his calling and he rid me of my collar's suffocating hold to the best of his ability. "But we were going to part ways then."

He nodded, and his eyes dimmed. "I know. I knew it was safest for you if we did. As the Dark Raider, you're automatically at risk if I'm ever caught, but I couldn't help but hope that maybe someday that would change. That our paths would cross again when I was no longer the Raider and you no longer hated me. I didn't know if that would ever be possible, but I wanted to be prepared for it just in case."

"I never hated you."

"You did. When I took your sight and sound on our way into Jaggedston, I felt your fear and utter anger. It nearly undid me."

"But that wasn't hate. I could never hate you."

A teasing smile lifted his lips, but it failed to reach his eyes. "Your scent spoke otherwise when I commanded Nellip to return you to your chambers and keep you there after you tried to escape."

I sighed. "Okay, maybe in that one moment, you're right, but that was only because you were controlling me as badly as Guardian Alleron had."

A look of utter guilt crossed over his features.

I squeezed his hand, my eyes misting. "But I've fully forgiven you now."

He leaned down and kissed me softly on the neck, then reached for the pad to open the portrait. "That's all in the past now," he whispered. "I will never hold you against your will again."

The painting swung open, and he made sure my flowing gown cleared the first floor's entrance before pressing the tab to close the painting behind us. Once it locked, it was entirely innocent-looking.

"You're very good at keeping secrets," I whispered.

"Yes, I am, but I'll never keep secrets from you." He tugged me forward, and we finally began to stride down the corridor.

I took in my new surroundings and knew we were still in Jax's private tower since I hadn't passed through another ward, but the double doors at the far end of the hall promised that our privacy would be ending soon.

"The dining hall is in the palace's central area, right?" I asked and tried to recall everything that Alec had shown me. If I remembered correctly, the large, opulent dining area overlooked the palace's central courtyard.

"That's correct."

With each step that our shoes made on the stone flooring, the tension around Jax's shoulders grew. Before my eyes, the crown prince of Stonewild was emerging, his more carefree counterpart—my mate, Jax, and the Dark Raider—vanishing.

"We'll find a way to convince them to accept me, my prince," I whispered, falling back into the role that was required of me. Outside of his private wing, I could no longer call him Jax. In public, he was either Prince Adarian or my prince.

He inhaled sharply. "Indeed."

At the hall's end, he swept open the doors and ushered me through them. The second we stepped into a common walkway, the doors to Jax's area sealed behind us, another ward falling into place that prickled the skin at my back.

Voices drifted to us from farther down the halls, and a servant passed us, carrying a large bucket with cleaning charms and supplies.

The second she saw us, she paled and scurried away.

Jax's brow furrowed, watching her. My mate's hand clamped even more around mine, and together we strode down the center of the hall.

My long navy gown swirled around me, moving easily with each step. I knew I looked the part. This gown made me appear as though I belonged here, but deep down, I knew I didn't.

Nerves began to tumble in my stomach, but for the first time in my life, my collar was no longer adding to my inner anxiety. I only had my emotions to deal with now since the suffocating collar was gone, and I took some comfort in that.

Jax led me around another turn, and more servants appeared. Each one that saw us either stopped in their tracks, jaw's dropping, or they turned and hurried away.

I frowned. "Why are they all acting strange?"

Jax's forehead furrowed. "I was wondering the same thing."

"So that's not normal?"

"No."

"Do you think it's because word's spread that I'm your mate and your parents found out and are angry?"

His nostrils flared. "Even if they are upset, that doesn't change anything."

We rounded the final turn to the dining hall, and the

guards standing near the entrance doors both stiffened, their shoulders drawing back.

"Prince Adarian," the one on the right called. "Your father's been looking for you."

"I'm sure he has. We're scheduled to meet him at eight," Jax replied, breezing right past the guards.

My heart began to pound frantically as the energy in the palace grew stranger with every step we took.

We swept through the narrow hall into the dining room, and the large chamber spread out before us. But instead of only the king and queen being in attendance, as Jax had requested, the entire hall was filled with noble fae.

But none of them were talking. Dead silence greeted us.

And at the center of the room, standing near the king and queen, waited my guardian.

I froze mid-step and blinked.

Then blinked again.

But Guardian Alleron was still *there*. He was free of his chambers. And he was *here*, with the king and queen.

Disbelief shook me first, but panic descended just as fast. At my side, Jax's entire body went rigid.

Footsteps came from my left and Jax's right. Before I could so much as glance to see who was approaching us, the king of Stonewild Kingdom leveled me and his son with a penetrating stare.

"Adarian, you have some explaining to do. This male is

insisting that you're the Dark Raider and that you abducted him and have been holding him captive in your tower."

My jaw dropped as an explosion of fear rose and whirled inside me. My magic responded just as fast, chasing and clawing through my limbs. Shadows unfurled within me, but somehow, I managed to lock them down until I realized the footsteps closing in on us weren't servants or guards of Stonewild palace.

They were kingsfae.

Two dozen kingsfae circled around us.

"Oh Gods." My gaze darted around the room, soaking up every detail rapid-fire.

Standing by the far wall, all of Jax's friends—Lars, Phillen, Lander, Bowan, Trivan, and Alec—stood with their heads dipped and their hands lassoed in magical bands.

"Stars Above," I whispered.

Jax's grip around my hand tightened. "Father, what is the meaning of this? Why are my guards and friends detained?"

"That's what we're hoping you can explain," the king replied, his eyes as cold as ice. "You told us you met Elowen in Fosterton, but you never said that you rescued her from the Dark Raider, yet that's exactly what a letter from King Paevin claims you told him. Yet this male, who was found in your tower, is claiming that's because *you're* the Dark Raider and that you never rescued Elowen at all."

Jax seethed, and his grip on me tightened even more. "I didn't feel it was necessary to reveal every detail about how Elowen and I met, and I have no idea who that male is or why he's accusing me of such things," Jax replied, pointing at my guardian. The lies rolled off his tongue so easily. So quickly. Once again, I was reminded of the many masks my mate wore.

Guardian Alleron glared at Jax but didn't speak. Heightened energy and crackling magic swirled around the kingsfae as they encircled us, and one thought and one thought only penetrated the fog that threatened to fill my mind.

Nobody would believe us.

Guardian Alleron had escaped and had somehow communicated what'd been done to him, which meant the kingsfae were here to arrest my mate.

They *knew* he was the Dark Raider. They *knew* Jax was lying now.

And it was all because Guardian Alleron had broken free and told them everything he'd seen.

# CHAPTER 14

"Stop!" Jax snarled at the advancing kingsfae.

They halted as one, and a male with an authoritative air about him paused just short of us. "You've been summoned by the courts, Prince Adarian." Six kingsfae moved in closer, flanking the commander's sides, yet all of them stared at Jax with uneasiness. "You're accused of being the Dark Raider."

"That's preposterous." Jax seethed. "I'm the crown prince of Stonewild Kingdom. I'm exactly the type of male the Dark Raider would steal from."

Another look of wariness passed between the kingsfae, but their commander, while looking more contrite, didn't dip his head. "We understand, but given what was discovered in your tower this morning, we have to take such accusations seriously until we can prove otherwise." The commander pointed at my guardian. "He was found in your private area after all, and he's accusing you of being the Dark Raider, of abducting him, and of holding him captive. We cannot ignore that."

Guardian Alleron stood tall beside the king and queen, his eyes shining with vengeful malice. Even though he had an unkempt beard and dark circles underneath his eyes, he looked anything but beaten.

A tremble of rage shook me, and it took everything in me not to curl my fingers into fists. Baring my teeth, I glared at him. "That male is a *liar*. The prince may not know who he is, but I do. He's my former guardian, and he probably smuggled himself in here as a way to get me back. Everything he says is a lie."

"But he was *locked* in a room in the prince's wing!" a female cried. "He didn't fake that. I found him there."

Jaw dropping, I swung toward who'd spoken.

Lady Aerobelle of House Dallinger stepped into view from around her parents. Puffy skirts swished with her movements. The garish, fluffy yellow gown she wore reminded me of sticky candy. "I found him this morning, knocking frantically on the inside of a locked chamber. It's truly a miracle I did. That area of the prince's wing was entirely empty of anyone else, and the lock on it was so complex that we had to call the Master of Spells to disarm it."

"You were in my tower?" Ice dripped in Jax's question. "How did you get in there?"

She raised her chin. "I . . . a servant helped me." Her pompous tone dropped, and she entwined her fingers, twisting them together. "I was simply looking for you, my prince. I'd heard rumors that you hadn't been seen lately in Leafton, and since we returned from the Match Finals this morning, I figured you might have as well."

"A servant allowed you access to my wing?" A flash of disbelief pulsed in Jax's aura. "I highly doubt that."

Lady Aerobelle's chin wobbled. Cheeks also flushing, she stammered, "It's . . . it's true. One of the servants was nice enough to let me enter at her side."

"She means that she forced the servant to allow her entry," Trivan barked from the edge of the great room, his lip curling. "She made the serving girl stay so close to her that your wards didn't detect her."

"You broke into my private wing by coercing a servant?" A cloud of fury rose from Jax, and his eyes emitted shards of sapphire sparks.

Lady Aerobelle shrank back. "I was just looking for you. That's all." She dropped her lashes. "I'd hoped we could enjoy lunch together."

"You hoped for a meal with him after *breaking into* his warded tower?" I challenged, my voice rising.

She shot me a haughty glare, her parents doing the same. Their looks were so similar to the disdainful glances they'd given me on the ship when we'd all sailed together to Faewood. But I didn't care what they thought of me. They were the reason for this disaster.

Aerobelle shifted her attention back to Jax. "I'm sorry, my prince. I didn't mean to cause any trouble, and it's ridiculous what you're being accused of, but I couldn't very well just walk past that door when someone was knocking frantically from within it, obviously unable to get out." She squared her shoulders. "I thought you would be pleased. I thought that I was saving one of your servants. I had no idea this male would be in there." She shuddered when she glanced at Guardian Alleron.

Jax's nostrils flared so slightly that if I wasn't standing close to him, I wouldn't have detected it. "Whatever Lady Aerobelle may have discovered in my tower, I can assure you I had nothing to do with it."

Guardian Alleron stomped his foot and made a motion with his hand to pieces of parchment on the table beside him.

The kingsfae nearest my guardian indicated for him to be quiet.

I stepped closer to Jax, and my heartbeat tripled. Because as much as I didn't want to deal with Aerobelle's meddling discovery, it'd been thrust upon us whether we liked it or not, and even though I'd truly thought any hold my guardian had on me had long disintegrated, he was now back in my life.

The king arched an eyebrow at his son. "If you've

never met this male before, then *how* is his presence in a locked chambers within your tower explained? Go on, tell them, Adarian, so this can all be put to rest."

Jax fisted his hands. "I. Don't. Know. Like Lady Elowen implied, maybe he smuggled himself in there."

"They won't listen to reason!" Bowan called from where he'd been restrained by the wall. "We've already told them it's absurd, that none of us have seen that male before today, and that none of us have had any part in the Dark Raider's crimes, but they won't listen."

Trivan grumbled something similar and spat on the floor, right by the feet of the kingsfae who stood over him. Lander and Alec seethed quietly next to Trivan. Beside them, Phillen and Lars also stood in cuffs. Only Quinn was missing.

My breath stuttered when I caught Phillen's worried expression. Both of the prince's private guards stood silently, but Phillen's attention kept swiveling around the room, as though searching for someone.

A wave of sickness came over me. He was probably looking for Saramel or Cassim. This was Phillen's greatest fear, that he would be caught, and his wife and child would pay the price for his crimes.

"Father." Jax swung toward the king again. "This is *absurd*."

Silence reigned.

The king of Stonewild stood with the queen

behind the front dining table, and the stare-off between them and their son was sharp enough to cut glass.

Food had already begun to be laid out on the long banquet-style table behind them in preparation for the supper meal. Numerous dishes and serving platters were filled to the brim with steaming selections, the serving ware enchanted to keep the nourishment hot, but all of the noble fae in the room appeared to be in attendance because of the spectacle. Not because of the impending meal.

I could only imagine what had gone on during the past two hours. While Jax and I had been making love in his tower, the kingsfae had been arresting his friends left and right and bringing them here. They'd probably been waiting for us to appear and *that* was the cause of the servants' strange reactions in the hall.

Haltingly, my gaze crawled over the king and queen. The king looked strikingly similar to Jax, but gray hair lined his temples, and his stomach wasn't quite as lean. His mother, however, was entirely fair. Unlike her husband, whose skin was a tanned light brown, she was as pale as me. Long blond hair was coiled around her head, and tepid blue eyes watched all of the commotion with stunned shock.

As though feeling me studying her, Queen Rashelle's attention slid my way, her eyes narrowing, and I hastily looked away before her stare could turn into an accusing glare.

"You still need to explain all of this," Lady Aerobelle's father decreed.

Standing near the king and queen were the Dallinger House nobles along with other House fae. Like the royal fae, they all appeared stunned. And given that one of the males had brown skin, a large build, and penetrating green eyes, I had a feeling I was looking at Bowan's father, the male who ruled his family's House.

"As I said, this is absurd," Jax exclaimed again, staring at his parents with fury streaming through his aura. "I've had nothing to do with this male."

"It's true," I added. "That male is my former guardian. He's been trying to get me back ever since he lost me, and he's now lying about everything. He and I were taken captive by the Dark Raider, but *the prince* saved me from him, although my guardian wasn't so lucky. He probably came here after the Dark Raider let him go, probably not only hoping to reclaim me but to also seek revenge since the prince hadn't saved him too."

Jax squeezed my hand lightly, and a pulse of his approval emitted to me along our bond.

Relief hit me that I'd made the right call. Because if we wanted to find a way out of this, we needed to keep our responses as close to the truth as possible. King Paevin knew that Guardian Alleron and I had been captured by the Dark Raider, but the Faewood king believed that the Stonewild prince had bartered for my release. If I told a new lie now, saying I didn't know who Guardian Alleron was or that I'd never met the Dark Raider, I would inevitably be caught in a lie.

"You're her *former* guardian?" The king turned on Guardian Alleron, confusion on his face. "You wrote that you're her current guardian."

Guardian Alleron's mouth opened and closed, indignation rising in his aura. It was obvious Jax's Ironcrest sense-stealing magic still kept his voice robbed. Seething anew, my guardian grabbed a piece of parchment that lay on the table next to the king and hastily wrote something down. And it hit me how he'd communicated everything to them. He couldn't speak, but he could *write*.

The king took the note, a look of disgust upon his face when my guardian edged closer to him. He read it, then zeroed in on me. "This male claims that you're still his property. He says the supernatural courts enslaved you to him and that my son was holding you hostage as well. He says everything you two are saying is a lie." The king scoffed and glanced back at my guardian, then the kings-fae. "Truly, this is getting ridiculous. I can assure you that my son is not lacking of females vying for his attention. He does not need to hold any female captive, and from the looks of it, this mistress he's taken is *not* a captive."

The king huffed out another breath, then raked his

gaze up and down my frame. "From what I heard from the other House families, this . . . *slave* has entirely captivated him." He eyed the Dallinger House, then glanced back at Jax. "Although, I must say, Adarian, one thing doesn't add up. You told the council you met this female in Fosterton and invited her back to see the palace. You never said anything about saving her from the Dark Raider. How did you even know the Dark Raider had her?"

A sheet of ice coated my stomach, and Jax's throat rolled in a swallow.

My guardian scribbled something else down, then handed it to the kingsfae nearest him.

The kingsfae took it and read it. His brow furrowed, and he wouldn't meet either Jax's eye nor mine when he addressed his commander. "He's claiming again that the prince is the Dark Raider, and that's how he and his enslaved female came to be here. He's saying the prince is lying, and so is the female because she's fallen in love with him."

I tried to keep my demeanor innocent-looking, but even I felt the blood drain from my face.

"It does support what another servant reported in our questioning this afternoon, Commander." A kingsfae stepped forward from the wall where Jax's friends were being held. "A staff member said he initially met this female when she was running frantically through the castle, as though she was trying to escape from here. She even had a broken arm."

Queen Rashelle's breath sucked in, and all of my limbs locked into place. I cursed myself a hundred times over for not trusting Jax and fleeing from his enchanted suite that day. If I'd only had faith in him, I wouldn't have tried to escape, and a servant wouldn't be sharing my strange behavior that day.

The commander sighed heavily. "All of this is certainly muddled and entirely conflicting, and I do apologize, my prince, but we still need you, this female, and the other males being accused of such crimes to come with us to the supernatural courts. King Paevin had also sent word to us that a male and female were abducted from his kingdom weeks ago by the Dark Raider, and he's been searching for them ever since, and both this female and this male claiming to be her guardian match their descriptions."

"And your name's Elowen, is it not?" the commander asked, turning toward me.

My throat rolled in a swallow. "Yes."

"King Paevin said his lorafin's name was Elowen, further proving that you're the female he's been looking for."

"But King Paevin already knows that I'm accounted for," I replied in a hurry. "He knows that the prince rescued me from the Dark Raider. We told him that when we were in Leafton."

The commander pointed at my former guardian and continued as though I hadn't even spoken, making the rising dread inside me increase. "Furthermore, the king said he's been searching for a male named Drevel Alleron, commonly called Guardian Alleron, and this male matches his description. King Paevin has also confirmed via dillemsill this afternoon that Elowen was once the enslaved lorafin of Guardian Alleron. At the moment, those are the facts that we solidly know."

The commander turned to the king and bowed. "Until we can sort everything out, these fae need to come with us, Your Majesty. I do beg your pardon, but we will need to take both the prince and this female, along with his guards and closest friends, in for questioning. I'm sure it will be a formality only, but the courts do demand that we conduct a proper investigation into this matter."

Jax snarled and stepped in front of me, blocking me from their view. "This female is my *mate*. She belongs to no one but herself, and you will not take her anywhere."

The king and queen gasped simultaneously.

"Your *mate*?" Ruddy color filled the king's cheeks.

Blood pounded through my ears, and icy sweat lined my palms. I hastily stepped around Jax so I could face them, but I was met with silence. Every single fairy in the large room, even the kingsfae, appeared speechless.

"Your . . . *mate*?" The queen repeated the same statement as her husband, and her mouth dropped open. "Is this some kind of joke?"

"Not at all. She's my mate." Jax's nostrils flared. "We were fated, and we've completed the bond."

Lady Aerobelle abruptly burst into tears, and her parents cast Jax a scathing look before ushering her away.

The king prowled toward Jax, his aura rising and growing more potent with every step he took. "You dared to defy us and your royal duties by *mating* yourself to this *slave?*"

That one-word accusation cut me so deep that all hope I'd ever had of being accepted by them died as though I'd been stabbed through the heart.

"I did." Jax bared his teeth at his father and kept his hand around mine. "And nobody, not even you, can take her from my side."

Silence again swept through the huge dining hall as the king and prince squared off.

Queen Rashelle scowled at me, that look telling me she blamed all of this entirely on me.

But I didn't try to defend myself. I knew there was no point. His parents had already made up their minds, and my guardian's accusations were only making everything a hundred times worse. But like Jax, I wasn't giving up on him. Even if they hated me, I *wasn't* leaving the prince's side.

Finally, the kingsfae commander cleared his throat, his

expression looking entirely uncomfortable as he gazed between Jax and his parents. "Mating duties aside, Your Majesties, if it is suitable with you, we will escort the prince, the other males being accused of such atrocities, and this female to the courts until this matter may be straightened out. I do apologize for the inconvenience."

The queen sneered and looked down her nose at Guardian Alleron. "Don't forget this one. I don't care for him to ever be present within the palace again."

Guardian Alleron shot her a contemptuous look and straightened his shoulders. I could practically taste the rising victory emitting from his soul despite her snub. He truly believed that he'd caught the Dark Raider, and inevitably, Jax and his friends would hang.

Sheer panic coated my insides because I'd seen that look on my guardian previously. It was a look he wore when he wanted something fiercely, and I'd never seen him lose when he'd set his ambitions.

"My prince and lady, if you would." The kingsfae commander gestured toward the door, and some of my panic calmed when I realized they weren't going to restrain us.

But Jax's expression hardened. "As I said earlier, Lady Elowen's not going anywhere. I won't say it again. She belongs to no one but herself. She will not be subjected to any questioning."

"Really, Adarian." The queen huffed. "You're making

this so difficult. Just do as they say so this matter may be cleared up." She eyed me again. "And I don't care to hear again that you're claiming a slave as your mate. That's beyond absurd. And if you truly have completely lost your head and mated yourself to this . . . *female*, we shall call upon a spellcaster and have the bond dissolved shortly upon your return."

I swayed, and it felt as though the floor had dropped out from under me. *Dissolve our bond by wielding a dark spell?* The queen actually wanted to cut the threads that wove Jax's and my souls together, but I would *never* allow such a thing. It was said one never recovered from a broken mate bond, and Jax and I had done nothing to deserve that kind of pain.

I locked my knees and met the royals' contemptuous stares squarely. "My king and queen, Guardian Alleron is my *former* guardian. As your son stated, he rules me no more. And despite your feelings for me, which I can partly understand given the circumstances, I hope that eventually you'll see me as a worthy mate for your son because I'm not going anywhere." I lifted my chin, and Guardian Alleron's eyes narrowed, but the second his attention dipped to my throat, his eyes widened.

*That's right.* I glared at him. *Your collar and adaptor are gone, which means that you can't control me anymore.*

Despite my respectful yet challenging tone and words, Jax's parents only gave me a dismissive wave, as though I was no more significant than a tiny beetle crawling in the soil.

Fresh pain cut through my heart at their obvious disgust of me, and a growl rumbled in Jax's chest.

"Just go and be done with this nonsense, and take that girl with you." The king pointed a finger at me and then Jax. "But be civil. Do not embarrass our great name by doing anything other than what they ask of you." The king shifted his attention to the commander. "And, Commander, we expect the same of you. Be mindful that Adarian is our *only son,* who you're taking in for questioning."

Jax's aura rose monumentally, and my concern shot to Bastian, confined within Jax's tower—the king's bastard son under this roof at this very moment, completely unbeknownst to any of them—and entirely at risk if he was discovered too.

And to make matters worse, since Jax hadn't delivered a looking glass to his brother yet, Bastian literally had no way of contacting anyone in the outside realm. Until Jax released him from the chambers, he was trapped. Just as I'd been.

*Oh Gods.*

The commander bowed. "Of course, Your Majesty. We understand the gravity of this situation." He signaled the other kingsfae, and they began closing in.

"You're coming with me," the kingsfae stated beside me and reached for my arm.

"Don't touch her." Jax snarled and shoved him away from me.

"Adarian!" the king yelled, fury lancing his tone. "Truly, if you're innocent of everything they're claiming, this will all be cleared up soon. And as for this female you've brought along, your mother is right. If she's a slave to this"—his gaze tracked up and down my guardian, his lip curling—"this *male*, then she best return home with him. Or she can handle her plea with the supernatural courts to be free of a guardian on her own time. Whatever the case, it has nothing to do with us. Neither your mother nor I wish to ever hear the word *mate* brought up again by you. Now go, and don't cause a scene." His voice dipped. "If you do, the only one who will pay the price is your supposed mate."

# CHAPTER 15

The king's threat hung heavily in the air, and a crushing sense of defeat filled me. Because even if Jax did manage to keep the kingsfae from questioning me, it wasn't like I had anywhere to go. Jax would be forced to either leave me in the palace, at his parents' mercy, or I would be dumped out into the streets.

"It's all right. I'll be fine," I said quietly to the prince. "I'll go to the courts."

"No, Elowen, you won't." He cast me a glance, and his look held a steely resolve. "You've done nothing wrong. You should remain free."

An aching pit opened in my stomach at the menace that filled his aura. Surges of it barreled into me along our bond, even more so when his attention shifted back to the kingsfae and the magic around Jax tripled.

"Adarian . . ." I said cautiously.

Nostrils flaring, Jax swung to his father, and a cruel smile curved his lips. "You're a fool, Father, if you think I'll let them take her. She's *my mate*. Don't you understand what that means?"

His father's eyes widened just as a huge rush of magic emitted from Jax, and something Jax had said to me, days ago when we'd been in Leafton staying at The Silver Hand, crashed to the front of my mind. *"I'll fucking kill* anyone *who tries to harm you or take you from me."*

My jaw dropped as the implication of that statement took root.

Jax was a mated fae male.

He wouldn't allow the kingsfae to apprehend me. It went against every instinct that commanded his soul. He *couldn't* let them touch me.

And he had the power to kill everybody in this room.

I yelled his name just as a rush of power barreled out of the prince and crashed through the massive dining hall. It hit every kingsfae in the vicinity at once, slamming them to the floor as the other fae in the room began to scream.

I reached for my mate, trying to rein him back in, but elemental wind whipped through the hall, snuffing out every candle. The dining room plunged into darkness, and the screaming increased.

Fumbling, I staggered toward Jax. Only the barest hint of light penetrated the underside of the doors, allowing me to see faint outlines.

"Adarian!" I called through the torrent of Jax's air element blasting through the room. "Stop! Don't do this. They'll only blame you more!"

"Stay down, Elowen." His voice was so faint even though he stood only an arm length away, and I realized he'd locked me in a void to protect me.

"My prince!" I called again, but it was no use.

On a rush of wind, Jax levitated into the air, careening through the dimly lit hall as he targeted every authority figure who had sought to take me into custody.

Kingsfae grunted, some screaming in pain, others yelling that they'd been blinded or couldn't hear. The dining hall became a cacophony of darkness, writhing figures, and unleashed elements. But Jax held his Mistvale magic at bay. He didn't command anyone. Whether that be because he knew such an act would surely implicate him as the Dark Raider or because he knew it was fruitless given the devices the kingsfae wore in their ears, I didn't know.

I squinted in the darkness, trying to see more.

A shuffling of feet and shifting of dark shapes pushed away from the wall. Jax's friends shoved off the kingsfae who'd bound them, trying to get to the prince, but a huge rush of new magic from the front of the dining table abruptly flooded the entire room in a torrent of water.

I screamed when water slammed through Jax's barrier into my shins and nearly knocked me to the floor.

Darkness.

Water.

Wind.

It was as if we'd been transported to an underground cave with rising flood waters and lashing currents. But in a moment of clarity, it hit me that the king commanded magic from more than one kingdom too, and given that Jax's mother was from Faewood and undoubtedly had elemental magic as well, it wasn't a surprise that the land had blessed their son with all four elements.

"Adarian, stop this now!" The king seethed as he wove his magic. Another tidal wave of water rose into the air, barely decipherable in the shadowy room.

The wave crested over the prince, swallowing Jax as he levitated in the air.

Heavy water crashed upon him, and my mate fell back to the floor. But the king didn't stop. Water cascaded over Jax. Soaking him. Pinning him. Drowning him as well if it didn't lift soon.

Light suddenly filled the room again, each candlewick bursting with flame. The queen's hands lifted, magic emitting from her palms, and the flames grew higher. Behind her, Guardian Alleron cowered, his eyes wide with panic.

The strength of the royal family's magic hit me at once. They had so much *power*.

Jax struggled against the water, and I shoved through the tide swirling around my calves, his void gone. I reached for him beneath the current holding him under. Magic rattled inside me as the prince fought against the water holding him down, but I tried to contain my instinctual reactions, knowing that diffusing this situation was the only way to salvage any peaceful resolution.

But I *couldn't* let them hurt my mate. "Release him!" I yelled at the king.

Disoriented kingsfae staggered to their feet, still blinded given their fumbling movements as they moved toward the prince, arms out.

More magic billowed inside me. The instinct to destroy anyone who harmed my mate rose in me so swiftly that shadows unfurled from my limbs of their own accord.

I rounded on the king, magic crackling all around me. "I said *release him*." Sheer power vibrated through my words, and I knew my eyes were shining like emeralds as my shadows grew.

The king staggered back, disbelief etching into his face as he beheld me.

But before I could act, a rush of stone exploded from the floor, shooting through the water holding the prince down and aiming straight for the king.

Jax's elemental magic shredded through the king's water, and King Stagthorn ducked at the last moment. If he hadn't, a jagged boulder would have taken his head off.

The queen shrieked, ducking to the side as well, just as a soaking-wet prince rose above the king's water element. Air instantly billowed around him, drying him completely, and he did the same for me, drying my dress entirely.

"Trying to drown me now, Father? Is that it?" Jax cast an anxious glance toward me, but when he saw me standing, shadows curling around me, he smiled darkly before facing his father once more. "Your abuse truly has no bounds."

"You are a disgrace to our name, Adarian," the king shouted.

"I'm a *mated male*, Father . . . what did you think would happen?"

The two royals squared off, each seething at the other while the blinded kingsfae remained entirely useless.

More screams sounded through the room as some nobles finally reached the exits and sprinted as fast as they could from the mayhem. Water soaked their gowns and pants, but the weighted-down fabric did little to slow their rapid pace.

Dozens of doors burst open in their haste to leave, and more light poured in from the hallways. The candles' fires flickered impossibly high, rising and rising until the flames nearly licked the ceiling.

The queen gasped, and she wove her hands through the air again, but the fire didn't relent.

A manic gleam filled the prince's expression, and he soared into the air, levitating once more. "You know my fire is stronger than yours, Mother."

He rose above his parents, and the walls trembled, the rock holding this palace together threatening to crumble.

Heat from the candles laved the walls as if bonfires sprouted from each wick.

"I'll pulverize this palace to the ground and then burn it into oblivion if they dare to take my mate." The prince's tone turned beastly. Antlers abruptly sprouted from his forehead, and the look on his face entirely transformed.

Gone was the playful male who had been with me in his chamber. Gone was the tender love I'd seen on his face when he rutted with me in his wardrobe.

The male who hovered above all of us was filled with potent rage, and the full strength of the prince's magic threatened to bring this city to its knees.

The king backed up, his eyes widening.

"Prince Adarian!" a kingsfae shouted. "Stop this at once before anyone gets hurt!"

"No one is touching my mate!" His words came out through clenched teeth, his voice barely fae.

Jax's friends all moved away from the wall, running through the remaining puddles to stand beneath their prince while forming a protective circle around me.

But I didn't need their protection. I was stronger than anyone here, save my mate whose horrific display of magic rivaled a god's.

Still, I held my magic at bay, not daring to unleash it given the consequences that would inevitably take hold.

"Adarian." I peered upward at the male who would decimate a city to protect me. "Not like this. They'll never let you go if you continue. Please, stop. For *me*. Stop."

The second my plea reached his ears, a crack formed in Jax's expression. Some of the visceral fury coating his features lessened. Eyes blazing like sapphire gems turned on me, and the briefest moment of awareness filled them.

"Stop. Please. For *me*." I stepped closer to him, gazing upward. "If you don't, they'll hunt you down and kill you for what you're doing. This is the beginning of the end for us if you don't stop."

My heartfelt words poured from my mouth. But even though they made me sick with worry, I also knew this was the only way, even if my guardian's damning accusations could result in the same outcome.

At least we had a chance if we went in for questioning. But if Jax continued as he was, he was as good as dead. The authorities couldn't allow someone with as much power as Jax to remain free if he did acts such as this. It would only be a matter of time before the kingsfae caught up to him. And he and I deserved a life better than being on the run.

"*Please*." I sent a huge rush of love along our bond, bathing Jax's senses. My request finally seemed to penetrate the rage pounding through my mate's aura, and a look of anger, then defeat, then sad acceptance filtered over him.

In a rush of wind, he lowered himself to the floor. The second Jax's feet touched the ground, he sucked his magic back inside him. At once, the fiery candles, trembling rock, and lashing wind calmed. Just as fast, the kingsfae blinked, and their outstretched arms dropped as their sight returned.

The king huffed in relief or irritation, I couldn't tell, but the remaining water winked out of existence.

In a single breath, the dining hall returned to normal, even if platters of upended food littered the floor.

A rush of relieved sighs came from the kingsfae. All of the males and females who'd come to arrest their prince gazed around in wonder, still blinking, as though to assure themselves they could fully see again.

With the spectacle over, a kingsfae rushed forward and grabbed my arm, but his grip was looser, and he didn't pull me, merely guided me away.

A low growl escaped Jax, but before he could react, several kingsfae rushed toward him and slapped glowing blue bands around his wrists.

Magic crackled around the restraints, and my heart sank. Jax's magic had just been doused. They'd subdued the prince's power with those bands, effectively locking his magic within him. I had a feeling that if they ever confronted the prince again, that would be the first thing they did after Jax's unhinged display of power today.

"Be careful with her," Jax called darkly to the kingsfae leading me away. "If you don't, you'll be dealing with me."

The kingsfae tugging me from the room glanced uneasily over his shoulder at the prince, but his grip loosened even more, and he gave the slightest bow toward his sovereign.

"I apologize for my son's behavior," the queen called from the front of the room. Panting breaths lifted her chest, but she straightened and smoothed her gown before glaring down her nose at me. "But we all know what mated males can be like. I do expect you to take that into consideration with how you're treating my son."

"So she finally admits that they're mated," Trivan muttered under his breath as Jax's friends were also led away.

The king, however, didn't utter a sound. Steely blue eyes shot daggers at his son, then me, as all of us were forced from the room.

Within minutes, me, Jax, his friends and guards, and Guardian Alleron were being marched down the hall.

Every servant we passed dropped their gazes. But the second we swept by, their whispers began.

It was entirely humiliating, and when we passed the double doors to Jax's tower, my throat constricted.

I hoped it wasn't the last time I would ever see those doors, because as much as I prayed that we could clear this matter up, the reality of what we were facing began to sink in more and more.

The kingsfae knew when each and every raid had occurred by the Dark Raider over the seasons.

Court records would show that Jax wasn't present in Jaggedston when each of those raids occurred. It was a big enough coincidence that they'd look into it more.

And Guardian Alleron's internal knowledge of all he'd seen and heard would be so damning.

He knew that Lordling Neeble had been killed. He could lead the kingsfae to the exact spot where Neeble's death had occurred in the Ustilly Mountains. They could even dig up his bones.

And the guards who had been employed by my guardian, that Jax had left alive because he refused to kill innocents, could all attest to the Dark Raider's abduction of me and Guardian Alleron.

Which would prove that my guardian *wasn't* lying.

There were so many things working against us, and with a heavy heart, I knew that even Jax's skill at wearing his secretive masks might not be enough to save us.

# CHAPTER 16

Outside of the palace, the kingsfae split us up. Every single one of us.

They called for nine enchanted carpets, and a moment of hysteria hit me when I realized I didn't have my story straight. I didn't know what Jax would say or what the others would admit, and I had no idea how much information would be demanded of me. It took everything in me to keep from crying out.

Jax's gaze cut to mine. I expected to see wildness growing in his eyes since he no doubt sensed the fear cascading through me along our bond. But I only saw calmness in his expression, and along our bond, his encouragement and belief in me flowed toward me, as though he was trying to instill that same peace in me.

I could tell from his resolve that he'd mentally prepared for such an event. He and his friends probably already had a story in place, aligned for full seasons in case their arrests ever came.

But I *wasn't* prepared.

Panic fired through me anew, my throat threatening to close. One of the kingsfae lifted me onto a carpet and propelled Jax onto another, but his calm peace over the matter doubled to me along our bond.

My erratic heartbeat began to slow. Jax didn't call out or try to say anything to me. He didn't need to. Our bond said it all. He felt I could do this. He thoroughly trusted my instincts to guide me, and he truly believed that I would know what to say when the time came. And that belief from him slowly helped instill confidence in me.

My pounding heart slowed even more. *I can do this. I'll tell them as little as possible, and I'll keep my answers as close to the truth as I can. I'll do exactly what Jax does.*

I nodded subtly at him, and a flare of pride shone on his face.

With a dip of his head, he silently wished me goodbye, and his relaxed stance only further encouraged me. We would see each other again.

I was able to maintain my blind faith on the entire ride to the supernatural courts. Even though I was alone with only my kingsfae beside me, since everyone's carpets took separate paths, it didn't matter. Jax and I would win this.

The carpet I rode on dipped around shops, winded

through neighborhoods, and traveled over several rivers as we headed southeast.

We passed the wharf where I'd boarded the ship to Faewood Kingdom. The last time I rode an enchanted carpet by the wharf, Jax and I had been heading to Leafton to search for Bastian. We hadn't been mated then. Only sizzling attraction had crackled between us.

I closed my eyes, and the evening breeze flowed over my cheeks. But despite trying to ground myself, it felt as though I was detaching from my body. None of this felt real. Just hours ago, Jax and I had made love in his private suite. We'd been dreaming of the future. Planning for our life together.

The regal navy gown still flowed around me. Jax had bought me this gown, and in a way, it symbolized what we hoped would come. So much had been on the precipice of what our future would bring.

But now, as much as I tried to maintain optimism, it felt as though our dream was slipping away.

*No.*

I took a deep breath and opened my eyes. All hope wasn't lost. My collar was gone, and I held immense magic at my fingertips. Bastian was back. We'd found him and saved him too, even if he was currently locked within the palace. And there was still so much that had to be done about King Paevin. We would find a way to continue as we'd been.

Tears threatened to fill my eyes, but I halted my thoughts from steering any further down a path of fear.

The enchanted carpet flew onward. The wharf fell far behind us, and the cobbled street widened when we careened around another corner, heading back inland.

After many more twists and turns, the street opened up completely, and at the end, a huge fountain waited in a large circular cobblestone section. And finally, just behind it stood the supernatural courts.

The huge stone building made of old, scarred rock rose two stories from its base. Large and wide stone steps led up to it. Several carpets holding other fae who'd been apprehended in the city flew around the building, flying to other areas I couldn't see. Kingsfae accompanied all of them.

Sweat lined my palms, but I fisted my hands and reminded myself to stay calm.

The carpet glided to a stop at the base of the steps. I searched for Jax and his friends, even for Guardian Alleron, but none of them were here yet. Either that, or they'd been taken to other entrances in this enormous building.

The kingsfae detaining me hopped off the carpet and extended his hand to help me down. "Follow me."

I took his outstretched palm, taking some comfort in the fact that he hadn't restrained me and was still being civil. Ever since Jax's warning, he hadn't been rough, and I hoped my mate's powerful sway would continue to hold.

Around us, fae walked by on the street, carrying on with their day as they traversed this part of Jaggedston. More than a few glanced toward me as I followed my jailer up the smooth steps. I did my best to ignore them, although as I reached the top, I began to question if it was me they were watching or the banners.

Columns graced the front of the courts, and banners hung along each one with magical renditions of criminals who were wanted by the law.

The Dark Raider's black-clad face hung front and center. His image moved left and right, the banner's three-dimensional magical images constantly changing, giving different views of his masked face. Of course, it was all a guess as to what he looked like. None of the authorities actually knew the Dark Raider's true appearance.

The banner billowed in the breeze, and it hit me anew that Jax was their most wanted criminal.

My insides chilled.

"This way." The kingsfae's armor clanked as he tugged me to the right. A single door stood off to the side at the top of the stairs, away from the large main entrance double doors.

Heart pounding, I followed him silently, and with each step I took, strange magic grew around me, prickling along my skin and cascading through my hair. It grew so thick that I wondered how anyone could breathe around here.

The kingsfae smirked when he caught my grimace.

"'Tis the wards. They're thickest here. But they'll thin out once we're inside. Don't worry. They're always the most uncomfortable the first time they assess you."

"What do the wards do?"

"They serve as a barrier should anyone decide to take action against the courts with weapons or spells. They also help to identify fae when brought to the courts, and they also serve as lockdown for anyone who tries to escape from their sentencing, so I'd think twice before running."

"I would never." I kept my voice small, falling back into the role my guardian had groomed me to play. I'd dealt with males having authority over me my entire life, and I'd learned that they usually treated me better if I acted meek and contrite, even if I wasn't.

The kingsfae grunted, seeming to appreciate my response.

My flowing navy gown swirled around me more as I followed him. He opened the door, indicating for me to go first, and when I stepped over the threshold, magic seized me in place.

A moment of panic hit me. Ice pressed against my skin. All air was sucked from my lungs. I couldn't breathe. Another bolt of fear swam in my veins, but the wards' hold was over before it'd begun, and then I was on the other side with the kingsfae right behind me.

He gave me a mocking smile. "Told you it takes longest the first time. I'm guessing you've never been here before?"

I shook my head. When I'd been five summers old, my guardian had presented me before the courts in Mistvale. But I'd been a child. Different measures had been used to bring me before the justices who had ultimately ruled to allow my enslavement. I'd never been subjected to the courts' wards before.

My jailer smirked. "Be warned, the wards have now cataloged your identity and internal magic. Even with a strong glamour or illusion, you'll never be able to fool the realm's courts. The magic is too ancient and too strong." The kingsfae nodded toward a row of desks near the wall on our right. "Processing is over there. Follow me."

A dozen fae sat on chairs behind their desks. Six other fae were being processed at different stations. Of them, five were males, but there was one female. Angry expressions covered most of their faces, but some looked as scared as I felt. And it wasn't lost on me that all of them wore cuffs.

I rubbed my wrists and wondered if those would eventually be placed on me.

Raising my chin, I did my best to quell my unease, but despite searching every corner of this admittance area, there was no sign of Jax, his friends, or my guardian. But I still felt Jax. Our bond perpetually connected us. He was alive, his confidence steady, but he wasn't near me. At least, I didn't think he was.

Across the wide hall, other kingsfae stood in small groups, talking with each other. The kingsfae socializing all looked at ease, and I realized this was just another day's work for them, while my entire realm was crashing down.

My breaths grew more rapid, and the earlier feeling of panic began to encroach upon my resolve, but I took a deep breath and ordered myself to stay calm.

"How long do you suppose this will take?" I asked the kingsfae as he marched me toward an empty desk.

He shrugged. "That depends upon how much you tell us."

"I've done nothing wrong."

"I don't assume you have, and hopefully neither has the prince, his guards, or the other nobles being accused of these heinous crimes, but until we can clear this matter up, it's our due diligence to thoroughly assess all accusations."

He stopped before the desk. Behind it, a siltenite male, wearing dark trousers and a silk button-up shirt, looked up at me from behind spectacles. "Name?"

"This is Elowen Emerson from Faewood," the kingsfae replied. "Brought in for questioning."

The male nodded toward a crystal sphere at the edge of his desk. "Place your palm upon that."

I did as he said, and the magical sphere's power lashed around me, holding my hand in place.

A ledger waited open before the male, and my name, address, and why I'd been brought to the courts appeared across it, being scrawled in elegant writing.

Once all of my information was cataloged, the male looked at the kingsfae. "No charges? Questioning only?"

My jailer clasped his hand around my elbow. "Correct. There have been accusations made against the prince, and she's part of it."

The attendant's eyes grew wide, looking even bigger behind his spectacles. He leaned forward and hissed, "I heard whisperings that royalty was on their way, but I assumed it was rumors."

*On their way.* I had to visibly keep my breaths calm. That likely meant Jax wasn't here yet.

The kingsfae shook his head, his voice dipping, "'Tis not rumors. They'll be processed as well."

The male nodded briskly. "Good to know. We're done here."

The kingsfae led me away, toward the hall's back corner, and I walked steadily at his side, his meaty hand still around my elbow. "What are you going to do with the prince and his friends?"

He grunted. "That's none of your concern."

He marched me down the hall. Doors, spaced only a body length apart, lined each side of it. Wailing, shouting, and a few sobs could be heard behind the closed doors we passed.

Stomach flipping, I begrudgingly followed him into an empty room.

"Sit." He pointed at the lone chair behind a table. Across from it, two unoccupied seats waited.

I did as I was told and settled my gown around me. Shoulders back, I kept my spine in a rigid line as I waited for whatever was to come.

The kingsfae moved to the corner of the room and stood stoically. Minutes later, two more fae bustled through the door.

I started at their abrupt arrival. A male and female, both wearing professional-looking clothes, appeared as no-nonsense siltenites. Without so much as a greeting, they pulled out the chairs across from me and sat.

The male had a folder with parchment inside. He opened it up, and a quick peek at it told me it held all of my identifying information that'd just been cataloged about me.

The female gazed at me with a shrewd expression. "Do you know why you're here?"

Her harsh tone made me flinch. "I think so. I was at the palace with the prince when my former guardian accused him of being the Dark Raider."

"And is he?"

I started again, slightly taken aback by her direct approach. "No, of course not."

She *hmmed*. "I'm Junior Justice Seewald, and this is Junior Justice Archmae. Before we continue, I must verify that you know it's a great offense to lie to the courts. Do you understand?"

My unease grew. "Yes." I paused. "Do I need a magistrate for this questioning?"

She arched an eyebrow and cocked her head. "I don't know, do you? Magistrates are only needed if one's guilty. Are you guilty?"

Flustered, I ran a hand through my hair. "No. Of course not. I just don't fully understand what's going on here or why these accusations are being made."

She offered a pacifying smile, but it didn't reach her eyes. "It's easy. Your guardian has accused our crown prince of being the Dark Raider. Such an accusation would have been easy to dismiss except for the fact that your guardian was locked within the palace and he's also been missing from Faewood Kingdom with the belief that the Dark Raider abducted him. Your guardian's claimed that our prince, masquerading in your kingdom as the Dark Raider, took both you and your guardian against your will. He's claiming that the prince has held both of you hostage." Her eyebrows rose.

From her expression, I couldn't tell if she believed any of that or if she felt it was as preposterous as it sounded. Or maybe she was waiting for me to say something.

Deciding to play innocent, I scoffed. "That's absurd. Prince Adarian *saved* me from the Dark Raider."

"So the Dark Raider did, in fact, abduct you?"

"He did, many weeks ago, after I'd done three callings for the Faewood king."

Junior Justice Archmae vigorously began to scribble on his parchment. I tried to catch a glimpse of his notes, but he angled the folder upward so I couldn't see.

Junior Justice Seewald inclined her head. "King Paevin also stated that you were supposedly rescued by our crown prince, stating that's what you told him, yet I have no proof that such a rescue occurred. Tell me more about that. Where were you saved? How did the prince do it? What happened? What did the prince say to the Dark Raider? Did he speak to him directly? Or was everything communicated another way?" She leaned forward. "And let me remind you, any lies told will be held against you."

I glanced around the room, wondering if they had the authority to force a truth potion into me. I swallowed the lump in my throat. If it came to that, I would insist on a magistrate before consuming anything. Although, as a slave to my former guardian and now the prince, I didn't fully understand my rights. Or if I even had rights. For all I knew, I would be forced to consume anything they demanded.

Licking my lips, I took a deep breath. "To be honest, I don't remember much of it. The Dark Raider commanded me with Mistvale magic. He has Mistvale magic. Did you know that?"

She pursed her lips but simply said, "Go on."

"The Dark Raider abducted me not far from my guardian's estate in Faewood after I did three callings for King Paevin." I recited the events of that night to her, being entirely truthful. There was no reason not to be.

She listened attentively, and Junior Justice Archmae took diligent notes of everything I shared.

When I finished replaying that night, she arched an eyebrow. "And he said he took you because he wanted you to find someone for him using your lorafin magic?"

I nodded, and she told me to continue explaining my abduction, going through each day, but when I got to the part about what had occurred in Lemos, I began to pick my words more carefully.

Junior Justice Seewald perked up. "So the Dark Raider captured you again in Lemos, along with your guardian, *after* your guardian found you at the Lemosilly Inn?"

I nodded. "That's correct."

"Why would the Dark Raider do that?"

"He knew that he couldn't access my lorafin magic without my guardian. He needed my guardian and his adapter to do so."

"What adaptor?"

I took another deep breath, knowing that I also needed to be honest about this. "It was a device used to control my magic. I used to wear a collar that suppressed my abilities, but it's since been taken off."

"Who took it off?"

"Someone the prince found. Prince Adarian has been trying to help me."

She glanced at her co-worker, and they shared a side-eye. "That's very gallant of our prince, but let's discuss the Dark Raider more. Do you know who he was looking for in the Veiled Between? Or why he needed you to find them with your lorafin magic?"

I shook my head. "I don't. Honestly, so much of my time with the Dark Raider is a blur. He kept me unconscious for hours at a time. The only reason I remember Lemos is because he allowed me to stay awake for supper before he took me upstairs for the night."

"And that's when he left you alone, and your guardian was able to help you escape?"

"Yes. I don't know where the Dark Raider was at that time, or what he was doing, but I took advantage of his absence."

For the first time, a twinge of sympathy covered her face. "That must've been a very scary event."

"It was. I've never been more terrified." And while I felt anything but afraid around Jax now, I wasn't being entirely untruthful with that response.

"Tell me about how your guardian rescued you in Lemos."

I told her everything about that as well, not lying or holding anything back. But when I got to the part where the Dark Raider abducted both me and my guardian when we'd been on Guardian Alleron's carpet departing Lemos, I told another lie. "The Dark Raider used his Mistvale magic on me again, and I fell unconscious."

She stared at me for a long moment, her expression giving away nothing. "Why do you suppose he did that?"

I shrugged. "I don't know, but maybe he does it to protect himself. At least, that's what I was guessing. Without me being able to recall anything, I couldn't bear witness to anything that he did."

Her shrewd expression didn't abate. "And throughout all of this, you never saw what he looked like? He never removed his mask or his bandanna or changed his clothing into anything that could be easier to identify?"

"No. Both he and the males he was with appeared the same throughout the entire time I was with them."

"And from Lemos, where did he take you?"

"The next memory I have is of arriving in Fosterton. That's where he handed me off to the prince." I paused, canting my head. "At least, I think that's where we were. Those details are kind of fuzzy too."

Her eyes narrowed. "And how did the prince come to learn that you were with the Dark Raider?"

I shrugged again. "I don't know that either. I suppose you'd have to ask the prince that."

Her eyebrows shot up. "You never asked him?"

I offered her a trembling smile, hoping she would think I was too traumatized to fully understand and remember everything. "I think I may have, but I don't think he told me." I looked down, fiddling with my fingers, and fell back on my seasons of play-acting. A few tears formed in my eyes, and one even rolled down my cheek. "Honestly, a lot of that time I don't remember. It's all a blur, and I would rather just forget it all anyway."

Some of the sternness around her faded. "I'm sorry. I'm sure it was very traumatic. I apologize for asking you to recount such horrific events."

I sniffed and wiped away my tears.

She sat straighter, and her tone returned to that of no-nonsense. "And once you were under the prince's care, did you learn anything about your guardian's fate?"

I vigorously shook my head, recalling what Jax and I had told King Paevin when we'd been at the Match Finals. My story had to match that precisely if I didn't want to get caught up in a lie. "No. All I know is that my guardian was still with the Dark Raider when the prince rescued me. I have no idea how my guardian got free of him or how he came to be in the palace."

The female glanced at Junior Justice Archmae again. They shared another veiled look, and a moment of panic hit me that perhaps they knew more than they were letting on. I desperately wished I knew what they were thinking.

"May I go now?" I asked quietly.

Junior Justice Seewald held up a finger. "Not quite.

One last question. Were you ever able to locate who the Dark Raider sought in the Veiled Between?"

I only had a split second to make my decision, and I shook my head. "No. I was rescued by the prince before I could. My lorafin magic was too fatigued for me to do a calling, so I never did travel to the Veiled Between on behalf of the Dark Raider."

She cocked her head. "Yet, the Dark Raider handed you over to the prince anyway? Even though he never got what he wanted from you?"

I knew immediately that I'd made a huge mistake. I should have said that I completed his calling and then made up some vague story about who the Dark Raider had wanted me to find.

Heart thumping, I only hoped she couldn't detect my pulse. "Maybe whatever the prince paid him made it worth it."

"That's another thing I can't put my finger on." She tapped her chin. "Why would our prince pay for a Faewood lorafin at all?"

"Perhaps because lorafins are coveted by everyone in power."

She *hmmed*, not giving away even an inkling of her thoughts, then gave a curt nod. "Archmae, did you get all that?"

The male nodded. "Yes, it's all recorded."

"Right then." She snapped her attention back to me.

"That's all for now. We shall release you for the time being, but since you are still an enslaved lorafin, you are to stay in Jaggedston until the courts decide your fate. You're not to leave until the courts have deemed it fine for you to do so. Understood?"

I nodded. "Of course. I understand. I'll stay in the city and wait to hear from you." I stood, then twisted my hands. "May I ask where the prince is or how long he'll be down here?"

She leveled me with a stony gaze. "No, Lady Emerson, you may not."

# CHAPTER 17

The kingsfae led me back to the courts' entrance and told me to keep an eye out for a messenger bird. "If you're needed again, you'll be summoned via dillemsill. You're to stay in Jaggedston until you hear otherwise."

I nodded, my heart pounding as I tried to recall everything I'd said to the junior justices and what I'd revealed. I just hoped I hadn't screwed up too much.

But the second we reached the admittance entryway, my focus changed. I searched everywhere for my mate and his friends in the vast hall, but they were nowhere to be found.

Several other fae I hadn't seen before were being processed at the desks, but other than that, there was nobody new present.

Stomach tumbling, I followed my jailer as he walked briskly ahead of me.

The kingsfae took me to the same door I'd entered and showed me out. The wards exiting the building weren't as horrible as when I'd been brought inside, but the magic still assessed me. I had no doubt that somewhere within this ancient and magical building, it had been cataloged that I'd just left and was no longer within its powerful walls.

Alone on the courts' paved platform outside, I gazed at the massive stone steps that spread out before me. Night-time had fully set in, and a slight breeze ruffled my navy gown around my legs. I was thankful the lightweight material was easy to move in, even if it didn't provide much warmth, and I quickly took the steps down two at a time.

At the bottom of the stairs, in the middle of the huge cobblestone circular street, the fountain sprayed water into the air. It was nothing like the Venapearl Fountains in Leafton with their colored water and dancing sprays that moved to the rhythm of music, but it was still a calming sight. And right now, I needed to be calm.

It was only as I turned back to gaze at the courts that I realized I'd never asked about becoming free of a guardian. I'd been so caught up in keeping my story straight and not revealing too much that it'd entirely slipped my mind. Someday, I would have to return here to plead my case for freedom, but that wasn't meant to be today.

Even though it was late, I walked swiftly around the entire building's perimeter to see if I could find Jax or anyone else. Two of the moons glowed brightly on the horizon, but it did little to lighten anything farther around the courts.

The capital's bells didn't ring once in my lap around the building, indicating it was indeed late since they never rang past ten.

Chest heaving, I finally stopped by the fountain again. My dash around the courts had confirmed that there were multiple entrances and exits. The prince and his friends could have been taken inside through any of those doors, but there was no sign of them. *If they're even here . . .*

I concentrated on the bond connecting my soul to Jax's. It burned brightly inside me. He was still alive and well, and instinct told me he was somewhere nearby, but the magic encasing the supernatural courts wouldn't allow me to decipher more.

Or, for all I knew, Jaggedston was big enough to have more than one supernatural court building. Perhaps there were multiple courts just like this one in different parts of the city. It was possible Jax was at one of those instead and he wasn't even here.

My mind raced with how I could find Jax or learn how he was doing. Twisting my hands, I searched for somebody I could ask.

But there was no one.

I twirled in a circle. A cool breeze billowed around me as sprays from the fountain misted across my face, and I realized that I was entirely alone. Unlike when I'd arrived earlier, there were no longer fae traversing the street, although I did catch sight of one fairy farther down the road, but they were walking quickly, obviously in a hurry to get to where they were headed.

It was late enough that most fae had retired for the night, and with stunning clarity, it hit me that I had nobody here. Nobody I could call. Nobody I could go home to.

Nobody.

I thought back to the bag of rulibs the prince had paid me for finding Bastian, but that was locked away within the palace, far from my reach. And I had a feeling if I returned to the king and queen's residence, asking for the coins that I'd been given, their door would be slammed in my face.

But it wasn't like I had any other option because I had nothing. Absolutely nothing. Not even a spare rulib or two sewn into a pocket. It hadn't even occurred to me to secure that small measure of safety before Jax and I had ventured down to the dining hall.

I began to walk away from the courts, my only saving grace being that the palace stood high in the distance, easy to see. I would have to return to it. I had no choice.

But while I doubted the royals would give me a place to stay for the night, I could insist that they return my things to me. I still had my bag with the clothes the prince had gotten for me in Fosterton. And then there were my rulibs.

As my feet tapped quietly on the silent street, I just hoped beyond hope that Jax's parents would have the decency to at least give me what was mine. Because I had to find a way to survive on my own until Jax was freed.

And my mate *had* to be freed. There was no other option I could accept.

Tightness coiled around my chest, threatening to constrict my lungs. I gulped in a breath and tried to reassure myself that all would be fine. Because it had to be. I couldn't imagine a future without Jax.

It took me two hours to walk back to the palace. Cold night wind had set in, leaving perpetual goosebumps on my arms. Despite the chill, a sheen of sweat covered me. It'd been a long walk across the city, gradually uphill the entire way, and I only thanked the gods and goddesses that nobody had accosted me on the long journey.

If I had been in Leafton, walking through one of the seedier areas of town, I had no doubt that someone would have assaulted me or attempted to rob me. But that wasn't the case in Jaggedston. I'd either lucked out, or Jax's father ruled his land with an iron fist and locked up any vagrants attempting to conduct a crime.

I shuddered, wondering what the king would do if he ever found out his own son truly was the Dark Raider and had committed more heinous crimes than all of the vagrants in Jaggedston combined.

Breathing heavily, I warily approached the gates surrounding the palace. Blisters had formed on my heels, making my steps unsteady. And even though my magic healed the open wounds quickly, it seemed as soon as one blister disappeared, another formed.

But even though I was sore and tired, when I beheld the palace's onyx walls, magic began to swirl like a tornado inside me. In the moonlight, the looming castle shone like obsidian.

Standing near the gates, the guards on night duty watched me approach, their eyes narrowing with every step I took.

When I reached them, one of them curled his lip at me. "You shouldn't be here."

"My belongings are within the palace. I need them."

The guard looked to the other across the lane. "Did you hear that? The whore wants us to retrieve her things."

My head snapped back, but just as fast, I seethed. "I am the prince's *mate*." I drew myself up taller and shot him an icy glare. "For your own sake, you may want to remember that."

A brief flash of uneasiness stole over his face, but just as fast, he rolled his eyes. "According to the king and queen, mate or no, you're to be arrested if you attempt to get within the palace again."

My eyes widened. Surely, they wouldn't be that cruel. "But my things. I need them. I literally have *nothing*. Absolutely nothing. The least that you can do is return my bag and coins to me."

"The least I can do is not call the kingsfae to have you arrested all over again." He bared his teeth, and the guard across the lane snickered.

My cheeks flushed. "And did the king and queen also order you to be so heartless?"

"They're none of your concern," he replied coldly. "Word of advice, you best be on your way before either of them learns that you've returned. They might not be so kind to you a second time."

A ball of worry knotted in my stomach. Without any clothes, rulibs, or a place to spend the night, I was in a much direr state than I'd ever dreamed possible. "Please, at least get me my bag. That's all I'm asking. I won't step a foot inside the palace."

"No," he replied coldly, and he made a move forward, as though he were going to strike me.

I jumped back, memories tumbling to the front of my mind of how Zale, my former guard at Emerson Estate, had treated me. But my abrupt movement had my foot catching on my gown. Stumbling, I almost fell backward on the pavement but caught myself just in time.

"Leave her be," the guard at the gate's other side said, a note of worry in his tone. "The prince won't like it if you hurt her."

I turned pleading eyes on him, hoping he had an ounce of mercy in his heart. "At least tell me where the prince is. Has he come back? Is he okay?"

But the guard only shook his head. "We're not to tell you anything about the prince. Now, like he said, you best get on your way." He nodded down the street.

Dejectedly, I was about to turn away, but then someone called from within the palace's large open front courtyard, "He's not back yet! But do as the guards said and go!"

I swung around to see Saramel standing on the other side of the gates. I nearly ran to her, tears instantly forming in my eyes at seeing a familiar face, but a quick shake of her head had me stopping.

She jerked her chin to the side, and her subtle communication had me schooling my expression into neutrality.

Turning on my heel, I scurried away from the palace and around the corner in the direction that she'd nodded.

On the opposite street, away from the palace wall but still visible should anyone walk by, I waited near the street corner, hidden just inside an alleyway.

Tapping my foot, I continually searched for Saramel on the dark street, but she didn't appear.

Above me, the moons slowly glided across the sky.

Stars danced in the galaxy, winking in pulsing light, and colors emitted from the visible planets.

I used the night sky to calm me, latching onto its beauty as I waited and waited and waited.

I finally sank to the ground, pulling my knees to my chest and wrapping the navy gown around my legs. I tried to ward off the chill, but it had to be after midnight, and I was freezing.

Hopelessness began to consume me, seeping deep into my bones as the night sky continued to shine.

I had no idea what I was going to do. I had no rulibs. No friends. No home to venture to. And even if I wanted to return to Emerson Estate since I had nowhere else to go, I had no way of getting there. Besides, I couldn't even leave. The courts had demanded that I stay in the city. Even if the city didn't want me.

I dropped my head onto my forearms, and tears sprang into my eyes. Fear bit me so hard that I couldn't contain it any longer. A soft, mewling sound escaped me as I let some of my worry gush out of me.

"Elowen," a soft voice said, then somebody dropped to the ground at my side.

I whipped my head up to see Saramel hunkered beside me. A shawl covered her hair, hiding most of her appearance. "I couldn't come any sooner. I'm so sorry."

I threw my arms around her. She didn't utter a sound, and just as quickly, her thin arms locked around my neck.

We held each other as tears rolled down my cheeks, and quiet sobs lifted her shoulders. The despair wafting from both of our auras was so acute that I could practically taste it.

Finally pulling back, I wiped my eyes. She did the same. I regarded her carefully. "How's Cassim?"

"Asleep, thankfully. He doesn't know yet what's happened. But he asked at bedtime why his da wasn't there to tuck him in, so I had to make up an excuse." She shrugged dejectedly. "He asked if he would see him in the morning, and I didn't know what to say."

New tears formed in her eyes, and I pulled her back in for another hug. She clung to me, and I couldn't help but wonder if anyone other than me knew the truth about her husband. She seemed as fearful and alone as I felt.

"Have you heard anything?" I asked when she pulled back. "Do you know where they are or what's happening to them?"

She shook her head. "I've been trying to stay close to the halls in case anyone says anything, but nobody knows what's happening. And if the king and queen are aware, they're not telling anyone. I even asked the queen's personal attendant, but she's oblivious too."

"They're not back? None of them?"

"No. Not one." She gripped my hands, and her throat rolled in a swallow. "It was pure luck I even saw you. I happened to walk outside to see if they were perhaps making their way back. I was hoping to catch a glimpse of them on the street, and that's when I saw you at the gate."

"I'm so glad you found me, and I looked for them too when I was at the courts, but I didn't see any of them."

"Stars, I nearly forgot that's where you've been!" Her tone turned anguished. "Elowen, I'm so sorry. How are you doing?"

"I'm okay, just scared, like you. They took me in for questioning, then let me go. I have no idea where they took the rest of them. They split us up when we left the palace. But even down there, I didn't see them."

Saramel nodded, her frown growing heavier in the moonlight. "They'll have to send word eventually. Prince Adarian is the crown prince, for goodness' sake. They can't keep him indefinitely without informing the king and queen."

"Do you suppose the king and queen already know what's happening, and they're just not telling anyone?"

She shrugged. "Your guess is as good as mine." She glanced over her shoulder, toward the palace. "But I should go back. Cassim's alone in our quarters. I don't want him to be afraid if he wakes up."

"Of course. I'm so sorry to keep you." I hastily stood and smoothed out my gown, wiping the dust and dirt off my backside.

Saramel looked me up and down. "You must be freezing."

"I am, but . . ." I shrugged. "I'll survive."

She cocked her head, her frown growing even more troubled. "Do you have anywhere to go?"

I considered lying to her. She didn't need my troubles to worry about on top of her own, but I couldn't. I'd lied enough today. I shook my head, not trusting myself to speak.

"Oh, Elowen." She clasped my hands. "I'm so sorry. I don't know what I was thinking. Of course, you have nowhere to go." She pulled something from her pocket and pressed it into my palm. I realized it was a handful of rulibs when she closed my fingers around them. "Take this. It's all I have on me, but I'll do my best to retrieve your things for you tomorrow. You have plenty of rulibs within the palace to sustain you. But for tonight, go down to the wharf. This will be enough to get you a room near the docks and a bit of food. It's not the most luxurious accommodations, but at least it'll be a roof over your head."

I squeezed her hand. "Thank you. I'll pay you back."

She gave me a weak smile, then shifted closer to my side and whispered, "They still don't have Quinn. I've already sent a dillemsill to try and find him."

My eyes widened. I'd completely forgotten about the eighth member of their raiding group in the interim. He'd disappeared days ago, after Jax and his friends had nearly been caught by the kingsfae in Possyrose Forrest.

"Do you think you can reach him?"

She shrugged. "It depends on the dillemsill. Sometimes they're able to find him. And sometimes they can't, but I'll hope for the best."

I nodded. "How will I find you again tomorrow?"

"Let's meet here at ten bells into the evening. With any luck, Nellip, the prince, and all the others will be back by then anyway, and all of this will be behind us."

"All right. Ten tomorrow. And you'll bring my things if they're still not free?"

She nodded. "Yes, I'll find a way to get everything."

"Is there any chance you can also grab a handful of portal keys from Quinn's stash? Just in case I need to get somewhere quickly?"

"Yes, I'll do my best to get all of that for you." She squeezed my hands again. "We'll survive this, somehow, Elowen. We will."

I dipped my head. "Yes, we will. And Saramel? Thank you."

She took a trembling breath. "Let's just hope by tomorrow, this nightmare is over."

# CHAPTER 18

I was exhausted by the time I found the inn Saramel had recommended by the wharf, and while she wasn't kidding about the less-than-luxurious accommodations, I didn't care. I fell asleep on the thin mattress, a scratchy blanket over me. Drunk siltenites lumbered by on the street, slurring and singing loudly, but I was asleep before my head hit the pillow.

In the morning, the sound of the bells woke me with a start. For a moment, I didn't know where I was. I gazed around the small chambers with only a single cot and lone table in it. A bowl sat on top to use as a latrine. There wasn't even a washroom.

The navy gown I still wore had ridden up, and my legs were chilled. Wrinkles covered the beautiful flowing material, but a quick burst of magic cleansed my body and gown. With my collar gone, I now had enough access to my magic to do so, not like last time, when I'd needed Jax to clean my clothing.

My heart twisted the second I thought of my mate. Perhaps he was being beaten, punished, or interrogated. Or, for all I knew, they'd released him, and he was looking for me at this very moment.

But my hope dimmed the second I thought that. If he was free, he would have come here. Saramel would have told him where to find me, or the bond would have led him.

But at least I knew he was alive. I closed my eyes and concentrated on the feel of our bond. Hot and bright, the strands linking our souls together still burned inside me, like a candle flame flickering in the wind. Jax was very much alive, and from how strongly I felt him, he was still in Jaggedston. They hadn't transported him elsewhere.

Taking comfort in that, I got up and grabbed the lone quarter-rulib I had left from Saramel's stash. It would be enough for a cup of tea and a pastry. I would literally be coinless after finding something to eat, and I could only pray to the gods that Saramel would be able to retrieve my bag and pile of rulibs tonight. Without them, I would soon be a vagrant on the streets.

Outside, the cool morning air swirled around me. I quickly checked out of the inn, then grabbed some meager food at a corner stall. The tea was bitter but hot, and the pastry dry, but it calmed some of my hunger pains.

Around me, sounds of the wharf filled the air. Banging,

shouting, and more than a few curses flowed through the wind. Down the port, at the last dock, the royal ship that I'd taken with Jax to Faewood was docked. Its beautiful navy sails were tied, its exterior gleaming from a fresh wash. Another twist of regret tore at my heart and nearly brought me to my knees.

*No, stay calm. You'll find Jax. You'll help free him. This isn't your new reality. All hope isn't lost.*

I was contemplating how to go about doing that when a dillemsill popped into existence at my feet. I jumped, nearly stepping on the poor thing.

"So sorry," I mumbled.

Its purple chest puffed up indignantly, and it swished its long furry yellow tail. "Elowen Emerson, you have a message," it chirped.

Heart pounding, I scooped it up and brought it to my ear. "Yes? I'm ready." Holding my breath, I waited and prayed that it was a message from Jax.

The small yellow bird tweeted into my ear, "The supernatural courts have summoned you. Please return promptly."

My shoulders fell, and with trembling hands, I set the little bird back on the street. It whirled in tiny little circles, spinning and spinning like a mini tornado, until it exploded out of existence and returned, most likely, to the dreaded courts.

Curling my fingers into my palms, I took off down the

street in the direction of the authorities. My hair flew around me, and a few sailors whistled when I ran past them.

But it was all noise to me. Meaningless noise. The courts wanted me to return, and that meant one of two things. They wanted further information from me, or Jax had asked for me so I could venture back to the palace with him at my side.

I vaguely remembered where the court building was in this huge city, but I still had to ask for directions multiple times, and it took me an hour of frantic walking and jogging to get there.

The air had warmed slightly by the time I reached the wide stone steps. In front of me, the imposing building waited, as though beckoning me into its mouth so it could devour me for breakfast. Behind me, the fountain shot water into the sky, its mist streaming down around it.

A sheen of sweat coated my entire body, and on shaky legs, I climbed the stairs and went to the door the kingsfae had shown me yesterday. Thick, prickly magic coasted over me, growing stronger with every step I took.

Struggling to breathe, I stopped at the door's threshold, and the same magic that had assessed me yesterday took root. Frozen to the spot, I was held. Its cold magic felt like an ice bath. It sucked all breath from my lungs, but at least it didn't take nearly as long as yesterday. I was on the other side within seconds. It'd obviously remembered me.

Stumbling, I hurried to the processing desk and stopped before a petite siltenite wearing a red dress. "I was summoned by a dillemsill this morning. My name is Elowen Emerson."

The female looked up from behind her desk, her lips pursed. "Ah, yes. You were summoned over an hour ago."

"I came as quickly as I could."

She glanced down and shuffled through a few pieces of parchment. "I see that Junior Justice Seewald requested your presence again." With a flick of her fingers, she summoned one of the kingsfae near the wall. He lumbered forward, his armor clinking.

My throat rolled in a swallow when he ground to a halt at my side.

The female nodded toward the hall, the same one I'd been escorted down yesterday. "Junior Justice Seewald wants to see her. Room thirteen."

"This way." The kingsfae lumbered in front of me, and with each step that I took, nerves fired through my limbs, making me tremble like a leaf in the wind.

I followed him to the room and stepped inside. Junior Justice Seewald was already seated behind the table. She waved toward the chair across from her. "I've been waiting for quite some time."

"I'm so sorry." I fell onto the seat and quickly smoothed my skirt around me. The kingsfae went to the corner and stood stoically. "Unfortunately, I have no way of traveling, so I had to walk. I left the second the dillemsill told me I'd been summoned."

She arched an eyebrow. "Walk? Do you not have any rulibs to hire a carpet or carriage?"

Shame fired through me, but I slowly shook my head.

Frowning, she assessed my clothing. A brief look of pity filled her face, and it wasn't lost on me that she was probably making note of the fact that I wore the same clothes as yesterday. "Did you sleep on the street?"

"No, I stayed at an inn."

"But you couldn't hire a carpet or carriage this morning?"

I swallowed the dryness in my throat. "My coins ran out."

She *hmmed* and pulled out one of her pieces of parchment. "In that case, especially if you have no rulibs or means to take care of yourself, it's probably for the best that you return to your guardian."

"*What?*"

Footsteps came in the hall, and she nodded toward the door. A sickening feeling coasted through me, and as though a phantom hand turned my head, I glanced at the door. Every line in my body went rigid. Guardian Alleron stood there, a smug look on his face, with a kingsfae just behind him.

I shot to standing. "You want me to go with *him?*"

The junior justice sighed. "You're still under the care of a guardian. You're not allowed to be free."

"But Prince Adarian is my new guardian."

Her look turned glacial. "No, he's not. The prince will not be anyone's guardian anytime soon."

"But . . . why not? Where is he?" A ball of worry tied my stomach in knots.

She straightened her pieces of parchment, not meeting my eye. "Still detained, as he will be for the foreseeable future. Now, you're to go with your guardian, and if anything further is needed from either of you, you'll be summoned."

"Come, Elowen," Guardian Alleron called. "Don't make a scene."

Just hearing his voice not only made my skin crawl, but it also caused fear to cascade through me because his voice was *back*. Somehow, the courts had either broken through Jax's Ironcrest magic, or Jax had been forced to remove it.

Not moving, I glued my feet to the floor, and my mind raced.

Breathing heavily, I finally said, "I would like to submit a plea to the courts for my freedom. I will *not* go with this male again. I'm now twenty-eight summers old, I've mastered my magic, and I'm no longer a danger to the public. I can prove that."

A soft huff came from my guardian, but Junior Justice Seewald sighed. "Very well, but such things take time. You may fill out a form to have your case brought before a King or Queen Justice." She gave the kingsfae in the corner a wave of her hand. "Please escort her to the necessary desk to fill out the requirements."

My guardian watched me with narrowed eyes. Annoyance emanated from him, like a swarm of stinging nettle insects, ready to descend upon me and sting every inch of my skin until my lungs seized and my heart stopped. But I ignored him. I had to. I couldn't fathom a life with him again. I could barely look at him without wanting to claw his eyes out.

Following the kingsfae, I strode past my guardian without saying a word.

With another huff, he followed.

But with each step I took, all I could think about was Jax. He was still being detained. My heart hammered as I contemplated why my guardian was free, but Jax wasn't.

Leaning forward, I asked quietly to the kingsfae, "Is Prince Adarian being charged with something?"

He glanced over his shoulder. "Indeed. He's been charged with the crimes of the Dark Raider."

My heart stopped.

My feet froze in place.

*No, no, no.* I'd misunderstood. That couldn't possibly be true.

The kingsfae turned to face me when he realized I'd stopped. Standing a few paces away, he crossed his arms and eyed me skeptically. "Did you know he was the Dark Raider?"

"No, because he's not!" The shout slipped past my lips before I could stop myself.

The kingsfae grumbled. "Watch your tone."

"He'll be hanged for what he did, Elowen," my guardian said from behind me, and the smug tone of his voice was like needles along my skin. "It's best you accept that now and remember your place in this realm."

I swung around to face him as heat blasted through my cheeks, and my hands curled into fists. "But he's *not* the Dark Raider."

A look of pity filled the kingsfae's face who stood behind my guardian. "It's best to forget all about him," he said gently. "All of the prince's crimes are being uncovered as we speak. Now, carry on to the entryway. You'll be with your true guardian until the courts deem otherwise."

His words penetrated the panic coasting through me like a burn. Stinging and scorching fear coated every inch of my skin. This couldn't be happening. None of this could be real.

Yet when they all looked at me expectantly, reality crashed upon me like a hammer.

I didn't know how I turned or walked. But somehow, I began to move as if invisible hands prodded me. But it felt as though a haze drifted around me, lifting me of its own accord. I no longer felt attached to my body. My legs moved automatically, one step in front of the other, but inside, my heart was shattering.

They were charging Jax with crimes as the Dark Raider. He would be hanged. Executed. And if he'd been identified as the Dark Raider, then all of his friends had likely also been accused of being his accomplices.

"And what of the others?" My voice sounded small. Broken. "What's to happen to his friends?"

We reached the main entrance, and the kingsfae gave me an irritated look. "They've all been charged. Court records have shown that all of them were gone during the Dark Raider's raids, so unless their magistrates are able to prove otherwise, every single one of them will be hanged."

I ground to a stop, my breath seizing in my chest.

Guardian Alleron grabbed my elbow from behind, his fingers digging into my flesh. "Enough of this, Elowen. You're coming home with me, where you belong."

I whipped my arm free, my lorafin magic crackling inside me. "Don't touch me!"

The kingsfae quickly moved in. "If you cause a scene here, it won't end well for you. Do what your guardian says and go home."

His expression remained hard, completely unforgiving. The kingsfae behind my guardian looked the same.

They were all working against me. I had no allies. No friends. No family. I had *no one* except for the horrific male who had murdered my mother and taken me from her in cold blood.

"And what of him?" I jerked my chin toward my guardian. "He murdered my mother when I was an infant so he could take me as his own. What charges are being brought against *him*?"

My guardian laughed. Actually *laughed*. "Elowen, enough with the hysterics. I never murdered your mother, as you well know. You're just lucky you're not in more trouble for lying since you knew the prince was the Dark Raider."

"I didn't know that because he's not."

The kingsfae grumbled again. "All right, I've had enough. Take her and get out," he said gruffly to my guardian.

"Gladly. I do apologize for her behavior." Guardian Alleron gripped me again, then hauled me to the processing desk. I tried to fight him, tried to work free of him, but his grip only strengthened, and I knew the only way he would release me was if I used my magic.

But if I did that here and now, they'd arrest me too.

I wanted to fall to the floor. To cry. Wail. Sob. I wanted to do all of those things, but I couldn't.

My mate was being tried as the Dark Raider. He would likely hang, and if I got arrested and shoved into a jail cell, then I couldn't do anything to help him.

I had to get myself together and think. There *had* to be a way out of this.

And as the female sitting at the processing desk handed me the parchment form to fill out, the form that I would submit to request freedom from my guardian, it hit me like lightning what I needed to do.

I glanced down at the parchment, at the questions and articles that would ensure my freedom now that I had complete control of my magic, but I knew as I held it, that if the courts found out what I was planning . . .

No. That didn't matter. Only Jax's freedom did.

# CHAPTER 19

Guardian Alleron stood rigidly at my side, his very presence like a cloud of malice. My hands shook as I filled out the form. *How has this happened? How has my guardian walked free, while Jax remains imprisoned?*

I couldn't comprehend how my mate was being held behind bars while my guardian—the most vile male I'd ever encountered, who'd *murdered* my mother—was being handed my leash once more.

"Don't forget that line." The processing employee pointed to a question near the end of the parchment. "Choose an option there, then sign here."

I did as she said, then handed it back to her.

She folded it precisely and dropped it into a small slot beside her desk. A whoosh of magic sucked it away through a narrow channel that disappeared into the floor. "We'll be in touch with your court date."

I clasped my hands tightly in front of me to hide my trembling. "How will I be notified?"

"Via dillemsill, like we do for all notifications."

My guardian grabbed my elbow again, but I dug my heels into the floor. "And will that dillemsill deliver my court date to me or my guardian?"

"Since you are of legal adult age, you will both be notified."

I breathed a sigh of relief, and my stiff stance relaxed. My guardian's fingernails dug into my skin once more, and with a firm wrench, he whisked me from the courts, back outside, then summoned an enchanted carpet.

I stood numbly on the steps, my magic roiling inside me. Tears threatened to fill my eyes as I thought of what Jax was going through at this moment. Our bond burned hotly inside me. He was here. I was sure of that now. Somewhere in this building was my mate, and I was being whisked away.

Pain nearly closed my throat. Being parted from him was like a knife cutting through my very soul, but I vowed to free him, no matter the cost.

The hired enchanted carpet glided to a stop at the bottom of the steps. Automatically, I hurried down the stairs, then stepped dutifully onto it.

"Sit," Guardian Alleron ordered.

Nostrils flaring, I did as he said while I contemplated my next step and tried to find a way *not* to partake in the idea that had struck me at the processing desk. But if Jax was being charged, if the courts had evidence to prove that he was always gone when the Dark Raider's crimes occurred, and if they had witnesses attesting that the Dark Raider *was* Jax . . .

There was too much going against him.

I couldn't possibly come up with a counterargument to prove how all of that wasn't possible while also proving that Jax wasn't the Dark Raider. And while I could hope that his parents would hire a genius magistrate to somehow wheedle Jax and our friends out of their crimes, I wasn't willing to take that chance. Which meant I was left with only one choice. I would have to travel to the Veiled Between. I would have to twist fate to stop this. It was the only way to guarantee Jax's freedom.

*But how?*

I chewed on my lip as my guardian whispered a command, and the carpet took off.

Hair blew in front of my face, but I didn't push it back. I closed my eyes and tried to figure everything out because I'd never changed the course of fate before, and I had no idea how to do such a thing. Never mind that it was illegal. Never mind that such an act was forbidden. If it was the only way, I would do it so my mate wouldn't hang.

I took a deep breath as a rush of hysteria threatened to rise in me. A part of me wanted to laugh maniacally at how upended my life had become. Just yesterday morning, Jax and I had been set on rallying the kingdoms to fight King Paevin. Yet now, I was fighting for my mate's life as the king continued with his horrifying plans to build his army.

And Bastian. Poor, innocent Bastian. What was to become of him?

A moment of panic hit me that I hadn't asked Saramel about him last night. I'd been too wrapped up in my mate's predicament and my coinless state, but I needed to find a way to help him too. Or who knew if he'd ever be freed of that enchanted chambers.

My mind raced.

*Okay, you need to find a way to get away from Guardian Alleron. Then you need to meet Saramel, get some rulibs so you actually have funds to support yourself, then you'll need to ask her to help with Bastian.* I nodded emphatically to myself. With Saramel having access to Jax's enchanted chambers, she would be the perfect help. And with any luck, she'd already realized that and was helping Bastian.

Wind blew across my skin as the carpet picked up speed. My guardian and I flew through the streets, but I refused to look at him.

*And after you have coins and know Bastian's safe, then you'll need to venture to the Veiled Between to save Jax and our friends. And then, you can figure out how to deal with King Paevin.*

I finally opened my eyes only to find Guardian Alleron glaring at me.

"What happened to your collar and my adaptor?" His cold tone flowed over my skin like ice.

I met his stare readily. "They've both been destroyed."

His breath sucked in. "That's impossible."

A spark of life flared inside me. Vengeful life. "It *is* possible. You may legally still be my guardian, but you control me no more. I will no longer be your puppet, and I *won't* do callings for you."

For the first time that I'd ever known him, his authoritative air slipped, and a moment of uncertainty stole over his face. "Elowen," he said, his voice gentling, "many things have happened in the past weeks. I know that it's been difficult to—"

"Don't even think you can manipulate your way out of this." The carpet shot around a street corner, heading toward the southern section of Jaggedston. "Even though you're still legally in control of me, you won't be for much longer, and I will *never* be your lorafin slave again."

His nostrils flared, and a flash of fury coasted over his face. But he sat back, shoulders stiff, and took a deep breath. "I had thought we could perhaps come to some sort of agreement."

I scoffed. "No."

His teeth grated together. "I can still provide you with

food, clothing, and shelter. You have nothing on your own. Without me—"

"Without *you*, I would still have a mother."

Red bloomed on his cheeks. He opened his mouth and then closed it. Silence passed as he studied me, and I could practically see the wheels churning in his mind. I knew he was going to try to manipulate me again. That he was contemplating how to spin this to his advantage. As always, he was going to twist everything around to make me feel like the guilty party while he was an innocent victim, but I saw through it now. Jax had helped me see him for who he truly was.

I met my guardian's gaze, unflinching. And when I held it, not backing down, not cowing, not showing the reverence I once had, his expression faltered.

He glanced away, anger still strumming from him in waves, but I caught the way his fingers picked at the carpet, aggressively tugging at loose strings. His nervous fidget spoke volumes, and a brief sense of victory barreled through me.

I would never be his slave again.

WE REACHED the city's edge, and my guardian commanded the carpet south, away from the palace, away from my rulibs, away from my freedom, and away from my *mate*.

With each mile that passed, the bond inside me burned less and less. Jax and I were being separated. Truly separated.

Hills and trees grew around us. Signs of civilization fell behind us until it was only Guardian Alleron and me on the barren road.

I finally broke the quiet. "Where are we going?"

Guardian Alleron glanced at me with disdain. He straightened his clothing and smoothed his hair. "We'll travel south until dark, then we'll stop at an inn and finish the rest of the journey in the coming days."

My eyebrows shot up. "We're going to Faewood?"

"Of course, to Faewood."

"You're truly taking me back to Emerson Estate? You actually think I'll live there with you?"

"You have to. You have nobody without me." His words were calm, but the edge of a threat loomed behind them.

I didn't bother replying. My lips pursed, and I glanced at the disappearing capital behind us, growing farther and farther away. I'd seen this view once before, when Jax and I had been atop Phillen as we'd ridden into Jaggedston following our night in Fosterton all of those weeks ago.

Jax had stopped us in the Wood so he could rob me of

my eyesight and change into his princely attire. That stretch of the Wood was just up ahead.

A ball of agony clogged my throat. How much had changed since that time.

I returned my attention to my guardian and crossed my arms. "And what about your voice? How did you get that back?"

He smiled smugly. "The courts hired an advanced spellcaster from Ironcrest, and once that spellcaster caught hold of Jax's magic, he verified that my stolen voice had indeed come from your beloved prince."

My eyes widened, and the implication of that statement wound around me like a coiling serpent, squeezing me so tightly that my breaths threatened to stop. The fact that my guardian's robbed voice had been identified as Jax's sense-stealing magic further proved his case that Jax *was* the Dark Raider. And if the courts knew that, it was possible that they would eventually view me as his accomplice, which meant my freedom wasn't guaranteed.

Magic roiled inside me. I had to stop this. All of this. *Now.*

I assessed the area more. Wind blew through the trees. The city was far enough away now that it was merely a glimmering speck. Houses and small dwellings from local fae had fallen behind us as well. Nobody was about.

My guardian regarded me from across the carpet, his

gaze gentling in mock sympathy. "Elowen? When we get back, I'd like you to see the king right away. He's—"

"No!" I loosened my crossed arms and shot to a stand. Rage erupted inside me.

"No?"

"Correct, *no*. Fuck this. Fuck *all* of this."

Before he knew what I was doing, I wrenched on my magic as fury blazed through me. Cold shadows lashed from my hands, shooting toward my guardian in a swell of power. He shrieked, but I wrapped my shadows around his mouth, neck, and chest.

"You will *not* command me anymore!"

His eyes bulged, and his hands rose. Fire shot from his palms, shooting toward me.

I dove to the side, and my guardian's fire element blasted right over me and hit a tree in the Wood. Smoke curled around its bark, and flames flickered at the tree's base.

Hands whipping through the air, I wrenched my guardian off the carpet with my magic. Power unfurled within me. Magnificent, heady power. All of the heartache this male had caused me roared through me like a quickly spreading wildfire.

He'd abused me.

Used me.

*Tortured* me since I was a child.

And now, he'd taken the only fairy in my life who had actually cared about me. Who had ever truly *loved* me.

"Elowen!" he muffled through my shadows, but I just gagged him more.

Another blast of fire shot from him, but it didn't matter. Magic exploded out of me, coating me in shadows and repelling his fire like it was harmless smoke.

"Don't you know what I am?" I asked, my voice rising. Power crackled around me. "I'm the queen of the semelees. The walker between the Veils. I am the enchantress of the shadows, and you will control me *no more!*"

I whispered a command to the carpet, and it stopped. My heart pounded as I stood, hands raised as I held my guardian aloft above me. He hovered in midair, his eyes widening with terror.

He tried to speak again, but I curled my shadows down his throat, stopping his breath.

I lifted him higher. It was so easy. So simple to manipulate him like this. Power flooded my limbs, crackling like lightning through my veins. Jax had once said that a lorafin's power was godlike, and in that moment, I knew he was right.

My shadows writhed and danced, snaking around my body as energy crackled in the air. I lifted my guardian higher, then higher, until he rose above the trees' canopy.

Fear shone upon his face, true fear, but I was done being merciful. I was done being his slave.

I. Was. Done.

My lips spread in a terrifying smile. "I hope you can swim."

With a huge surge of power, I shot him through the sky, catapulting him through the air. I used so much magic that he flew toward the sea.

I commanded the carpet to lift, taking me above the tree line until the ocean's sparkling view appeared in the distance. My guardian was still hurtling toward it, moving so high and so fast that he was just a speck amidst the clouds.

I didn't release my shadowed hold on him until he was miles out to sea, but I watched him the entire time, reveling in his fury mixed with sheer terror, which streamed toward me on my shadowed hands.

His plummet into the Adriastic Sea was so distant I could barely see him, and his splash into the water was nearly non-existent.

His magic wouldn't help him there. Water doused fire. He was entirely on his own, miles out to sea, and despite my taunt to him, both me and my guardian knew that he'd never learned to swim.

# CHAPTER 20

I stayed in the Wood, hidden from view on the enchanted carpet. Hours had passed since I'd killed my guardian, but I didn't feel one speck of regret or sadness. I felt nothing but firm resolve.

Only one thing mattered now.

So I waited until the time was right. Waited for the sun to set and the moons to rise.

My stomach howled with hunger, and my lips were dry from thirst. I'd had nothing since the tea and pastry in the morning, but my hunger and parched throat would have to wait because I had nothing other than the carpet beneath my feet.

It was only after I'd flung my guardian to his death that I wished I'd emptied his pockets first. But I hadn't. My rage had taken over me, so I was now entirely dependent upon Saramel.

Once the three moons were shining brightly, I whispered a command to the carpet, and I took off. I sailed through the Wood, around the curves, back onto the road until the billowing night lights of Jaggedston appeared like twinkling jewels.

I kept the carpet at an even pace, and as I grew closer to the city, other fae became present. Some also traveled on the road, and others tended to the yards of their small homes. I rode the carpet, doing my best to remain inconspicuous.

The navy gown I still wore flew around me, the long skirt fluttering in the wind, but my focus was fierce, my goal set.

My heart thrummed in a steady rhythm on the ride to the palace, but I didn't slow. I coasted toward its onyx spires until I reached the streets surrounding it.

I only stopped when I glided into the alleyway where I would meet Saramel. I commanded the carpet to settle on the ground, and then . . . I waited.

My teeth were chattering, and the carpet was rolled up beside me by the time I heard Saramel's pattering feet. Ten bells had rung a few minutes ago, the last bells of the night, and the palace guards had done a shift swap. It was amazing how much one could see and learn about the palace's going-ons simply by lurking in the shadows.

"Elowen?" Saramel whispered from the mouth of the alley. A shawl covered her hair, hiding part of her face.

"I'm here." I rushed forward, her doing the same, and we collided in a hug halfway down the narrow lane.

"Oh, thank the stars, I didn't know if you'd still be free." She pulled back and quickly unstrapped a pack from her back. "I have your bag, clothes, rulibs, and a few portal keys as you requested. I also swiped some food and drink from the kitchens. I thought you may be hungry."

As though to confirm her suspicions, my stomach let out a loud grumble. "Thank you, you've done so much for me. Thank you, Saramel."

She shoved the pack in my hands, her eyes as sharp as the moonlight. "Have you heard what happened today?"

"I know they've been charged, but that's all I know." I tensed. "What do you know?"

Tears formed in her eyes, shimmering like pearls in the dim light. "Exactly that. They've all been officially charged. It was announced today in the Jaggedston Herald. It said they have irrefutable proof, and the whole city now knows." A tear fell onto her cheek. "The prince, my husband, and all of our friends will be going to trial in the coming weeks before a King or Queen Justice."

The ground swayed beneath me, and I reached a hand to the alley's wall to steady myself. Just as fast, I pulled myself up straight. No, I wouldn't allow that to happen. I would save them.

I swallowed the dryness in my throat and gripped Saramel's hands in an iron-tight hold. All day I'd been able to think of what I needed to do, and now the time was finally upon me.

"Saramel, this is very important. Do you know what scholar Jax consulted about lorafins? He always knew so much about my kind, yet I never asked him how he'd acquired his knowledge."

Her eyes turned to saucers, and she nodded vigorously. "Yes, of course. Nellip accompanied him on that journey. The prince went to the Isle of Song to ask what the great scholars there knew of how to locate someone who couldn't be found."

The Isle of Song. *Of course.* The island off the east coast of our continent held the most prestigious university and library of our land. Our continent's greatest scholars lived there.

"That makes sense." Hands trembling, I released her and grabbed some food and drink from the pack. I quickly ate a few bites and took a few drinks. "And what about Bastian? Did you know he's staying in the enchanted chambers? Has anyone—"

"He's fine." She laid a hand on my arm, and some of my trembling stopped. "Nellip told me you brought him back, before the kingsfae came and took him." She looked down, and her aura fluttered with grief. "I checked on Bastian this morning, and he asked for a looking glass, so I brought him one. Obviously, he's as worried as us, but at least he has Anna now to talk to, even if he can't reveal any details about the prince to her."

"Thank the stars." I sagged in relief. "I was concerned he'd be trapped and alone in the palace forever."

"No, he won't be, but Nellip said it's not safe for him to return home yet. Do you know when it will be?"

"No, I don't, but Nellip's right. It's not safe for him right now. He needs to stay in the chambers for the time being." I took another bite of the cold ham she'd brought as I mulled over the other looming problem that had been in the back of my mind—King Paevin. He was still capturing half-breeds and planning to build an army. He needed to be stopped, but for the life of me, I didn't know how I could stop a king while also trying to free my mate, unless I . . .

I nearly dropped the ham I was chewing.

"Of course! I can do *both*!" I quickly chewed another bite of food. "Oh stars, Saramel. I just had the biggest revelation." I quickly stuffed the rest of the ham into my mouth and chewed vigorously. "But I have to go. I have so much to do. But are you able to look after Bastian? I know you're already dealing with so much, and I hate to ask that but—"

"Yes." She squeezed me. "It's all right, Elowen. I'll take care of him. Please don't worry about the prince's brother."

I nodded curtly and finished consuming the food and drink, then fished a portal key from the pack. "I have to go."

Saramel canted her head. "Where are you going?"

I slung the bag over my shoulder, then grabbed the rolled-up carpet. "I'm going to the Isle of Song so I can learn how to fully use my magic, and then I'm going to save our mates and friends and stop the king."

"The king?"

"King Paevin."

When her confused expression grew, I realized Nellip hadn't told her everything we'd discovered before the kingsfae had apprehended him. But at least Nellip had told her of Bastian, and Saramel had looked after Jax's brother since their arrest.

I finished securing my pack. "I'm sorry. It's a long story, so I don't have time to fully explain, but the Faewood king was behind Bastian's abduction. And he's doing many atrocious things. He's trying to build a half-breed army, and he wants to march on the kingdoms and start a war, and—"

"*What?*" Her shocked whisper rang through the alleyway.

I nodded vigorously. "It's true. The semelees revealed it to me, so I need to stop him *and* save our mates and our friends. And I just realized that I can do *all* of that by twisting fate. It's the only way to stop everything."

Her jaw dropped. "You mean . . . you're going to . . ."

Her hands flew to her mouth. "But if the courts find out that you—"

"I know, and if that happens, I'll deal with it. But right now, too much is at stake. I have to do it. It's the only way."

She dropped her hands, and for the briefest moment, a flare of hope shone upon her face. "Okay, but please be careful, and don't worry about anything here. I'll take care of Bastian, Cassim, and myself. We'll all be fine."

A breath of relief left me, and Saramel's lips lifted in a quivering smile. And in that moment, I realized I *wasn't* alone. I might not have much, but I had Saramel. I did have a friend in this realm.

I sighed in relief. "Deal. You look after the three of you, and I'll save our mates."

She pulled me into a fierce hug. "May the stars, moons, galaxy, and all the gods and goddesses bless you, Elowen."

"And you."

She squeezed me one last time. "And, Elowen? Good luck."

I forced a smile, then gripped the portal key tighter. "Open key for thou I ask, I need a door for this new task."

The realm swirled around me, and the ground dropped out from beneath me. But I kept my concentration steady, my mind clear.

*The Isle of Song. Take me to the university on the Isle of Song.*

THE PORTAL KEY dropped me off at the bottom of the university's steps on the large island.

Moonlight illuminated the huge stone stairs, cut into natural rock, that climbed to the monstrous monolith in front of me. I'd never been here before and had only heard of this prestigious school, and for a moment, all I could do was stare. The building before me was more like a temple, and it was *huge*.

Tales wove through our land about the university's imposing magic. Everything I'd ever heard about this place rang true. Heady power pulsed around the school, which was carved from the scarred rock on the side of the natural mountain that rose from this lone isle far out in the Adriastic Sea.

Waves crashed below on the distant shores beneath the mountain, so faint I could barely hear them. I searched my surroundings, gazing at the wild grasses swaying in the breeze behind me. But nobody was about. I wasn't surprised. Other than this ginormous building holding the university and library, there was nothing else on this isle, and it was said the scholars and the handful of students here rarely left their chambers.

Pillars waited at the top of the stairs, and intricate mystical engravings decorated each one. It was rumored those engravings had come from the time of the gods and that this architectural marvel was just as old.

I had no idea who'd built this place, and no one else did either, but the magic here was thick and ancient, and it was said to have come from the stars. It caressed me on the wind, as though trying to seek the power inside me while humming through my veins.

Some said it was why the scholars here were so knowledgeable—that the land fed their minds, linking them to a time when our realm was first born and our magic was ignited by the galaxy. It was a time that no longer existed. An ancient time.

*No wonder Jax knew so much about lorafins if he consulted the scholars here.*

I dropped the rolled carpet at my feet. It was too heavy and cumbersome to carry with me, and I had no need for it at the moment, so I gripped my pack instead.

With deliberate footsteps, I began to climb the stairs, and with each press of my soles into the rock beneath my feet, an answering pulse—a beat of acknowledgment—vibrated through my limbs.

This land knew what I was, and perhaps I was crazy to think it, but it felt as though it welcomed me.

At the top of the stairs, torches lit rock doors that stood twenty feet high. But there were no guards. No sentries. Yet the doors opened automatically the moment I stepped toward them.

They swung inward, and a long stretch of an immense hallway appeared before me, reminding me of darkly buried tombs long forgotten. Pillars graced the halls on the inside as well, and like the outdoors, torches lit the way.

I stopped at the threshold, gazing at the cavern in front of me. Not a soul could be seen.

"Hello?" I called, my voice echoing down the vast chamber.

"Welcome, Lorafin." The whispered words carried on the breeze, and I swung around, my heart hammering as I searched for who'd spoken.

No one was about.

"Don't be afraid." The whisper again came from nowhere and everywhere at once. "We've been waiting for you."

I took a deep breath, reminding myself that this was the only way to save Jax and that the magic here was not to be feared. Respected, yes, but I'd never heard of this isle hurting anyone maliciously. Not yet, at least.

Tentatively, I stepped over the threshold, and a wall of magic instantly encased me. Thick, potent power swirled around me but released me just as fast on the other side.

I gasped, my eyes widening. The hall that I'd seen from the outside was no more. Instead, a large chambers stood before me, lined with books, tomes, and rolled scripts. I swung around. The twenty-foot-tall doors were gone. Only a simple arched doorway waited behind me.

Fear cascaded through me. I had no idea where I was or how to get out, and perhaps the whisperings I'd heard about this place were wrong after all.

"Do not be afraid," a voice called. "'Tis the land's magic. It knew what you wanted, and it transported you to where you seek within the school."

I swung around, my breaths so short and quick that I had to consciously slow them. My eyes popped. A gargoyle waited before me, no more than four feet tall. He wore a long crimson robe, and his clawed feet poked out from beneath it.

"My name is Master Fistideeous, and I'm to be your teacher."

I blinked. I'd heard that the universities and great libraries on the continents employed gargoyle scholars, but I'd never seen one. And I'd always thought at night they returned to stone, yet the gargoyle standing before me was very much alive.

The creature grinned, revealing a mouthful of wickedly sharp teeth. Black solemn eyes gazed upward at me. His face was truly horrific, yet his voice was pleasant when he said, "Time moves differently on this isle. Come. I have the answers you seek."

"You . . ." I licked my dry lips. "You know why I'm here?"

"Of course. The magic told me." He hobbled to the

shelves behind him, his crimson robe trailing along the floor.

Numbly, I followed, my feet making quiet tapping sounds on the stone. "Do you know who I am?"

"You are Elowen Emerson of Emerson Estate, a lorafin from Faewood, or at least, that is what you believe."

I cocked my head at his cryptic words. "Was the crown prince of Stonewild here recently?"

The gargoyle glanced over his shoulder. "Oh, yes. He came looking for answers as well, just like you. He hoped to find the one he lost. But that answer eluded him. It was I who told him that only a lorafin could find who he sought, and that *you* were the only lorafin currently in our kingdoms."

My eyes widened. "You met with the prince too? Does that mean you're able to help me? The prince has been captured by the authorities, and I must twist fate to save him . . . and do some other things too, yet I don't know how."

The gargoyle smiled. "Yes, Lorafin. I know how you can twist fate."

"And you'll tell me, even though such a practice is illegal?"

The gargoyle made a motion with his hand. "Why should mere fae decide what magic can be wielded in our great universe? Especially when that magic was born of the gods."

"Born of the gods?" I repeated.

"Oh yes, did you not know? The magic within your veins carries power from the Goddess of Time, Verasellee herself."

I froze. "Are—" I licked my lips. "Are you serious?"

"I am. Did you not know?" He grinned again, his features even more terrifying than they'd been a second ago. "Are you also ignorant of the fact that the gods and goddesses once walked our land?"

"No, I've heard that before, but that was so long ago."

"It was, but in the ancient times, some gods and goddesses bred with fae. As a result, some fae in our realm still carry traces of the gods' blood. That magic passes at the will of the gods, not following genealogy, but instead it picks those that it believes are worthy, and it chose you." He canted his head. "Have you never wondered how a mere fairy is able to travel through the cosmos and reach areas of our universe that only the gods can walk?"

I paused again and thought of what my magic allowed me to do. "I suppose I never really considered it."

"Hmm, such a shame, but then I guess if you've spent your entire life enslaved, you probably had other things to worry about, but no matter. The gods and goddesses gave you your power for a reason. We pass no judgment here. You may twist fate all you want."

A blast of relief nearly bowled me over. If he wasn't going to turn me into the kingsfae, then it was possible I *could* save Jax and our friends. If only I learned how. "Thank you for being willing to help me."

He bobbed his head and pulled out a scroll. "Of course. Now, to acquire such knowledge has a price. Even a goddess's descendent must pay."

I surged toward him, ripping off my pack and reaching inside. "I can do that. I have rulibs. How much do you need?"

He shook his head. "Not rulibs, Elowen. The library doesn't barter in coin. We require something else, something much more powerful."

A skittering of dread slithered through me, and I clutched my bag to my chest. "What is it you want?"

"Knowledge, Lorafin. The magic here continually seeks *knowledge*. If I teach you how to twist fate, you must return and report everything you learned in the Veiled Between when you do such an act. This knowledge must be recorded for the ages."

I nodded vigorously. "Of course, whatever you want is yours."

He *tsked*. "Such desperation can land one in trouble. Be mindful of that. You should be glad that our school functions in neutrality. I fear if you went to the wrong creature, begging for help, more dire consequences could result."

I took a deep breath. He was right. I was being foolish. I was so desperate to save my mate that I was willing to do anything, but if I traveled to the underworld and made a deal with Lucifer . . .

I shuddered. No, that wasn't happening. I wouldn't allow myself to be that stupid.

Squaring my shoulders, I met his solemn gaze. "I will give you the knowledge you seek in exchange for instruction on how to twist fate."

He grinned, his black eyes shining. "Very well, then let us begin."

# CHAPTER 21

I'd naïvely thought Master Fistideeous would simply give me a list of directions on how to twist fate, and I would be on my way. But it wasn't that easy. He insisted that I learn much more than just my magic.

Days passed on the Isle of Song. Days and days that eventually turned into weeks.

Master Fistideeous made me read scroll after scroll and tome after tome. He refused to just tell me what to do. Instead, he insisted that to wield the power of a goddess required more than mere skill.

I needed to learn. To understand. To respect all of the magic that I'd been given.

And the only way to do that was through knowledge, which required endless days of studying.

My mind felt as though it would burst from all that he

was teaching me. He taught me everything . . . theories about the Veiled Between, history about the mighty semelees, knowledge about a goddess's lineage, and instruction about my magic.

More than once, I was tempted to flee to the Veiled Between and attempt to twist fate on my own, but the university's magic didn't let me. I would know. I'd tried.

On one desperate night, when I'd received word through the daily news castings from the continent that Jax was going to trial, I'd fled to my quarters and dove my magic inward, willing it to take me to the Veiled Between so I could try to twist fate before my teacher said I was ready.

But my magic didn't work. The island's magic had trapped my power inside me. After I'd realized that and returned to Master Fistideeous's work area, he'd patted my hand and told me everything would come *in good time*.

So I'd gone back to work as instructed, even though life carried on outside of these ancient walls as though my fate wasn't hanging in the balance.

And *so many* things were occurring. The Final Match selection had ended. The official Centennial Matches had begun, yet I had no idea how far King Paevin was coming along in his plans to enslave more half-breeds and build his army. Of course, that wasn't covered in the daily updates we received from the continent.

The only solace I took was knowing that as a lorafin with the ability to twist fate, I could also alter time—something I'd learned in my studies.

But the only question my teacher couldn't answer for me was what would happen if Jax was executed before I twisted fate. Even Master Fistideeous didn't know if my mate could still be saved if his soul had crossed to the afterlife.

SIX WEEKS after venturing to the Isle of Song, Master Fistideeous finally declared me ready to leave and gave me his blessing to fully use my magic.

I was an anxious mess by the time we said our goodbyes. Word had arrived that both Lars and Phillen had been found guilty during their trials. It'd been proved that neither of them had been on hunting exhibitions with the prince during the times they'd been away from court, and their executions were set to take place next week.

The others' trials were still ongoing, Jax's included, yet it'd also been proved none of them had been hunting either. Their excuse for being away from court when they'd been conducting raids, that they'd used for full seasons, had failed.

The Centennial Matches were also drawing to a close,

only a few days remaining, and the continent's excitement had turned away from Faewood and to the upcoming Iron-crest Ball. I still had no idea what was going on with my court date to secure my freedom. A dillemsill had never arrived, but perhaps it hadn't been able to find me, considering where I was.

Yet all I cared about was finally returning to Stonewild and using what I'd learned to save my mate and our friends, and to stop the king. My freedom from a guardian could come after that.

Bending down, I wrapped the small gargoyle in a hug. "Thank you, Master Fistideeous, for all that you've done for me. I'll never forget it."

He patted me on the back. "It's been an honor, Elowen, truly. Now, don't forget what's required. We still need you to return and share what you learn after you twist fate. And I would be lying if I said I also wasn't looking forward to seeing you again."

I straightened and secured my bag to my back. "I won't forget. I give you my word that I'll return, and I look forward to seeing you again too."

He smiled up at me, his face no longer terrifying even though it truly looked like a nightmare. "I'll see you soon."

I STOOD on the island's shores, portal key in hand, not bothering to retrieve the enchanted carpet I'd left outside all those weeks ago. The sun shone above me, but time moved so strangely on the island that I didn't know if it would be day or night, morning or evening, when I materialized back on the mainland. Locked within the island's magic, time had taken on no meaning. The only way I'd been able to keep track of it at all was through the daily news castings from the continent.

But I'd accomplished what I set out to do. Master Fistideeous had taught me what was needed to twist fate. Now, all that was left was to actually do it.

Taking a deep breath, I gripped the key and whispered the words to activate it. I thought of Jaggedston, of where I wanted to go.

The realm swirled around me, dropping out from beneath me as the portal key transported me back to Stonewild's capital.

Only moments later, I landed on solid ground, swaying slightly. My pack was still secured to my back, and in my hand, the portal key fizzled out of existence. Above, the night sky shone, yet I had no idea what time it was.

Materialized once more, I surveyed where I'd been dropped. The palace's black towers soared in the distance, only blocks away, and an inn stood just behind me. Master Fistideeous had told me it was the closest inn to the palace, and I quickly rushed inside to secure a room.

A wildling stood behind a desk, and he was the only fairy present. A clock ticked on the wall behind him. It was the wee hours of the morning, so I wasn't surprised that he blinked sleepily.

I dropped five rulibs on the counter, and my heart began to pound at what I was about to do. "One room, please."

The wildling took the coin with automatic movements and nodded toward the crystal sphere at the end of his counter. "Hand there, if you would."

I placed my hand on it, and my details scrawled across the ledger before him. He took his time checking me in, even though I was so anxious to get moving that my aura was practically crackling. It wasn't lost on me that there could be a warrant out for my arrest. I needed to hurry in case the kingsfae were summoned.

It felt as though it took ages before the wildling dangled a key in front of me. I snatched it from his hand, murmuring my thanks, then hurried to my chambers on the second floor.

Once inside, I closed and locked the door behind me, then whispered a spell to hold the lock in place. If the kingsfae came, that would delay them for a while.

A lone bed with a cream coverlet and dainty pillows strewn across it greeted me. A latrine also waited in the chambers' corner, and a thick rug covered the clean wood floor. It was a huge step up from the hovel I'd slept in weeks ago near the wharf.

My heart began to pound as I stood there.

This was it.

This was the moment I'd spent the past six weeks working toward.

Never mind that I'd never attempted such a thing before, and perhaps I was a fool to do it, considering what would happen if the courts found out, but if it meant my mate would be free, our friends would be saved, and King Paevin would be stopped, then I'd spend the rest of my life dealing with the consequences if it came to that.

I dropped my bag at my feet, and the heavy weight of it sank like a stone. Another anxious breath lifted my chest, but I climbed onto the bed, lay down, and closed my eyes.

The mattress dipped, soft and comfortable, but I would have lain on a hard rock in the freezing cold if needed.

Forcing my breaths to slow, I took one last moment to steady my fear, then dove myself inward, downward to my bottomless depth of power.

*Take me away.*

The silent command was all that was needed to call upon my lorafin magic. It rose up inside me, the power of a goddess, so quickly and easily. Without my collar and with the new skills I'd learned, it was as simple as breathing.

Cold shadows coasted through me, and then I was

blazing across the galaxy, shooting through the stars until I arrived at the Veiled Between.

My ghostlike essence parted the Veil as immense power hummed inside me. I'd never felt magic like this before. It burned and soared, extending all of the way to my toes, lighting up my fingers, beating through my soul. Without my collar, I was truly *free*.

And for the first time in my life, I understood my potential.

The second my being fully drifted through the Veil, several semelees rushed forward.

*Queen of Darkness, Commander of Fate, you've come. What do you seek?* They all bowed to me, their potent magic swirling around me like billowing stars.

I took another deep breath, knowing Jax's survival depended on me and this moment, and I hung onto the knowledge of what my gargoyle scholar had taught me. *Engulf the semelees. You and they become one. It is the only way for a lorafin to command the fates.*

I ran a hand along the semelee nearest me, my fingers trailing across its cold scales. Stepping closer to it, I did as Master Fistideeous instructed. I imagined my magic opening like a well inside me, a bottomless hole that allowed the semelees to join with me.

The semelee's energy rose, its silent understanding like an approving teacher. *You've learned much since the last time we saw you, Lorafin.* It slithered inside me, and the feel of its power connecting with mine made me gasp.

I took a moment to steady myself as my magic grew. Already, the single semelee's power was combining with mine. Energy radiated from me. Blazing, potent power. The power of a goddess.

Billowing beyond the Veil, I anchored myself to this new feeling, and once the strangeness of it began to pass, I moved to the next semelee.

*You as well*, I commanded it, my voice echoing with the strength of the cosmos.

It surged forward, its power rushing into me. Again, the strangeness of it took my breath away, but I didn't stop.

I turned to the next semelee, then the next, sucking each one inside me as their power joined with mine.

Moments passed as my power grew, brimming with energy, crackling with sheer force. It was *so much* power— a galaxy of might.

The semelees grew in numbers, overpowering time itself, until I was swirling in shadowed darkness.

Each and every one connected inside me, power bursting from my limbs, until finally, at last, I was the queen of fate.

I paused momentarily, knowing there was no going back after this moment, but also knowing I would give my life to save my mate's.

And I'd spent the past six weeks considering each of

my next words over and over. One wrong word, one tiny mistake, and the rippling effect could stretch through eons.

Whispering, I said the words that could damn me or save us completely.

*I command you to twist fate. I command you to free the crown prince of Stonewild, Prince Adarian, and all of his Dark Raider band. I command you to set them free by rewriting time so that my guardian was never allowed to escape his chambers and accuse them. And I command you to have King Paevin's evil plan abolished so that we may save the captured half-breeds and their enslaved children, eradicating the king's plan in the process to wield an army and destroy the kingdoms. I command you to venture with me to the fae lands and rewrite history and time itself.*

A clash of power reverberated through the cosmos.

*It is as you wish,* the semelees hissed inside me as one.

I shot through the galaxy, the semelees riding inside me, morphing into the terrifying shadow creatures that the history books had spoken of. Master Fistideeous had taught me of this power, of times in our pasts when previous lorafins had commanded the fates. The potential of a lorafin queen made me one of the most powerful and dangerous creatures of our land. Yet I would never be a slave because of it again.

The semelees and I collided with my realm in a sizzling crash, shooting through the sky, barreling toward

Stonewild's capital, and gliding right through the wards of the supernatural courts as though they were tissue paper.

We came to a crashing halt. Floating in the large entryway, high above the kingsfae and processing staff, the semelees and I hovered. The huge creatures coasted out of me and through the air, their deadly fangs coated with venom, gnashing the air as they waited for my final command.

Screams sounded.

Fae ran.

Eyes wide with horror gazed up at us.

It was the same looks I'd seen when I'd been five summers old. The one other time I'd brought several semelees back with me, not even realizing what I'd done.

But this time it was different. When I was five, they'd simply joined me on my journey. I hadn't pulled them inside me, and I hadn't controlled them. I hadn't even realized what I'd done.

But now I did. I was a lorafin by birthright. The gods and goddesses had chosen to give me this power, and it was mine to command.

And I was choosing to wield it.

I hovered in the courts' terrified midst as the shadow creatures billowed around me.

And I lifted a hand, knowing once I said the words, there was no turning back.

But Jax needed me.

Our friends needed me.

Bastian needed me.

The half-breeds needed me.

The kingdoms needed me.

My voice echoed through the chambers, mighty, godlike, and entirely *mine*.

*I command you to rewrite time. I command you to twist fate.*

*Yes, my queen,* they hissed simultaneously.

And then the semelees unleashed.

# CHAPTER 22

I awoke on the bed at the inn, only blocks away from the palace. Fatigue made my eyes feel heavy. My skin felt cold, and unbearable soreness plagued me, yet after taking a few deep breaths, it began to pass. Yet I still felt drained. Used. As though my magic had been tapped out.

But even as I lay there, exhausted from what I'd done, a kernel of magic began to swirl inside me, cool and fluttering. With each breath I took, it grew.

Amazingly, already my magic was returning, and I recalled what the gargoyle scholar had told me, that I carried a goddess's blood.

The inn's wooden ceiling stared back at me, and I closed my eyes again, struggling to recall all that had happened. I'd gone to the Veiled Between. I'd twisted fate. I knew that much. Yet after appearing in the supernatural courts with the semelees around me, it all became fuzzy. Especially after they unleashed.

I knew that the semelees had done as I'd commanded and that I'd returned them to the Veiled Between when they'd finished, but when time had been altered, it'd created an explosion of power, so much that fragments of time and space had shifted. The cosmos had been rewritten, and even to me, it'd all turned hazy.

Disoriented, I forced myself to sitting and gazed out the window. An evening sky loomed with the sun disappearing beneath the horizon. Wind blew through the streets, but here at the inn, it was quiet.

Frowning, I glanced down and realized the simple breeches and top I'd worn when I'd ventured to the Veiled Between were gone. The navy gown that I'd worn when Jax and I had planned to meet his parents all those weeks ago swirled around me instead.

I started. I wasn't sure if that was a good sign or not.

Even though every part of my body ached, I swung my legs over the bed, then grabbed for my bag . . . but my bag wasn't there.

I crouched to search under the bed, stumbling in the process, but my belongings weren't there either. I checked under the nightstand and in the closet, too, but nothing. It wasn't in the room and neither was the room key.

Frowning, I figured that, like my clothes, my bag and the key were no longer here in this new reality. A memory stirred, of what Master Fistideeous had taught me. Previous lorafins always returned to where they'd been physically when they'd commanded fate. Otherwise, two bodies of oneself would exist at once.

My confusion disappeared, and I finally made my way down the stairs and out into the city.

My legs throbbed in time with my footsteps, but I forced myself to walk one foot in front of the other until I reached the palace. Black gates greeted me. Two guards stood at them, one on each side. More guards patrolled the perimeter.

When I approached, the guard on the right frowned. "Are you all right?"

I stopped dead in my tracks. *Is he speaking to me?*

The guard took a step toward me. "Lady Elowen, are you all right?"

I glanced at the guard on the left. Like the other, concern knitted his brow. They watched me with befuddled expressions, as though they were actually . . . *worried.*

Hope surged through me. If I'd truly rewritten time, then their behavior would be explained. The crown prince had let the servants know that I was his guest, and the guards had likely been told that as well. And if I'd been successful in commanding the semelees to undo Jax being caught, and to right the atrocities that King Paevin had committed with the half-breeds, the guards wouldn't be surprised at my appearance. My arrest and visit to the supernatural courts would have no longer occurred in this reality.

My heart began to pound even more, and I blinked away the grittiness in my eyes and tried to ignore what would happen if anyone found out what I'd done. My godlike power was why lorafins were allowed to be enslaved. Our power was too great and could be used for selfish or malicious purposes. A lorafin queen could literally mold anything in the realm to her bidding. It was total and complete control of our lands. It was the power of a goddess, of Verasellee herself.

But I'd only done it to save Jax, to save our friends, to save the half-breeds, and to prevent King Paevin from creating his army. I hadn't done anything for myself. My intentions had been *good*, even if others might not see it that way.

"Lady Elowen?" the guard said again when I just stood there.

Forcing myself to move despite the tiredness spiraling through me, I reached the guards, then licked my dry lips. My throat felt so parched. I could have drunk an ocean of water, and it wouldn't have been enough.

"What day is it?" I asked them in a scratchy voice.

His troubled look grew, but he rattled off the date, and my eyes widened. The current time was the day when Jax and I were supposed to meet his parents—*the day Jax's arrest had initially taken place.* The semelees had transported me back in time after doing as I'd asked. It was liter-ally *weeks* ago.

"And where's the prince?"

"I . . . I don't know." The one on the right assessed me carefully. "But I believe he's been looking for you."

A sharp sense of relief pierced me. It was so sharp that I staggered back. "And he's . . . free? He's not detained by the supernatural courts?"

The guards shared a side-eye, and then the one on the right said in a slow, patient tone, "No, Lady Elowen. The prince has not been detained by the courts." He frowned even more. "My lady, are you all right? Shall I call someone for you?"

"Yes!" I cried. "Please get the prince."

The guards again shared a wary look, but with a swift nod, the one on the right jerked his chin toward the palace and called to an interior guard, "Please let the prince know his guest is here."

The interior guard lifted a device and said something into it. Magic shimmered around the apparatus and projected his voice to somewhere else in the palace.

The gate's guard gestured for me to step forward. "Come, Lady Elowen, let's get you inside."

The gates swung open, and the guard led me across the large stone courtyard to the palace steps. But before I could place a foot on the first stair, the palace doors crashed open.

"Elowen!" Jax was down the steps, flying toward me with a panicked look on his face.

My heart soared, and our mate bond hummed.

The second Jax reached me, he crushed me to him, and my arms wrapped around him just as hard.

Pine and spice. Magic and fire. Strength and warmth. Everything I'd ever felt in my mate's presence cascaded through me.

I clung to him, feeling him, soaking up his presence, relishing that he was here and I was touching him again. "Stars Above. I worried I'd never see you again," I whispered.

My trembling words had him pulling back, concern evident on his features. "Where were you? I've been looking for you."

I shook my head and memorized his face, tracing my fingers over each sculpted line. A heavy brow. Crashing and blazing irises. A strong nose. Firm yet full lips. A defined jaw. Everything about him looked so familiar, yet it also felt like I was looking at him for the first time.

My mate bond burned with renewed intensity, and my heart flooded with relief. He was safe. Alive. *Here.* I soaked up his appearance like the desert drank in its first rain, and just thanked the stars and galaxy that I was with him again.

He cupped my cheeks, seeming to understand that *something* had happened to me but obviously not knowing what. "Come with me, my love. We need to meet my parents."

He kissed me once, his lips molding to mine, then he clasped my hand and pulled me along.

We ventured up the stairs, side by side. Like me, he was wearing the same navy clothing that he'd changed into after we'd made love in his wardrobe. Even more of the panic in me eased. I'd been transported to the past. I'd truly *twisted fate.*

With my mate at my side, I entered the palace, and we began making our way to the main dining hall. Familiar walls passed us. Elegant chambers filled my view. Everywhere I looked, all appeared calm and normal. No kingsfae were in sight.

But that didn't mean everything was safe.

"Did anyone check on my guardian today?" I asked him quietly.

He inclined his head. "Lars was going to."

"So Guardian Alleron's still alive?"

Jax frowned. "Of course, I haven't killed him. Not yet, at least."

I gripped Jax's hand. "Are you certain that Guardian Alleron's still locked in his chambers?"

Jax canted his head, and he was so devastatingly beautiful that I could have looked at him all night. "I haven't heard otherwise."

My eyes widened as that implication took root. If my

guardian was alive in this reality, then that meant someone who'd passed to the afterlife *could* be brought back to life if I twisted fate. Either that, or my guardian had somehow miraculously survived after I'd thrown him miles out to sea. But I doubted that was possible. Guardian Alleron couldn't swim, and I'd seen no ships that could have rescued him. Apparently, if I rewrote time, fae *could be brought back to life.* When I returned to the Isle of Song, I would have to report that to Master Fistideeous.

But that was assuming that Guardian Alleron truly lived . . .

My slippers dug into the soft carpet fibers beneath my soles. "Jax, are you certain that my guardian is still alive and is still locked in his chambers?"

Jax's brow furrowed, and he turned to face me. "I haven't spoken with Lars since we parted, if that's what you mean, but he said he was going to check on him, so I'm sure he did."

I gripped Jax's arm, my nails digging into him. "This is *very* important. If my guardian's still alive, we need to ensure that he's still in his chambers and hasn't escaped."

Worry began emitting in my mate's aura, and his gaze flitted across my face. "I'll be right back." He disappeared in a blur of speed, leaving me alone in the hall.

I wrung my hands and scanned the area to see if any servants looked to be acting strange or fearful, but none were about.

Yet I'd been transported *back in time*. I took some comfort in that. I'd obviously done something with my magic, and I didn't have to wait long for Jax. He whizzed back to my side only minutes later, barely winded thanks to his shifter-enhanced run.

"He's still in his chambers, as angry as ever, but he's there, and he's alive."

I sagged in relief, and my mate cupped my cheeks, tilting my head up. "Elowen, *what's wrong?*"

But I shook my head. "It'll take too long to explain now, but I will, I promise. And what about your"—I glanced around to ensure nobody would hear me—"brother . . . is he okay too?"

Jax angled his head toward me and nodded. "Yes, he's still in his suite, again, as far as I'm aware. Do you want me to check on him too?"

I shook my head. "No, I don't think you need to. I just wanted to make sure nothing else had changed. We should keep going since your parents are expecting us."

"All right." He clasped my hand, and we resumed walking, but he constantly glanced down at me.

I could tell from his wary looks that he knew something had happened that he was unaware of, but I was thankful he didn't push me for answers. Given that I was about to meet his parents, and since my guardian was still locked away and the kingsfae hadn't been called, I really needed to concentrate on winning them over. The arrest that had once been made was no longer occurring.

"What if they hate me?" I whispered.

"How could anybody hate you?"

"They might."

He growled. "I'll make it clear to them that hating you *isn't* an option. Besides, after they hear what you've learned of King Paevin and that you acquired that knowledge by using your magic, they'll realize how extraordinary you are, whether they want to admit it or not."

My eyes widened, and I froze in place again, forcing Jax to stop too. "You mean the king's plan hasn't been stopped?"

Worry again puffed in Jax's aura, and he pulled me close, slipping an arm around my waist. He frowned again, his look intent. "Something's obviously happened, and given what you're saying, I suspect I might know, but tell me, my love, what's wrong?"

But all I could do was shake my head. "Not here. It's too much to explain. I'll tell you later." I squeezed his hand again, trying to reassure him and myself, but my attempts at that only strengthened his frown.

And perhaps his concern was warranted, because if the king's plan *hadn't* been stopped, then my attempt to twist fate hadn't fully worked. Jax had remained free—thank the stars—but if *nothing* had changed with King Paevin, then I'd failed, and that meant the half-breeds were still at risk.

I numbly followed Jax down the hall toward the dining area, looking every which way as I waited for disaster to strike. I thought I'd fully grasped what Master Fistideeous had taught me about twisting fate, but I apparently hadn't.

"Are you ready to meet your future parents-in-law?" Jax asked carefully, his aura still vibrating with concern. "Or would you rather we postpone this? We can meet them another time."

I shook my head. "No, they're expecting us. Let's do this now. If we postpone, that could be something they hold against me."

"Are you sure?"

"Yes."

We rounded the final turn of the wide hall, but before we were halfway there, a flurry of shadows emitted near the wall. In my next blink, Quinn stood before us.

My eyes bulged, and Jax's attention whipped in all directions. "What in the realm? Someone could see you here."

The crowfy shifter stepped forward, his movements quick. "I know. I was careful to ensure nobody was about before materializing, but I had to get to you so you knew." He pulled Jax and me into an alcove, hiding us from view, then said under his breath, "King Paevin was the one behind your brother's disappearance, my prince. I heard him talking about Bastian this morning."

Jax's tensed shoulders relaxed, and a smile tugged at

his lips. "We're way ahead of you. Elowen already uncovered that."

But Quinn's look stayed intent, his jaw locking. "That's not all. There's another reason I'm here. The *real* reason. King Paevin is dead."

It felt as though my heart stopped. "He is?"

Jax's eyebrows shot up. "Truly? But how? And when?"

Quinn's light-blue eyes turned as frosty as ice. "This evening, only hours ago. I was in the Faewood palace, still watching King Paevin and listening to his whisperings with his less-than-scrupulous staff, when he had an accident. He fell down the stairs. Broke his neck. It killed him instantly. The Faewood court hasn't officially announced it yet, but his daughter will take the throne. Everything's a mess there at the moment, especially with the Centennial Matches starting soon. It's pure chaos."

My mouth parted, understanding hitting me. *So that's how the semelees stopped the king's malicious plan.* A rush of relief flowed through me. I *had* fully commanded fate after all. I just hadn't realized it yet since I hadn't known the king was already dead.

"And the half-breeds? Where are they?" I asked quietly.

Quinn's attention shifted to me. "Still in the caverns."

Another rush of relief hit me. They hadn't moved them, which meant we could save them since we still knew how to reach them.

I sagged against the wall as gratitude filled me. I'd been so careful when I'd considered what to alter with fate. I'd had six weeks to plan for it, and I'd realized that if I commanded the semelees to free the half-breeds too, that could have meant the semelees would have had to venture back *full seasons* in time to alter fate since the king had captured some of his half-breeds many summers ago.

And altering time and fate over that long of a period would only ensure more ripple effects through the space and time continuum, something Master Fistideeous had warned me about.

Because of that, I hadn't felt it wise to risk it, especially knowing that we could still rescue the half-breeds in the caverns under the Wood ourselves.

Straightening, I addressed Quinn again. "And the children, particularly the one gifted with psychic power that was able to tell the king about the raid in Possyrose Forest, where is she and the rest of the children that were born in captivity?"

"The same. All of the children are still in the caverns."

I released another breath. "Thank the stars."

Jax glanced down at me again. His brow knitted together in a heavy frown, and his jaw tightened even more. Potent concern from him strummed toward me on our bond. "We'll have to free them soon, even tomorrow. If the king's truly dead, the guards taking care of the half-breeds are likely to scatter without anyone commanding them. Or, they may murder all of the half-breeds to hide their crimes."

My thoughts rushed back to what I'd experienced as a child. "Or, they could hurt them or take them. The child psychic especially would be considered extremely valuable, and if she has an anklet on, and one of the guards or Paevin's cohorts has a device to control her . . ." I shuddered. "She's very much at risk of being enslaved as I was."

Jax pulled me close to him again, his pine and spice scent flooding me. "We *won't* let that happen."

Brow furrowing, Quinn added, "The fortunate aspect of the king's death is that his plan to build his army and attack the kingdoms has stopped, but you're right about the half-breeds. They're still at risk."

"Indeed. We still have a lot of work to do." Jax kept one arm slung around me, but with the other, he raked a hand through his hair. "Let's meet tonight to figure this out. I'll let the others know. Tomorrow, we'll—"

The prince cut himself off when the faint sound of approaching footsteps carried to us.

Quinn glanced over his shoulder. "Someone's coming. I'll go, but I'm glad I found you. This news was too big not to share right away."

"Agreed. Thank you." Jax dipped his chin. "We'll meet at ten tonight, our usual spot."

Quinn nodded, and then in a swirl of shadows, disappeared.

The air settled around us, and a servant appeared from around the corner, carrying a pile of linens. She bowed toward the prince when she passed us, but she didn't scurry away. And she didn't look concerned. It was so different from last time.

My pounding heart slowed even more. I'd truly twisted fate, which meant everything was actually okay.

Jax and I resumed our walk, and my mate scratched his chin. "It's quite fortuitous that King Paevin's dead. What are the chances of the king breaking his neck just when we needed him stopped?" He glanced down at me again, as though waiting for me to confirm what he likely already suspected.

I squeezed his hand but pressed my lips together because the dining hall appeared ahead. Although, I did mutter, "You're right. It's quite fortuitous." A small smile slid across my face.

A look of absolute wonder crossed his features, but he didn't have time to comment further.

We swept through the doors, and I had such a strong sense of déjà vu that I nearly stumbled. And when I saw what lay before me, I nearly did.

Because the entire hall was *full* of noble fae, even though Jax had asked the king and queen to meet us privately before the supper meal.

I quickly scanned the room for kingsfae, but there were none. Conversation and the sound of clinking glasses drifted through the air. Dozens of fae were scattered throughout the room, chatting and laughing as the servants bustled about, readying for the impending meal.

The king and queen stood near the head of the table while noble families, including House Dallinger, hovered nearby.

I scanned that House's attendants, but Lady Aerobelle was nowhere to be found. Yet Bowan's father, as well as Trivan, Lander, Alec, and Bowan, were all present. All three of them stood with their respective Houses. In addition to them, there were dozens more that I'd never met before.

"I thought we were meeting your parents privately," I said.

Jax hissed a breath through his teeth. "So did I."

"My prince!" a noble called that I'd never seen before. "Welcome back from the Match Finals!"

Irritation swelled in Jax's aura, and a low growl escaped him. His gaze cut to his parents, but they were too busy speaking with other nobles to acknowledge us.

I quickly finished scanning the room and realized that Lars and Phillen were missing, but since Jax's personal guards weren't needed for duty at the moment, I could only surmise that they were with their families or elsewhere in the palace. That also meant Cassim would likely be tucked into bed by his da tonight.

*At least there's that.* Despite irritation also filling me that Jax's parents had blatantly defied his request for a private meeting, I took some comfort in knowing that everything else was falling into place.

My plan to twist fate had *worked*.

For the first time since waking in the inn, I took a deep, unencumbered breath. All it'd taken was for me to venture to the Veiled Between and demand complete submission of the semelees. And now, with my magic fully free, they'd done as I asked.

The only side effect of the entire thing was my fatigue, not to mention I still had to return to the Isle of Song to share my knowledge. Yet those things were trivial compared to what had been at stake and was now rectified.

Another tentative sense of triumph coasted through me. Perhaps everything truly would be fine.

Jax ushered me forward, and the navy gown swirled around my legs.

"Father. Mother," Jax said to his parents when we reached them. "I thought I asked to meet with you in private."

I faced the king and queen and automatically curtsied, but one look at the royals had my hope at everything working out dying.

Annoyed expressions covered their faces, and they both stared at me with cold eyes.

"I didn't see why we would need to do that," the king replied. He looked exactly as I remembered him, similar in coloring and features to Jax, but older and slightly heavier.

His mother was the same too. Pale skin, tepid blue eyes, and blond hair. And the way she glanced down her nose at me was no different from the first time we'd met—unbeknownst to her.

I straightened from my curtsy, my smile slipping, but then I reminded myself I'd done the right thing by not manipulating fate to suit my needs. I could have commanded the semelees to have Jax's parents accept me, but the more one interfered with reality, the more threads were woven . . . and the more likely it was that a thread would tangle. Master Fistideeous had taught me that too.

I took a deep breath and braced myself for what was to come. One thing I knew . . . this was a battle I *would* have to fight. I wouldn't twist fate again to make his parents accept me.

Standing tall, the king's chest puffed up. He wore the same clothes as the first night I'd met him, and he had the same air of disapproval radiating from him. "So this is the young lady I keep hearing about that you wanted us to meet in private?"

"This is," Jax said stiffly. Everyone was watching us, yet Jax's voice didn't falter when he said, "This is Lady Elowen Emerson of Faewood Kingdom."

I dipped into another respectful curtsy, but when I glanced up, the king's nostrils were flaring, and his mother's eyes were shooting daggers at me.

My stomach tumbled, but I still said, "Your Majesties. It's an honor to officially meet you both."

His mother arched an eyebrow, then lifted her chin and focused on Jax. "Adarian, you may seat your guest at the end of the table. There's a free chair down there."

Jax's aura pulsed. "Actually, Mother, I plan to have Elowen sit beside me."

"Adarian," the king growled. "Don't make a scene. Do as your mother said. We're eating in a few minutes as we had to change our plans to dine earlier than normal. An unexpected meeting's come up for me after supper. Apparently, something's happened in Faewood."

"Oh?" Jax asked, eyebrows rising. "What's that?"

The king waved his hand. "Who knows. They said it's urgent, but they always say that, so I told them it can wait. We shall dine first and give you a chance to explain this *female* you've brought along."

"Yet you didn't give us the courtesy of a private meeting beforehand, and now you're insisting she not sit with me." Jax's free hand curled into a fist, but before an argument could begin, I squeezed his arm.

"I'm fine to sit wherever. Thank you for having me." I curtsied again to his parents.

Neither the king nor queen so much as glanced my way.

Jax's aura puffed even more in irritation, but I squeezed him again, my fingers firm on his arm. I had to try to win over his parents *without* the use of my magic, if it could even be done, but it would be harder if he began to fight them here and now.

And a fight it would undoubtedly be. Because the fact remained that I was a commoner. Granted, I was a commoner with immense magic, but I wasn't of royal or noble blood, and that would work against me at all turns.

But Jax didn't move.

I tugged him. "It's fine," I whispered. "Please."

Finally, Jax turned stiffly and escorted me to the end of the table. We passed House Dallinger on the way, and I subtly looked for Aerobelle again, but I didn't see her anywhere.

Once I was seated, Jax leaned down, and his fingers dug into my chair's armrest. "I'm sorry about this."

I forced a smile. "Don't be. We'll figure it out."

Jaw locking, he returned to the head of the table to sit by his parents.

The second the royals were all seated, all of the other nobles followed suit, and then the hall erupted into a flurry of activity. Servants glided about. Silverware clanked. Glasses were lifted. It was obvious this type of meal was the norm for most of them, and I was the only anomaly.

Thankfully, the seat that I'd been directed to wasn't next to any of the spiteful females or House members that had been on the ship with us to Faewood. Instead, I'd been seated by a young girl who couldn't have been older than fifteen.

"And what House are you from?" I asked her as a servant placed a plate of food before me. Rich scents of roasted hen and succulent vegetables rose from it.

She arched an eyebrow at me. "House Luvinteen. And you?"

I hastily took a drink of water. Wine was present and freely flowing, but all I wanted was the crystal-clear water in my goblet. I downed all of it because I was so thirsty, and a servant immediately refilled it. "I'm not from a House."

Her eyebrows shot up. "You're not? Then what are you doing here?"

Her direct question was so youthful that I actually smiled. "I'm a friend of the prince."

Her lips curved. "Oh, I see what you mean."

Heat rose in my cheeks. "No, I'm not his, I mean—"

She laughed lightly. "Don't worry about it. You're not the first *friend* he's brought to a meal, and I'm sure you won't be the last, not even after he marries. You know he's to marry one of the females his parents have chosen, right?"

I gripped my goblet harder, my fingers curling around the smooth glass. "I've heard. Speaking of which, do you know where Lady Aerobelle is? I would have thought she'd be here tonight."

The girl waved her hand. "They arrived back from Faewood this morning, but she wasn't feeling well. I guess she got sick on the ship, so is currently at home."

A flare of triumph coasted through me. So that was how the semelees had taken care of her meddling.

I picked up my fork and began to eat, although my eyes drooped. The events of the past six weeks and the huge use of my power were catching up with me. And now that everything was calming, my utter exhaustion was creeping in.

But I took some comfort in this new reality. Even though things still looked disastrous for Jax's and my future, at least he was free, Bastian was well, King Paevin had been stopped, and tomorrow, we would find a way to free the half-breeds.

Yet a part of me wondered what this new reality would be like if I'd asked the semelees to twist fate in Jax's and my favor. Perhaps the king and queen would have welcomed me with open arms, likely insisting that I sit with them.

But I hadn't changed the course of our realm more than what was necessary. It was dangerous enough what I'd done. Time had been rewritten. New paths had been forged, and with each turn of fate, new possibilities arose.

And who was to say those possibilities would be positive.

I took another bite of food, chewing slowly. No, it was best that I'd kept it to the necessities only. Everything else between Jax and I would eventually be made right. We would have to see to it ourselves, and surely, we would find a way.

# CHAPTER 23

The second the supper meal was over, Jax was up from his chair and striding toward me. He ignored everyone else, even when some of the House nobles tried to engage him in conversation on his way past.

His focus had settled on me, his intent clear, and from the rising tide of anger in his aura, it was apparent he wasn't happy with his parents' treatment of me.

I sighed. I wasn't exactly happy about it either. They'd ignored me all night and had sent sharp looks to any House that had tried to engage me. Their snub hadn't even been subtle.

It'd reminded me of what Jax had told me of them. He'd suffered abuse at his father's hand, and his mother had always turned a blind eye to it. These fae were to be my future family despite that. Granted, I'd never known a loving family either, but the Stonewild royals certainly weren't a family I would have ever chosen willingly.

Yet, they were still the king and queen. They were still Jax's parents, as much as I didn't like it. So, not wanting to make a scene, I bid goodnight to the girl I'd sat beside—literally the only fairy who had talked to me—and took Jax's outstretched hand. His warm, smooth palm closed over mine, and his thumb brushed against my knuckles.

Everyone watched, and a hush fell over the hall.

Stomach tumbling, I rose from my seat.

At the front of the table, the king and queen were still sipping their wine, but their gazes tracked our movements. The slight flare to his mother's nostrils and the king's curling lip told me they were not impressed with their son's behavior.

But Jax said loudly enough for everyone in attendance to hear, "Elowen? May I escort you from the hall back to my tower?"

His devotion was so fierce. So purposeful. My mate bond hummed with love, and his lips curved in a satisfied smile.

Despite the royals' rebuff, we would find a way to make his parents accept me. But that obviously wasn't happening anytime soon.

I dipped into a curtsy and snagged a quick look at Alec, Bowan, Lander, and Trivan. They were still seated, but I had a feeling eventually they would all make their way out to join us at ten when we met with Quinn.

Fatigue made my legs feel heavy when Jax and I walked from the hall, but the second we were released from prying eyes, the prince stopped and tugged me into a dark corner.

"Gods, my love. I'm so sorry. It was atrocious how my parents treated you." His aura billowed around me, and his arms slipped around my waist. "Please forgive me for allowing that."

I shook my head. "You didn't allow anything. We expected as much, right?"

He huffed. "It doesn't make it any better." He brushed his knuckles against my cheek. "Are you going to tell me now what's going on with you or why I found you outside earlier when I could have sworn you'd been walking at my side on our way to supper?"

I nodded. A chill swept over me at what I'd done, but then I reminded myself that nothing adverse had happened. I'd simply used my lorafin magic to the extent of my capabilities. Nobody was any the wiser. And no innocents had been harmed.

I squeezed his hand and tugged him back to the center of the hall. "Let's go to your tower. This conversation is best held behind a warded and locked door."

My eyes were drooping so badly by the time I finished telling Jax everything that had happened in the past six weeks that I was nodding off.

We were in his suite, and I was lying on his bed. Jax, however, jumped up from where he'd been sitting beside me and began to pace. "Guardian Alleron broke free and reported me to the kingsfae, and *all* of us were arrested and likely to be executed?"

I nodded. "His accusations worked, and the kingsfae began an investigation. I don't know all of what they uncovered, but they said they had irrefutable proof. Your trial was still ongoing when I twisted fate, but both Lars's and Phillen's had ended. They were set to be executed the week following. There was no way to free any of you, so I did the only thing I could think of to ensure your freedom."

"Gods." Jax raked both hands through his hair. Behind him, the night sky shone through the window. "*I* did that to you. I'm the reason you had to go through all of that agony, and spend all of those weeks on the Isle of Song, and change the course of our realm, putting yourself at risk in the process."

"What? No, you didn't." I straightened more from where I lay on his bed. "You didn't do anything to me. My *guardian* caused that mess. Well, him and Lady Aerobelle."

Jax returned to my side, his brow furrowing as a look of pure anguish covered his features. "No, Elowen, as much as I would like to blame the both of them too, I can't. If I wasn't the Dark Raider, *none* of that would have happened. It's exactly what I've always feared—that I would be caught, and you would be the one to suffer because of it. It's why I knew I needed to let you go when we first met." He ran his finger along my cheek. "But I was too weak. I couldn't let you go."

I forced myself to shake off my fatigue and face him more. "I don't *want you* to let me go. If needed, I would twist fate a hundred times over to save you."

A low snarl rumbled in his chest, and he jumped up from the bed again. "No, that's never going to happen. I will *never* put you in that position again." His movements grew more agitated, his strides even longer.

"What are you saying?"

He paced a few more times, then returned to my side, sitting on the bed again, but energy streamed out of him. "I'm saying that I think the time has come for me to no longer be the Dark Raider."

My eyes widened. "Are you serious? But you've been doing it for so many summers. It's who you are. It's how you feel you're making a difference and helping others."

"True, but I'm also a crown prince. There are other ways I can help those in our kingdoms who don't have a voice. It'll be harder and require more political dealings and will probably have fewer rewarding payoffs." His look turned dark, and I couldn't help but think that he was imagining what he'd done to Lordling Neeble. "But if that role puts you at risk, I'm hanging up my mask tonight."

My chest tightened, and his love for me flooded toward me on our bond. "You would really do that for *me*?"

Blazing devotion shone in his eyes when he met my gaze. "I would do *anything* for you, my love."

I lay back, and he followed me. His large body pressed into my side.

"Whatever made you become the Dark Raider anyway?" I asked. "You told me once that something specific had set it off. What was it?"

A sad smile lifted his lips. "It was Bastian."

"Your brother?"

He nodded. "Seeing how my father treated him, watching him struggle, and knowing there wasn't a greater life for him"—he paused—"it made me feel hopeless. I couldn't do anything to change that, so I thought of things I *could* change. I may not be able to change the laws as a prince, but someday I'll have more sway as the king, but in the here and now, I could take action if I developed a plan to avenge those who had no voice."

"That's what brought it on?" Of course, now that he'd voiced it, it made sense. Jax loved his brother so fiercely. I could only imagine how gut-wrenching it would have been for him to see his brother mistreated so egregiously season after season.

"But now, I'll find another way." Jax traced his finger along my jaw and down my neck, then kissed me softly.

"You'll really give it all up? Just like that?"

"For you? Yes."

"But what about everyone else in your band? What if they want to continue?"

He shrugged. "I'll ask them, but I highly doubt they will. Several have been having second thoughts about it, especially Phillen, and it was me who was the driving factor behind it to begin with. If I tell them I'm done, my guess is they'll all follow suit."

He kissed me again, and I closed my eyes, savoring his taste and feel. He rumbled in pleasure and kissed along my neck. "My mate. So strong. So fierce. You never cease to amaze me," he murmured. "You twisted fate for me. All because of your love for me."

"And I'd do it all again," I whispered. I arched into him, loving the feel of him after being parted for so long, but I pulled back, placing my hands on his chest. "But what I did isn't to be taken lightly. I learned that much on the Isle of Song." A heartbeat of fear pulsed through me. "And if you're going to change your ways and no longer be the Dark Raider, it's important that I change too. I can never twist fate again. It's incredibly dangerous to do so and could carry lasting effects that I can't foresee. Not to mention, if anyone were to ever find out that I've already done it once, I would be arrested."

His nostrils flared, and his aura rose in agitation, but I pushed on.

"Having the ability to do what I did . . . that's exactly why I was allowed to be enslaved. The amount of power I wield in the Veiled Between, and now being able to command the semelees fully, it's not natural, and it scares fae. It's not unlike how half-breeds are treated. They're punished for just having the potential to be powerful and able to breed faster than siltenites. Imagine the fear fae would have if they *knew* what I'd just done."

A thunderous expression grew on his face, and Jax's aura wrapped around me. "Their fear is *their* problem. The gods gave you that much power for a reason, and anyone who tries to control you because of it, or hurt you, will meet the end of my blade." A glow filled his irises, and his potent protectiveness swirled around me and strummed along our bond.

"That's all good and well, my love, but if the supernatural courts ever found out—"

"They *won't*." He ran his hand down my side, cupping my waist and pulling me closer. "The only fairy who's truly a threat to you is your guardian, and I still have him, which means that I can do what I want with him. But nobody knows that you twisted fate, only you and me, and we'll keep it that way. We tell no one what you did."

"You're not going to tell your friends?"

"No, not even them." He kissed me again, his lips firm and warm. "The less that know, the safer you'll be."

I was breathless by the time he finally pulled back. "What are you going to do with Guardian Alleron?"

He smiled, the look dark, but his eyes gleamed. "Consider it my last act as the Dark Raider."

I held my breath, certain that my guardian's death was coming. But not an ounce of me cared. After all, in my initial reality, I'd killed him myself, and I had yet to regret it.

"Meaning . . ." I said, waiting for him to continue.

Jax ran his hand up my side again, his fingers dancing across my skin. "I'm not going to end him, my love. Death is too easy of a punishment for all that he's done to you."

"Then what are you going to do?"

"That's a very good question." He glanced at the clock. Ten bells were nearly upon us, and night had fully set in. The three moons glowed in the sky, and our galaxy was awash with color.

"I'll talk with the boys about that tonight, and we'll work out a plan." He leaned down and kissed me again. My body thrummed, and he hardened against me, but he still pulled back. "As much as I want to rut with you here and now before I meet with them, you look beyond exhausted, my love. And you've been through so much, more than you should have ever had to deal with. Go to sleep. By tomorrow, this will all be fixed."

Exhaustion claimed me so fully that despite wanting to join Jax and our friends, I hadn't been able to keep my eyes open. A dreamless, heavy sleep had pulled me under all night, but I awoke in the morning to Jax's heavy arm around me.

Soft puffs of his breath filled my ear, and the distant morning bells in the capital filtered quietly through the window.

It was just past seven. I'd slept like a stone, so exhausted from commanding the semelees and the chaos of Jax's arrest and the past six weeks that I'd been dead to the realm.

Stretching, I rose. Or rather, I tried to.

Jax's arm tightened around my waist, his fingers dancing across my skin. I thought he'd been asleep, but his aura strummed higher with every breath.

"Good morning, my love," he whispered in my ear.

"You're awake?"

"I have been for some time. I didn't want to disturb you, but now . . ." A smile entered his voice, and he lifted the hem of my shirt and splayed his palm across my belly. Warmth billowed from his body, and he shifted closer until his broad chest brushed my back.

I snuggled into him, loving the feel of his heat taking the morning chill away. And loving that he was here with me and *safe*. I'd been dreaming of this moment for so long. Aching for it. At times during the previous weeks, I thought it'd never come true.

"Stars, I want to wake up to you every morning," I murmured.

He kissed my neck, then nipped at my skin. Behind me, he hardened, growing thicker and longer with every breath, and I pushed my backside into him. A low growl rumbled his chest. "You will. From now on, this is where you wake. In our bed. With me."

"Where's Guardian Alleron?" I asked quietly, my eyes closed when his hand trailed across my skin, over my hip, and down my thigh. His movements were soft and lulling, yet arousing too.

"He's no longer in the palace."

His hand danced up my side, and a smattering of goosebumps broke out across my skin. "Where did you take him?"

"Away. He's currently without a tongue or fingers, and he's en route to one of the Lochen islands."

I flipped over to face him, my eyes flying open. "*What?*"

Jax smiled lazily at me, his dark hair tousled and his eyes bright despite the early hour. His chest was bare, his tanned skin beautiful and smooth in the morning sunshine. The scar that had once grazed his skin right below his breastbone, from Lordling Neeble's attack, was now so faint it was hard to see. "Quinn's had a few run-ins with the Lochen. He knows some of the more unsavory individuals who inhabit their isles, and he sold your guardian to one of them."

My jaw dropped. "Sold him? Like a slave?"

"Exactly."

"But slavery is outlawed, not only on our continent but the other continents too."

Jax shrugged and tucked a strand of hair behind my ear. "Just because slavery is outlawed doesn't mean that it doesn't occur. Slavery will always exist in the darker parts of society. You just don't see it."

His finger trailed along my jaw, and he tugged me closer. I breathed in his scent. Pine and spice tickled my senses, helping to alleviate some of the panic coursing through me.

"So my former guardian is now a slave?"

Jax dipped his head to kiss my neck. "He is. It's a fitting end for him, don't you think?" His lips trailed along my collarbone, and with his other hand, he worked my shirt free until it was up and over my head. "My Ironcrest magic has kept his voice robbed and will continue to do so. But even if it wore off—or an Ironcrest spellcaster dissolved it like you said happened initially—without a tongue, he'd be hard pressed to talk, and without fingers, he'll be unable to write. Besides, as a slave, nobody will listen to him anyway. Even if he could tell the entire realm that I was the Dark Raider, nobody would believe him."

A shudder ran through me. It was so cruel. So vicious. Yet the fierceness billowing along my mate's bond told me he'd do it all over again. Jax's ruthlessness, especially when it came to protecting those he loved, had no bounds. And even though his dark nature might disturb some, it'd never made me feel anything but safe. It was who he was. Dark and light. Vengeful yet capable of breathtaking kindness. He was my mate, and to me, he was perfect.

"I'll never see him again." I tilted my head back when his mouth returned to my lips.

He kissed me deeply, then pulled back enough to say, "No, my love. He's gone for good."

"And now that King Paevin's dead, Bastian can return home."

Jax's lips found the soft spot on my neck that always caused a stirring to inflame my core. He kissed there, grumbling in pleasure when I gasped. He kissed me again softly, reverently, then nodded.

"Yes, we'll take Bastian home today and take you back to the Isle of Song so you can report the knowledge they require, and then we'll return to Faewood to ensure the other half-breeds are freed. They're still wearing those anklets, although without the king commanding them, I'm unsure what state they'll be in. But once we save them, we'll return here, and then we'll find a way to make my parents accept you."

I wrapped my arms around him, allowing myself to get lost in his touch. In a flurry of magic, all of my clothes were off, and then Jax's hard naked body was atop mine.

And when we began to move together, his hard length filling me in the most perfect way, a flicker of hope burned inside me. Maybe, just maybe, all of this would end up as we'd always hoped it would.

Maybe everything finally, *truly*, would be okay.

## CHAPTER 24

We made love twice before getting up. Still, it was hard to leave the bed. Jax and I had enjoyed so little time together since completing our bond, and given the predatory gleam in his eyes when we finally both rose to get dressed for the day, I had a feeling it wouldn't be long before his magic whisked my clothes off once more.

A delicious ache curled in my lower belly at the thought of him rutting with me again, but I reminded myself we still had so much to do.

I bathed quickly, then went to the wardrobe, which Jax insisted I now call *our* wardrobe, and slipped into a long-sleeved top and simple black leggings.

Jax, dressed in breeches and a tunic, then came up behind me and kissed me on the neck. Hands settling on my hips, he whispered huskily into my ear, "When this is all said and done, mate, I'm locking you in this chambers and fucking you for a week straight."

I shivered, and he nipped at my ear. "Promise?" I whispered.

His fingers dug into me. "Oh yes, mate. That's a promise."

Reluctantly, we both slipped into boots, then Jax retrieved a portal key. The jar that Quinn had produced of the small magical keys was now half empty, and I couldn't help but wonder if he could procure more since they certainly made traveling easier.

My eyebrows rose when Jax clasped my hand. "The others aren't joining us?"

"Not yet. We'll go to the Isle of Song first and then take Bastian home. After that, they'll join us when we go to Faewood."

"I'm so excited for Bastian to finally get back to Anna." A grin bloomed across my face, and knowing that Bastian could finally return to his life made my smile widen even more.

Chuckling, Jax whispered the words to activate the key, and the realm tilted around us. The portal transfer crushed and stretched us in a discombobulating way until our feet landed on solid ground.

The great university loomed in front of us. Salt kissed the air, the sea's breeze whipping around us. Tall swaying grasses swished by my hands, and above, the pale-green sky was filled with stars. This island's strange way of commanding time never ceased to amaze me.

In the nighttime, the building's exterior looked even older than I remembered. Crumbling rock infused with ancient magic waited before us. The heavy throb of it slid over my skin like a ghostly touch.

"You truly spent six weeks here?" Jax asked, gazing down at me.

"The longest six weeks of my life."

His jaw locked, and his guilt bled into our bond. I knew he was thinking again of what we'd discussed last night—that he was no longer going to be the Dark Raider so I would never be put in a position like that again.

I still wasn't sure how I felt about that. I didn't want to rob him of that role, but I also knew it was pointless to argue. Jax had always put my safety first, and I knew that once his mind was made up, it wouldn't change.

Together, we climbed the steps and headed toward the tall, imposing doors. Like the other time I'd been here, they opened automatically. Inside, the familiar pillars and torches waited. I'd spent so much time in this school, and everything looked so familiar.

"Ready?" Jax asked.

I nodded, and hand in hand, we stepped over the threshold and were swept away to Master Fistideeous's chambers.

It all happened so fast, as though we were in the entry

and then in the small chambers in a blink. Despite experiencing transfers like that for weeks on end when I'd stayed here, I still wasn't used to it. So much magic infused this place.

I blinked and acclimated myself to our new surroundings. Pristine books and tomes graced all of the shelves, and standing near the far wall was the four-foot scholar.

"Ah, dear Elowen, you've returned!" The gargoyle swirled on his clawed feet to face us. Dark eyes gazed our way, and his lips lifted in a terrifying smile. "And I see you've brought your mate with you, which means you must have twisted fate after all."

Jax dipped his head. "Indeed. It's nice to see you again."

Master Fistideeous's smile widened. "Likewise, my prince."

Confusion filled me, and I froze in place. "Wait, you remember me?" In our current reality, I'd never met Master Fistideeous before—unlike Jax, who met him months prior when he'd been searching for ways to locate his brother. But since I'd changed the course of our realm, I figured the gargoyle scholar wouldn't know who I was.

Master Fistideeous's smile dimmed. "Unfortunately, no, I don't actually remember you, Elowen. But the ancient magic here told me that a lorafin by your name had been tutored by me and that you were returning today to share what you learned."

Jax and I both glanced at the walls around us. Ancient magic pulsed in this land, and the rock this building was constructed of had stronger magic than I could fully comprehend. The same powerful feel filled the supernatural court's building and other buildings of our realm forged of similar stone.

Whatever the gods and goddesses, who had once walked our realm, had done to these rocks and parcels of land had left a lasting impression that stood the test of time. Their magic was so complex I doubted few could fully comprehend it. If any could.

Shaking off that mesmerizing thought, I rolled my shoulders and approached my former tutor. "You're right. Even though you don't remember me, I certainly remember you, and I'm here to share what I learned by twisting fate."

"Very good. This way." He led me to a low bench at the end of the room and opened a scroll, then nodded toward a crystal sphere. "Place your hand on the sphere. The magic will siphon the knowledge from you."

I did as he said, but unlike the spheres used at the inns and the courts that simply cataloged identifying information, the feel of the magic in his sphere encompassed my thoughts. Power swirled through my mind and took whatever it wished.

Words flowed across the page, and my eyes widened as detail upon detail of my time with the semelees appeared before me. Every single second I'd commanded the fates was documented. It didn't name me, and there was nothing identifying, but in the centuries to come, if a new lorafin was born and walked the land, if she came to the Isle of Song, she too could learn from the history books.

By the time the magic finished, it left me with an unsettled feeling. My mind had literally just been plundered, but it had only taken from my time with the semelees. No more. It was a small price to pay for all that Master Fistideeous had done for me.

Still, I shook the feeling off. It was definitely strange.

"Thank you," I said, when the knowledge-sharing was complete. "If not for you, the prince and I would not be together right now, and a horrible plan that had been brewing on the continent would be taking form."

The scholar's smile stretched wide once more, and he twisted the scroll up and secured it with a leather strap. "I'm glad to hear that I tutored you well and that you were mindful of whatever you changed. And might I say, the pleasure was all mine, even if I can't remember you, and I do thank you for what you've done." He tapped the scroll with one of his claws. "The day may come when another lorafin will need our help, and what you've shared today may be exactly what she seeks."

I leaned down and gave him a kiss, his skin cool and rough like stone, and I could have sworn a blush rose in him when I pulled back.

"We can't thank you enough, Master Fistideeous." Jax bowed toward him.

The gargoyle cleared his throat, hopping from foot to foot, then bowed as well. "I wish you both many moons and stars of happiness to come."

We said our goodbyes, and then magic swirled around us, taking us back to the university's front steps. Both Jax and I gazed upward at the ancient building that had changed both of our lives.

Silently, we said goodbye to it and then used a portal key to whisk us back to the continent.

We returned to Jaggedston to find the others. It wasn't hard. A dillemsill was waiting for us on the windowsill of Jax's suite, letting us know everyone was waiting for us in Bastian's enchanted chambers.

"I can only imagine what they're all up to," Jax said, a smile in his voice as the dillemsill began to spin with magic.

We headed to the third floor of Jax's tower, using the magical lift he'd created within the walls. He let me operate it, so I closed the painting that covered the creation and then told the lift to descend. On the third floor, I tapped the button shining green, which indicated that the coast was clear. The portrait swung open, and the familiar third floor greeted us.

Out of the lift, the carpet made our steps silent as we strode toward the enchanted suite. Jax knocked briskly on the door once, then let himself in.

Bastian looked up from where he was sitting in the seating area. Everyone else was either lounging on the furniture around him or casually standing.

A huge tray of food sat before them, and from the looks of it, all of them were enjoying it.

"I hope those goblets aren't filled with leminai." Jax put his hands on his hips, his voice stern, but a smile tugged at his lips.

"Of course not. What do you take us for?" Trivan replied, lifting his glass. "Drunkards?"

"Bro, I can't get enough of this cheese. Seriously, it's the best." Bastian picked up a thick wedge of it and placed it on a slice of bread before shoving the entire thing into his mouth. Beside him, on the couch, lay a looking glass.

I laughed lightly at the sheer joy emitting from him and had a feeling it was due to the males' company and the fact that he could speak with Anna whenever he wanted. That, and he'd only been in this room for a day. He hadn't been imprisoned for weeks in this reality, with Saramel caring for him while I studied furiously at the Isle of Song.

Chuckling, Jax joined Bastian and the others.

Bowan leaned forward on the chair across from Bastian

and picked up a piece of cheese too, but Bastian swatted his fingers away. "That's my breakfast you're taking."

Bowan grinned and popped the cheese in his mouth. "Yes, it is, and it's quite delicious."

Trivan snickered and also snagged a few pieces from the tray while Lars and Phillen stood near the door. Both held beverages.

Lander and Alec lounged near the wall, and Quinn was nowhere to be seen. One thing I was quickly learning about the crowfy shifter, he came and went readily within the group, and nobody seemed to think anything of it.

Jax dropped down beside his brother and clapped him on the shoulder. "Are you ready to go home?"

Bastian's eyes widened, and his antler rack swung so quickly when he turned his head, that if anyone had been standing closer, they'd likely been knocked over. "Seriously?"

Jax nodded. "King Paevin's dead. He can't hurt you again."

"I get to go home today?" Bastian leaped from the couch, a whoop of joy emitting from him. He did it so quickly that the tray knocked over in front of him, and cheese flew everywhere.

Bowan caught a piece and popped it into his mouth. Lander wasn't so lucky. The tray landed on his head.

Grumbling, he knocked it to the side.

I laughed, unable to help it as Bastian pulled his brother into a fierce hug.

"I take it nobody told you?" Jax said, laughing.

Lander shook his head. "We figured we'd let you surprise him with that."

Bastian was still cheering. "I'm going home? Today? Does Anna know?" He pulled his brother into another hug.

Jax snorted and hugged his brother back just as fast. "Not yet, so you can surprise her if you want."

"Ooh, good idea. I'll surprise her at home." He finally released his brother and glanced around. "When do we go?"

Jax pulled a portal key from his pocket. "Now, if you want."

Bastian grinned, the look so similar to Jax when he was in a good mood that my heart swelled. "Now sounds good."

JAX TOOK Bastian back to the north alone. Even though I wanted to see where he lived and meet Anna, and even though I knew Jax would have loved to spend time with his brother there, too, the fact remained that nobody knew Bastian was the crown prince's brother. Not even the female that Bastian wanted to marry.

Even though Jax and Bastian had been meeting

secretly for full seasons, almost nobody knew that. And the more members from the palace's court who showed up in Bastian's town, the more illusions that Jax had to weave to conceal their arrival. Because of that, Jax oftentimes visited his brother alone.

Until the time came when Jax could declare to the realm that his brother was a half-breed, they would continue the ruse, and I had a feeling that once Jax became king, that would be the first thing he did.

My mate returned less than an hour later, but none of us had been sitting idly in his absence. We'd packed bags of healing potions, food, and saggerwire plants for the half-breeds who we anticipated rescuing.

Jax nodded approvingly at our quick work, and while I knew that he would have loved to spend more time with his brother, the clock was still ticking.

It'd already been a day since the king's death, and who knew what was happening in Leafton or what the guards were doing to the half-breeds. With the chaos of the Centennial Matches beginning—*if* the Matches were still scheduled—Faewood's capital was likely the prime place for nefarious individuals to take whatever enslaved half-breeds they wanted.

We needed to move. Now.

We all stood in the enchanted suite, and Jax pulled out another portal key, then held out his hand to me. The others also stepped forward until we were all locked together.

None of the males wore their black masks or raider clothing. As several of them had explained to me while Jax had been gone, their days as the Dark Raider's band had officially come to an end. As Jax had suspected, they hadn't put up too much of a fight about it. Phillen had even looked relieved, and seeing that had quelled any remaining guilt I'd been harboring at their raider roles coming to an end.

Jax squeezed the portal key between our linked palms and whispered the words to activate it.

In a swirl of magic and potent power, the floor dropped from beneath my feet, and then we were spiraling through the realm in a blink of magic.

WE REAPPEARED outside of the capital, near the wildling trail that would lead us to the caverns. A somber feeling coated the air, and the activity I would have normally expected to see around the distant stadiums and fields was absent.

"Have the Matches been called off?" I smoothed out the top I wore and tucked a few strands of hair behind my ear.

Phillen shook his head. "No, but the Jaggedston

Herald reported this morning that they've been delayed for two weeks, and the Ironcrest Ball has been delayed as well. Everything will still carry on as usual after the king's funeral has concluded and the new monarch takes Faewood's throne. But it's now all running behind."

Trivan grunted and nodded toward one of the stadiums in the distance. A banner hung from it, highlighting which competitions would be taking place on each day. "In all honesty, I'm surprised the palace is still allowing the Centennial Matches at all given the king's death."

"That probably has something to do with his daughter," Lander replied. "They announced this morning that the princess of Faewood will take the throne, and she's known for not giving way to her emotions. In all likelihood, she insisted the Matches continue since the fae of her kingdom have been looking forward to them, and so many competitors have arrived to take part in it."

"Do you think the traditional funeral customs will be upheld, despite the Matches?" I asked.

"From what the Herald said, yes," Phillen replied. "The official mourning period will start tomorrow. It'll last for a week as usual, prior to a monarch's burial. But not all of us will observe that." His jaw locked. "That scum got exactly what he deserved."

"Agreed," Lars remarked.

I nodded, my lips pursing. Death happened, it was

inevitable, but siltenites had long lifespans, so when a king or queen died, it usually shook the entire continent, even if we were glad to be rid of Faewood's king.

"This may work to our advantage," Alec remarked. "Everyone will be readying themselves for the king's funeral, then the princess's succession to the throne, and then the Matches. Nobody's going to be paying any attention to what's going on in the Wood."

Jax nodded. "It will give us more time to document everything too. We won't be rushed." Jax pulled several looking glasses from his pocket.

Last night while I'd been sleeping and the group had been discussing the best way to free the half-breeds, it'd been agreed that it was important to document everything that King Paevin had done.

On the rare chance that anyone tried to further hurt the half-breeds or accuse them of being a part of the king's devious plan—should it ever come to light—documentation would prove that the half-breeds had all been innocent. Especially if anyone tried to accuse them of breeding since such an act was punishable by death.

"Let's get to work." Jax took off down the wildling trail, the rest of us following.

The scent of the Wood wrapped around me, and the familiarity of it breathed life into my soul. A few of my old wildling friends made appearances in the trees and shrubs, and I called greetings to them, but try as I might to find Esopeel, she wasn't one of them.

When we reached the clearing that held the trap door to the caverns below, a pulse of sickly, dark magic tingled against my skin.

"The repulsion spell surrounding this place is obviously still intact." I shuddered. Everything about this part of the Wood made me want to run.

"Push through it," Jax instructed everyone. "Hold your breath if you need to."

We all stepped through the slimy spell that screamed at one's instincts to flee. Once free of it, I breathed easier, but the pulse of its repelling magic still beat against my skin.

Not wasting any time, Phillen dropped to one knee and pushed colorful leaves that had fallen over the trap door out of the way. When the door's small blue handle appeared, he slipped his hand around it and yanked it open.

A stairwell cut into the rock appeared, but despite all of the males being ready to jump into action should any guards be present, the stairway was empty. The fusterill guards who had previously been at the bottom of the staircase were nowhere to be seen.

"Follow me." Magic shimmered around my mate as he descended below. He held a looking glass in front of him, recording everything as he plunged into the caverns.

One by one, we joined him, moving in a single-file line down the stairs, then through the tunnels cut into the damp rock.

Nerves clenched my stomach, but the tunnels were eerily quiet. The only sound that greeted us was the steady *drip drip* of water dropping from the tunnel's ceiling.

We went single file down the winding dark walkways, and I called upon what the semelees had shown me of these caverns, remembering the way. But unlike the first time we'd ventured here, there weren't any illusions covering any tunnels or turns.

"Is the magic already starting to wear off in here?" Bowan asked, cocking his head.

"It's hard to say," Jax replied, still moving forward. "It's possible it needs to be activated each day, and nobody's done that yet this morning."

We finally reached the cavern that Bastian had been kept in. The circular room opened up before us. Eerie silence filled the space. Only a single torch remained lit high above. Like before, chamber doors cut into the rock were all closed and locked. But the dead bodies that we'd left in our wake last time we'd been here had all been removed. Not even blood stains remained. Someone had thoroughly removed all evidence of Bastian's rescue.

Jax nodded toward the door closest to us. "We'll likely have to break through them to make sure nobody's being chained inside. We'll have to check each room and each cell in every tunnel and cavern down here."

Bowan sighed. "This is going to take a while."

Bowan and Trivan broke through the first door while Phillen and Lars set about getting into the second.

I called upon my knowledge of unlocking spells and quickly undid the locking mechanisms upon the rest of the doors. One by one, we opened them and peered inside.

And behind each door, we found half-breeds either lying despondently on the ground or slumped against the walls. Most of them had their eyes open, dazed looks upon their faces, while others appeared to be sleeping.

Rage thrummed from Jax's aura. "It's exactly as we feared. They left them here to die."

"And even worse, the anklets' power is still caging them." I waved toward the rhifilyte gemstones. Just seeing that stone made me want to recoil. For so many summers, I'd been caged too.

Phillen's nostrils flared. "Cowards ran this place. It's appalling that all of the guards have fled."

Jax's lips thinned, and his fury coasted toward me along our bond. "Everyone activate your looking glasses. All of this needs to be documented."

One by one, we did as he said. Looking glass in hand, I crouched by a female's side. Her lips were dry, her skin covered in dust.

And when we checked on the others in this large

cavern, just to ensure each still lived, none of the half-breeds moved or even seemed to know we were there.

"We'll need to move everyone out of the cells and place them in the open areas," Jax said. "Once that's done, we count every single half-breed here."

We all set to work, lifting the half-breeds and grunting under their weight. Similar to how Bastian had been when we'd rescued him, they all remained unresponsive. None of them even blinked when we laid them down on the ground outside their cells.

By the time we were done in this cavern, two dozen half-breeds lay unmoving before us. We used saggerwire plants to hydrate all of them. The water held in the leaf's inner surface allowed us to rehydrate each one with only a drop. Some looked so parched that I had a feeling it'd likely been days since they'd drunk at all.

Panting heavily, I glanced back toward the winding tunnels in the cavern. "There are dozens of other half-breeds down here, along with children. We have to find all of them."

Jax nodded. "We don't finish until we've got everyone."

It took us over a week to free all of the half-breeds within the caverns. There were so many of them, and not enough of us to make their rescue go any faster.

During that time, none of the half-breeds roused, and no guards returned. It soon became apparent they'd truly been left here to die. Even the children.

My heart broke when the kids remained just as catatonic as their parents. Like the adults, the children also wore anklets.

I had no idea which child had found Jax in Possyrose Forest. All of them had glazed eyes that stared up at us, entirely unseeing, and it took everything in me not to begin sobbing every time I saw them.

These children had known nothing but slavery and abuse in their short lives. But I couldn't help but notice that none of them had antlers. None of those already born could have come from Bastian, but we discovered that three of the adult females were pregnant, their bellies round and swollen. I cringed to think what would happen to their infants.

The only comfort I took was knowing that none of these children or adults would remember any of this. Bastian still couldn't recall any of his time locked away under the king's spell, which meant these tiny, innocent souls and the adults who'd bred them would likely not remember anything either.

Still, it didn't make their abuse any less horrific.

The only saving grace about all of it was that Alec had been right about the court's and kingsfae's attention being distracted. So much activity was occurring in Faewood with the king's funeral, the princess's succession, and then the Centennial Matches set to begin, that nobody was paying any attention to the Wood.

It allowed us to come and go each day, only stopping long enough to rest and eat when our aching muscles demanded it.

Dust perpetually coated my skin each night when we left the tunnels, but by the end of the eighth day, we'd discovered every tunnel and cavern, and after I did a quick venture to the Veiled Between, the semelees confirmed that we'd found every enslaved half-breed.

"How long do you think it'll take Saroly to correct all of this?" I asked Jax as we gazed at the tunnel lined with dozens of unconscious half-breeds.

His lips thinned. "As long as it takes." He pulled a portal key from his pocket. "Speaking of which, I think it's time we let Norivun know about all that's gone on. We'll let him decide how this should be handled from here." He turned to his friends. "Stay here and keep feeding and hydrating them. Elowen and I are heading back to the Solis continent."

# CHAPTER 25

Norivun's huge black wings folded behind him as he stood next to us in the underground caverns. His four guards stood behind him, all of them wearing grim expressions. Fury emanated from the Solis's auras.

Norivun's silver eyebrows slanted together. "We can't keep them in these conditions. It could take weeks for Saroly to successfully remove each anklet from them. We'll have to transport them back to Solisarium and keep them there unless you want the entirety of Faewood knowing what's gone on down here?"

I swallowed the ball in my throat, but before I could respond, Jax shook his head. "No, that'll bring up too many questions that we'd rather avoid." He subtly reached for my hand and squeezed it.

As we'd promised each other, nobody, save us, knew that I'd twisted fate. And Jax had already decided that he wouldn't allow any questions to ever be brought my way. Protecting me from any potential fallout was his number one priority, so if it meant concealing what King Paevin had done, then he would.

Norivun nodded. "In that case, we'll mistphase them out, and I'll hire staff to care for them until each anklet can be removed."

"And the children?" I asked, my voice catching. "What's to become of them?"

The Solis royal's voice gentled. "We'll see to them first."

"And when you're done?" Jax asked.

Sandus, one of his guards, stepped forward. "We'll return them to wherever their homes are."

Jax's brow furrowed. "Questions will undoubtably be asked when they return home. Some of them now have children. *Illegal* children. Will you keep me posted on their recoveries? I'll likely have to get involved once they return here, wielding whatever illusions are necessary to conceal their children until they've grown and have learned to hide their immense magic."

"Of course," Norivun replied.

I sighed. Despite Norivun's help relieving a mountain of pressure from my shoulders, Jax was right. This wouldn't be something we could walk away from. We would have to continue working over the seasons to ensure the half-breeds' safety. But one look at everyone around me, and I knew we would take on whatever task was needed to protect all of them.

"Thank you." Jax dipped his head at Norivun and added, "Truly, thank you for helping them. I'm in your debt."

"I'm afraid it's the other way around. We're in *your* debt." Norivun scowled. "It's my duty to clear up this atrocity since my continent's mines grew the gems that are responsible for this, and one of my fae forged the anklets. I shall ensure this is made right."

Jax brought his fist to his chest and bowed. Norivun did the same.

Formalities concluded, Norivun placed his hands on his hips. "You can all be on your way. We'll take it from here."

By the time we returned to Stonewild's palace, King Paevin's funeral processions were over, the new queen had taken her throne, and the entire continent was looking forward to the Centennial Matches finally beginning.

But I couldn't have cared less about all of it. I was exhausted, both mentally and physically, but even though Jax's and my future was still uncertain, we at least had several hurdles behind us even if I hadn't gone to the courts yet to officially plead for my freedom. Thankfully, in this reality, there was no rush to do so. Everyone believed that the crown prince of Stonewild Kingdom was my new guardian since Guardian Alleron had officially been declared missing.

Evening had arrived by the time the portal key transferred us back to Jaggedston. We'd arrived just in time for the evening meal, the first one we would be attending since we'd left the capital over a week ago.

And even though I wasn't looking forward to another tense meal with his parents, I knew that it was necessary. I wasn't going anywhere, and unless the king and queen of Stonewild wanted their son to abdicate, eventually, they would have to accept me.

After a quick bath to scrub away all of the grime that'd accumulated on us in the caverns, hand in hand, Jax and I left his private chambers and took his secret lift to the first floor. Once out of his tower, we strode together toward the dining hall.

"Prince Adarian!"

We turned simultaneously to see several palace guards racing toward us from the front of the palace. "My prince, apologies for interrupting you and your"—the guard's gaze slid my way—"guest, but urgent matters have arisen in your absence."

Jax cocked his head. "They have? I wasn't aware."

The guard twisted his hands. "Yes, I'm sorry, my

prince. Every dillemsill we've sent hasn't been able to reach you."

Jax and I shared a side-eye. That wasn't entirely surprising, given the potent magic surrounding the caverns in Faewood. I doubted any dillemsill was able to see through its dark magic.

"And what's this about?" Jax asked coolly.

The guards shared an uneasy look before the first addressed Jax again. "Authorities from the supernatural courts have been looking for you and . . ." His focus slipped my way again, and a pulse of fear grew on his face.

I frowned, and a swell of uneasiness erupted inside me. "Is something the matter?"

But the guard returned his attention to Jax. "I'm sorry, my prince, but we were instructed to inform you immediately when you returned that you and your guest have been summoned to the supernatural courts."

My stomach dropped.

Jax scowled, and his grip tightened around my hand. "What's the meaning of this?"

"I'm sorry, my prince." The guard bowed. "I am unsure as well. I'm simply passing along the message that we were instructed to tell you."

Jax's jaw ground together. "Message received. You may return to your duties."

The guards both bowed and marched back to the front of the palace.

Jax wheeled on his heel and pulled me with him toward the dining hall.

"Jax, aren't we supposed to—"

"We're not going down to the supernatural courts. You've been through enough."

"But Jax—"

"Elowen"—he stopped and spun toward me—"you've been running yourself into the ground for weeks. *Weeks*, my love. I won't allow it to continue." His voice gentled, and a pulse of his protectiveness surged toward me on our bond. "Come, let's dine, and then we'll return to my tower. I don't want any further stress put on you. You deserve a break. The courts can wait."

A swell of uneasiness still rose in me as I followed my mate toward the double doors ahead. The guards at the dining hall's entrance immediately opened them when Jax strode forward. However, their side-eye when they beheld me wasn't subtle.

My uneasiness surged when we strode into the hall. Scents of mouthwatering food drifted through the air, but the room was surprisingly empty save for another servant who rushed forward.

"My prince! Everyone has been looking for you."

Jax stopped in his tracks, keeping me locked in close to his side. "What now?"

The servant bowed respectfully. "We've all been instructed to alert you immediately that your presence has been requested at the supernatural courts as well as your guest's." His attention drifted my way momentarily before snapping back to Jax's.

Jax growled. "Elowen is my *mate*. You may call her as such, or you may call her by her name. I no longer want her referred to as my guest."

The servant bowed. "I had no idea, of course, my prince. I apologize."

"As for whatever it is the courts want, it can wait until tomorrow."

"Actually, it can't." The king's authoritative tone drifted to my ears.

I spun around to see the king of Stonewild striding into the dining hall behind us. His air was regal, yet his focus had zeroed in on me.

The king stopped before his son, his aura like prickling thorns poking out around him. "Where have you been? You've been gone for over a week. Nobody could find you."

Jax met his father's gaze, unflinching. "I was out."

"Where?"

"Not here."

The king seethed. "I've had enough of your insolence." His gaze slid my way, then returned to Jax. "Your guest has been summoned by the supernatural courts. She's to be taken down there immediately."

Jax stepped in front of me, blocking his father from my view. "Why?"

I peered around Jax's side.

The king narrowed his gaze on his son. "I'm sure they'll tell you when you arrive. And you must go down there. She's been summoned. You can't ignore that, especially since, for over a week, the kingsfae have been prowling around this palace and Jaggedston looking for her. It's becoming an embarrassment to the royal family that we're even associated with this female."

My entire stomach dropped. *Kingsfae are looking for me?*

Jax's nostrils flared, and his jaw muscle ticked. "Elowen is *my mate.* I expect her to be treated with respect."

The king's head whipped back. "Mate?"

"Yes, we're mated."

Color burst across the king's cheeks, and it took me a second to recall in this reality that Jax had never told him that before. "You can't be serious."

"I'm deadly serious, Father."

"That's another matter entirely that will be dealt with." The king's nostrils flared. "But mate or not, she's been summoned. She needs to leave here. Now."

My heart picked up a wild beat. "And you don't know why the courts have summoned me, Your Majesty?"

For the first time, the king looked me directly in the eye, but instead of replying, he sneered. He whirled away, his footsteps tapping on the stone floor. "On your way, Adarian."

The aura around Jax soared. He took a menacing step closer to his father, starting to follow him. "Answer her! Why do they want her?"

The king paused and glanced over his shoulder. Disgust was evident in his tone when he replied, "I don't know, but you best take her down there. Your mother and I are growing weary of your disobedience, and this female's presence has caused nothing but problems. Now, *go*. That's a direct order from your king."

I was trembling like a leaf when Jax and I climbed the steps to the supernatural courts. It was late, the air cool, and the streets were mostly empty, yet I'd never felt the feel of the city closing in on me as much as it was. It felt as if heavy sand pressed into me from all sides. I was drowning. Suffocating. I could barely breathe. It felt so thick.

We went to the same court building I'd been to previously. According to Jax, it was the main court in the city. There were several other smaller courts located within Jaggedston, but this one was the largest of them all.

At the top of the steps, the same assessing wards that had prickled my skin in my initial reality washed over my senses. But their assessment didn't take as long as it had the first time. A stirring in my conscience alerted me to the fact that the wards should have taken longer. In this reality, I'd never been here. They should have held me for as long as they had following my arrest, but they hadn't, and that only happened if . . .

They recognized someone.

My breaths grew shallower. Despite the fact that I'd altered time with my lorafin magic, the wards here still knew me. Just like the university's magic on the Isle of Song had recognized me. And it hit me that the courts' building was constructed of the same, ancient rock—stone that the gods had formed.

It felt like my heart was going to explode from that devastating revelation, but before we could even reach the main doors to enter the courts, the doors sprang open, and a rush of kingsfae erupted from within. Their armor clinked, and their stares were deadly.

Magic rising, Jax immediately positioned himself in front of me. "What's the meaning of this?"

The kingsfae ground to a halt as potent power billowed around them. "Step aside, my prince. This doesn't concern you."

A growl rumbled in his chest. "Like fuck, it doesn't. She's my mate. Why has Elowen been summoned?"

My eyes widened when the kingsfae commander, the same one who'd appeared in the dining hall the night Jax and all of his friends had been arrested, pushed forward to the front of the group.

His gaze settled on me, but there wasn't even a flicker of recognition. He'd obviously never seen me before.

Some of my panic eased, but then I remembered the wards. The courts' wards had known who I was.

"Elowen Emerson?" The commander drew himself up to his full height and looked me square in the eye.

"Yes?" I hated that my voice shook.

His nostrils flared. "You've been summoned to appear before the supernatural courts for breach of unified kingdom law. You will present before a King Justice to hear your charges. You are to follow me immediately."

It felt as though the realm had dropped out from beneath me. I swayed, but Jax caught me before I could fall. His large hands closed around me, his snarl following.

"What in the realm is going on?" A rush of magic barreled out from him. "She's done *nothing* wrong. I demand to know why she's been summoned."

The commander turned his frosty gaze on the prince. "Your mate is being charged with using her lorafin magic illegally. She twisted fate. The ancient wards have spoken, alerting us to this atrocity, and as you may know"—his unwavering glare slid my way—"that is a crime punishable by death."

# CHAPTER 26

The prison's walls closed in around me. Rock. Magic. Suffocating chains. Everywhere I looked was the darkness of my future.

I'd only been here a day, yet already it felt like a lifetime. The King Justice had sent me to the maximum-security prison on the Nolus continent as soon as my charges had been read. He hadn't even listened to me when I tried to tell him I'd twisted fate to protect the realm. That I'd tried to *stop* King Paevin from destroying the kingdoms. That I'd done it to save fae.

Instead, a sneer had marred his lips when I'd spoken so unbecomingly of a recently deceased monarch. Jax had grown so irate of his treatment of me that they'd slapped the magic-stealing cuffs on him to stop him from exacting his power. His cries of rage when I'd been dragged away and forced into a bright jumpsuit still echoed through my ears. At least they hadn't arrested him too. It was the only saving grace.

To make matters even worse, the magic used in the maximum-security prison was the same as the ancient magic surrounding the supernatural courts in Jaggedston and the Isle of Song, and since I couldn't access my magic, I couldn't command the fates again to break me out.

I shook my head and closed my eyes. Everything had happened so fast. *So* fast. All of it felt like a blur.

But one thing I knew. The courts considered me an extreme threat. They wouldn't even allow me to walk freely before my trial. And that was all because the ancient wards had told them what I'd done. It was only the remnant of the gods' magic that had the power to do so.

*Fate has been altered*, their wards had whispered to them . . . and since there was only one lorafin currently alive on the Silten continent, they'd known it was me.

I didn't even know such intricate magic existed before becoming involved with Jax, and it'd all worked against me.

Head pounding, I lay on the simple cot that my cell provided. A hard, scratchy pillow felt like a brick beneath my throbbing skull. Tears threatened to fill my eyes.

I was now contained in the most feared prison of our realm. As if I was a lethal criminal who couldn't be trusted within a normal prison cell. As though I truly was a danger to everyone around me.

"Emerson!" a guard barked from the outside hallway. "Time for your potion."

I blinked the tears back and winced, then brought a hand to my aching temple. *Not again.* They'd forced one down me after being arrested yesterday. The potion had been a sickly sweet concoction and had tasted like poisoned syrup sliding down my throat. Even worse, it had instantly suppressed my magic, and not only that, it'd hidden my mate bond too.

I could no longer feel the threads of magic linking me to Jax. Of everything that had occurred, that was the hardest part of all of this.

But I knew Jax still lived. They'd done nothing to him other than remove him from the premises in Jaggedston, but after that, my awareness of everything got fuzzy, as if the potion had clogged my mind too. I wasn't sure how I'd been transported here, yet I knew it all occurred yesterday since the morning alarm that woke me up today had confirmed the day and time.

The slide of the guard's baton clinked against the bars. He stopped just outside of my cell. The Nolus fairy's hair was nearly as bright as my jumpsuit, pink strands shaved close to his head.

Sparks emitted from his baton, painful *zaps* that would sting a prisoner into catatonic submission if used. I would know. I'd seen a guard using one firsthand on a prisoner several blocks down from me just a few hours ago.

"Up!" The guard rapped his baton on my cell. A *zap* zinged from it.

Groggily, I stood. Cobwebs filled my mind, but I stumbled dutifully to where he stood.

"Turn around, hands behind your back."

"Is that truly necessary? I'm not going to hurt anybody."

"Turn. *Now*." He bared his sharp teeth at me.

Sighing, I complied, as I had so many times in my life.

Once positioned as he wanted, he slipped cuffs around my wrists, securing me completely, then shifted me until I faced him again.

"Mouth open, head back."

I winced when the movement jarred my aching skull, but I parted my lips as instructed. There was no point fighting this. He'd likely call more guards to hold me down if I refused.

He tipped the potion's contents into my mouth, and the syrup was just like yesterday. It was so thick I wanted to gag.

"Swallow. All of it."

Somehow, I forced myself to ingest the sticky liquid. It slid down my throat in a rush, its effects instantaneous. Horrible magic washed through me, suppressing and stifling everything inside me. My lorafin powers, already subdued from the previous potion, disappeared even further, falling down, down, down until I could no longer feel them, access them, *use* them. It was as if my magic had been snuffed out inside me like a blown-out flame.

"Open your mouth."

My head spun, and the realm tilted, but I opened my mouth, and the guard inspected every corner to ensure I'd fully swallowed the magic-suppressing potion.

He grunted and removed the cuffs. "We're done. You may return to your cot."

I toppled toward the bed, barely making it before I fell onto it. Mouth now dry from the potion's after-effects and head still pounding, I turned on my side just as magic reverberated through the walls.

Rock groaned. Stone shifted. Before my eyes, my cell moved as the ancient magic of this impenetrable fortress transported my cell to somewhere else within its bowels. When it finally stopped, the rock grew still.

I closed my eyes, not even wanting to contemplate any of this. For all I knew, I was now on the second floor or perhaps a subterranean floor. Only the guards knew.

Maniacal laughter suddenly burst from down the corridor.

I winced anew and rubbed my temples, but it did little to alleviate the pain.

"This is just great," I grumbled. It seemed I had a new cellmate in this wing. Cackling sounds emitted from whoever else had been moved to this section.

I pulled the thin blanket up and over my head, trying

to drown out the sounds. Drown out my new existence. And drown out the reality that I'd created.

But one tiny part of me felt relief. Jax was still free. So was Phillen. So was Alec. All of the Dark Raider's band remained unimplicated of any crimes. Bastian was also back home, and all of the half-breeds would be healed and returned to where they lived after Norivun forced Saroly to remove their anklets. The king's plan had been abolished. War would never come between the kingdoms because of that. All of that had been accomplished because I twisted fate.

A moment of lightness hit me as I clung to that. Because while my current state was severe, it hadn't been for nothing. Because of my lorafin magic, all of those lives would continue as they'd been. And while I'd never relished nor wanted to go to prison, I grasped onto the fact that my magic hadn't been used in vain.

So many lives had been saved because of me.

"Emerson! You have a visitor."

My head lifted, my neck twinging from the abrupt movement. Crustiness filled my eyelids, and bleary-eyed, I wiped it away.

A guard stood at my door, waiting expectantly.

"Someone's here?" I croaked. I'd lost count of how

many days I'd been imprisoned, but I thought it was close to a week.

"You have an hour. I suggest you get moving."

Somehow, I staggered to my feet and went through the motions required of me to leave my cell. The prison shuddered around me, and I knew the time limit had almost been reached for when the walls would shift again.

Once I was cuffed and had my shoes on, the guard led me down a hall to another secure portion of the wing. He guided me into a small room. It was empty save for a chair.

"Sit there." He pointed at it.

Once I was seated, he chained me to the chair using glowing strands of magic that lassoed around me. I stared at the opaque wall in front of me. "Where am I?"

"Visiting room. Keep your eyes on the wall." The guard shuffled to the corner and stood stoically.

I peered ahead, searching for my visitor, but no one was visible on the other side. "Where—"

The milky wall abruptly shimmered, and my eyes widened when Jax and a female appeared on the other side. Both sat on chairs facing me.

My heart soared. *Jax.* Even sitting, he looked tall and broad. A crisp white button-up shirt covered his top. It looked clean and freshly laundered. Yet his eyes were bloodshot, his midnight hair tousled, and several days' worth of beard grew on his cheeks.

His gaze traveled over my appearance, and his lips

parted. Anguish and a flash of rage twisted his features. His hands fisted, his attention whipping to the side, and he said something rapid-fire to the female beside him.

I felt frantically for our bond. Jax was so close to me. *So close.* Yet, like my magic, our mate bond was too suppressed for me to feel him.

The female sitting beside Jax pursed her lips, and she indicated something to the guard behind them.

Another shimmer of magic, and Jax's voice abruptly filled my cell.

"Elowen? Can you hear me?" His raspy words filled the air around me.

I closed my eyes, and love thrummed steadily in my chest. My mate. My love. Just hearing him was like a soothing balm smeared over a scorched wound. My lips curved as tears threatened to moisten my eyes. "Yes, I hear you."

I opened my eyes just in time to see his jaw lock and a flare of light shining in his irises.

Gods, how I wished I could feel him, touch him. But just looking at him helped calm some of the panic that was perpetually coating my soul in this horrid place.

But my mate looked anything but relieved at seeing me. Veins swelled in his neck, and his fisted hands were shaking.

He inched forward, his gaze skating over me. "Goddess, what have they done to you?" He whipped his attention to the female at his side. "This cannot be allowed. She's *not* a danger to anyone."

The female nodded and leveled her focus on me. "Elowen, my name is Magistrate Fortifine. I've been hired by the prince to represent you during your trial."

My heart throbbed, its beat picking up. "You're my magistrate?"

"Indeed. I've looked over your case, and I agree with the prince. The court's decision to imprison you immediately while awaiting your trial, and at the maximum-security prison across the sea nonetheless, was done hastily without full evidence of all that has occurred. They acted only upon one bit of evidence from the ancient wards, not fully understanding the complexity of your actions. This is an egregious error, which the prince has hired me to correct. And I'm confident once your trial ends, you'll be walking free."

I canted my head. "But the ancient magic alerted them to what I'd done. They know that I—"

"Yes, they know you've twisted fate, correct. That fact cannot be denied." She huffed, and I would have guessed that if I'd been in the same room as her, I would have felt her indignation rising. "But what they don't know is *why* you twisted fate. The prince told me that you tried to explain that to the King Justice, but he wouldn't listen, so I've petitioned the courts to expedite your trial. The prince has brought forth evidence that the appointed Justice who will oversee your trial needs to consider. We'll be returning to the Jaggedston courts by the end of the week." Her sharp eyes coasted over me, taking in every detail of my pathetic state. "You will need to stay as you are until then, but have faith that this will all come right in the end."

My lips parted, and despite feeling like everything was moving in slow motion, I gazed imploringly at Jax. While I wanted to believe that the courts would only find out about King Paevin's plans, I didn't know how much their investigations would uncover if he truly tried to free me. It was possible they would also find out that I'd twisted fate to save the Dark Raider, in which case, we would both be damned.

Jax leaned forward, his eyes locking with mine, and I could have sworn that the intensity of his devotion slid through the wall. "My love, trust me on this. I will not allow you to stay in this prison. Do you hear me? I won't rest until you're free."

I could only nod because I knew when that look entered Jax's eyes, there was no stopping him. No matter what I would say, his mind had been made up. *But at what cost?*

The worried question swirled through my foggy mind because I also knew that Jax would give up everything to save me, just like I would do for him, in which case he'd surrender himself as the Dark Raider if it meant that there was any chance of me walking free.

A WEEK LATER, the magic-killing potion hummed through my system as the guards brought me into the courts for my trial. I'd been transported back to Jaggedston, to the same courts where the ancient wards had alerted the kingsfae to the illegal use of my lorafin power.

Imposing stone walls pressed in around me. I tried to focus and see everything clearly, but I'd been subjected to the magic subduing potion for so many days now that my head felt perpetually coated in shadows.

But my mind was made up. I wanted to trust Jax, but I also wouldn't allow him to surrender himself to save me, so I would lie if needed. Yell. Plead. I would do whatever was necessary to keep him safe.

But I didn't know if it would be enough.

Shuffling in my worn prison shoes, I somehow managed to put one foot in front of the other as two guards flanked me.

My magistrate was already seated behind the table the guards prodded me toward. Jax sat just behind her, in the area where fae from the public were allowed. Beside him sat all of our friends.

Shocked, I realized that they'd *all* come: Lars, Bowan, Lander, Trivan, Alec, Quinn, Phillen, and Saramel. All of them were there. Every single one of them had shown up for me.

And when I spotted two wildlings sitting right next to Saramel, who I initially hadn't seen because Phillen's bulk had been blocking them from view, tears sprang into my eyes. Lillivel and Esopeel were here too.

Love burst through my heart, ripping through the cloud that caged me, as I gazed at the fae in this realm who truly cared about me. Loved me even.

My gaze found Jax again as I shuffled closer to my magistrate.

Jax's hair still looked tousled, as though he'd been running his fingers through it repeatedly for days on end, but his eyes were bright and determined, his demeanor foreboding, and his aura palpable as the guard brought me forward.

"Sit." The guard pulled out a chair beside my magistrate, and I fell onto it.

Jax growled from behind the bench that separated him from me and my magistrate and eyed the guard with a lethal stare.

The guard's throat bobbed, but he kept his head high.

Before I'd even fully settled myself, Jax leaned forward and placed his hand on my shoulder. The contact was like an instant balm to my nerves, and his heat warmed my chilled skin in the thin jumpsuit. That simple touch had my eyes closing and my pounding heart slowing.

Sluggish from so many potions forced into my system, I

turned slightly so I could see him. "Did you invite Lillivel and Esopeel?"

He shook his head. "They reached out to me when they heard what happened to you, but I provided their transport and a place for them to stay in Jaggedston."

Another ray of love wove through my veins, and I dipped my head at my wildling friends. My former attendant, Lillivel, and my cerlikan wilding friend, Esopeel, both gave me signs of encouragement from where they sat, and just as fast, Jax's friends, or rather *our* friends, also leaned forward and offered me words of support.

"We won't let them keep you in that place, lovely," Phillen grunted. "You can count on that."

"It's the last place you deserve to be, Elowen," Bowan added.

"Arseholes, all of them for keeping you in there," Trivan muttered.

"Don't worry, Elowen. We'll ensure you're set free." Lander crossed his arms. "You'll see."

Alec nodded. "We're not giving up until you're out, Elowen."

Quinn and Saramel also murmured words of support and affection, and by the time everyone finished, my eyes were entirely filled with tears.

I glanced back at my mate. Jax's irises shone like glimmering gemstones, and his jaw was tight. Determination radiated from him, and something Bastian had told me once flitted through my mind. *My brother's unstoppable when something's driving him.*

"What do you have planned?" I whispered.

A sly smile lifted his lips just as the Queen Justice and two other judges paraded into the courtroom. He squeezed my shoulder once more before letting go. "You'll see."

# CHAPTER 27

Flowing robes fluttered around the Queen Justice and the two judges that entered the courtroom. They settled themselves behind a long wooden bench. Each judge flanked the Queen Justice, and all of them looked at us expectantly.

My magistrate immediately stood, indicating for me to do the same. The potion still fogged my mind, but I managed to stand without swaying too badly.

The Queen Justice sat stoically behind her bench, her lips pursed and her expression severe. A gong sounded in the corner of the room, and magic reverberated through me. It made my head spin.

"The courts are now in session." She eyed my magistrate and me on one side and then the kingsfae commander and their magistrate on the other. "Elowen Emerson has been charged as a lorafin who twisted fate. This is considered an illegal offense, punishable by death. I shall hear both sides' testimonies today and in the coming week." She glanced at the two judges beside her. "We shall make our decision at the end of the argument and decide upon the extent of Lady Emerson's punishment then." Lips pursing, she focused on my magistrate. "Magistrate Fortifine, you may begin."

The Queen Justice's words penetrated my mind briefly but then disappeared like a scent on the breeze. My mind was so muddled. It took everything in me to simply stay standing without swaying.

My magistrate indicated for me to sit. Sluggishly, I sank onto my seat.

Jax squeezed my shoulder again from behind but let go when the guard gave him a stern look.

Magistrate Fortifine, still standing, smoothed her fitted wool coat and slacks, then clasped her hands behind her back. "Queen Justice, as we all know, Elowen Emerson did indeed twist fate using her lorafin magic. The ancient wards have spoken, and that cannot be denied. In fact, even she doesn't deny it. She never did. She's taken responsibility for her actions, however, the true reason behind such an act has not been fully revealed."

Magistrate Fortifine paused in front of the bench. "We shall be presenting new evidence to the courts that hasn't been previously seen. It will be shocking, appalling, but also enlightening as to why Lady Emerson did what she did. I have full faith that once the courts have learned the extent of what has occurred, and *would have* occurred, had she not twisted fate . . . why, I even go so far as to say the courts will be thanking her."

The Queen Justice's eyes narrowed, and the magistrate and kingsfae commander on the other side leaned together to whisper something to one another.

My magistrate turned to me, her eyes bright and alert while I merely gazed at her, trying to stop her image from blurring. Tired. I was *so* tired, but I forced my eyes to stay open and my head to remain up.

"Prince Adarian is here today as well, as he has evidence to present to the courts of what was occurring within the kingdoms." She held out her hand to Jax. "Queen Justice, may he enter the courtroom?"

The Queen Justice waved her hand. "Proceed."

Jax stood and slipped through the opening near the corner, then strode to my table. He carried a bag at his side, and when he reached my magistrate, he dipped his hand into the bag and pulled out a looking glass.

For the briefest moment, my head cleared. The looking glass he handed to my magistrate was the one he used when we'd saved the half-breeds from Faewood. We'd recorded everything, having agreed that King Paevin's atrocious acts needed to be captured in case the innocent half-breeds were blamed, and it suddenly struck me what Jax had planned.

Magistrate Fortifine swirled back to the judges. "I present to you a looking glass that contains damning information about the now-deceased King Paevin of Faewood Kingdom." She handed it to the court's kingsfae who brought it to the Queen Justice and judges. They studied it before turning it over to a magic wielder.

The magic wielder inspected it further, muttering a few spells in the process, then nodded. "'Tis an authentic looking glass." He handed it back to my magistrate.

"Thank you." Magistrate Fortifine held the looking glass up and whispered a few words to command it. A picture projected above, high in the air so all in the courtroom could see it. An image flashed to life, showing the Wood outside of Faewood's palace and the trapdoor buried in the soil.

The Queen Justice's brow furrowed, and the judges gazed upward, their attention on the image.

"What is it we're looking at?" the Queen Justice asked.

"This is in the Wood, just outside of Leafton." My magistrate waved toward the image that showed everything we were doing in the clearing as though it were happening in real life. "Prince Adarian became aware of unusual activities during his recent trip to the Final Matches in Faewood Kingdom. He, along with his guards, a few House nobles, and Lady Emerson, investigated further and came upon a shocking find."

The looking-glass image changed, showing a lifelike

rendition of us disappearing into the cavern's tunnels, finding the half-breeds, studying the anklets they wore . . . Everything we'd done when we returned to rescue them was shown to the courts.

"Unbeknownst to the other kingdoms, King Paevin was playing a dangerous game. He'd captured half-breeds who had ventured to his kingdom to compete in the Matches and had enslaved them by using magical anklets that controlled their minds." She waved toward the image of the catatonic half-breeds. "The king's plan was to breed the half-breeds he'd captured, harnessing their superior fertility in order to create an army to do his bidding. His ultimate goal was to march upon all of the kingdoms to take control of them." She released the looking glass, but its magic kept it aloft, the images continuing to play.

"Fertility, you say?" One of the judges raised his hand. "But half-breeds are rendered sterile at birth."

"Very true." My magistrate again clasped her hands behind her back. "But as you'll learn in the coming week— when more witnesses are brought forward—King Paevin discovered a way to make them fertile again, all so he could enact his plan. We've learned since King Paevin's death that he was enthralled by what King Novakin had done on the Solis continent. As we all know, centuries ago, the Solis king marched upon all of the territories on the northern continent and united them under his rule. Apparently, and this was confirmed by the new queen of Faewood, King

Paevin had idolized King Novakin because of that, and unfortunately, as we've come to learn since his death, he also had secret ambitions to do the same on our continent."

A hush fell over the courtroom, and the judges all glanced at one another.

The magistrate nodded her head. "You heard me correctly. King Paevin also wanted complete control over our continent. He planned to build his army of superior magical half-breeds and go to war with the kingdoms. He wanted the other thrones to fall so only his remained standing, and it is only because of Lady Emerson"—she pointed at me and paused dramatically—"that his plan was stopped."

The looking glass's images kept playing, showing the days' worth of our activities in a sped-up rate. When the image's from Jax's looking glass ended, he pulled another from his bag, and then another. Each looking glass we'd used during the half-breeds' rescue was surrendered to the court.

It all played out in front of the courtroom, every damning piece of evidence bared for everyone to see of what King Paevin had been doing. Even the opposing kingsfae commander and his magistrate appeared speechless.

Magistrate Fortifine stopped before the judges. "As we all know, looking-glass magic does not allow it to lie or be altered. What you're witnessing is true and occurred not long ago in Faewood Kingdom." My magistrate turned and pointed to me. "Elowen Emerson understood the gravity of the situation. She knew the chances of the king being stopped before many lives were lost was unlikely to occur, so she took matters into her own hands and twisted fate. She *stopped* the king's plan from occurring. That is why she twisted fate, and that is why she should be pardoned of her crimes and set free."

The Queen Justice's eyebrows rose. "Where are these half-breeds now?"

"On the Solis continent," Magistrate Fortifine replied. "It's been learned that the magic controlling the half-breeds originated there and was procured secretly by King Paevin. The Solis royal family is working to remove that magic from all of the half-breeds so they may return home."

The kingsfae commander raised his hand, and the Queen Justice inclined her head. "Yes, Commander?"

"Queen Justice, with the court's permission, the kingsfae would like to dig more into these accusations to uncover exactly what happened. This is all new information to us."

"Of course, Commander. We would expect nothing less, and I'm sure the Faewood kingsfae will also be working to uncover the truth of what's been revealed." The Queen Justice returned her attention to my magistrate. "Now, Magistrate, back to Lady Elowen. Are you telling me she changed fate to have King Paevin murdered upon learning of his crimes?"

My eyes opened wide, and I frantically shook my head.

"Queen Justice, if it pleases you, may Lady Emerson speak for herself?" my magistrate asked.

The justice nodded. "Very well."

I tried to stand, but I swayed and almost fell. Jax caught me just in time, a low growl rumbling in his chest.

"Is she unwell?" the Queen Justice asked my magistrate.

My magistrate's lips pursed. "She's been heavily sedated with magic-suppressing potions since entering the prison system. I dare say her mind is addled right now."

The Queen Justice's nostrils flared. "Yet she's to testify of what she knows?"

"If the courts would allow her daily potions to be halted, I'm sure her mind would be much clearer."

But the Queen Justice shook her head. "Absolutely not. Until this trial is over, she shall remain suppressed for the safety of the entire realm."

Stumbling and with Jax's help, I managed to reach the bench with the three judges. Once standing before them, I peered up at the Queen Justice and the two judges flanking her.

They all gazed down at me, their faces stern masks and hard lines.

"Tell me, Lady Emerson," the Queen Justice began. "Did you command the fates to murder King Paevin?"

I shook my head. "No, Queen Justice, but I did tell the semelees to stop King Paevin's plan to enslave the half-breeds and march his newly formed army on the kingdoms, but I didn't specify how. The semelees decided that path on their own."

The Queen Justice leaned toward the two judges, and they began to whisper. After a few terse exchanges, she straightened. "When her official testimony begins, we shall need Lady Emerson to ingest a truth potion to ensure her statements are honest."

"Another potion?" Jax growled. "Her mind is already entirely fogged."

The Queen Justice snapped her attention to him. "Prince Adarian, while I understand you're next in line to be the king of Stonewild, let me remind you that your presence here is on my terms only. I allowed you to enter this courtroom with your looking glasses as a sign of good faith between the supernatural courts and the crown, based upon your involvement of what's occurred. Don't make me regret that decision."

Jax clamped his mouth shut and didn't say more, but his eyes turned into deadly chips of ice.

"Now," the Queen Justice turned back to my magistrate. "Lady Elowen may return to her seat, and you may finish presenting what you plan to show the court."

# CHAPTER 28

The first day of my trial was a formality more than anything. My magistrate outlined what she planned to reveal to the courts over the duration of my trial, and I learned what witnesses would be called forth and what evidence she planned to submit. Following that, I was taken to a smaller prison than the one I'd been kept in on the Nolus continent. The guards hauled me out immediately, not even allowing me to say goodbye to Jax or my friends.

My new cell was just outside of Jaggedston. It was just as forbidding, but the rock walls didn't shift like they did on the Nolus continent, but the potions continued.

Each day of my trial blurred from one day to the next. My head was perpetually fuzzy. Muddled. And I was so unbearably tired, but I tried my best to focus.

Each witness who my magistrate had found came

forward, one after another. I was vaguely able to understand why my magistrate was presenting them, but it was
too hard to fully comprehend what they were saying.

And when the day finally arrived when it was my turn
to testify, my heart turned into a galloping beast. Because
the courts would not allow me to speak without taking a
truth potion.

"Bring the truth potion." The Queen Justice signaled
the guard, who disappeared back into a room in the court's
corner. He re-emerged a few minutes later carrying a tiny
vial.

"Drink." The Queen Justice made a motion toward
me. "And then we'll get to the bottom of all of this."

Behind me, Jax's aura pulsed steadily around him. The
Queen Justice didn't like him touching me or talking to me,
as she'd made clear on the second day of my trial, so
instead of laying a hand on my shoulder as he'd done the
first day, he instead used his magic to soothe me as best he
could.

Pine and spice wrapped around me, filling my senses
as he projected his aura outward. Warmth from his air
element billowed against my back next, warming my
perpetually cool skin. There was only so much he could do
to help me in the courtroom, but he was constantly doing
something.

The guard stopped beside me and handed me the
small vial.

Reluctantly, I took it, my fingers shaking. I knew that whatever words tumbled from my mouth in the coming hour would be pulled from me as though Jax's commanding Mistvale magic had taken hold.

For the briefest moment, I glanced at Jax behind me, my stomach tumbling, because if the judges asked me to reveal more than just King Paevin's plan . . . if they asked me to tell them what else I'd had the semelees change, the truth potion magic would ensure that I revealed all.

Which would mean that Jax and all of our friends would be damned.

AFTER I DRANK the potion and the necessary time was allotted to have it in full effect, they placed me on a seat to the side of the judges, thankfully allowing me to sit down so I didn't topple over right in front of them. The hard chair pressed into my back, hitting every bump in my spine, but I kept my back rigid.

Jax, Esopeel, Lillivel, and all of my Stonewild friends watched on, their expressions encouraging and their eyes sharp.

My magistrate stood astutely at her table, her no-nonsense persona clouding around her.

"Now, let us begin." The Queen Justice turned in her seat to face me more. "State your full name."

I parted my lips, my mouth still dry from the multiple potions I'd been forced to ingest, but my voice was clear when I replied, "Elowen Emerson of Faewood Kingdom."

"Your age?"

"Twenty-eight summers."

"Your magic?"

"I'm a lorafin."

The Queen Justice canted her head. "And how many times in your life have you commanded the fates?"

The truth potion's magic coursed through me, responding for me before I even knew what I was going to say. "Once."

"And when was that?"

My brow furrowed, and the magic pulled at me, seeking an answer. Yet, I didn't know. "I apologize, Queen Justice, but I've lost track of time. I'm unsure of the exact day that I twisted fate, but it was sometime in the previous month."

Her lips pursed. "And *why* did you command the fates?"

Panic engulfed me, but my mouth opened, the words bubbling up from inside me as though pulled of their own accord, but just as I was about to speak, an arrow of magic struck me.

Commanding Mistvale magic spiraled down my throat, entwining with the truth potion's serum. The magic was so precisely aimed, so perfectly concealed, that nobody in the courtroom blinked. Everyone was entirely unaware of it.

My eyes widened, my foggy mind barely understanding what was happening, but the second I did, my breaths quickened.

Jax sat quietly in the courtroom, his expression masked, his demeanor non-threatening, yet he was wielding his magic so subtly, so *precisely*, that nobody was any the wiser.

His magic wrestled with the truth potion as the truth potion struggled to erupt the words from me.

"I commanded the fates to—" I licked my lips, the truth of wanting to save the Dark Raider trying to break free of me, but Jax's magic continued to subdue the potion. My gaze darted around, but other than the Queen Justice and the judges waiting with expectantly raised eyebrows, nobody was acting unsettled.

Jax's magic heightened. Just a touch more of it entered my system, and the words spilled out of me. "I commanded the fates to stop King Paevin. I commanded them to stop him from marching on the kingdoms and destroying our continent as we know it." I gasped, my head now pounding from the effects of the truth serum warring against Jax's potent magic.

The Queen Justice arched an eyebrow. "Is that the only reason?"

My lips parted, the truth again desperately trying to break free, but Jax's magic engulfed it once more. "Yes."

She leaned back, her brow furrowing. "I see. And why didn't you go to the kingsfae to report what you found? Why did you take matters into your own hands?"

"There wasn't time," I replied readily, and that was close enough to the truth that not even Jax's magic or the potion were needed to supply my answer. "Half-breeds were being bred against their will. Several females were already pregnant, and other children had already been born. The longer King Paevin's plan was continued, the more innocent half-breeds would be targeted. I felt that I needed to act immediately to stop his heinous crimes."

The Queen Justice and the judges shared another veiled look, and several fae watching my trial began talking.

"Silence!" the Queen Justice roared.

Quiet descended in the courtroom once more.

The Queen Justice angled toward me again. "And have you ever considered twisting fate to your own advantage?" She arched an eyebrow. "Have you ever wanted to use your magic to give yourself immense power or to give someone else an advantage, something that they would not have otherwise been privy to had you not altered fate?"

My mouth opened again, the truth potion demanding that I say yes I'd done such a thing for the Dark Raider, that I'd granted his freedom, but my mate's magic again pulsed steadily inside me. "No."

Her eyes widened. For one brief, infinitesimal moment, she looked at me with a flash of guilt.

Even the kingsfae commander and magistrate on the other side shared uneasy looks.

Frowning, the Queen Justice leaned back, a wash of sympathy radiating across her face. Another moment of silence fell over the courtroom, but the Queen Justice straightened, her expression turning shrewd again.

Questions resuming, she didn't relent. She came at me from all angles, digging into my past, asking me more personal questions, commanding me to reveal every intrusive detail about myself.

Yet each time the truth potion demanded me to reveal anything that might implicate Jax as the Dark Raider or something that would hurt Bastian or our friends, Jax's magic saved me from responding.

However, as her questioning wore on, Jax's magic was needed less and less. Most of her questions became more focused on my character, as though she thoroughly wanted to understand my motivations and nothing more.

It seemed the Queen Justice was more interested in learning about my risk to others versus trying to uncover details about the king's malicious plan.

And by the time her questioning finished and the truth potion began to wear off, she at last stopped.

"I believe that's enough for today. We shall adjourn and begin questioning again tomorrow."

My trial continued for the rest of the week. Each day, the prison system continued to force the magic-suppressing potion down my throat, and my head was constantly swimming, so much so that I could barely walk, let alone fully understand all that was happening.

Yet, as my trial wore on, my surprise and love for my mate grew. Fae were brought in to testify on my behalf. Fae who only Jax could have told my magistrate about. Lillivel, Esopeel, Saramel, and even my former Emerson Estate guards were all called to stand witness to my character.

When Mushil was brought into the courtroom, I nearly wept. He looked healthy and whole, his walk smooth and even. And when he sat before the judges, he turned kind eyes on me and told the entire courtroom of the horrific abuse I'd suffered my entire life under Guardian Alleron's care. And he further revealed that despite that upbringing, my demeanor remained kind and true. He testified that I was a rare fairy who the realm did not need to fear despite my immense magic.

But it was the last fairy to testify who truly seemed to capture everyone's attention. When Norivun walked into the courtroom, every fairy in attendance took notice. The Solis royal's huge black wings folded behind him, and his demeanor was as commanding and icy as his northern realm.

Norivun even ingested a truth potion as a sign of good faith before telling the courts of how the prince and I had uncovered what King Paevin had done with the gems mined from his continent. He further explained how it was the prince and me who'd worked tirelessly to ensure all of the half-breeds King Paevin had egregiously used be returned to their normal state of mind.

And he then went on to explain that a similar gem had been used to control me throughout my lifetime. That I'd worn a collar, like a slave, and that my guardian—who the courts had appointed to own me—had viciously used that gem's control over me only to benefit himself.

Gasps had emitted from the crowd when that knowledge was shared.

Yet, despite all of that, Norivun testified that he'd never seen anything but me wanting to do good in the realm. That, despite all of the suffering I'd been subjected to in my lifetime, I still wanted what was best for others.

And even when the opposing magistrate and kingsfae commander had their turn to argue their side, it wasn't lost on me that they didn't seem enthralled with the idea of imprisoning me. Magistrate Fortifine's case had been too strong, too convincing,

At last, as the trial came to a close and the Queen Justice had me stand before her, she handed down her sentence.

"Elowen Emerson, lorafin of Faewood Kingdom, the supernatural courts have ruled that you are not a danger to the realm. They have further ruled that you enacted your lorafin magic to twist fate as a way to save the realm from further misgivings." She banged the gong near her bench. "Your charges have been dropped, and you are free to go, Lady Emerson, but let me remind you, should you use your lorafin magic to twist fate again, without the permission of the courts, you run the risk of being imprisoned once more. Do I make myself clear?"

Tears filled my eyes, and an explosion of satisfaction burst from Jax's aura.

I dipped my head and nodded emphatically. "Yes, Queen Justice. I understand, and I can assure you that I will never twist fate again."

# CHAPTER 29

The bright sunlight hit my face when I walked free from the supernatural courts. Jax brushed against my side, his presence heavy and pulsing with magic. I paused, standing on the top of the wide stone steps as the hustle of Jagged-ston filled the view in front of me. The potions still clogged my mind, dulling my senses and suppressing my magic, but as I inhaled the fresh afternoon air, for the first time in weeks, fear didn't grip me.

My mate looped an arm around my waist, drawing me close. I'd been allowed to change out of the hideous Nolus jumpsuit into my own clothes again. And despite the potions' nauseating effects, that simple act helped to ground me further.

All of our friends followed us out onto the steps too, including Esopeel and Lillivel. Smiles broke across every-one's faces, and they all rushed forward to hug me.

"It's good to see you free at last," Phillen said quietly. "I'll never forget what you—" But he swallowed his words that were thick with emotion.

I met his eye and nodded. I knew what the guard was referring to. Because of what I'd done, not only was Jax still free, but all of them were too. Since the fact that I'd twisted fate had come to light, Jax had told his band everything about what had occurred in the initial reality I'd saved us from. Phillen knew he was to be hanged and that his son would have grown up without a da.

"No words need to be said," I replied.

Phillen bowed, Lars doing the same, and the rest of our friends followed, each and every one of them bowing to me, and that simple act portrayed so much more than any declaration.

Lillivel and Esopeel both rushed forward after my Stonewild friends moved out of the way, and I bent down to hug Lillivel and then take Esopeel's tiny palm in my hand. "I cannot believe you both stayed for the entirety of my trial. I shall always remember that kindness."

"Oh, Elowen, I'm just so pleased to see you free and happy." Lillivel hugged me again, and I realized she truly was my friend, and she cared for me even though she'd been paid to be my attendant.

Pulling back, I gazed down at the small cerlikan. "And, Esopeel, you actually left the Wood to be here."

She shrugged her furry shoulders. "It was a small price

to pay for all that you've done for us. Finally, the caverns in the Wood have been wiped clean of that horrible dark magic and returned to normal once again. And the half-breeds you saved . . ." She sighed. "The realm should be thanking you."

We all embraced again, and I spoke to them for a few more minutes, but when I began to sway from fatigue, Jax helped me stand, and I finally said my goodbyes.

"Don't forget to visit every time you're in Faewood!" my wildling friends called.

I waved one last time. "I will, I promise."

With my goodbyes complete, Jax kept his arm locked around my waist. "Let's get you home."

He flicked his fingers toward an attendant, who summoned an enchanted carpet, and when we were finally seated upon it, my mate enacted his right as a royal and commanded the carpet to rise high in the sky, drifting over the buildings and homes as we sailed clear over all of Jaggedston. The pale-green sky shone above, and intermittent pastel clouds dotted the horizon.

The ten Houses north of the city came into view, the glittering Adriastic Sea to our right, and the palace dark and foreboding off to our left, standing taller than any building in the capital.

My stomach twisted slightly as the palace grew closer. Trying to veer my mind away from what lay ahead, I asked, "How's Bastian doing?"

Jax's crashing blue eyes met mine, and his fingers curled around my hip. "He's well. He wanted to be here, but we all decided it was best that he wait to see you until after your trial."

I nodded, knowing that for all of us to be seen together in public would require many things to change first. Changes that likely wouldn't occur until Jax took the throne.

"And is Bastian back with Anna?" I asked as the others spoke quietly behind us, and the palace grew closer with each second.

Jax nodded. "He's not only back with Anna, but he's back to work and back to his everyday life." A look of regret cleaved his face. "He so wished he could have been down here for your trial. He asked me multiple times to convey his apologies."

I gave him a sad smile, and while I knew that we'd done so much to help our continent and all of the fae on it, laws were still in place that didn't protect everyone.

"And the enslaved half-breeds? What's the latest update on them?"

"Saroly has removed anklets from most of them. Those half-breeds have been returned to their homes. Norivun thinks she'll have the rest removed as well in the coming weeks."

"Do the authorities know about their illegal children?"

Jax's expression turned grim. "They do, but given what

was revealed in your trial, at least the courts understand why those children exist. Still, I'm not taking any chances. I've hired magistrates to represent all of those who birthed children."

I sighed heavily. "I shall pray each night that none of them are executed."

A moment of silence passed over us as I thought of all of the half-breeds on our continent and what they still endured. "Do you think you'll ever be able to acknowledge Bastian as your true brother for the entire realm to know?"

The wind brushed against Jax's face, pushing a lock of hair into his eyes. He feathered it back and shook his head. "While my father sits on the throne? No. But one day, when the crown has passed to me, I plan to let the entire realm know that my brother is a half-breed, and a powerful one at that."

A smile spread across my face, and my love for Jax magnified a thousand times over. "And your role as the Dark Raider? Is it truly over?"

He folded his hands together and nodded solemnly. "Fully over. I'd already made up my mind that I was done, but after seeing what you've gone through while being imprisoned, on top of what you went through the six weeks prior to that on the Isle of Song . . ." A sharp rise of his aura pounded out of him. "I will never do anything that could put you in such a position again."

I squeezed Jax, and his long fingers closed over mine. "I

would do it all again in a heartbeat, you know. Even if it meant I ended up back in that prison again. I meant it when I told the Queen Justice that I have no plans to twist fate again, but if I had to go back in time, if I had to do what I've already done all over again, I would still command the fates. You all have to know that I could never allow you to hang when all you've tried to do is make our realm a better place."

"Which is why you'll never be forced into that position again." The finality of Jax's words carried on the breeze, and I knew that he meant every word of it. "We'll find another way to help those less fortunate. The days of the Dark Raider are over."

A slight throb came from my temples. I rubbed my head, and Jax's brow furrowed. "Are you all right?"

"It's just the potions. They haven't fully worn off yet."

He growled slightly and moved his hand to my lower back, then rubbed me up and down in soothing motions. "What do you need right now?" Warmth from his palm seared through my clothing.

"Just you."

My words brought a devastating smile to his lips.

We passed over the final buildings just south of the palace and glided over its mighty black gates toward the large open courtyard beyond. The gates' guards watched us, bowing when the crown prince passed over them.

The carpet sailed downward, stopping just shy of the

palace's main steps. Jax helped me off, steadying me when my body swayed.

"I'm taking you to my tower. And please, my love, allow me this one courtesy."

Before I could ask what he meant, Jax swept me off my feet and bounded up the steps two at a time. I squealed, and all of our friends laughed as they departed the carpet.

The guards standing at the main doors opened them in a flourish, and then Jax and I were back inside, within the Stonewild palace once more.

It was as we'd always planned. Somehow, things were once again on track. We saved Bastian, I commanded the fates and got away with it, we stopped King Paevin, and we freed the half-breeds. Yet despite all of that, one niggling detail remained that neither Jax nor I had acknowledged.

He was still the crown prince whose parents required he be married to another royal or noble.

And I would never be that female.

# CHAPTER 30

Jax pushed open the doors to his private suite at the top of the west tower. I took in the large circular room, huge bed, plush furnishings, and sweeping views. A moment of disbelief filled me that I was back in his chambers.

"I never thought I would be here again," I whispered.

A pulse throbbed from Jax's aura, and his arms tightened around me. "This is your home now, Elowen. This will always be your home as long as I take breaths and my heart still beats."

He strode toward the bathing chamber and didn't stop until he reached the tub. "A bath, I'm assuming?"

I glanced down at the huge tub that was perched by the window. In the distance, the Adriastic Sea glistened, and this high up, it felt as if I could see the entire realm.

"A bath would be perfect." I'd never been allowed to bathe while I'd been imprisoned. Most inmates had probably used self-cleansing, but with my magic so suppressed, I hadn't even been able to manage that. "Stars Above, I must stink."

His lips curved. "You don't smell fresh, I will admit that."

I slugged him lightly in the shoulder but couldn't help my smile. "Be careful, or I might choose to begin living this way."

He nuzzled my neck. "I'll take you stinky, fresh, dirty, or clean. Just as long as you're with me."

My heart fluttered at his tender words.

He set me down, then got to work filling the tub, adding a soothing elixir, summoning food, and grabbing fresh towels. Even when I tried to help, he stopped me. "No. Let me do this for you."

It was only as I was about to undress, and he placed a tray of food on a small table near the tub, that I saw his hands were shaking.

I reached for him. The bond inside me was slowly coming alive again, tugging and commanding. "Jax? What is it?"

He turned, pulling me into such a fierce embrace I could hardly breathe. He held me, buried against his chest as his arms were like steel enclosed around me. Leaning down, he settled his face in the crook of my neck. "I almost lost you."

Fear tumbled from his aura, and for the first time, some

of the fog parted in my mind, allowing me to see, truly *see*, what state he was in. His hair was unkempt, his clothes wrinkled, and a beard graced his cheeks.

"Jax," I whispered achingly. I ran a hand over his face. Coarse hair met my fingertips. "My Gods, my love, I'm so sorry."

"What for? It is *I* who should be apologizing."

"No." I pressed my fingers to his lips. "It wasn't only me who's been suffering, and I'm only just seeing that. I'm so sorry."

So much had been at stake during the past few weeks, but while I'd been nearly comatose from the potions forced upon me, he hadn't. He'd been living free and alone, thinking that I might never leave that prison.

I could *feel* his fear. It tingled in his aura, even though he was trying to hide it.

"I'm here," I whispered. "I'll always be here with you." I slowly began to undress him.

"What are you doing?"

"You're joining me. I think we both need this bath and food."

He gently clasped my hands. "No, I want to care for you. I must—"

I again stopped him with my fingers pressed to his lips. "And *I* must care for *you*. I want to do this for you as much as you want to do it for me." A throb came inside me, our bond warming and growing with him so near. I gasped and placed a hand on my stomach. It was the first time in weeks that I'd felt our mate bond, and galaxy and stars, had I missed it. "'Tis not only you who feels the need to care for the other."

His throat bobbed, and I continued undressing him. Inch by inch of perfect golden skin was revealed with every layer of clothing that fell. Naked before me, his gaze turned heated. My clothes were soon peeled off and my hair unbound.

Together, we stepped into the tub, now filled with steaming water that smelled faintly of jasmine. He lathered a cloth, filling it with soapy suds, then washed me head to toe. He did it so gently, so reverently, and with each pass of his hands, his love beat toward me.

Memories of the first bath I'd taken in this palace came back to me. The bath I'd had after doing Jax's calling to find Bastian. Like then, Jax's hands were just as gentle, just as tender.

My heart swelled under his strong yet soothing touch, and when he finished, I took the cloth and did the same to him. My hands traveled over his broad shoulders, defined chest, and chiseled limbs. With every swipe of my fingers upon his skin, he shuddered, and the need in his aura grew.

The fog in my mind cleared even more as the potions' potent effects faded, and for the first time in weeks, a tingle of my magic glowed inside me.

"It's coming back." I dropped a hand to my stomach,

near my shadow mark that signified I was a lorafin. "I can feel a tiny bit of my magic."

Jax's eyes grew hooded, and he pulled me closer until I sat on his lap. I straddled him, my legs parting automatically.

He pulled a piece of food off the tray sitting by the tub and fed me. Piece after piece he placed into my mouth, watching my lips close over them and feeling the swipe of my tongue against his fingertips.

Longing curled in my lower belly, and lust grew on his expression, stronger and more heated with every scrape of my teeth. And with each morsel that I swallowed, his aura swelled and grew, pulsing with want and *hunger*.

"Let me love you," he whispered. "I need to feel you, hold you, rut with you—" His throat bobbed.

I slanted my mouth over his, and an answering pulse of desire shot through my core. He was already rock hard beneath me. Water lapped against my waist, and his hands, still slick with soap, trailed over me, sliding along my skin, cupping my backside, and palming my breasts.

Our kiss turned frantic and raw. His hands fisted in my hair, a groan coming from deep in his throat. He lifted and lowered me onto his length, and I sucked in a breath as the perfect feel of him began to fill me.

He slid inside me, inch by inch, filling me completely, and then hissed when I was fully seated atop him.

"I can't live without you." His voice was hoarse, his eyes glowing when I pulled back just enough to see them.

"You don't have to."

And as we made love in the bath, the water lapping around us, I only hoped that somehow, we could make that declaration come true.

I AWOKE FROM A LONG NAP, happy and content after several restful hours of slumber. Jax lay beside me, awake and stretched out as he watched me. Dark hair fell over his forehead, and smoothly shaven cheeks brushed against me when he dipped down to kiss me awake. Outside, the capital's bells began to toll.

A smile curved my lips. "You shaved."

He rubbed a cheek. "It was about time. I grew neglectful while you were away."

"What time is it?" I asked sleepily.

"It's almost time for the evening meal. But we don't need to go down. We can stay up here and have food delivered."

"No." I shook my head, my head clearing more. "I want to go. I refuse to let your parents chase me away. Not even time in prison can do that."

A fierce flare of pride shone in his eyes, and together we got up and dressed.

Similar to the navy gown I wore the last time I'd donned such garments, the new blood-red dress that hugged my frame was light and airy. Movement was easy, and the material was soft. I felt like a queen in the stunning deep-crimson gown that was encrusted with jewels and sewn with sparkling thread.

Like me, Jax wore a top of dark red. Both of us had forsaken Stonewild colors tonight, perhaps in solidarity with one another. Or perhaps not. But we'd both been drawn to the bold color when we'd chosen our formal clothing.

Jax held my hand when we walked down the hall toward the dining chambers. Two servants lined the doors ahead of us, and din from the preparations in the great room carried through the doors toward us.

"Do your parents know I'm here?" I asked quietly.

"I'm sure they've heard by now."

I gripped my mate's hand tightly. The potions had completely worn off, and the bath, food, and long nap had helped immensely. My magic was once again fully awake inside me, and for the first time in weeks, I felt like myself.

The doors drew nearer. "Do you think they'll try to kick me out? Or just make me sit at the end of the table again?"

"They won't be doing either," he all but snarled.

"But they could."

His hand tightened around mine. "Then they'll be kicking me out too. If you go, I go."

A fierce resolve had formed around Jax, as though he would move a mountain, slay the stars, capture the moons . . . I'd seen him determined before, but nothing like this.

As though sensing the prince's malevolent magic swirling around him, the servants opened the main doors with a flourish, stepping back as we neared, and we strode inside.

Similar to the last meal I'd had here, the dining hall was overflowing with nobles as the king and queen sat at the head of the table.

All conversation stopped when we appeared in their line of sight.

The king sighed, his expression morphing into irritation.

The queen's nostrils flared. "Adarian? What's the meaning of this?"

I ground to a halt when the queen's sharp words pierced my ears.

But Jax merely ushered me toward a seat near the head of the table. He pulled the chair out, and even though everyone's gaze prickled over my skin like stinging needles, I sat.

"Adarian," the king boomed. "Answer your mother."

Jax turned his frosty gaze on them both. "I'm unsure

why you're making a fuss. I'm simply sitting down for supper with my *mate*."

The king's cheeks turned ruddy, and the queen gasped.

"But she was . . . arrested!" Queen Rashelle hissed under her breath.

"And now she's not," Jax replied calmly.

I pressed my lips together. Even knowing I needed to win them over, a laugh threatened to bubble out of me at Jax's wry response.

Steaming plates of food sat on the tables near the wall, and the servants waiting to begin the service gave one another side-eyes.

With a growl, the king barked to them, "Begin."

In a flourish, the servants set to work, and our plates were filled with food, and our goblets poured full of drink. Everyone began to eat, but you could have cut the tension with a knife. Automatically, I cut into the roast in front of me even though my stomach was roiling.

A sneer came from my side.

Lady Aerobelle sat two seats down. "That's the wrong fork."

I glanced Jax's way to see that he'd picked up the fork near the end of his silverware, not the second one in like I had. Etiquette lessons my guardian had insisted on had taught me what silverware to use, but even though I felt better, I was still tired. I'd simply grabbed a fork, not bothering to check which one it was.

Despite Aerobelle's snub, I didn't change what fork I held. "Is it?" I raised my eyebrows and speared another piece of meat. "Thank you for that fascinating lesson, Lady Aerobelle."

Lady Aerobelle harrumphed and said something under her breath to another female at her side. Both began to laugh.

I rolled my eyes but refused to cower. After all, it was *silverware*. I'd literally just stopped a king from marching upon the continent. I'd prevented a literal war. The last thing I was going to stress over was a fork.

But my mate was another story. A low snarl came from Jax, directed entirely at Aerobelle. "Truly, Aerobelle, have you never learned any manners? Or anything truly interesting to say? Considering your comments are reserved for silverware, apparently not."

Her eyes widened, and Bowan and Trivan, seated across the massive table from us, both laughed openly.

Lander's mouth slanted in a smile, and he lifted his glass. "I toast to Lady Aerobelle's continued etiquette classes. Apparently, she never mastered them."

Aerobelle's mouth fell open, and her parents, who were seated near her, puffed up with indignation.

"Prince Adarian," her father huffed. "My daughter has been thoroughly—"

"Thoroughly rude?" Jax cocked an eyebrow. "Yes, you're right. She has been. And unless she learns to treat my mate with more respect, then she has no place at this table." Ice lined his words. "And that goes for anyone else who cares to insult Elowen." His gaze cut to the female Aerobelle had been tittering with.

The female slunk so low in her seat that it was a miracle her head was still above the table.

Lady Aerobelle's mouth opened, then closed. Tears sprang forth in her eyes, and I couldn't help but wonder if it was the first time the prince had ever insulted a female so blatantly.

"My prince, I was just—"

"About to apologize?" Jax's question was said so low but was filled with so much menace that she paled. "I certainly hope that's what you were about to say, Lady Aerobelle. If not, the door's right there." He used his fork to point toward the hall.

Lady Aerobelle's cheeks reddened. She stood, her chair scraping against the stone floor. Huffing, she threw her napkin onto the table and stormed from the room.

Her parents gaped, and her mother stood and scurried after her.

I sat speechless. The fierceness Jax had just exuded was simmering all around him.

"Does anyone else care to insult my mate?" His voice

carried through the hall, and even the king and queen appeared to be at a loss for words.

I couldn't help but wonder if Jax had ever acted this brazenly, this *hostilely*, before.

"No?" The crown prince lifted his wine glass. "In that case, solls."

A few of the nobles automatically clinked glasses, wariness coating their expressions, but across the table, Alec, Bowan, Lander, and Trivan all smirked.

"Adarian," the queen called, then cleared her throat. A flush had worked up her neck, and I had a feeling she was two seconds away from throwing me out. Or maybe not. For the first time, she was watching her son with a mixture of hesitation and wariness. "We were all just chatting about the Ironcrest Ball before you arrived. It's next week, as I'm sure you remember. We shall be leaving soon for it, so the coming days will be busy." The queen sipped from her goblet, her gaze darting to me. "Quite busy, my darling."

For the first time, some of her haughtiness evaporated, yet I had a feeling that had less to do with me and more to do with the swirling cyclone seated at my side.

Jax tapped his fingers against his wine glass. "I haven't forgotten, Mother. And in case you're unaware, Elowen will be joining us for that trip."

The king sighed heavily and tossed his napkin onto the table. "Adarian, a word if you would." He pushed to standing and strode from the hall, not looking back to see if his son was joining him.

Jax's nostrils flared, but he dutifully stood, then lowered to kiss me on the neck. "I'm sorry, my love. I'll be back shortly. If anyone tries to make you leave . . ." He shot a look at his four friends across the table.

Bowan and Alec lifted their glasses, and Trivan's eyes danced with mischief. Even Lander looked ready for a fight.

I inclined my head, and my mate bond hummed. "I'll stay put."

Jax followed his father out of the dining hall, leaving me alone with the others. Conversation quickly erupted, nervous words and awkward mutterings from the other nobles and guests dining with their sovereign tonight.

I forced myself to eat, and even though I refused to leave Jax's side, no matter what was to come, I couldn't help but wonder if every night would be this hostile.

I certainly hoped not.

A presence suddenly penetrated my senses, and before I could glance toward it, the queen was sliding into Jax's chair.

Her large gown ruffled around her, brushing against my thigh.

Everyone else carried on talking, nobody commenting that the queen had just left her place at the head of the table to sit near a commoner.

I took a sip of wine and kept my chin up. "Good evening, Your Majesty."

"Elowen, is it?" A smile danced on her lips, but it didn't reach her eyes. Her expression, as sharp as glass, assessed me. "I can see that my son is very enamored with you."

"He is. He's my mate. So with all due respect, of course he's enamored with me, my queen."

Her smile tightened, tiny lines forming around the forced expression. "Even so, I thought perhaps we should talk, female to female. Surely, that's not too much to ask. Is it?"

"No, of course not."

"Come." She stood and waited for me to join her.

I shot a look at Bowan, Lander, Trivan, and Alec across the table. They all watched me. Bowan made a move as though he was going to stand to follow us, but I shook my head.

The queen led me from the dining hall, and it wasn't lost on me that she exited the room from across where Jax and the king had departed.

Once alone in the hall, away from prying eyes, she walked languidly, her hands clasped behind her back.

"You and my son are in love."

I kept pace at her side. "Yes, we are."

She laughed, the sound filled with scorn. "Love isn't what's needed to run a kingdom."

I had no response to that, so I kept my lips pressed together.

"And love, even to one's mate, can cause a plethora of problems. Surely, you understand, as a female of the realm, that sometimes we have to do things for others and not for ourselves."

My feet ground to a halt. "Your Majesty, I just spent several weeks in the prison system due to helping others, so please, don't lecture me on such matters. I've spent my entire life serving others."

Her lips pursed. "Ah, yes. You were a slave. Entrusted to your guardian because you're a lorafin." She eyed me and continued walking. I was forced to follow or be left behind. "Your magic is quite potent, I will give you that. I can sense it, simmering just beneath your skin, and your aura is quite powerful. Perhaps that's why my son is so taken with you. He does love a challenge, and I have no doubt you've been exactly that."

"I'm more than just a challenge, my queen. Your son and I were meant for one another. The gods declared it so by creating the mate bond between us. I'm sorry that's not what you or the king wanted, but Adarian and I plan to be together, with or without your consent, but in all honesty, I have no desire to fight you. And I do hope that perhaps you'll grow to accept me one day."

She stopped and faced me again. Piercing blue eyes stared at me, so much like Jax's that for a moment, I could only stare. We were around the corner now, away from the dining hall and the servants' prying eyes who stood outside of it. "Ah, the mate bond. Of course. How silly of me not to discuss it more. And despite what you've just claimed, about refusing to leave my son's side, it's brought up a very interesting question. May I ask you something?"

I inclined my head.

"Is a mate bond worth strife throughout a kingdom? Is your love for my son so selfish that you would put your own desires above all others?"

My brow furrowed. "Of course not, but we're not hurting anyone by being together."

Her gaze sharpened, and she stepped closer to me. "You're not? Do you know what will happen if Jax doesn't marry a female of his standing?"

When I didn't reply, the queen clucked her tongue.

"No, you don't know, because you know nothing of what it's like to rule a kingdom or what's required to keep the ten Houses in line, or what's needed to appease those Houses who've made alliances with neighboring kingdoms. You know nothing of the politics that ensures peace remains and prosperity continues. You know none of this because you're not one of us."

Each word from her was like a blow to my heart. Every. Single. One. But I squared my shoulders and didn't back down. "Yet, it was *me* who stopped a king from creating a war throughout our continent. Doesn't that deserve some kind of respect?"

She laughed lightly. "Ah, the charges that were brought against you that you somehow managed to wheedle your way out of." Her smile turned razor-sharp. "And is that how you'll solve issues as they arise? By visiting the Veiled Between and altering fate every time something doesn't go your way?"

My head snapped back as though she'd slapped me. "No, of course not."

"That's good. We wouldn't want a heretic sitting on the throne who flaunts the laws of our land in everyone's faces, now would we?"

A flush worked across my neck, yet despite the rage building inside me, I kept my voice calm. "My queen, I can see that you're doing everything in your power to disrespect me and try to scare me away, so I'll say this once. I won't let you."

Her eyes widened.

"And to answer your concerns that I cannot possibly lead because I'm not royal, or that a union between Adarian and I could never work because of the ten Houses . . . I disagree. The Houses may be angry that one of their daughters wasn't chosen, but that doesn't mean they can't be appeased in other ways, and I can learn to lead. I'm educated, willing, and determined to do what's best for Stonewild. And I love your son more than any other ever could. He and I will rule together, side by side, doing what's best for our kingdom. And I can assure you, every decision *I* ever make will be to benefit Stonewild. I promise you that. So, whether you choose to accept me is up to you, but I'm telling you this now, I'm *not* going anywhere."

For a moment, she just stared at me, her gaze as consuming as her son's.

She shook her head and laughed softly, yet the sound wasn't scorning. It was more . . . pitying.

She sighed and laid a hand over mine. Her palm was smooth, warm, and soft. It was the hand of a female who'd been doted on her entire life and had never needed to lift a finger to obtain what was needed. Unlike Jax, whose hands were rough and calloused. He had the hands of someone who got in the fray.

"Truly, Elowen," she said quietly, and a ring of sincerity filled her voice. "I mean this from the bottom of my heart. I have nothing against you. I can see that you mean well, and my son wholly cares for you. But I'm asking you to step back. I'm asking you to do what's best for others. If Jax doesn't marry a woman of noble birth, we'll have broken our vows to the ten Houses. The reason they've never risen up against the crown, or threatened to try and steal it from the Stagthorn line, or bickered too valiantly when their king asks for them to put his needs before their own is because of promises that have been made and must be kept. And one of those promises is to keep the crown pure with royal blood."

*Pure.* A dirty feeling washed over me. "And I'm not . . . pure."

"No, Elowen. You're a lorafin whose magic has been treated as a whore." I made a noise, low in my throat, and her face dimmed. "I don't say that to insult you. I'm merely speaking plainly. The ten Houses will never view you as an equal because you're not. You don't belong with my son, and you don't belong here, so please, I'm asking you to do what's best for everyone else around you and leave Stonewild once and for all." She stepped closer to me, her voice like steel. "And, Elowen, I ask that you *never* come back."

# CHAPTER 31

The queen's words cut me so deeply with hurt and rage that I didn't trust myself to return to the dining hall. Because apparently, the queen hadn't heard me. Despite her threats, despite her attempts at manipulation, I wasn't leaving, and I saw what all of her words truly were.

A way to try and trick me.

A way to twist my emotions to suit her.

But I'd grown up with a master manipulator. Now, I could spy those acts miles away, and I wasn't going anywhere.

Even though the queen wanted me to leave because it would be easier for her and the king, I had no intention of doing so. Still, I couldn't help the fury her meddling had born.

I scoffed and paced back and forth in Jax's suite. So

much anger had worked up inside me that I needed to burn off some steam.

I sneered when I reached the far wall and turned. His mother had even used the ten Houses as a scare tactic to try and *make me* leave her son, yet I'd seen enough of our realm to know that the ten Houses could change at a king's whim. And as much as she tried to declare that the throne needed the Houses, the opposite was, in fact, true. The Houses needed the throne.

The law of our land gave the power to the courts and the throne. Not the ten Houses of each kingdom. So while I knew that it made life easier for the throne if the ten Houses were functioning amicably, I also knew it wasn't the be-all and end-all. It just made a king and queen's life less encumbered.

And as for the promise Jax's parents made to the Houses that their son would marry one of their daughters. Well, that was just too damn bad. *They'd* made that promise. Jax hadn't, and I hadn't either.

I paced even faster in Jax's tower. I knew that Jax was still downstairs. I could feel him within the palace, and from the tug of his location along the mate bond, I was guessing he was still with his father. Most likely, he was getting an earful too.

Seething, I threw my hands up in disgust that his parents were being so difficult, and stormed across the room again. Magic crackled around me. The bedsheets flapped wildly against the mattress. The walls trembled. I was seriously ready to combust.

Taking a deep breath, I stopped and realized that I needed to expel some energy. My magic was roiling inside me so violently that I worried I would blow off the top of Jax's tower if I didn't calm down.

Tapping my foot, I tried to figure out the best way to do that. I could exercise, perhaps even grab Trivan or Lander or Lars and ask if they'd spar with me, even though I had no idea how to spar.

Or, I could leap from the window and see how well my shadow magic protected me in the wind's currents. I'd learned on the Isle of Song that such a thing was possible for a lorafin who fully controlled her shadow magic. I'd just never had the opportunity to try yet. But apparently, my shadows could work as one with the air, and if I learned how to master that part of my magic, I could literally fly.

I made a face. No, that probably wasn't very wise. I could just as likely end up on the cobblestones below, a bloody mess, if I didn't do it right. It was probably best to try and master that skill with a location closer to the ground.

With a huff, I sat down on the sofa and realized the easiest option to expel my energy was to simply venture to the Veiled Between and speak with the semelees. In fact, there was no reason I couldn't do a calling for myself right now.

My spine stiffened as soon as that thought struck me. I was free of my collar. Neither it nor the prison's potions were suppressing my magic any longer. I once again had full access to my power, and I was finally at a place in my life where I truly could do a calling of my own in which I *wasn't* going there to twist fate.

Just as I'd always dreamed of doing.

My thoughts turned to what I'd wanted to do my entire life when my thirtieth birthday arrived. Find my family and find where I'd truly come from. It suddenly struck me that just because my mother was dead, that didn't mean *all* of my family had passed to the afterlife. Perhaps I had other family members somewhere on the continent.

*And they're probably not nearly as snobbish as Jax's parents.*

My heart began to pound with pent-up excitement, and I couldn't believe I hadn't thought of it sooner. But so much had happened since my collar had been removed. So much. And just because the queen accused me of being selfish didn't mean that I was. I knew that I wasn't. The entire reason the thought of doing my own calling to find my blood family had never occurred to me in the previous weeks was because I'd been thinking of others and what had needed to be done for them. Not what I could do for myself.

I sneered again when I thought of Queen Rashelle, then went to the bed and lay down. I was determined to put her nasty words behind me, and there wasn't a better distraction than traveling to the Veiled Between and finally asking the semelees about my family.

Closing my eyes, I thanked the stars that the potions' effects had finally worn off. Once again, it was as easy to access my magic as breathing, so I called upon my power and commanded it to take me away.

My lorafin magic instantly responded, and I shot across the galaxy, through the stars, and to the Veil.

I entered it just as fast, and the semelees surged forth.

*My queen.* They collectively bowed as one. *You've come. What is it you seek?*

I paused momentarily and allowed myself a second to appreciate the enormity of this situation. Finally, I was going to learn about my blood family. *Tell me if I have any family in the fae lands. Tell me if any of them are still alive.*

The one nearest me swirled around my ghostly limbs, its cool black scales sliding along my essence. *Your mother is dead, but your father is alive.*

It felt as though my heart stopped. *He is?*

Another semelee surged forth. *Yes, and you have a sister, several aunts, an uncle, and many, many cousins.*

*I have a sister? Aunts and an uncle, cousins too?* It felt as though I couldn't breathe. *Where? Where can I find my sister, my father, and the rest of my family?*

*Ironcrest. You hail from Ironcrest Kingdom, my queen. Your guardian found you outside of Parvol in the Wood.*

*That is where your mother perished at the hand of your former guardian.*

In other words, Guardian Alleron hadn't lied about killing her. Of course not. He hadn't been able to lie once Jax's Mistvale commanding magic had seized him.

*Did my guardian know of my other family members?*

*No, my queen. You were the only one with your mother when he happened upon you. He knew nothing beyond her.*

I tried to take some comfort in that, even though there was nothing noble about it. I could only thank the gods and goddesses that my sister hadn't been with us when my mother was killed. Surely, Guardian Alleron would have murdered her too.

I thought of my dead mother, her soul in the afterlife. I could summon her, speak with her directly. I could do so right now.

At just the thought my heart raced, and I decided against it at the moment. I would find my blood family first, then I would summon my mother, after I knew more about her. Meeting her, even if she'd died, was going to be so emotional that I needed to mentally prepare myself.

I took a deep breath. *Where can I find my sister?*

*She'll be at the Ironcrest Ball next week.* The semelee on my other side showed me a picture of her. I gasped. She looked similar to me yet different. We shared the same green eyes, but whereas my hair was chestnut brown, hers was golden. Yet our mouths had a similar shape, and our ears the same curved point.

*What's her name?*

*Lorasbelle.*

*And my father? Will he be at the ball too?*

*Yes,* one of the semelees replied. *The fates have woven for the entirety of that night. Their fate is sealed. Both will be there. Unless you would like to twist fate again and make it otherwise?*

*No, I won't be doing that again anytime soon.*

A smile spread across my ghostly face as I thought of what next week would bring. I had a father who was alive and a *sister*. I had an actual blood sister, and her name was Lorasbelle, and next week she and my father would be at the Ironcrest Ball. I could meet her. Meet *him*. Finally, I could meet my family.

*What does my father look like?*

They readily showed me an image of him. He had blond hair, like my sister, and a mouth shaped like mine.

Tears threatened to form in my eyes. I had a real blood family. *Thank you,* I said to all of them.

The semelees bowed as one. *Yes, my queen.*

I shot back through the galaxy and came awake upon Jax's bed. A smile danced upon my lips, and I couldn't wait to tell him about it.

I didn't have to wait long. Jax stepped over the

threshold into his chambers a short while later, looking as irritated and angry as I'd felt initially arriving here.

"Gods, they're *impossible*," he groaned.

Laughing, I launched myself at him and wrapped my arms around his neck. I kissed him frantically, excitedly, my energy so exuberant that he instantly started laughing too.

"I take it that you had a better evening than me?" he said, chuckling between my kisses.

"No, not at all. Your mother was absolutely horrendous to me, but I don't even care anymore because I have the most exciting news."

I quickly told him what the semelees had revealed to me, and his eyes grew wider with every sentence I shared.

"And not only do I have a father, but I have a sister too, and her name's Lorasbelle. She and my father still live in Ironcrest Kingdom, and they'll be at the ball next week. I can go there, and I can meet them. I have a family, Jax, a true *family*!"

A wide grin burst across his face. He whooped and picked me up, spinning me around the room until I was laughing so hard I could barely breathe.

Finally setting me down, he cupped my cheeks and kissed me soundly. "Then next week we'll be at the ball, my love. We'll attend Ironcrest's Ball together, and you're finally going to meet them."

## CHAPTER 32

It felt as though a thousand dancing butterflies were flapping in my stomach. The carriage we rode in had all of the windows open, and music from the outdoor Ironcrest Ball carried to us on the country lane.

Ahead of us, many fae were also arriving, since it was the first official day of the ball. A whole line of carriages traveled on the narrow road as fae from all of the kingdoms ventured here for the huge Ironcrest Ball that took place every hundred summers after the Centennial Matches.

The supreme winner of the Matches, a fairy from Mistvale, would also be in attendance. She was to be awarded a noble title on the last day of the celebrations, and all of the other Match competitors would likely be wearing their medals and posing for many portraits in the coming days.

A part of me mourned that I hadn't been able to see

any of the actual Matches since I'd been on the Isle of Song in my first reality and then imprisoned and under the effect of potions in my second, but I figured in another hundred summers, I could actually attend the next one.

Jax slipped an arm around my waist as we drew closer to the ball. Our carriage rolled along, slowing as the area to depart from one's ride grew closer. This far south, the heat pressed in on all sides, making my gown stick to my lower back. A burst of cool air abruptly filled the carriage, and I shot a grateful look at my mate. His air element chilled the breeze, soothing my heated frame, while a small smile curved his lips.

"You look as though you're about to jump out of your skin," Jax said with a smile in his voice.

Bowan laughed. He sat beside the prince and wore Stonewild colors, just like all of us did.

"Don't worry, El." Trivan clapped me on the back. "Surely tonight will go fine. I mean, what's the worst that can happen? Your sister or father tells you that they want nothing to do with you? Totally won't occur."

Jax cut our friend a sharp glare, and Phillen rolled his eyes. Even Saramel made a face at Trivan while Cassim jostled on her knee.

"Subtle. Real subtle," Lander said in a bland voice.

"I'm joking. She knows I'm joking, right, El?" A moment of guilt stole over Trivan's face, and I didn't have the heart to chastise him.

"Even if they don't want me in their lives, at least we'll have met." I smoothed my cobalt-blue gown and tried not to think about that or the fact that the king and queen of Stonewild Kingdom followed in the carriage behind us.

It was only Jax threatening to reveal Bastian's lineage to all of Stonewild that had made his parents finally back off on their attempts to get rid of me. Still, the past week had been tense, to say the least.

My relationship with his parents probably also hadn't been helped by the fact that Jax had paraded me before all of the kingdom as often as he could—at every meal, at every outing, at every noble event in the past week. He'd told anyone who would listen that I was not only his mate but his upcoming bride, and he'd further declared that if his parents didn't like it, then he would choose abdication versus taking the crown.

I sighed. It'd definitely been a tense week.

Of course, while I shared in his sentiments, my presence in the palace was so strained now that it was a miracle his parents hadn't hired an assassin to execute me in the night.

I took a deep breath and put those worries to the side. Tonight, it was about *my* family. Not Jax's. Tonight, I would finally learn where I truly came from.

"What time's Bastian arriving tomorrow?" I asked Jax.

He cocked his head. "His last dillemsill message said he and Anna will be arriving mid-morning."

"But they're staying with us, right?"

Jax grinned. "Yes, he finally told Anna who he really is, since he proposed, and she said yes."

I laughed. Like Jax, I still hadn't met Anna, so we were both looking forward to tomorrow, and I was dying to meet my future sister-in-law.

"Are you going to let Bastian pick out what glamour he wears this time?" Alec asked Bowan.

Bowan shrugged, his devious smile getting a sly smirk from Quinn. "I haven't decided yet. Depends on if he lets me beat him in *storggers* or not."

Alec chuckled, and even Lars sported a smile.

I'd never been to the infamous Ironcrest Ball before, but all week, the males had been talking about how many games were played at the huge outdoor event. Apparently, it was what most of them were looking forward to in the coming days. Well, that and the leminai tent.

The carriage finally pulled to a stop outside of a huge pavilion. The ball was in full swing outside, on the palace grounds of the king and queen of Ironcrest. The capital, Metalwick, gleamed in the distance, but here it was only rolling countryside, with the palace perched on the top of the highest hill.

The palace's opulent structure was pure silver that gleamed in the sunlight. Magenta and burnt orange banners hung from every window. Flags flew, highlighting this kingdom's colors, and at each flag's center sat a six-pointed star, highlighting the six senses—sight, touch, taste, scent, sound, and magic. We'd truly arrived in the sensory kingdom, and the magic that wafted up from the land at the border had pulsed through me.

I gazed around, unable to stop my curious stare. Thousands upon thousands of fae dotted the land. My jaw dropped when I saw how many fae were already here. As was tradition, all four kingdoms were invited, and it didn't matter if you weren't a noble or royal. Commoners were also included, even if most couldn't afford the travel expense to attend the grand event.

Still, my heart warmed to know that the royal family in Ironcrest wasn't nearly as snobbish as Jax's parents.

"What do you think she's like?" I whispered to Jax as two attendants outside opened the carriage's door and provided a stool so we could step down. We'd decided we would find my sister first, since the semelees had told me she'd be easier to find, before I looked for my father.

"If she's halfway as lovely as you, I'm sure she's marvelous," he replied.

My hands were shaking when I stepped out of the carriage, and I feared my knees would give out.

Jax was instantly there, slipping an arm around my waist and holding me close.

I surveyed the surrounding landscape. The ball was swimming with so many fae that my heart fell. "How am I going to find her?"

But Jax just swept forward, pulling me with him. "We'll find her. We're not leaving until we do. Where did the semelees show you meeting her?"

My brow furrowed as I recalled the details they'd revealed in the two additional callings I'd done since last week as I peppered them with more questions. I'd not only gone to learn more about my family but to also fulfill a promise to Bastian that he'd hesitantly reminded me about.

The semelees confirmed that Bastian had never sired a child when he'd been under the anklet's spell, and after telling me that, they'd also revealed further details about my sister. "It was near a table filled with food and drink. She was standing beside a large chocolate fountain, dipping fruit into the drizzling liquid. They said she would be there the first day, close to this time."

"That's easy enough. There can't be that many chocolate fountains."

But as my gaze scoured the hillside, my excitement dimmed. There were literally tens of thousands of fae present, and from what I could see, there were dozens upon dozens of food stands and banquet tables dotting the rolling countryside.

"We better split up." Lander crossed his arms, gazing at the landscape.

Bowan scratched his head. "I was thinking the same. So everyone needs to find a chocolate fountain, then look for a female who looks slightly like Elowen but has golden hair. Remind me again, what was she wearing?"

I replied readily. "A silver gown. It's shiny and refracts the light, as though it's scattered with diamonds. At her ears, she's wearing magenta earrings."

"It sounds like a lovely gown befitting an Ironcrest fairy." Saramel smiled at me and held Cassim at her hip, jostling the wee boy. The toddler had three fingers stuffed in his mouth that he removed intermittently in order to point at things.

Phillen stood just behind them, grinning as he stared down at his son. During the past week, as I'd spent more time with Phillen and his family, it'd become clear Phillen was absolutely smitten with his boy.

Alec straightened his lapels when two females sauntered by us, giving him appreciating stares.

Quinn, however, had a rather intent look on his face. Even though I knew him the least of the group, I was coming to learn that he relished a challenge, and tonight would certainly be that.

I smoothed my gown as energy grew at my back. I didn't have to turn around to know that Jax's parents had just departed from their carriage. The cheers and greetings called to them said enough.

Bristling, Jax ushered me forward. "Is everyone ready to start looking?"

One by one, all of our friends nodded.

I took a deep breath. The butterflies were dancing so vigorously in my stomach I felt nauseous.

Lars moved silently to stand by my side. "We'll find her, Elowen. Fear not."

I gave him a grateful smile.

"If anyone happens to see her, signal the rest of us immediately. Does everyone have their charm?" Jax pulled his from his pocket, a small ball that looked like a marble. It'd been spelled to glow and warm if one was trying to communicate. Depending on who signaled it, the glow would change color, and a tracking spell would be triggered, pulling the others toward them.

"We all have ours." Bowan tucked his back into his pocket. "Let's go."

The entire group split up, Jax's guards not bothering to accompany us as they usually did. Given how large the outdoor field was that the ball was being held at, the numerous food stands, the plethora of entertainment venues, the multiple game areas, and the various dancing floors that had been constructed for a huge gathering, it would truly be a miracle if we found Lorasbelle before the night's end even if the semelees had shared specific images with me.

Jax's hand pressed to my lower back, and I could have sworn that a hiss came from behind us. I didn't turn. I'd come to learn that disapproving sound from his father all too well.

Jax steered us away from the carriages. "Forget about them." He leaned down and nipped at my ear. "Tonight is about you."

We meandered through the crowds, some people recognizing Jax, others not. A few times we were stopped so fae could pay their respects to him. I barely even heard what was said.

I couldn't stop scanning the field, but as I took in the crowd, scents, and warm breeze, some of my anxiety faded. There were more commoners here than nobles, so surely she was here. Most were dressed finely, and I knew that many of the fae present had likely spent full seasons saving up for their gowns and tunics, my sister probably no exception.

Jax propelled me along, and our feet stepped over the colorful grass brushing against our ankles. Music rang throughout the hill, a lively and jovial sound. It called to me, igniting my senses, and my hand tapped on my thigh as I searched and searched for a golden-haired female in a silver dress.

"There's a chocolate fountain over there." Jax pointed toward a long table. At its center, a three-tiered fountain looked like a dripping chocolate waterfall. Surrounding it were platters of fruits and sweets that fae were spearing with long toothpicks before dunking under the cascading chocolate.

"I suppose we should wait here. This looks like what

the semelees showed me." I stopped close by the fountain, nervously turning and searching the crowd. Across the hillside, I caught sight of another chocolate fountain, so far that I could barely see it, but a flash of red hair near it alerted me to Lars. He'd stopped himself by that one and was also scanning the crowd.

I took some comfort in that. The landscape appeared so similar everywhere I looked, that even though the chocolate fountain I waited at looked identical to what the semelees had shown me, I wasn't entirely certain I was in the right spot.

"How many fountains do you suppose there are?" I asked Jax quietly as someone brushed by my side to grab a pastry from the table.

Jax's brow furrowed, and he assessed the numerous venues. "I count at least six banquet tables that I can easily see, so if each hillside has that many . . ."

My heart felt about to burst. Despite what the semelees had shown me, it would be near impossible to find her.

But Jax just leaned down and ran his hand soothingly up and down my back. "We'll find her, my love. We will."

We waited near the fountain, and the sun slowly set, allowing the galaxy to come alive. The music grew louder, the crowd thicker, and the laughter and conversation livelier. Drink was freely flowing, fae were dancing, and everywhere I looked were smiling and happy fae.

It was as though the entire continent was celebrating.

I twisted my fingers in my gown, but as I was about to turn away from the fountain to search the crowd again, a flash of silver caught in my peripheral vision.

I turned as though in slow motion, my body moving as though attached to a string.

Golden hair cascaded down a female's back as a bright, glittering silver gown fell around her. It brushed against the grass, and a flash of magenta caught my eye when she tucked a strand of hair behind her ear.

My breath stopped.

My heart pounded.

"Jax," I whispered.

The female grabbed a toothpick and speared a berry, then drizzled it under the chocolate. She brought it to her mouth, turning as she did so.

I was so close to her that all I would have to do was reach out, and I could touch her.

The female faced me fully, the berry popping into her mouth. Her eyes widened when we stood face-to-face.

"Lorasbelle?" I said, and it felt as though someone else said the word. My heart was beating so fast I could hear blood rushing through my ears.

Her brows puckered together as her gaze traveled over my face. She quickly swallowed her food, then her jaw slowly dropped, her eyes growing round with shock.

"Hi," I said, my voice nearly breathless. "I'm Elowen, and I'm . . . I mean, I think I'm your—"

"Lorasbelle!" someone called through the crowd, and the fae parted as though the tide had pulled them away.

My jaw dropped just as the king of Ironcrest bustled through the crowd. He stood tall, with a lean figure and blond hair. A crown of silver, studded with magenta and orange stones, graced his head. "I've been looking for you, Belle. We're about to—"

The king stopped dead in his tracks when he saw me standing near his daughter. His smile disappeared.

For a moment, all I could do was stare at him. His face paled, and he gazed at me as though he was seeing a ghost.

Time slowed. I glanced between him and Lorasbelle, the female the semelees said was my sister, and then I looked at the male who they said was my father.

"Miramim?" The king took a hesitant step toward me, his gaze skating over my face and down my frame. "Gods and Goddesses, Miramim? Is that you?"

I licked my lips, then glanced at Jax, who stood with a shocked look on his face.

Jax cleared his throat. "This is Elowen Emerson of Faewood Kingdom," Jax finally replied, finding his voice. "And I'm her mate, Prince Adarian Willip Jackson Stagthorn, crown prince of Stonewild Kingdom." He bowed to the king, and somehow, my legs dipped into a curtsy.

But the king—my *father*—didn't respond. He stepped

closer to me, his gaze traveling over my face so fast, his complexion still white. "My Gods, you look just like my first wife." He glanced at Lorasbelle, who was also staring at me as though she'd seen a ghost.

"My mother," she finally said. "That's what my father meant to say. You look just like my dead mother."

It felt as though a thousand volts of lightning hit me. Shock billowed through me, yet all of my senses zeroed in on the female and male who the semelees had told me was my family.

"They told me you're my sister," I whispered to her. "And that you're my father," I said to him. "I'm a lorafin who can travel to the Veiled Between, and the semelees said you're my family."

The king gasped, his hand flying to his mouth. "What? That can't be."

I forced myself to reply, even though dread was growing in my stomach that they would reject me. "It's what they said, and the semelees know all."

My father and sister shared a look, and the king finally said, "You're saying that you're my daughter, but . . . you died."

"She did?" Jax cut in. "How?"

The king licked his lips. He still looked entirely pale, but he managed to get out, "A seer told my wife that we would have a daughter who would be feared by all, and Miramim grew so afraid that someone would try to kill our daughter upon her birth that she fled to Parvol to hide so no one could find her, and then she fled to the Wood to have our child alone when her contractions started." A look of utter devastation filled his face. "I was away at the time. Her labor pains started several weeks earlier than anticipated, and when I was finally able to reach her—" Grief made his face crumple.

Lorasbelle cleared her throat and laid a hand on her father. "Nobody ever truly knew what happened to her. I was only eleven at the time, but when my mother's body was finally found in the river, it was determined that she'd drowned, but you . . ." Her gaze slid my way. "Nobody ever knew what became of my sister. The healers knew that my mother had given birth as the child was no longer in her womb, but there was no sign of you. We'd all assumed a predator in the Wood had perhaps taken you. We all thought you died."

Tears filled my eyes. "I didn't die. I was taken."

My throat became so clogged that I couldn't speak more, so Jax placed his hand against my lower back and slowly explained to them what not only Guardian Alleron had told us but the semelees too.

"You're a lorafin?" the king finally managed after Jax finished explaining. "*That's* why the seer said you would be feared by all?"

I could only nod. I was still so clogged with emotion that it was hard to speak.

My father brought a hand to his forehead. "Stars Above. I've *heard of you* during the past twenty summers. That a lorafin was traveling through the kingdoms with her guardian, her services open to any who had the coin. I've even had nobles in my court use your magic for their bidding." His knees buckled, and those near us gasped.

An attendant rushed forward, bringing a seat for their sovereign.

The king of Ironcrest lifted himself just enough to seat himself upon it, and Lorasbelle crouched at his side, tears in her eyes too. "Oh, Da, are you all right?"

He just shook his head. "I can't believe it." He gazed up at me again, his eyes traveling over my face. "But it has to be true. You look just like her but even more beautiful in a way."

"That's my lorafin magic at work." Tentatively, I crouched on his other side and looked at him and then Lorasbelle. "I never knew about the two of you either. The male who stole me, he told me that I'd been abandoned in the Wood and that my family didn't want me because I was a lorafin."

Ruddy indignation filled my father's cheeks. "Where is this male?" he all but seethed.

"Gone," Jax replied readily, his voice clipped. "He'll never hurt Elowen again."

Tears began to spill down my cheeks as my family and I gazed at one another in wonder, and deep in my heart, I *knew* that I'd found my family. The king of Ironcrest was my father, and the princess of Ironcrest was my sister. My mother had been the queen, and with a thunderstruck memory, I recalled a detail about Ironcrest that I'd learned long ago but had never even considered was related to me.

Miramim, the queen of Ironcrest Kingdom, had died a tragic death twenty-eight summers ago. She'd gone into the Wood, as she was privy to do, and had tragically drowned in a river. It'd happened so long ago, but the king had eventually married again, many summers later, giving his surviving daughter a stepmother to call her own.

More tears fell down my cheeks, and tears fell down Lorasbelle's too as we both stared at each other in shock.

Jax slipped an arm around my waist, hope growing in his aura as he stared at the Ironcrest royal family. "King Bronwan and Princess Lorasbelle, may we go somewhere more private? Elowen and I have much to tell you."

# CHAPTER 33

We all sat in the large receiving room in Ironcrest's palace. Outside, the bonfires, music, and celebrations continued as the great Ironcrest Ball carried on into the night. Jax, Saramel, Cassim, and all of our friends were seated with us while my father and sister, along with the current Ironcrest queen sat across from us.

"Your guardian killed my wife." The king still looked as though he'd seen a ghost, and Lorasbelle was looking just as shocked.

Disbelief and amazement coursed through me continually too. These fae were my family. My actual *family*. "He did. I guess Guardian Alleron happened upon us in the Wood. He said he saw me lying on a blanket near the river while my mother was bathing. That must have been after she'd given birth to me, and she was perhaps cleaning herself off. He saw my shadow mark and jumped at the opportunity to capitalize on that, so he killed her and took me. Until recently, he was my guardian and had complete control of me."

"He *took* you. And he murdered my Miramim." The king abruptly stood, his face reddening and his hands fisting. "What did he do to you after he had you?"

Given the tortured expression that filled the king's—my father's—face, I didn't have the heart to tell him of my guardian's manipulative ways and seasons of abuse. "He raised me as a daughter and sold my magic, similar to what you've heard."

"Did he hurt you?"

I swallowed, unable to meet his eyes.

The king's nostrils flared sharply. "And where is this murderer now?" he all but growled.

Jax placed a hand over mine. I gripped him tightly. I was shaking so badly I felt like a trembling leaf in the wind. "Like I said before, he's gone. Nobody's seen or heard from him since he ran into the Dark Raider several months ago."

The king scoffed, but some of the redness cooled from his cheeks. Finally taking a deep breath, he said, "Well, I suppose that's fitting. If his last encounter was with the Dark Raider, one would think he got what he deserved."

"Yes, that's what I've been hoping too." I could barely sit still as I stared across the small table at the fae in front of me. It was still sinking in that I was staring at my lost family. My lost *royal* family.

Lorasbelle and I darted looks at one another again, just as the king finally sat once more, then brought both hands up to his face.

He scrubbed his cheeks. "I've been tortured with grief ever since that day." The queen, the king's new wife, laid a hand on his shoulder and gave him a sympathetic look. He finally dropped his hands, his shoulders folding inward. "And to think, you were alive and so close all this time."

Lorasbelle scooted closer to him and laid a comforting hand on him as well.

My attention alighted on the casual affection the three of them showed one another. Touching, soothing pats. Until Jax, I'd never known someone to give me that kind of care before.

A ball thickened my throat, tears forming in my eyes. If I'd grown up here, I had no doubt I would have experienced that regularly.

"If I had known you were alive—" Tears filled the king's eyes when he looked at me. "My darling girl. I don't know how you'll ever forgive me, but I should have found you. I should have felt that you were alive. I should have—"

Something in me broke. Before he could utter another word, I was up from my seat and flying toward him.

He caught me in his embrace, his lean arms closing around me. The rich scent of wood mixed with cinnamon hit my senses. A memory stirred, so distant and fleeting that I didn't know if my mind was playing tricks on me, but

I could have sworn that I'd smell that scent before. That I'd smelled *him* perhaps on my mother's clothes.

"I'm so sorry, my darling girl," he sobbed, holding me close. "I'm so sorry that I wasn't there for you."

I clung to him, and for the first time in my life, for the first time in my entire existence, it felt as though all of the puzzle pieces within me finally clicked into place, forming a full picture of the history of who I was and who I was going to be.

"It's all right, Da," I managed in a choked whisper. "Everything's going to be all right now."

# EPILOGUE

Jax and I stood in Jaggedston's throne room, our hands entwined, our heads held high. Our fathers stood in front of us. Crowns sat upon their heads. Jewels dripped from their cloaks, and they held a sealing cloth between the two of them.

Behind them, the rest of our families sat in the first row of seating, and Lorasbelle couldn't stop grinning. Upon the other seats, the ten noble Houses from each kingdom watched on. Other fae were present too, both nobles and commoners of Stonewild and Ironcrest.

I'd come to learn that my birth name wasn't Elowen, but instead Isobel, or at least, that was the name my parents had intended to give me upon birth if I'd been born a girl.

But Jax and I had agreed that in private we would continue using the names we'd always called one another—

Jax and Elowen—but to the continent, I was now Princess Isobel Miramim Cerullee Riverling, a princess of Ironcrest Kingdom.

Jax's father walked toward us, the side of his cloth held in his hands. His gaze kept drifting to mine, and I could have sworn that the tiniest bit of shame lay there. The queen of Stonewild Kingdom wore a similar expression from where she watched in the front row, and while I didn't revel in their guilt, I was thankful for it. Finally, the friction that had existed between us was gone, even if it angered me that it hadn't stopped until they learned I was of noble birth. I should have been worthy before they'd found that out, but I pushed that thought aside.

They were to be my new family, and despite how abusive they'd been to Jax and me, I vowed to create a peaceful relationship with them in the coming seasons. I'd had enough strife in my life. I didn't want more, but I also knew that while Jax and I could remain civil with them, a loving relationship was never in the cards for us. They weren't the kind of fae that was even possible with. But civility we could maintain.

Jax's father draped the silk cloth over Jax's and my joined hands while my father wrapped it around us. Then the two kings turned to the kingdoms, and they both declared at the same time, "Prince Adarian and Princess Isobel are hereby joined in engagement for the entire realm to bear witness. We look forward to joining the might of our two kingdoms as their upcoming marriage signifies the beginning of a new dawn."

A burst of applause and cheer exploded in the throne room. From the corner of my eye, I saw my sister beaming. My new stepmother was also grinning.

I winked in their direction, and Lorasbelle blew me a kiss, then I faced my mate.

Jax gazed down at me, his blue eyes shining like sapphires. He pulled me close, his mouth descending to mine. We kissed before the realm, the cheers increasing.

When he finally pulled back, his mouth moved to my ear. "I told you we would find a way, my love."

I laughed softly at the swagger in his words. Still laughing, I gazed up at him, all of the love for this male shining through me. Playfully, I said, "It probably helps that I'm a royal."

He groaned, but the sound was still joyous and carefree. "I'm pretty sure that's made my parents happier."

Hand in hand, we descended the stairs, newly engaged for the entire realm to see. We walked together past the cheering crowd, passing all of our friends who were whistling and cheering, and under a glamour, Bastian's eyes shone with happiness as he and Anna watched on.

Outside on the streets, the passing fae whistled and called congratulatory comments to Jax and me. The Jaggedston bells tolled, and in the distance, the palace sparkled like black sand.

Jax and I waved and thanked everyone who called out.

Still grinning, Jax's expression took on a devious look. "You know it's tradition that when a male and female are engaged in Stonewild, that the female rides her mate in his animal-form back to their dwelling."

My throat bobbed. Jax had told me this yesterday, and a part of me couldn't wait. I still hadn't seen him in his stag form. The opportunity had simply never arisen.

"Ready?" he asked, arching a midnight eyebrow.

I nodded.

He stepped back, and in a flash of magic, Jax disappeared, and a huge black stag stood before me.

"Jax, you're so *big*."

He pawed at the ground and chuffed, getting a laugh out of me.

In his stag form, Jax was enormous, so tall that his antlers would have tangled in vines in the Wood's canopy if we'd been in a denser part of the forest.

He lowered a front leg, bowing before me, and in a flash of my own magic heating my muscles, I jumped on him.

The second my seat was secure, a billow of his air element flared in the air around me, then he took off through the streets, exacting his magic as we flew to the palace.

I clung to his mane as his air element kept me in a bubble atop him, the wind not pushing me off. And it was only when we arrived back at the palace that he shifted back to his fae form in the huge open courtyard.

Dressed once more in his royal attire, he tucked a lock of hair behind my ear. "Well, what did you think?"

"You're fast, maybe even faster than Phillen."

He smirked. "Way faster."

I laughed anew, and he swept me up in his embrace, then bounded inside the palace, through his wards, and up the circular stairwell to the top of his tower.

It was only when we were alone in the privacy of our bed chambers that he finally released me.

Outside, the bells continued tolling, and in the central courtyard far below, sounds drifted up to us of the huge feast that would take place in an hour to celebrate our new engagement.

Jax cupped my cheeks, his sapphire eyes shining bright. "I love you, Princess Elowen, and royal or not, I was never going to let you go."

"And I love you, mate of my heart. Dark Raider or royal, you have my love forever."

Jax hadn't mentioned his former raider role once since deciding to leave that life behind him. His friends hadn't either. It truly seemed that they were fine with forging a new path forward, a just and fair one in their royal and noble roles.

Jax kissed me fiercely, and our clothes came flying off.

We fell in a tangle on the sheets, the mate bond brimming with love inside us as we began our true first day together as an engaged couple from two of the mighty thrones on the Silten continent.

Prince Adarian and Princess Isobel, the future king and queen of Stonewild Kingdom.

# ABOUT THE AUTHOR

Krista Street is a Minnesota native but has lived throughout the U.S. and in another country or two. She loves to travel, read, and spend time in the great outdoors. When not writing, Krista is either chasing her children, spending time with her husband and friends, sipping a cup of tea, or enjoying the hidden gems of beauty that Minnesota has to offer.

# THANK YOU

Thank you for reading *Queen of Fate* the final book in the *Fae of Woodlands & Wild* trilogy.

Would you like a free bonus chapter that gives you a glimpse into Elowen and Jax's life in the future? If you do, and you live in the USA or Canada, sign up for Krista's new release text messaging service, and you'll receive a free digital bonus chapter.

Simply text the word **ELOWEN** to **888-403-4316** on your mobile phone.

Message and data rates may apply, and you can opt out at any time. If you live outside of North America, and you would like to receive the bonus chapter, visit:

www.kristastreet.com/elowenbonus

To learn more about Krista's other books and series, visit her website. Links to all of her books, along with links to her social media platforms, are available on every page.

**www.kristastreet.com**